EAGLE WING

Other novels by Alfred Dennis

Chiricahua
Lone Eagle
Elkhorn Divide
Brant's Fort
Catamount
The Mustangers
Rover
Sandigras Canyon
Yellowstone Brigade
Shawnee Trail
Fort Reno
Yuma
Ride the Rough String
Trail to Medicine Mound
Arapaho Lance: Crow Killer Series - Book 1
Lance Bearer: Crow Killer Series - Book 2
Track of the Grizzly: Crow Killer Series - Book 3
Bear Claw: Crow Killer Series - Book 4
Blood on the Lance: Crow Killer Series - Book 5
Slocum

To see more books by Alfred Dennis visit
www.alfreddennis.com

EAGLE WING

Crow Killer Series - Book 6

by

Alfred Dennis

Walnut Creek Publishing
Tuskahoma, Oklahoma

Eagle Wing: Crow Killer Series - Book 6

ISBN: 978-1-942869-39-9
First Edition, Paperback
Published 2021 by Walnut Creek Publishing
Front cover: iStock.com/Daniel Eskridge "Native American Warrior and Hawk"
Library of Congress Control Number: 2021944273

Books may be purchased in quantity and/or special sales by contacting
the publisher;
Walnut Creek Publishing
PO Box 820
Talihina, OK 74571
www.wc-books.com

This book is dedicated to my good friends,
James & Brenda Cobb. We sure nuff been
down the trail together.

Chapter 1

Two sets of dark eyes watched the party of white hunters as they moved slowly down the mountain trail. Hidden from sight, behind the dense foliage of cedar, cottonwood, and pine growing abundantly along the north pass, the two figures waited quietly. Standing far back in the shadows bordering the trail, the oval eyes missed nothing. A frown creased the forehead of the taller watcher. This was the valley of his father, Crow Killer, and these whites had no business in his mountains. Both watchers were young; one in his late teens and the other even younger. Silently, the two youngsters stood unmoving as five heavily armed men descended the steep trail, down from the pass, moving steadily closer to where they sat concealed. Both youngsters had piercing black eyes that were as sharp as the eagle or hawk watching for prey from the high peaks that guarded the huge valley.

"They come like thieves in the night." The older boy looked down at the thirty-caliber Hawken rifle he carried. "See how they move very slow and silent down the trail."

"I have seen these white hunters somewhere before." The younger of the two studied the bearded faces closely.

"These whites were at Bridger back in spring when we sold our furs, little brother."

"Yes, I remember now. That's where I saw them." The dark face nodded slowly. "I can smell the stink of them even from here."

"Quickly, Red Horse, run to our lodge and warn our father."

"What will Eagle Wing do?" Red Horse glanced up the mountain trail. "They are very close, my brother. You are right, they are trying to remain unheard and unseen."

"I will stop them before they reach our lodge." The grim set face of the taller youth looked back at his younger brother. "Go quickly, Red Horse, bring Crow Killer here. Hurry now."

"I will miss out on all the fun."

"Hurry, bring our father here." Eagle Wing shook his head at his younger brother. The younger muscular youth was fourteen summers now and he didn't know the meaning of fear. "Hurry, Red Horse, let your legs carry you like the deer."

"Run? I'd rather fight."

"Go!"

"I go, Brother, but you be careful." The younger lad started away. "These men may be white, but their rifles reach far and will sting you."

Eagle Wing watched as Red Horse disappeared into the mountain cedar and pine that covered the edges of the great valley. Luckily, they had been out looking for their grandfather's cow when the bright sun flashed off a gun barrel, drawing their attention. They hid for an hour, watching as five hunters moved slowly down the north trail of the canyon. Their cabin was less than two miles from where Eagle Wing watched the interlopers. He knew the whites were up to no good. They were too cautious as they held their horses to a slow walk, barely letting them move as they descended the trail. The tall youth knew they were trying to keep the noise of their approach as secret as possible. In these mountains, and especially along the canyon trails, sound carried far. The whites were experienced hunters and trappers, and they would know the echoes reverberating against the canyon walls would warn their approach.

Eagle Wing knew these men weren't here to trap beaver. Since the passing of the Shining Times of the early trappers, the skins of the flat tails were worth practically nothing at the trading posts. Also, it was far too early in the summer for trapping. The hides of the fur bearers needed the colder weather to thicken and bring top prices at the trader's store. He studied the five men closely, without them being aware of his presence. The youngster knew they didn't come for beaver and there were no buffalo in this valley. Deer and elk were plentiful, but the fleet-footed ones inhabited every valley in these vast mountains. Eagle Wing knew they had ridden far for something else.

He was curious as to why these men had come. Looking up the trail, he could clearly make out the bearded faces. They were the typical filthy-haired faces of greasy white hunters and trappers. Eagle Wing had seen this breed of men several times when he rode with Crow Killer to Bridger's Post to sell his furs. Some of these hunters were extremely cruel men who would kill and rob the weak and helpless ones.

Now, less than a quarter mile separated him from where they stopped to study the lower valley. One of the men motioned with his arm, as two others moved to the left, flanking the trail as it widened. From their movements, he could tell they were planning on approaching the cabin from two sides without being discovered. Their actions spoke plainly to the tall youth. These men were coming into the valley to cause trouble of some kind. Whatever mischief they were up to, it wasn't good.

Slipping beside a tall oak, covered with shrubs, Eagle Wing checked the priming on his rifle and waited. They were very close now, and he would permit these riders to ride no closer to the cabin.

"That Nez Perce said the cabin would be less than two miles from the base of the trail." A filthy, tobacco-stained hunter grinned. "Smile, boys, a hot meal, good-looking women, and many fine horses are just ahead for the taking."

"We're close alright, and I doubt we have been discovered yet." The smaller of the men agreed.

"You know who we're riding against, Maud?" Another filthy one spat tobacco, letting it dribble down his crusty beard. "You know what old Squirrel Tooth told you."

"I know. Just cause that Nez Perce is scared of Crow Killer, sure ain't no reason for us to turn tail and run, is it?"

"Maybe we should think this over." The one called Joe shook his head. "I've heard Crow Killer has done for a lot of men, white and red."

"I hear he's deadly as a riled up rattler, Maud." The filthy bearded one added.

"There are five of us and he's got something I want." The brown-stained teeth of the big hunter showed again as he grinned. "Two somethings, that is."

"The girl I seen, Maud, but the gold that's supposed to be up here is just talk. Rumor and tongue wagging, nothing more."

"Maybe, but if it's here, I aim to find it." Maud grinned and nodded at a thin, sad-faced young man dressed in store clothes, not the typical skins of a hunter. "That's why we brought this pilgrim with us."

"How do we know he can even find gold?" Joe shook his head. "I don't like that we forced him to come with us. He may be some kind of government man. They might be looking for him."

"He's a gold hunter, just like us." Maud looked hard at the young man. "He finds it for us, he lives. If not, well, there's a lot of bodies buried up in these mountains. You hear me good, pilgrim."

Eagle Wing moved in closer, standing within hearing distance of where the three riders sat their horses talking. Their voices were loud, and he clearly heard what they were talking about. Now, he recognized the big man in the lead. He remembered at Bridger when the same man had questioned McGraw, the liveryman, about Jedidiah Bracket and his valley. Last year his mother, Bright Moon, had wanted to ride to Bridger when they took their pelts in to sell. His father had argued with her, but she had insisted on visiting the post. Her old friend, Alex Caldwell, was getting on in years and she wanted to see him before his time came. Also, she had figured her brother, He Dog, might be at the post trading his furs. It had been two years since she had seen He Dog and her family. Finally, the whole family had made the journey, except for Grandfather Wilson, who wanted no part of the trip.

At Bridger, the same white hunter had seen his sister, Ellie Thunder. Eagle Wing remembered how the white's eyes had narrowed as he watched them as they walked around the post. When the filthy white had approached them, the blacksmith McGraw and another white, had stepped between Eagle Wing's sharp skinning knife and the white, preventing trouble. A bitter taste formed in his mouth. Yes, he remembered this one well.

Faintly, he heard the name Squirrel Tooth mentioned as the men talked. The Nez Perce was the hated enemy of Crow Killer. He had sent whites to the valley before to kill his father. Eagle Wing knew nothing of the yellow iron that came from the ground, but he did know when whites were told of it, they seemed to go crazy with greed. This was the bait the Nez Perce used to lure the whites to the high valley of Crow Killer. His father should have killed the Nez Perce many moons ago. One day, Eagle Wing vowed to visit the village of Squirrel Tooth. But for today, he had other problems to worry about.

"What's your plan, Maud?"

"We'll let Case and Percy get themselves in position, then we'll just ride in like we're passing through."

"And?"

"When he shows himself." Maud grinned widely. "Bang."

"That's murder." The city man swallowed hard.

"You just stay clear of it, pilgrim, and you'll be fine." Maud kicked his tired horse. "Let's go, they've had plenty of time to get in position along the trail."

Red Horse could hear the little black mule's warning bray as he crossed the small creek below the cabin. He saw his father already had his rifle and was sprinting to the horse corral. Bridling the bay horse, he had kept up for the day, Jed looked as his youngest son raced afoot toward him. His chest heaved and sweat ran down the boy's face from the long run back to the cabin.

"The mule warns us, my son. What's wrong?"

"Five white men come down the trail." Red Horse pointed his bow to the north. "They are not friends, my father. By their actions, they come here seeking trouble."

"Stay here and help protect your mother and sister." Jed swung on the bay horse.

"I would go fight with you, my father."

"Your mother may need you." Jed looked to where Bright Moon and Ellie Thunder stood. "Barricade the door and see to your weapons, Bright Moon."

"Where is Eagle Wing?" The tall, slim older woman looked at her youngest son worriedly. "Where is my other son?"

"He watches the white hunters."

"Hurry, my husband." The woman turned her eyes to the north trail. "Eagle Wing will fight them."

Maud, and the two with him, had barely ridden fifty feet, when Eagle Wing called out a warning from behind a box elder tree. Reining in, the three men looked around for the voice that had spoken to them.

"Whoever you are, where you at?" Maud strained to see inside the maze that hid the voice. "We're friends, show yourself."

"I am here, white man." The voice was strong with no fear. "You will come no further until Crow Killer gets here."

"And you, one lone man, are fixing to stop us?"

"I warn you, white man, not another step or you'll have your answer."

Jed heard the roar of the thirty-caliber rifle as he raced up the north trail. He knew the shot came from his son's rifle. The noise had the distinct sound of the smaller caliber rifle, he had given Eagle Wing on his thirteenth birthday. Kicking the horse hard, he raced ahead, reining in as he saw three men sitting crossways on the trail. Two other men were off to the side of the trail, and one was on the ground holding his arm.

Eagle Wing stepped from behind the box elder as Jed rode closer to the three men waiting on the trail. He quickly recognized the men as some of the hunters from Bridger.

"What do you men want here?"

"We were just passing through, heading south, when that heathen there shot one of my men." Maud glared over to where Eagle Wing stood. "That Injun shot poor old Percy for no reason."

"The heathen, as you call him, is my son." Jed looked hard at the hunter. "You're lucky he shot to warn you, or your man would be dead."

"Well, now, that ain't a very sociable way to greet one of your own." The big man shrugged. "Shooting at us like that."

"You men turn around now and leave this valley." Jed pointed his rifle back up the trail. "Now!"

"Percy needs doctoring before he bleeds out."

"You're probably right about that." Kicking his bay forward Jed rode alongside the big hunter. "Your last chance to turn them horses around."

As the man started to speak, the hard slap of Jed's hand sounded, knocking the hunter from his horse. Dismounting, Jed let the man get to his feet before knocking him to the ground again. Standing over the bleeding man, Jed started to strike again as the man held up his hand.

"Alright, we're leaving." Maud got up and struggled aboard his horse. "Don't come back, ever."

"This is a free country." Maud felt safer on his horse. "The law will hear about this."

"This is the only law in these mountains." Jed held up his rifle. "Leave now, mister, last time I'm gonna tell you."

"We're going."

"Mister." The tall man with the store-bought clothes spoke up. "May I speak with you?"

"Speak, but make it quick." Jed's eyes settled on the man.

"These men abducted me from Bridger's Trading Post." The slender young man trembled. "They brought me here against my will."

"They did?" Jed looked over the city man closely. "Why would they do that?"

"Yes, sir, they did." The Adam's apple swallowed hard. "I fear for my life if I leave here with them. May I remain here with you, until you can get me back to the post?"

"Tell me, mister. How do you know I even go to Bridger?"

"Shut your mouth, pilgrim." Maud glared. "Don't say nothing."

"My name is Oliver Bass. These men said they saw you and your family at Bridger's Post this spring." Oliver swallowed hard. "I heard them say they came here for your daughter and gold."

Eagle Wing spoke softly in Arapaho. "He speaks the truth, my father. This big one tried to attack Ellie at the post this spring."

"You did not tell me of this, my son."

"It was of no importance. Nothing happened. Our friend McGraw and another stopped him." Eagle Wing frowned.

"What are you two saying?" Maud looked nervously at Eagle Wing. "Speak English."

"He just pronounced your death sentence, mister."

The big face turned pale as the blue eyes blinked wide in alarm. "What, what did I do?"

Handing his rifle to Eagle Wing, Jed pulled Maud from his horse and unsheathed his skinning knife. "You've got a knife, use it."

The roar of a pistol went off, then the thirty-caliber rifle sounded again. With a look of surprise, the one called Joe slipped slowly from his saddle. A pistol fell from his hand as blood quickly covered the front of his filthy hunting shirt. Jed looked to where Eagle Wing had dropped both rifles and was pulling his own knife.

"Wait, my father." Advancing threateningly at Maud, the youngster pointed the razor-sharp blade at the scared hunter. "This one is mine."

"Alright, we're going." Maud begged. "Keep him away from me."

Stumbling for his horse, Maud started to mount when he felt Eagle Wing's blade touch his throat. "You still want my sister, white man?"

"No." Swallowing hard and shaking, the big man shook his head, then collapsed against his horse. "I was only fooling, Injun."

"And I only fool now, white man."

The sharp point of the blade notched a hole in the hunter's right ear before Jed could stop his son. "Enough, Eagle Wing. Let him go."

Blood flowed brightly down the man's neck, covering his hunting shirt. "We will meet again, this I promise."

Jed looked at the scared young white. "Mister, you can stay here with us if you want."

"Will I be safe?" Oliver stared at Eagle Wing's hard face, then at Joe's dead body.

"Safe enough, I reckon. Your choice, young feller, you'll have to take your chances either with us or them."

"Then, sir, I'll stay here with you."

Jed hadn't taken his eyes from the mounted hunters. "You men get back across the Snake and don't come back into these mountains again."

"I reckon you'd kill us?" Maud held a filthy cloth to his split ear.

"Maybe I wouldn't." Jed looked at Eagle Wing. "But, he would."

Watching the riders disappear up the trail, Eagle Wing turned as Red Horse pounded up the trail. "My father, we should have killed them."

"It was not the civilized thing to do, my son, and we are civilized, aren't we?" Jed frowned at his oldest.

"Maybe, but these whites are not civilized." Eagle Wing retrieved the rifles from where he had dropped them as he sprang on Maud. "The big one has looked at Ellie Thunder, and someday he will return for her."

Jed shook his head as he knew the white man's mind. He had seen the same thing happen when the trapper Squires and the Metis from the north had followed him to his valley to take Ellie Medicine Thunder many years ago. Eagle Wing was right. He should have killed these men, but he was still civilized. To kill in cold blood was not his way.

"Perhaps we should have, my son." Jed nodded as Red Horse reined in his horse. "Red Horse was told to stay and protect his mother."

"We heard the noise of the rifle and Mother sent me." Red Horse stared his father in the eye. "I could not stay behind, my father."

"It's alright, my son. It is over now."

"Is it?" Eagle Wing watched as the white hunters disappeared from his sight. "I do not think this."

"Come, let us take our guest to the cabin." Jed swung up on his horse.

"Who is this one?" Red Horse looked to where Oliver sat on his horse nervously.

"He is our guest for a spell." Jed looked at Red Horse. "This is my youngest son, Red Horse."

Taking in the dark eyes and fierce face of the youngster, the white man nodded. "Great."

"I must find Grandfather's cow before I return."

"Eagle Wing will not follow the whites." Jed stared hard at his older son. "Let them leave this place without further trouble."

"I hear your words, Crow Killer." Eagle Wing swung on the horse in front of Red Horse. "If they leave our mountains, I will do as you say."

"Your son seems very hard for one so young."

"He came into this world during a bloody battle." Jed nodded. "He's a product of his times."

"But, he is so cold and cruel acting."

"He is of age to become a warrior." Jed smiled. "Young Arapaho warriors are pretty tough sometimes."

"But, Maud said you were white."

"He was wrong." Jed kicked his horse. "We are Arapaho."

"The boy would have cut Maud's throat if you hadn't stopped him." Oliver shook his head. "I do not understand such cruelty."

"Yes, I suppose he would have." Jed turned to look back at his sons. He knew Oliver's words were true. Eagle Wing was hard beyond his years. "A few years back, I would have done the same myself."

"That's barbaric."

"Perhaps, Oliver, but I'll tell you what's barbaric." Jed explained.

"Those white hunters would have slit your throat and dumped you when they were finished with your services."

"You're probably right about that, sir." Oliver shivered slightly. "I do have to admit what you say is the truth."

"This is a wild and savage country." Jed kicked the bay into a trot. "Why would they want you to come here with them?"

"I am an assayer and also a lawyer."

"What's an assayer?"

"An assayer is a person that studies minerals, such as gold and silver."

"Come, we ride to my lodge." Jed thought of the shining light. After finding the source of the light, he hadn't disturbed the rocks. Planting a few pine trees and covering the wall to protect its hiding place was all he had done. With his pelts bringing in good money, he had no need for gold. Bringing a sack of nuggets into Baxter Springs, would be like waving a red flag at a bull and his secret would be out. Every man in the country would come into his mountains looking for the yellow iron.

Oliver looked at the broad back of the man before him and shook his head. The ones at Bridger's Post said he was white. They must have been wrong as this was no white man. He dressed, looked, and talked like an Indian. Had he jumped from the frying pan into the fire? Well, at least he was still alive. Hopefully, he would remain that way until he could get back to Bridger. He couldn't wait to leave these heathen lands forever and return back east to civilization.

Riding up to the cabin, Oliver blinked in surprise. For some reason, he figured he would see a hide lodge before him, same as the ones at the post. Two Indian women stood before the cabin with their long deerskin dresses almost touching the ground.

"Great, more Indians." He muttered to himself.

Dismounting, Jed tried to hide his smile. He could tell what the tall young man was thinking. "This is my wife, Bright Moon, and my daughter, Ellie Thunder."

Removing his hat, Oliver bowed slightly. "My pleasure, ladies. Oliver Bass at your service.

Oliver was surprised when Bright Moon answered him in perfect English. "You are welcome here, Mister Bass."

"He'll stay over at Pa's cabin while he's here."

"Great, another Indian." Oliver mumbled.

"Ellie, take Mister Bass to meet your grandfather." Jed pulled the bridle from his horse. "He can unsaddle his horse over there."

The distance between the two cabins was less than two hundred feet. Oliver followed the young girl along the small path that led to Ed Wilson's cabin. The tall young man could not take his eyes from the form of the beautiful girl walking ahead of him. He had to admit, she was the most breathtaking girl he had ever seen in his lifetime. The light-tanned deerskin dress clung to the girl's figure, cloaking her like a glove. The girl hadn't spoken yet, but Oliver was already in awe of the beauty before him. Ed Wilson stood up from where he had been sitting, whittling on a pine limb. Studying the tall stranger following Ellie, he laid the wood aside.

"Grandpa, this is Oliver Bass. He will stay with us for a few days." The voice was soft, musical to Oliver's ears. Never had he heard or seen anything like this girl.

"Oliver Bass, is it?"

"Pa wants you to put him up here with you."

"Well, Mister Bass, is that alright with you?"

""Yes, sir. Thank you, sir." Oliver was surprised to see the white man, but he couldn't take his eyes from Ellie.

"You're to bring him over for supper after you milk."

"I've got to get that blame cow back before I can milk her, Ellie." Wilson laughed. The young man seemed dumbstruck looking at the girl as she spoke.

"The boys are out looking for her now." Her laugh was soft with a tone that hit a man in the pit of his stomach.

"She's probably been ate by that dat burn mountain cat." Wilson scratched his beard. "Poor old Beauty, first one cow gets eaten by the Metis, and now she may be ate by a mountain cat."

"They'll find her." Ellie looked directly into Oliver's staring eyes. "We will see you at supper, Mister Bass."

"Yes, ma'am."

Wilson watched Ellie walk away, and then looked over at Oliver. "Put your eyes back in your head, boy, before you trip over them."

"Yes, sir,"

"Yes, she's pretty, ain't she?" Wilson was amused. He had seen men's breath taken away by Ellie's beauty at Bridger when he had gone to the trading post, his first and only time to trade Jed's pelts.

"She's the prettiest creature I've ever seen, Mister Wilson."

"Don't say that too loud in front of her older brother." Wilson resumed his whittling. "He might take offense."

"No offense intended, just pure fact." Oliver nodded. "I've met her brother and I wouldn't want to rile him."

"That wouldn't be wise, son."

"Where do I put my horse?"

"Strip the saddle and get your trappings off him, then turn him loose." Wilson's long knife cut a piece of shaving from the soft wood.

"He won't run off?"

"Run where, youngster?" Wilson shook his head at the pilgrim. "Ain't nowhere for him to go that we can't find him."

"I s'pect you're right." Oliver loosened the cinch on the animal. "Tell me something, Mister Wilson."

"And just what would that be?"

"The one called Crow Killer calls you pa, but he says he's Arapaho." Oliver slapped the horse on the rump as he turned him loose. "Is he Indian or white?"

"A little of both." Wilson replied. "He's my adopted son."

"I guess a man wouldn't want to get him mad at you either?"

"Nope, that wouldn't be wise."

"I figured that."

"Tell me, Oliver." Wilson stared at the tall one. "What is a city feller like you doing way up here in these mountains?"

"That, Mister Wilson, is a very good question." Oliver shook his head. "I was kidnapped."

"Kidnapped?" Wilson blinked. "Kidnapped by who?"

"Yes, sir." Oliver related the events that wound him up there on the old man's porch. "And as quick as I can, I'll be heading back east to civilization."

"That's quite a tale, young man." Wilson grinned. "So you're one of them eastern lawyers?"

"Yes, sir." Oliver nodded as he took a seat on the porch. "I'm from Philadelphia, studied law, and also became a land surveyor and geologist."

Wilson knew all about lawyers. "That's why I'm out here. A high-minded Philadelphia lawyer got me cheated out of my farm back in Pennsylvania."

"Weren't me, sir."

"Nope, but he was a lawyer just the same." Wilson shook his head in disgust. "Probably a land surveyor too."

"Where are we going?" Red Horse asked as Eagle Wing started the horse up the mountain trail. "The cow will not be up this high."

"We will follow the whites over the pass."

"Crow Killer said for you to leave them alone." Red Horse shook his head. "And this one does not wish to disobey our father."

"He only said they were not to be harmed." The older youth shrugged. "Get down and return to the cabin if you do not want to come with me."

"To the cabin, am I such a baby?"

"Then remain quiet as you should." Eagle Wing scolded his younger brother. "We will stay out of sight and watch these whites until they start down the other side of the mountain."

The horse, blowing slightly from carrying double and the hard pace Eagle Wing was setting, made Red Horse shake his head. He knew his brother wanted the whites to give him a reason to fight. "You've blooded them. The cowards won't stop until they reach Bridger."

"We will see." Eagle Wing shrugged. "At Bridger they will tell how we ambushed them and killed for no reason."

"It's not right, my brother. Do not disobey our father." Red Horse grabbed Eagle Wing's arm. "Crow Killer has permitted them to leave this place with their dead and wounded without further harm."

The dark eyes of the older youth were like piercing coals as they glanced back over his shoulder at the smaller boy. Looking down at the cabin in the far distance, then back up the trail, Eagle Wing nodded. He had never disobeyed his father, but he had heard the white's words about his sister. The big hunter deserved to die. He knew his sister, Ellie Thunder, was beautiful, and he knew the white men were dangerous.

They would come again. They would drink their strong firewater, build their courage, and one day, they would return to these mountains.

Nodding, the fire faded from his eyes. "You're right. We will only follow to make sure they leave our valley, then we'll hunt for the cow."

"I will help you kill these white hunters if you wish." Red Horse shrugged. "But, Crow Killer will find out we have dishonored him by not doing as he says."

"No, we will just make sure they leave." The dark eyes looked up the trail. "Nothing more."

Oliver sat on the porch, watching the old man whittle on a pine stick, steadily reducing the limb to only a pile of shavings. Looking out across the small creek and the broad valley, he had to smile. These mountains, like the girl, were all beautiful, not a blemish on them.

"Here they come with old Beauty now." Wilson slapped his knee in relief. "I was feared that old mountain cat might have had her for supper."

"Mountain cat?"

"Yes, sir, we've been troubled with a big one prowling around after dark these last few weeks."

"We got her for you, Grandpa." Red Horse led the cow through the corral gate.

"Took you boys long enough."

"She's back, that's enough." Eagle Wing stared at Oliver.

"Tell your ma we'll be over just soon as I milk."

"Yes, sir." Red Horse grinned at Oliver, then followed Eagle Wing down the small trail.

"The older boy don't seem to cotton to me much, Mister Wilson."

"He'll warm up to you soon enough." Wilson reached for his milk bucket. "But, were I you, I wouldn't be looking too hard at his sister."

"Don't worry about that." Oliver shook his head. "I've seen that young man in action."

"What do you mean?"

Oliver quickly finished telling Wilson of the trouble with Maud, the white trappers, and how Eagle Wing shot one of the men and cut another.

"Your grandson is a rough one, Mister Wilson."

"That he is."

CHAPTER 2

E agle Wing's powerful legs carried him silently along the mountain trails as he trotted south toward the far end of the huge valley. With the long black flowing hair, dark skin, and dress, he could easily be mistaken for one of the many wild tribes that frequented these mountains. Armed only with a longbow, quiver of arrows, and sharp skinning knife, the wide black eyes took in every part of the small trail he traversed. Today, Eagle Wing, the eldest son of Jed Bracket, was out hunting for deer.

A lone runner arrived at the cabin, ahead of the other approaching warriors. His uncle, Walking Horse the Arapaho, blood brother to Jed Bracket whom most called Crow Killer, would arrive in two days. Eagle Wing was excited and could hardly wait for his uncle's arrival. Almost a year passed since Walking Horse had come for a visit to their valley. Now, in his eighteenth summer, it was time for the young son of Crow Killer to go with his uncle, to learn the ways of the Arapaho Lance Bearers. It was also the time for him to go alone on a vision quest. The vision, after being translated by the medicine man of the tribe, would guide him along the path he would follow throughout his life. Many younger boys sought out their vision at an earlier age, but Spotted Panther, Medicine Man of the Cheyenne, had told Crow Killer that Eagle Wing was to wait until his eighteenth summer.

Jed and his mother, Bright Moon, were not happy knowing their beloved son would be leaving their valley and riding into unknown faraway dangerous lands. However, they both knew it was the Arapaho way and Eagle Wing was Arapaho, at least half. His mother was full-blood Cheyenne, from the northern band of his uncle He Dog's village. He had turned eighteen years of age and now, his obligation as a young Arapaho coming-of-age, was to learn of his heritage and experience the vision he hoped would be revealed to him. Every young Arapaho boy yearned for the day he would become a man and take his rightful place among the warriors of the Arapaho Tribe. His uncle, Walking Horse, Chief of the Northern Branch of the Arapaho, was the greatest of warriors and he would be the one to teach Eagle Wing of the war trail. As the boy's uncle, it was his place to teach his nephew everything he would need to know to become a man. This warrior was the same one who had taught Jed Bracket the ways of the Lance Bearer. With Walking Horse's guidance, the young white had been molded into the fearless Lance Bearer all the tribes feared. The warrior they called Crow Killer, the great bear hunter.

Every time the Arapaho warriors or Crow warriors of Red Hawk had arrived, Eagle Wing would hear the stories of his father's bravery and the many battles he had fought in their valley. Time had passed so slowly, that he couldn't wait to become a man and ride the war trails of his people. Since he was old enough to hunt alone, he had sought out the burial scaffolds of the warlike Nez Perce and Pawnee. He would look up at them in awe, wondering what they had been like. His father seldom spoke of them or his battles, only saying they had been very brave warriors and formidable enemies. The youngster dreamed at night of fighting these same battles and warriors. Yes, he was eager to follow Walking Horse south into the lands of their enemies to find adventure, as his father before him had done. Even as huge as the high valley of Jed Bracket was, it seemed small to him. Their valley didn't contain the enemy warriors or battles he had dreamed about at night as he slept. Something deep inside drove him, setting a fire in his boundless spirit.

Slipping quietly through the green grass, lining the valley, the hunter placed his feet so the leather moccasins that covered them made little to no sound. The bedded down deer were close, and he could sense them. Testing the wind, the youngster notched an arrow and slipped silently forward. The late spring grass was tall enough already to hide the deer so Eagle Wing knew they were there. He wanted to get close enough for a clean kill before they sensed his presence and bolted. To go home empty-handed, without fresh meat for the coming guests, would be humiliating. Never once had he failed his father, the great Crow Killer. Never had his father had cause to rebuke him for anything in his short life. Eagle Wing, even at his young age, was strong and proud, and he could never disappoint his parents by failing in any way.

Slipping from tree to tree, the hunter finally spotted the twitching ears of a resting deer as the animal swished away the tormenting flies that swarmed the herds continually during the summer months. Setting his feet, the youngster whistled softly, causing several deer to stand suspiciously to their feet with their ears pointing straight at him. Only the hiss of the arrow and the slap of the bowstring hitting his arm guard sounded, as it flew straight and true to its target. Seeing the deer spring into the air as the shaft found its mark, Eagle Wing quickly notched another arrow, hoping for another shot. Again, an arrow took flight, as another deer whirled away in fright as it sensed danger lurking in the woods nearby.

Whistling loudly, the hunter knelt over the dead deer, then walked to where he had last seen the other deer as it disappeared into the thick tree line. A heavy trail of blood spattered along the ground showed Eagle Wing his arrow had flown true and found its target. To leave such a blood trail meant a killing lung shot. The wounded animal would not travel far before lying down. Hearing the sound of running horses, he looked at the valley floor. Red Horse came into view, leading two horses.

"Eagle Wing has done well today." The younger boy grinned as he looked down at the deer. "Uncle Walking Horse and his warriors will have fresh meat to fill their bellies when they arrive."

Eagle Wing nodded at the grinning youth. "Gut this deer, Red Horse. I will look for the other one."

"Two deer? You have indeed done well today, Brother." The youngster laughed. "Our father will be very pleased."

"Don't count the deer, little brother, until they are in our hands." Eagle Wing shook his head as the younger lad slid down from his horse. "Clean this one, I will return shortly."

"We should have brought Oliver to help with the skinning, or Wolf's Head." Red Horse shrugged as he pulled his skinning knife.

"The white knows nothing of such things." Eagle Wing continued. "And Wolf's Head is tired from his long journey here."

"Oliver should learn." Red Horse suggested. "And an Arapaho Lance Bearer should never get tired."

"Why? The white returns to the east soon, and Wolf's Head is not yet a Lance Bearer." Eagle Wing replied.

"Don't the whites eat deer and elk in the east?"

"How should I know?"

"At least we could keep him away from our sister."

"Dress the deer, Red Horse." Eagle Wing shook his head. Today, he had other things on his mind. He didn't have time to listen to his younger brother goading him about the white and Ellie Thunder. He knew the young one was right. The tall white was always hanging around talking with their sister. "I'll return."

"Don't get lost, Brother."

Eagle Wing frowned. Red Horse was four years younger than his sister, Ellie Thunder. Not as serious as his older brother, Red Horse already had the height and frame that told one day he would be a magnificent looking warrior. That is, if he survived to manhood. His carefree and fearless attitude sometimes worried his older brother.

The younger son of Crow Killer could never be serious about anything. Fear of anything was not in his vocabulary. Once, Eagle Wing had found his younger brother hanging onto the head of a live rattlesnake that was wrapped around the boy's leg buzzing away. The youngster hadn't called out for help, nor did he intend to. With a firm grip on the snake's head, he was hanging on for dear life. Begging his brother not to tell their father, after Eagle Wing had parted the reptile's head from his body, Red Horse only laughed. He was more afraid of his father finding out, than he was of the snake. Quickly skinning the huge reptile, the younger boy had held the snake's skin out for his brother to see.

"It will make our mother a beautiful belt." The dark eyes laughed as he proudly displayed the skin. "Just don't tell Crow Killer exactly how we got it."

Eagle Wing remembered asking Red Horse how he had managed to get in such a fix.

The boy only shrugged. "He wanted to be friends."

"Well, little brother, what if he had bitten you?"

"I would have bitten him back."

Eagle Wing shook his head. That was Red Horse, and he doubted his young brother would ever survive to become a man. The youngster feared neither man nor beast which could one day be his downfall.

The deer hadn't run far. Eagle Wing waited several minutes, giving it time to bleed out before he trailed the blood trail to where the animal laid down. Returning to Red Horse, he helped the younger boy load the first deer on the packhorse, then they loaded the second one.

Laying his dark hand across the deer's chest, Eagle Wing looked up at the blue sky. "Forgive me, my friends, but I needed your meat to feed the great Arapaho Lance Bearers who are coming. The afterworld will welcome such brave warriors as you."

"I do not think they will thank you for taking their bodies to feed others." Red Horse disagreed. "I wouldn't."

"You, my brother, would be too bitter to eat."

Early next morning, the dark eyes of Eagle Wing studied the south pass of the huge valley for any sign of riders. Dressed in the typical buckskin leggings and doeskin hunting shirt, most trappers wore, the young one sat on the Appaloosa horse quietly. The sharp black eyes, encased in a broad handsome face, took in everything that surrounded him. His father, Crow Killer, had taught him well to always stay alert and aware of his surroundings, if he wanted to survive. The long straight black hair lay unfettered, as it fell down his back, almost reaching the horse's rump. Even dressed as a white trapper, there was no mistaking this rider for a white. His dark skin and eyes marked him as Indian. Although, still in his youth, the young one's tall, muscular frame and powerful toned physique, already promised he would grow to be a magnificent looking warrior.

Today was Eagle Wing's eighteenth summer, the day his uncle Walking Horse, had promised to come for him. The young one wondered if Red Hawk, his other uncle of the Crow Tribe, would ride with him. In the Arapaho villages, eighteen was considered the age for a boy to learn to be a man. It was time for him to pass the ceremonial tests to prove he was worthy. Now was the time for him to ride with Walking Horse on the path to becoming an Arapaho warrior. As with all young men, their uncles were in charge of teaching their nephews the ways of the Arapaho Lance Bearers. If he failed to pass these rituals, he would be shamed, as his teacher would be. Many things were expected of a young man, as he followed the path of a warrior. He had to be cunning like the wolf, silent like the mountain cat, and brave as a buffalo bull, fighting for his cows. He could never show pain or hardship, as it was not the Arapaho way.

The Lance Bearers were the greatest of fighters, willing to die for their brothers in battle. To become an Arapaho Lance Bearer, every young man was expected to pass many tests. Not all who undertook the rituals succeeded, and some couldn't endure the tremendous feats of endurance needed to pass. The ones who failed were still Arapaho, but they were not the great elite Lance Bearers. Anyone among the Arapaho lodges could spot a Lance Bearer immediately. They had a proud, arrogant tilt of their head, a ramrod straight back, and a short lance protruding from their arrow quiver. Also, unless a young man passed into adulthood and became a warrior, he would never be allowed to take the woman of his choice in marriage. The young maiden's father would refuse the horses brought for her bride price. The tests were difficult and dangerous. Some young men were killed by an enemy and others went away in shame, if they failed for any reason.

He had heard from other warriors how his father had gone into the enemy Crow camp and stole the headdress of the great Plenty Coups. Plus, he had taken the great spotted horse of his other uncle, Red Hawk. He would not fail and he would become a Lance Bearer of the Arapaho people or die trying. The powerful heart that beats in his chest was given to him by his father, the great Crow Killer, and Bright Moon, his Cheyenne mother. He would rather die first before being shamed by showing fear or by failing.

Eagle Wing's father, Jedidiah Bracket, better known in the tribes as Crow Killer, had already taught all the things the youngster needed to know. Ever since he could lift the heavy Hawken rifle and war club, his father had taught him how to shoot and how to fight. Jed Bracket had taught both of his sons how to kick and fight with their feet as well as their hands. Most Indian warriors would not strike an enemy with their bare hands, giving the advantage to Eagle Wing and Red Horse. Many times, at Bridger's Post, the boys had been challenged by the young Arickaree boys. With every challenge, Eagle Wing and Red Horse had defeated their opponents, gaining them much fame.

Knowing the Arapaho Lance Bearer's ways was permitted, but it was still Walking Horse's duty to teach and keep the young one for many moons. Neither Crow Killer nor his mother, Bright Moon, had been happy knowing soon their oldest son would ride south into Arapaho country and danger.

Jed Bracket worried as he remembered the tests he had been required to perform as a youngster, and he remembered the prophecy spoken by Spotted Panther, the Cheyenne Medicine Man. For the last eighteen years, Jed Bracket had been awoken many times from his sleep, by the prophetic words of the old medicine man of the Cheyenne.

"Your son will become a great warrior, a Lance Bearer of the Arapaho." Jed recalled the old man's coal-like eyes as they stared across the fire at him. "He will ride and fight beside another great warrior and Chief of the Sioux."

Spotted Panther's words were burned into Jed's mind and he wondered about his son's future.

The spotted horse pricked his ears as he sensed the presence of other horses coming down the steep trail, leading to the valley floor. Eagle Wing checked the priming on his rifle, then looked up at five riders as they wound their way along the path. Kicking the horse forward, the young one smiled and raised his hand in greeting as four Arapaho warriors and one Crow rode out onto the valley floor.

"My nephew." Walking Horse took the outstretched hand of the youngster.

"Uncles, it is good to see you." Eagle Wing greeted his uncles and the other warriors.

"You have grown, young one." Red Hawk nodded. "You have become tall like our brother Crow Killer."

"Did Wolf's Head tell of our coming?"

"Yes, he arrived two sleeps ago."

"Where is your father?" Walking Horse looked about the valley floor.

"He stays behind at our lodge." Eagle Wing pointed to the north. "He says his bones are getting too old for the long journey to this place."

Walking Horse laughed at the words. He knew Crow Killer wanted his son to have the honor of escorting his uncles to the cabin. "Our brother will be riding this valley long after we are in our soft robes."

"Are they well?" Red Hawk followed the young one's gaze to the north end of the valley.

"Yes, he and my mother are well." The youngster nodded, then looked at the other warriors sitting behind his uncles. "It's my birthday. He says it is my place to ride here to greet my people."

"And the old one, your grandfather?"

"He grows old and grey headed, but he's still feisty."

"And your sister, Ellie Thunder and your brother, Red Horse?"

"They are fine, Red Hawk, my uncle."

"Well, let us ride to see them." Walking Horse kicked his horse. "It has been many sleeps since I have spoken with my brother."

"There has been no trouble here?" Red Hawk looked at the youngster, noticing the scar on the youngster's face.

"No trouble, except for a party of white trappers that came to our valley."

"Tell us of this."

"My father defeated their leader and the rest left our valley quickly."

"Did Crow Killer kill the white?" Walking Horse questioned him.

"No, but the white man was probably sore for many sleeps." Eagle Wing thought of the white hunter's bloody ear.

Red Hawk laughed. "Your father is a terrible warrior to get mad."

"Yes." Eagle Wing smiled. "I watched his face as the white hunter bled."

"Is that all?"

"No, I believe one day these whites will return to our land." Eagle Wing shrugged. "Their leader has looked at my sister, Ellie Thunder."

"Why did my brother not kill this one?" Walking Horse was curious. "Does Crow Killer believe this?"

"He believed, but would not kill." Eagle Wing shrugged.

"What else has happened since we were here last?"

"My father rode to the village of Baxter Springs with a young white man named Oliver. He was gone many sleeps and when they returned, he had a piece of paper saying this valley belongs to him and cannot be taken from him for all time to come."

"Own the land?" Walking Horse shook his head. "No one can own the land. Mother earth is for all to enjoy."

"The young white is some kind of white medicine man that knows the writing on paper." Eagle Wing added. "He says the land belongs for all time to Crow Killer."

"This cannot be." Red Hawk shook his head. "No."

"I hope my uncle is wrong." Eagle Wing replied. "Crow Killer paid many bags of his hide money for the paper."

"The white man's paper is worth nothing."

"The paper says Jedidiah Bracket owns this valley and the valley that lies to the west." Eagle Wing explained. "I have read it and the one, Oliver, said it was so."

Red Hawk smiled. "Your father has taught you to read the white man's marks on paper?"

"Yes, all of us and even my mother."

"My woman, your Aunt Ellie Medicine Thunder, has tried to teach me the scratches, but she gave up." Red Hawk shrugged. "What need does a Crow have to learn such things?"

"A Crow needs all the help he can get." Walking Horse laughed as their horses plodded down the valley floor.

"Why, I am pretty, have the greatest of horses, and a beautiful wife and children."

"And, my brother, you are not the least bit boastful, are you?"

"When the words are true, my Arapaho friend, it is not boasting, it is fact."

Laughing as his uncles argued, Eagle Wing kicked his young Appaloosa into a short lope toward the far-off smoke coming from the cabin's chimney.

Riding alongside the easy striding spotted horse, Red Hawk smiled. "My nephew rides a strong horse."

"He is one of many we have raised from the stallion you gave my mother many years ago."

"He was the first colt from the old stallion I took from the Nez Perce."

"Stole is the right word, Uncle." Eagle Wing shrugged. "I have heard the story many times."

Walking Horse laughed out loud. "Your uncle, Red Hawk, does not steal horses, my nephew. He just borrows them from time to time."

Eagle Wing agreed. "Yes, I have heard this."

"This is another son of the mighty spotted horse, I borrowed." Red Hawk patted the sleek neck of the Appaloosa stallion he rode.

"Where is the old one?"

"He just runs with his squaws now. He is too old to make such a long journey as we are on." Red Hawk nodded sadly. "We have ridden many a war trail together. Now, it is his time to rest."

Walking Horse laughed. "Perhaps, Red Hawk should rest too. He grows old."

"Never, my brother, never."

Jed Bracket and Bright Moon sat outside their cabin, studying the swells of grass covering the huge valley. They knew Walking Horse would be coming soon. Thrilled to see their brother again, the parents of Eagle Wing still dreaded losing their son. They knew Eagle Wing would be leaving soon to become a full-fledged warrior of the Arapaho, and neither could object.

Bright Moon looked at her son's rolled sleeping robe, and the bags she had packed and laid out on the table. Tears formed in her eyes as she recalled the wonderful times they had the last eighteen years. Since the coming of their third child, Red Horse, named for each of his uncles, time had passed so quickly. She thought back to the fight with the Pawnees and the birth of her twins. Yes, time had passed far too quickly. Bright Moon wouldn't have missed these years for anything. They were magical times that she had experienced with her husband and children, tucked back in this beautiful valley. Their life had been carefree and blissful, but now, these days were forever at an end.

Bright Moon also remembered the words of the old Cheyenne Medicine Man. She knew if his prophecy held true, her son, Eagle Wing, would become a great warrior, but his life would always be in danger as he rode against his enemies. She was Cheyenne, and it was a

Cheyenne warrior's duty to protect his people. Bright Moon knew it also bothered her husband, Crow Killer, that the old one had predicted their son would fight not only against their hereditary enemies, but the whites as well. Both knew the future held extreme dangers for their eldest, but it was Eagle Wing's destiny to ride the war trail against his enemies.

The small black mule of Silent One brayed out long and loud when she smelled the approaching horses. Rising from the table, Jed and Bright Moon stood waiting, as the approaching horsemen splashed across the shallow creek and rode up to the cabin. With the stately and proud forbearance of their people, the warriors smiled slightly as they shook hands.

Suddenly, Walking Horse laughed and grabbed Bright Moon, lifting her high over his head. "Ah, Sister, it is good to see you."

"Put me down, you overgrown buffalo." Bright Moon laughed as Walking Horse set her down gently. Her feet had hardly touched the ground when Red Hawk gathered her to him. "You too, Crow."

"Your tongue is as sharp as your sister's."

Bright Moon smiled and nodded at the other warriors. "Where are my sisters, Little Antelope and Ellie Medicine Thunder?"

"One of you at a time is enough, three would be unbearable." Red Hawk shrugged.

"Tell me, why didn't you bring them?"

"Little Antelope would not leave the children to come here, and Medicine Thunder has sick ones in our village that she could not leave."

For so long Little Antelope had been saddened that she had no children. Now, she and Walking Horse had two little ones that they were so proud of.

"I would like to see the children again." Bright Moon smiled.

"Perhaps, when Eagle Wing has finished his novice time, you will ride to the village and see all your people." Walking Horse nodded. "We will have a great celebration when his time of learning is finished."

"After that, my nephew will come to the Crow village to learn how to become a true warrior." Red Hawk laughed. "The Crow way."

"Perhaps we should wait until he becomes an Arapaho Lance Bearer before we celebrate." Hearing the soft, pleasant voice, all eyes turned to the cabin door, as Ellie Thunder walked outside to greet her uncles and the others.

"Who is this beautiful one?" Red Hawk seemed shocked. "She must be of the spirit world with all her beauty."

The lithe, slender young woman smiled with her bright white teeth gleaming in the sunlight as she stood in the doorway. A long doeskin dress of pure white reached all the way to the ground, covering her moccasins. The young warriors that had ridden with Walking Horse swallowed hard, as they were mesmerized by her beauty. Long black hair cascaded down her back, framing the most flawless smooth face and oval eyes. The young daughter of Crow Killer and Bright Moon was a raving beauty in any society.

Stepping forward, she embraced her uncles and smiled at the other warriors. "It is good you are here, my uncles."

"The small, ugly caterpillar has turned into a beautiful butterfly." Walking Horse held her hand for several minutes. "It is good to see my niece again, it has been far too long."

"Yes, my uncle, it has been far too long a time." Ellie Thunder smiled her beautiful smile, captivating the young warriors who had accompanied Walking Horse.

"Where is your brother, Red Horse?" Jed looked questioningly at Eagle Wing.

"Only Red Horse knows where Red Horse is, my father." Eagle Wing looked around the cabin. "He will be here soon. He knows his uncles are here."

"I think he and Wolf's Head hunt for fresh meat." Bright Moon spoke up.

Jed nodded, as Eagle Wing spoke the truth. He knew his younger son well. The young one had a mind of his own. When he was away from the cabin hunting, time seemed to stand still for his younger son.

Once again, Jed was with his brothers. Ushering the warriors to seats in the shade, they sat talking of bygone days. Suddenly, from across the creek, they heard the sound of a horse running full out toward the cabin. Shielding their eyes from the bright afternoon sun, the warriors watched in amazement as Red Horse thundered across the valley toward them, sitting backwards on his racing horse.

Flipping around on the hard running animal, the youngster rolled under the horse's belly and came up on the other side. However, he misjudged the nearness of the creek in his desire to show off. Red Horse was almost back on top of the plunging horse when the animal slid to a sliding bone-jarring stop, flinging the youngster head first into the creek. After seeing the boy wasn't hurt, all the warriors started laughing at the soaked youngster, who sputtered and coughed as he regained his feet.

Completely drenched, Red Horse walked shamefaced to the cabin, cussing the horse as it raced toward the pasture and the other horses. The others started to feel sorry for the embarrassed, pitiful acting youth, when suddenly the youngster's contagious smile broke out and he started laughing. Only Red Horse could turn an embarrassing moment into a laughable one. Charm and humor was a major factor of his persona. Nobody could dislike the likeable youngster for long.

"I told him not to do it." Wolf's Head dismounted from his horse.

"Well, Nephew, is that the new way of dismounting a horse or the Arapaho way?" Red Hawk could only shake his head and smile.

"Either way, it was much faster, Uncle."

"Maybe so, but it is very hard on the head." Walking Horse laughed.

"No worry, nothing could hurt that head." Eagle Wing assured him.

Moving closer to the other warriors, Red Horse laughed as they poked at him, ribbing him about falling from his horse. Jovial, always with a smile, the youth drew everyone to him.

"Soon, Red Horse will be old enough to ride with the Arapaho warriors against our enemies." Two-Eyed Dog, a Lance Bearer, chided the youngster. "But first, perhaps he should learn to ride better."

"Be careful, I think he rides better than you do already." Grey Hair laughed.

Two-Eyed Dog laughed. "Grey Hair may be right."

The handsome warrior called Grey Hair, had a strip of grey hair growing down the middle of his head. A glancing blow from a Pawnee war axe had ripped across his head when he was just a novice warrior. The hair had turned grey, where the axe had laid his scalp open, clean to the bone. The village medicine man had seen this coloring as a good omen and had given the young warrior his new name, Grey Hair. The warrior, except for the skunk colored hair, was an unblemished young man, very handsome, straight, and proud. It was a fitting name, and it marked him in battle. Every enemy warrior desired his long black and grey hair for their scalp pole. Many had tried to take it, but so far, none had succeeded. The warrior with the white hair, although still young, was becoming a great, fearless, and well-known Lance Bearer.

Grey Hair was a cousin of Walking Horse, and although still young, Walking Horse called on him when he was in need of strong counsel. Other warriors, and even elders of the tribe, respected and followed the warrior. Like his father, Big Owl before him, the young warrior was a born leader of men, with great strength and an indomitable fighting spirit. Since the fight at the big river, with the Comanche and Big Owl's death, Walking Horse missed the strong right arm and wisdom of his friend, Big Owl. In time, Grey Hair replaced his father, lacking only his father's size and huge appetite.

Wilson and Oliver walked up to the cabin and stopped before the warriors.

Jed grinned as he knew exactly what the tall white was thinking. "Yes, Oliver, more Indians."

"I didn't say that, Jed." Holding up his hands, the young white grinned nervously.

After introducing everyone to Oliver, Wilson shook hands and greeted the warriors. "It's good to see my friends."

Oliver did not understand when Grey Hair spoke to Eagle Wing in Arapaho. "Is this the one from the east that is a medicine man?"

"He is a medicine man with paper, Grey Hair." Jed answered the question. "Not a healer of men."

"I do not understand this paper." The warrior shook his head.

"White man's writings are like the treaties your chiefs signed with the white government."

"Then, I do not like this one." Two-Eyed Dog growled. "Their words were as worthless as the paper that held them."

Jed looked hard at the young warrior. "This white has done me a great service and saved this valley for us, my friends. Honor him and be his friend."

"If this is what Crow Killer wishes, it will be so." The warriors shook hands with Oliver.

After Bright Moon greeted the newcomers, she and Ellie Thunder went into the cabin to prepare a meal for their hungry visitors. Motioning for Red Horse to follow, Bright Moon quickly mixed fresh milk and flour for biscuits. She wanted the food to be hot on their arrival so she had delayed starting the meal.

"Red Horse, go to the spring house and bring fresh meat for your uncles."

Red Horse nodded as he looked back out the door where the warriors were talking. Trotting up the trail behind the cabin, he moved quickly to a small heavily-constructed log shed. Opening the heavy door, he felt the cool rush of air when he entered. Several carcasses were hanging from the rafters, each salted and encased in light cloth. The small structure was built over a natural spring that ran underground from the mountains, and came to the surface inside the building. The cool spring water kept the temperature inside the shed very cool, preserving the meat. His father and mother smoked the hams from elk and deer, keeping them from spoiling. Dried meat also hung in strips from the rafters of the spring house.

Resting a side of deer across his shoulder, Red Horse closed the door and returned to the cabin. Laying the carcass on the table, the youngster looked at his mother.

"Do you need me to help?"

Bright Moon knew her younger son wanted to go back outside with the warriors, to listen to their tales of battle and great deeds. Her son, Eagle Wing, was proud, stoic, and reserved, whereas, Red Horse, was carefree and forever getting himself in trouble. His father, Crow Killer, would shake his head at the youngster's antics, hoping one day the boy would mature and grow out of his childish ways.

"Go listen to the warriors, my son." She smiled.

"Thank you, Mother." The youngster was carefree and hardheaded, but he respected his mother, Bright Moon. He would not do anything to shame himself in her eyes.

"You could stay and wash the dishes, Red Horse." Ellie Thunder teased.

"Washing dishes is not a warrior's place, my sister." Red Horse hurried from the cabin. "We do the hunting and fighting."

"Warrior, you are just a boy." The pretty girl laughed.

"One day, he will be a warrior, my daughter." Bright Moon smiled, then clucked her tongue.

"Does my brother, Eagle Wing, return to the Arapaho people to fulfill the words of Spotted Panther?" Ellie knew about the prophecy.

"If Spotted Panther's words come true, your brother has a hard, dangerous trail in front of him. His will be a path of many hardships, glory, and death." Bright Moon thought of the old medicine man's words.

"Which one will it be, Mother, glory or death?" Ellie Thunder looked fearfully at Bright Moon. She and Eagle Wing were identical twins, which entwined them together stronger, more than normal siblings.

"It is your brother's destiny. Many moons ago, it was seen in the stones and smoke of Spotted Panther's fire." Bright Moon shook her greying head.

"What is written, is written then?" Ellie Thunder asked.

"I am afraid for your brother." Bright Moon replied sadly. "What will be will be, my daughter. We cannot change what the spirits have shown."

CHAPTER 3

Walking Horse studied his muscular nephew, who sat quietly as the other warriors told their stories. He watched as the young one listened politely, paying close attention to the words of the older warriors. Only if asked a question, would Eagle Wing speak, and then answer in a direct manner with his voice strong and clear. Even at a young age, muscles rippled in the youth's biceps with every move of his powerful arms. Walking Horse knew this one, even though still young, was special and would one day become a great warrior. He would mold Eagle Wing into a Lance Bearer of the Arapaho, as he had done his father, Crow Killer.

As Bright Moon and Ellie Thunder passed out steaming deer and elk steaks to the assembled warriors, Walking Horse thought about the words of the medicine man. Spotted Panther had foretold of the trail he had seen for this youth, a hard and dangerous path. Someday, Eagle Wing would be a great warrior, fighting not only his hereditary enemies, the Pawnee and Shoshone, but the whites as well.

Crow Killer told the gathered warriors how Eagle Wing, in early summer, had wounded one white and killed another. Then, he slit the ear of a third, as they fired on him, striking the youngster with a passing bullet from their pistol. The hot piece of lead had left a shallow scar on Eagle Wing's smooth dark face.

Walking Horse thought the mark gave the youth character and an air of prominence. He wondered about Eagle Wing's future. The jagged scar, where the white man's bullet had plowed its furrow across the youth's high cheekbone seemed to point upward into the clouds where the spirit people lived. He also had the birthmark of the lance on his back, the same as his father.

As Crow Killer spoke of the fight with the whites, there was no doubt in the listening warriors' minds that one day, this one would be a leader of men, courageous and steady in battle. From what Walking Horse now observed, he was humble and unobtrusive. The youth was quiet in the presence of his elders, a trait not to be mistaken for fear or timidity. There was no doubt in the forbearance and carriage of this young one. He was a serious one, and if he had reason, he would be a very dangerous foe.

The meal finished, and the warriors with Red Horse following, walked to the creek for a swim and a bath, to get rid of the trail dust from their long journey from the south. Moving upstream to the deep swimming hole, out of sight of the cabin and women, the warriors removed their leggings and vests, and dove into the clear water. As usual, Red Horse was the first into the water.

Grey Hair grabbed the laughing youngster, and ducked him under the water several times. Swimming like a fish, Red Horse slipped from the warrior's hands and came up laughing his contagious laugh.

"The water feels good, Nephew." Red Hawk pushed water at Red Horse.

Jed nodded as he watched the merriment. He wondered if Ellie Medicine Thunder ever told Red Hawk about them swimming together in this pool of water so many moons ago. He hoped not, Red Hawk was his brother and he never wanted anything to come between them. Their swimming here had been completely innocent between two young people who thought they were in love. In time, they had grown apart, knowing they were of two different cultures. At the time, he and Ellie knew nothing of love. Then, she had married Red Hawk, a warrior who was even wilder than Jed had been. It was funny, in the end Ellie had married a warrior living in the very same society she thought she had no place in. Jed was happy for them, his best friend and a woman he thought so much of. They were brothers, and nothing would ever come between the two of them.

"You are quiet and serious, my brother." Walking Horse scrubbed his arms and chest with the clean sand from the creek bottom. "Do you worry for the boy?"

Jed looked to where Eagle Wing was talking quietly with Grey Hair. "His journey begins soon. The path sometimes can be dangerous for one so young. Yes, I worry."

"I too worry, my friend, but the prophecy has been spoken for all to hear." Walking Horse rinsed the sand from his body. "I believe Eagle Wing was sent by the spirit ones above. He must follow his true path."

"I know." Jed agreed. "When White Swan gave me the same choice to go with you and become a Lance Bearer, it was the same. I accepted the dangers that lay before me."

"The difference this time, it is your son, not you." Walking Horse understood his feelings and fear, not for himself, but for his son. He knew Crow Killer feared nothing, but he did fear losing a beloved son whom he loved more than life itself. "The old one saw glory and good things in his fire for the young one, nothing more."

"I know, but sometimes, maybe the stones do not see all things."

Walking Horse smiled. "We have held each other's lives in our hands many times, my friend. I would die before I let anything happen to Eagle Wing."

"I know, my brother. I don't want anything happening to you either." Jed smiled.

"My oldest son will be of age in a few years. Then, he will come here with you." Walking Horse laughed. "Then it will be my time to worry."

"The children must have grown a lot since we saw them last."

"They have grown, like spotted fawns losing their spots."

"And how is Little Antelope?"

"She wanted to come, but our trail was to be fast, maybe dangerous, and our return will be the same. It is no place for a woman and children."

"You will leave soon then?"

"We will ride with the coming of the new sun." Walking Horse relaxed in the warm sun letting his body dry. "I cannot be gone long from the village."

"Do you foresee trouble ahead on your return trail?" Jed watched the warriors at play with Red Horse. "Should I ride south with you?"

"No, we will be fine." Walking Horse nodded. "But, with the passing of

Plenty Coups, the peace between the Pawnee and the Arapaho is very fragile, maybe it no longer exists."

"Do they raid the Arapaho villages?"

"Yes, and the Crow also." Walking Horse frowned. "Several moons ago, Red Hawk killed two Pawnee raiders, when they raided his pony herd."

"The Pawnee must have grown brave to raid the Crows."

"They now scout for the white-eye pony soldiers and they have several white traders as friends. This makes them brave." Walking Horse nodded sadly. "The Pawnee warriors are many, with many guns given to them by the whites."

"It is the white soldiers that make them brave enough to ride against us." Two-Eyed Dog hissed with hatred. "Without their help, they would not dare attack the Arapaho."

"Two-Eyed Dog speaks the truth." Walking Horse nodded.

"Have you spoken about this with Red Hawk?"

"Red Hawk is Crow." Walking Horse looked to where Red Hawk and another warrior were talking. "The Crow are also the hereditary enemies of the Arapaho."

"He is our brother by blood and by marriage." Jed shook his head. "He could never be our enemy."

"The old chief, Plenty Coups, no longer walks the earth." Two-Eyed Dog shrugged. "Many of the Crow do not follow Red Hawk as they did the old one."

"Red Hawk has many enemies in the Crow villages that do not want peace with the Arapaho." Walking Horse added.

"Who, the elders?"

"No, only the younger warriors who follow Long Leaper."

"Ah yes, Long Leaper." Jed nodded, remembering when he had killed Wild Wind, the father of Long Leaper. The warrior had always hated Jed for killing his father and Red Hawk for being Crow Killer's friend and blood brother. "Someone should have killed that one long ago."

"Red Hawk is loved by his people as Plenty Coups was, but Long Leaper has a poison tongue that wags always." Walking Horse shrugged. "And he has matured and made a name for himself."

Two-Eyed Dog nodded. "And there are always young fools willing to follow one such as that braggart."

Walking Horse looked over at Red Hawk. "As Chief of the Crow, it is forbidden by tribal law for Red Hawk to kill another Crow."

"Perhaps, I will ride south in a few sleeps, and pay Long Leaper a visit." Jed looked at the two warriors. "The peace the Crow and Arapaho enjoyed while Plenty Coups lived was good."

"Long Leaper has earned prominence in the tribe by killing many enemies, Comanche, Sioux, and Pawnee." Two-Eyed Dog smiled. "I would like to see his face if Crow Killer challenged him to a fight in front of the whole Crow Nation."

"No, my friend, this cannot be." Walking Horse held up his hand. "Red Hawk waits for the right time, then he will take care of Long Leaper himself."

"We'll see." Jed looked to where Red Horse had pounced on Grey Head's back. "I owe Red Hawk much."

"Your youngest reminds me of He Dog of the Cheyenne, in his youth." Walking Horse laughed as Grey Head tossed the laughing youngster far out into the creek. "Yes, he acts exactly as He Dog did before the death of his brother."

"Bright Moon wishes to see her brother, He Dog." Jed nodded. "Perhaps, before the cold times come, we will travel to the Cheyenne village."

"He has not come here?"

"No, he sent Crazy Cat and a few warriors here last fall." Jed shook his head. "His people have many enemies from the north. He is afraid to leave his village for very long."

"There has been trouble with the Rics." Walking Horse shook his head.

"The ones from the north challenged him last fall, during the meat taking time." Two-Eyed Dog added.

"What happened?" Jed was curious. "Crazy Cat spoke nothing of any trouble when he was last here."

"He Dog accepted the challenge. He had a warrior return to the village to bring back the old yellow horse he had taken from the Rics when he killed their greatest warrior." Walking Horse retold the story as

Crazy Cat had related to him. "The cowards, upon seeing He Dog astride the old horse, turned and rode away."

"Superstitious, aren't they?"

"It is a good thing for them." Walking Horse laughed. "He Dog has matured into a mighty warrior. When mad, he can become extremely dangerous."

"I saw him last year at Bridger." Two-Eyed Dog shrugged. "He Dog has changed. His eyes are wild. I would not like him to get mad at me."

Jed remembered the young chief of the Cheyenne. He had been just a fun loving youngster as Red Horse was until the Arickaree had killed his brother, Yellow Dog, from ambush. Now, he was Chief of the Northern Cheyenne, and there was no longer any play or foolishness in the young chief.

"He has become a great chief." Jed nodded slowly. He wanted his sons to be strong, but he did not want them to be hard and cold as He Dog had become. His cruelty in battle was known by all the tribes. Yellow Dog's death had changed the fun loving young Cheyenne. Jed had seen it himself as He Dog battled the scar-faced warrior. The young chief had killed, then scalped the ferocious Arickaree warrior, the one with the blue lightning bolt splashed across his torso and face.

"Yes, my brother, tomorrow we will ride for our village."

"Bright Moon and I hate to see Walking Horse and his warriors leave so soon." Jed frowned. "You have just arrived."

"We must go." Walking Horse nodded. "Red Hawk says he will remain here and visit a few sleeps."

"Will it not be dangerous for Red Hawk to ride alone back across the many miles to his village?" Two-Eyed Dog questioned.

"Not for Red Hawk." Walking Horse laughed. "He is like a ghost in the dark. No enemy will find him, if he does not wish it to be so."

Jed knew the warrior was right. Red Hawk was like a whisper in the wind. He was seemingly invisible to an enemy's eyes or ears. Jed remembered when the Crow had ridden to the north following the Blackfoot, Bear Claw. Like a thief in the night, he had managed to rescue Little Antelope from the warrior. Then, after returning Little Antelope safely back to Walking Horse, the Crow had appeared magically and watched from a hillside, as Jed battled with the Blackfoot chief. No, there was little to worry about. Red Hawk would always be safe, riding the lands alone.

Early morning, after a huge breakfast of deer steaks, flapjacks, and sweet syrup, Jed, Bright Moon, Red Hawk, Oliver, and Wilson waved good-bye as Walking Horse departed to the south with his warriors. Ellie Thunder and Red Horse rode alongside Eagle Wing, following the warriors. Tears formed in Bright Moon's eyes as she watched her eldest son ride away from the cabin. For eighteen years, she knew this day would come, but she hadn't resigned herself to it actually happening. Bright Moon had fought many battles beside her husband, Crow Killer. She knew about life and death, and no one knew what a new day would bring. In these mountains, life and death were alike, both could be very short. To a warrior, death was welcomed, providing his dying in battle was honorable. To die as a coward was not acceptable, and the spirit people would not let a warrior enter the hunting grounds above.

With one final look at their disappearing backs, Bright Moon turned sadly for the cabin. Jed watched as his beautiful woman walked away with her back straight and proud. He knew what she felt.

Red Hawk nodded slowly. "It is a hard thing to see a son ride away."

"Spotted Panther says he will have a very long and dangerous trail to follow." Jed let his dark eyes follow the riders.

"Then, he will become a great warrior for his people." Red Hawk nodded proudly. "He will be honored by all, and he has Walking Horse to guide him as he learns."

"There is none better."

"Yes, Walking Horse is a great warrior."

"Let us go hunting, my friend." Jed turned for the horse corral.

"What will we hunt?"

"I wish to check the north pass. Perhaps up high, we will find a mountain cat for you to fight with."

At the base of the south trail, Eagle Wing reined in his Appaloosa horse and looked at his brother and sister. "You can go no further. You must return to the cabin now."

"Just a few more miles, Brother." Red Horse begged. "The day is early yet. We can ride with you to the top of the pass."

"You know our father's wishes." Eagle Wing frowned.

"Ride safely, my brother." Ellie Thunder smiled at her twin brother.

"We will keep him safe." Grey Hair assured her.

"I will hold Grey Hair to that promise." The snow-white teeth flashed as she laughed. "You must come and visit with us again soon."

"I would like to see Ellie Thunder again." The warrior seemed to blush at his words.

"Grey Hair will have to bring many horses if he wishes to see Ellie Thunder." Red Horse laughed. "And remember, there is Oliver."

"Why do you two speak of me like I'm not even here?" Ellie looked at Grey Hair and blushed.

"I will come. Your sister is worth many horses, young one." The warrior nodded, then turned for the pass. "The daughter of Crow Killer demands many. Oliver is a white, he owns no horses. I will return."

Walking Horse said his good-byes, then with Eagle Wing and Grey Hair following, he started up the south trail. Red Horse and Ellie Thunder waited at the bottom until they disappeared from their sight, among the mountain cedar, shrub oak, and pine trees. The long, low call of the grey wolf sounded, as they started to turn their horses.

"The old one calls out." Red Horse looked up at the tall mountain peaks where the wolf's lonely howl had echoed down to them. "He knows our brother leaves us."

"How does Red Horse know it's the old wolf?"

"His call trails away into a shrill yip at the end." The youngster nodded knowingly. "The young ones only howl."

"I have never noticed before, but my ears say you are right, my brother."

"Women don't know about such things." Red Horse shrugged. "Only warriors do."

"Tell me, what do women know about then?"

"Food!" The youngster laughed and kicked his horse into a slow lope across the flat, flower-filled meadows. "And I'm hungry."

"You're always hungry." Ellie Thunder took a final look up the trail, then followed Red Horse. She was saddened, already missing her twin brother. They had been born in the midst of a terrible battle with the Pawnee. Blood tied them together as no other siblings were.

Jed slid from his horse at the top of the north trail, as a smaller rock strewn path started its descent away from the larger trail. Taking only his bow and quiver of arrows, he started down the trail, studying the ground as he passed.

"What does my brother look for?" Red Hawk watched as Jed examined the path closely.

"I have seen the track of a large cat many times along this small trail that angles down into the small place below."

"He hunts your horses, maybe?" Red Hawk studied the path, then looked below where the horses were grazing peacefully on the large meadow. "These are his hunting grounds."

"I think he hunts my father's cow." Jed pointed at a large cat track the animal had left in the sand during the night. "Last week we found claw marks on her side."

"This one is indeed a big cat." Red Hawk traced the fresh track with his finger.

"And a smart one." Jed nodded. "He is hard to spot."

"If you want him so bad, where is your rifle?"

"To kill him with only the bow will be more of a challenge."

"For you or the cat?" Red Hawk questioned. "This one must have great medicine to live to be so old."

"The cat has lived many seasons. He deserves to die from a warrior's weapon, not a rifle."

"As the old bear did?"

"That was different. I only had an arrow, then." Jed thought back when he had killed the mother grizzly. He had dropped his rifle where the chase had begun and could only retrieve his bow and arrows. "Yes, that was very different."

"How so, my friend?" Red Hawk was curious.

"The bear was a man killer, very dangerous. This cat only kills to eat."

"Do not be fooled. If this one is cornered, he will become very dangerous and may eat you."

"This one will die by the bow." Jed nodded slowly.

"I doubt if the cow would care how you kill him." Red Hawk laughed lightly. "As long as you kill him before he has her for dinner."

"This one has lived many seasons. He should die like a warrior in the old way."

"Perhaps, you are right." Red Hawk shrugged. "But, one as large as this one is old and has grown very smart."

"Surely not as smart as a Crow?" Jed laughed.

"We shall see."

Jed started forward, carefully watching the trail for spoor of any kind. The dark eyes missed nothing as they carefully surveyed the narrow pathway. Many fresh tracks of the cat showed along the trail. Jed knew the animal's lair was ahead. He had been down the rocky track before, looking for the mysterious shining light, not realizing the cat's den was down there too. Many times in his searching, he had probably walked within feet of the hidden cat, without realizing the danger. The trail was a dead end, leading to the edge of a small stream that raced down the mountain through a narrow gorge that was impossible to navigate. Sheer walls of granite and rock made escape from the small flat meadow impossible. Escape from any source, other than the trail, was not possible, even for a powerful mountain cat. Sands of time and heavy rains had made this small hideaway a good place to hide from enemies, but also a good place to be trapped in.

At the stream's edge, Jed ran his hand into the ice-cold water, then looked up at the mountain ledge. From where he stood, Jed could see where the stream started as it gushed from the side of the mountain, one of earth's truly magnificent wonders. Jed knew somewhere in this thick scrub oak and brush lined gorge, the old cat probably had his lair. A cave or an outcropping of some kind lay hidden in the jumble of rock. Here, the cat felt he could rest safely during the heat of the day.

Once before, he had discovered the cat's track as he rode the mountain trails, but until the cow was attacked, he hadn't thought much about the animal. Now, he wanted to track the cougar down and kill it before he could attack the cow again. In these high meadows, mountain cats were plentiful, but a good milk cow was as scarce as hen's teeth.

"I feel his presence. He is here somewhere." Red Hawk whispered. "He watches. He knows we are here."

"How does Red Hawk know this?" Jed let his eyes roam across the thick mountain cedar, sumac, and dwarf pine. The aroma of the trees and flowers down in the gorge lingered, as there was no wind to carry it away.

"I can smell him." The warrior sniffed with his nose. "He has the pungent smell of a fresh kill on his hide."

"Then, my friend, let your nose carry us to this warrior." Jed couldn't smell anything.

Red Hawk moved quietly ahead, studying every pile of rock and clump of trees. In the canyon, all the trees were dwarfed for lack of sunshine and deep soil to plant their roots to find water. Stopping, as he was about to step from behind a clump of cedar, Red Hawk held his hand out, then pointed above them to a rock ledge.

"The old one is there." The muscled arm pointed to the ledge that probably concealed a cave higher up. "The path up there will be difficult."

"I'll go first." Jed studied the narrow path that was worn smooth from the cat's goings and coming. "When I reach the ledge, I will cover you."

"I hope your aim with the bow has gotten better than the last time we hunted."

"My brother is not afraid of a little old cat, is he?" Jed grinned.

"This little old cat has four razor sharp feet to rip a warrior open, not to mention several very long teeth."

"Perhaps, he is not at home." Jed started forward but he knew better, the cat was ahead and waiting.

Looking up at the midday sun, Red Hawk shook his head. "Be careful, my friend, this time of day he will be in his lodge. When cornered, he will become very angry."

For a four-legged creature, like the nimble cat, the climb up the narrow ledge would be no problem. However, for a man, the poor handholds and steep narrow path was extremely hard to navigate. Near the top, with only a couple more steps to go, Jed looked down at the fifteen foot drop to where Red Hawk waited with his arrow notched and ready. Giving Jed the nod, the warrior watched expectantly as Jed pulled himself up high enough to peer over the lip of the ledge.

His head and eyes barely cleared the rock escarpment so he could see, when a black hissing shadow charged straight at him, moving with the speed of a charging grizzly. Falling, as the cat passed across his head, swiping at him with its huge claws, Jed fell backward, landing on top of Red Hawk. An arrow with the bloodred markings of Red Hawk, stuck from Jed's arrow quiver. Only the quiver, and the good graces of the spirit people, had diverted the arrow from his body.

Red Hawk was as surprised as Jed was, that the cat came over the ledge, hurling itself downward, clearing the warrior's head by only inches. The arrow half drawn had been knocked loose and imbedded itself in Jed's arrow quiver. The weight from Jed's body landing on him temporarily knocked the wind from Red Hawk.

Both men lay where they had landed, looking up at the ledge in astonishment. Suddenly, as each saw the other wasn't hurt, they began to laugh.

"The old one has counted coup on both of us today." Red Hawk was rolling in hysterics. "The great Crow Killer was defeated this day."

"And what of Red Hawk, Chief of the Crow?" Jed shook his head, trying to control himself. "You missed the whole cat and hit me."

"Yes, my friend." The warrior seemed to blush. "But, I will not speak of this, unless you do."

"I think that would be wise." Jed looked up at the high ledge and he could see Red Horse laughing himself sick. "We will meet again, old one."

CHAPTER 4

Walking Horse held the warriors in a steady trot to the southeast. They followed the ancient game trail, leading to the big river, and then on to the ancestral hunting grounds of the Crow and Arapaho. Grey Hair brought up the tail end of the riders, as they passed in single file, toward the south. The day passed uneventfully, with nothing to disturb their thoughts, passing only a few deer and a band of wild horses. Eagle Wing rode straight and proud, thrilled to be in the company of such warriors as these Lance Bearers. He could see the pointed handles of their lances, sticking out from their arrow quivers. Each shaft was decorated with the carving of an animal. Each warrior had carved on their lance shafts, the ceremonial token they had seen in their visions. Only the young one, Wolf's Head, had not passed his novice time to become a Lance Bearer.

Eagle Wing could hardly wait until it was time for him to seek his own vision and become a Lance Bearer. No coup or battle could surpass the honor of stepping into the ceremonial ring before the whole Arapaho Tribe and be handed the short-pointed lance, pronouncing him a member of such a mighty society. It was an honor all Arapaho boys dreamed of, from the time they could ride a horse.

"What does my nephew think of?" Walking Horse without Eagle Wing's awareness, had moved alongside him.

Startled, the voice was so near, the youngster turned to the speaker, embarrassed. "Nothing, Uncle."

"Out here…" Walking Horse moved his massive arm to point out the flat meadows and far trees. "Out here, a warrior should always be aware of everything that passes by."

"Yes, Uncle, I will heed your words."

"You will, if you wish to live long enough to become a Lance Bearer."

"Yes, Uncle." Eagle Wing nodded, as Walking Horse kicked his horse and took the lead again. "Now, how did he know what I was thinking?"

Grey Hair smiled. "Eagle Wing is young. What else would he be thinking of?"

"And Grey Hair, what does he think of?"

"I am already a Lance Bearer, young one." The young warrior smiled. "So, it is not that."

"Maybe you think about my sister, Ellie Thunder?" It was Eagle Wing's turn to smile.

"Would you disapprove of my thinking of her?"

"No, but it is not my place to approve or disapprove."

"And, Crow Killer, would he approve?"

"My father thinks like the white man, in such matters." Eagle Wing smiled. "I think you will have to win over my sister first to get such a question answered."

"You mean your sister can choose her own husband?" Grey Hair was puzzled. "She cannot be bought with horses?"

"Buying a wife is not the white man's way."

"Perhaps, my young friend, you will tell me how to do this."

Eagle Wing liked this young warrior. There already seemed to be a bond forming between them. "I will tell Grey Hair this. Horses will not be the price for her."

"Then what?" Grey Hair was curious since horses had always been the bridal payment for a woman. "How do I win her for my wife?"

"You will have to figure that one out yourself."

"But, your father's lodge is so far away." Grey Hair shrugged. "It will be very difficult to play my flute or court her."

"A fast horse and eager heart makes the distance short." Eagle Wing smiled. "Does Grey Hair not think my sister is worth a little riding?"

"Your sister is worth much riding." The grey-haired one seemed to blush. "But, I am still a Lance Bearer, protector of my people."

"This is true, my friend." Eagle Wing understood. "But, my father says anything worth having is worth working hard for."

The warrior smiled. "For one so young, you speak wisely."

Reining in behind a small clump of trees, Walking Horse and the warriors watched, as Two-Eyed Dog loped his horse toward them. He pulled the horse to a stop beside the waiting riders.

"Many warriors camp alongside the crossing of the great river." The warrior looked at the river. "We will not be able to cross here."

"What warriors would be here?"

"Arickaree, I counted ten of the dog eaters."

"What are they doing so far from the north country?" Grey Hair questioned. "This land is many sleeps from their hunting grounds."

"They have women and many extra horses." The warrior shrugged. "I think they have been on a raid."

"Against who?" Walking Horse looked to the east. "There are no tribes near this place."

"These warriors have many spotted horses and I think two squaws of the Nez Perce Tribe."

"Nez Perce?"

"Yes, my chief, the women are their captives." The warrior nodded. "They treat them very badly. The squaws have many red welts and bruises on them. These warriors beat them with their rawhide quirts."

"You must have gotten close to them."

Two-Eyed Dog replied. "No my chief, they got very close to me, before I knew they were there."

"Did they see you?"

"No, they did not see this one." The warrior shook his head. "They make camp for the night. Many swim in the river. Only two watch over the horses and women."

"Can we pass in the night?"

"It would be very dangerous, but perhaps we could do this thing."

"Let us attack them while they swim." Grey Hair spoke up, then looked at Eagle Wing. "The young one could have his first taste of battle."

"Do not forget the beautiful Appaloosas of the Nez Perce, my chief." Two-Eyed Dog's mouth watered. "They are worth much."

"There are only four of us." Walking Horse looked to where Eagle Wing and Wolf's Head sat their horses listening.

"Six with Wolf's Head and Eagle Wing." Grey Hair pointed out. "Crow Killer says the young one has counted coup already on trappers."

"We should attack quickly, my chief, before they realize we are here." Hide Belt spoke up. "We do not want them to discover us."

"They are enemy of the Arapaho and their horses are magnificent." Two-Eyed Dog repeated. "To kill them would bring much honor."

Seeing all his warriors were in agreement and wanting to fight, Walking Horse gave in. "Grey Hair and Two-Eyed Dog will kill the two guarding the horses. Then, join us where the others swim."

The eyes of the two warriors seemed to light up in pride as they were picked for such a dangerous task. Honor and scalps would be theirs this day, providing they succeeded. The Arapaho were a warlike society, and nothing gave the warriors more pride in battle than a chance to display their bravery against such an enemy. To them, the Arickaree were an age-old detested tribe of dung eaters.

"We go." Grey Hair nodded at Walking Horse. "Today, my chief, we will count many coups."

"Give us time to get in place and use only your bows so there will be no warning given to the ones swimming."

"Yes, my chief."

Walking Horse did not want this coming fight, but his warriors did and a good chief had to lead his men or they would lose faith in him. Only a brave and respected leader would retain loyalty and allegiance of his people. Warriors could not be ordered into battle like the whites. They fought only if they wished and if the signs were right.

"Eagle Wing, Hide Belt, and Wolf's Head will stay behind me." Walking Horse looked at the youngsters, seeing eagerness in their faces. "Use your rifles when Grey Hair calls out."

"Yes, my uncle." Eagle Wing and Hide Belt carried a rifle, but Wolf's Head was armed only with a bow.

The six riders moved cautiously forward, keeping their horses in a slow walk. The river was less than a quarter mile ahead when Walking Horse had them dismount and hobble their horses. Motioning at Grey

Hair and Two-Eyed Dog; Walking Horse led the other three warriors to the right where he knew the enemy would be swimming. Outnumbered, almost two to one, this fight had to be finished quickly. The Arickaree were great fighters and all would be armed with the far-reaching rifles of the whites. If Two-Eyed Dog was correct, these warriors had just come from killing and stealing horses, and squaws from the Nez Perce.

No, he had no qualms about killing the Arickaree warriors without warning. They had killed Yellow Dog, his great friend and brother-in-law, in the same way. Today, was a good day for them to meet their ancestors. He only worried about Eagle Wing. If anything should happen to the youngster, he would be unable to look Crow Killer or Bright Moon in the eyes again.

Four sets of dark eyes watched from the trees, only yards away, as eight enemy warriors bathed themselves in the slow moving waters of the great river. Their bows, rifles, and leather clothing lay in piles on the far shore. The warriors were young, foolish, and loud. Their voices carried across the water as they joked and played. Walking Horse figured the way the young warriors were playing without a posted guard, this was their first raid into enemy lands without older warriors to advise them. They were in high spirits following a successful raid, after stealing horses and women from the mighty Nez Perce. They knew there would be a great celebration in their honor when they returned to their village. The maidens of the village would look upon them with great admiration. He raised his Hawken rifle, there would be no celebration for these foolish ones.

From across the river, they waited for the call of the dove to sound, telling Walking Horse the two warriors guarding the women were dead. The call would also tell the waiting warriors, they were in place and ready to attack. Standing up in plain sight of the Arickaree, as the dove call sounded, the Arapaho warriors appeared out of the brush on the far bank of the river. With a shrill war cry of alarm, the young Rics lunged from the water and raced for their weapons. Three rifles exploded across the river, knocking two of the Ric warriors face down in the sandy bank.

Seeing the remaining six warriors running for their rifles, Grey Hair sprung from his place of concealment and plunged his war axe into the head of a screaming warrior. Dropping his empty rifle, Eagle Wing plunged into the river and started across, moving through the deep water with incredible speed. Walking Horse tried to call the excited youngster back, but to no avail. Hide Belt and Wolf's Head plunged into the river behind Eagle Wing.

Four Arickaree raced for their weapons while the fifth grappled with Grey Hair, trying to tear loose from the Arapaho who had tackled him. Reaching for his rifle, one of the Rics fired at Grey Hair, knocking him loose from the warrior he had pinned down. Rolling free from the wounded Lance Bearer, the warrior pulled his hunting knife and lunged at Grey Hair. Trying to defend himself with just one good arm, Grey Hair fell beneath the strong Ric. Straddling the wounded Arapaho, the warrior was so intent on plunging his knife into the struggling Grey Hair that he wasn't aware of the onrushing warrior.

As the young Ric wrenched his knife arm loose from the wounded Lance Bearer's grip, he screamed his war cry and raised the knife victoriously. He waited too long, as he started to plunge his sharp knife into Grey Hair's chest, Eagle Wing dove feet first into the fight. His powerful kick knocked the Ric sideways and away from Grey Hair. Rolling in the sandy bank, both fighters came to their feet with their knives reaching out in front of them. Frantically, Walking Horse tried to reload his rifle and kill the Ric. Eagle Wing was just a youngster, and Walking Horse knew he was no match for the muscular warrior who circled him. In fear for the youngster, he watched helpless as the two bodies clashed together with their knives flashing in the sunlight.

Many times, Eagle Wing had fought mock fights with the huge skinning knife against his father, Crow Killer. He had no fear of the Ric or his knife, because he knew few warriors could match his father with a knife. He had been taught by the best. Seeing the four other warriors racing toward the knife fight, Walking Horse took a steady bead on the lead Ric and slowly squeezed the trigger. The warrior was thrown backward, dead before he hit the ground. Laying down his rifle, Walking Horse raced to the riverbank and dove far out into the river. Exiting the water, Hide Belt caught up with another Ric, driving his war club into the warrior. Seeing they were alone and badly outnumbered, the last two surviving Arickaree warriors melted silently into the surrounding trees.

Wading hurriedly from the water, Walking Horse could only blink as Eagle Wing raised the Ric easily above his head and flung him mightily against the ground. Again, the flash of the blade showed in the sunlight as the Ric breathed his last breath. Blood mixed with bubbles came from the dying warrior as his head rolled sideways.

Running up, Walking Horse looked at the blood covering Eagle Wing. "Are you hurt, Nephew?"

"No, I am not hurt." Eagle Wing stepped away from the body. "But, Grey Hair is injured."

"It is nothing, my young friend." Grey Hair limped toward them. "It would have been much worse if you hadn't knocked him from me."

"Your shoulder is bloody." Walking Horse pointed to the blood running down the warrior's torso.

"Only a slight wound, my chief." Grey Hair shrugged. "It will mend."

"Where is Two-Eyed Dog?" Walking Horse watched as Hide Belt and Wolf's Head searched the thickets for the last two Rics. All the Aricakree were accounted for except for the two warriors that ran off.

"He watches the women and horses." Grey Hair smiled. "One of the squaws is very comely."

"Eagle Wing and Hide Belt will get our horses and bring them across the river." Walking Horse looked down river. "We will gather these weapons, then go to where Two-Eyed Dog waits."

Watching the two warriors walk away, Grey Hair shook his head. "That one has much courage. Did you see the way he killed the Ric?"

"Yes, the young one is mighty in battle." Walking Horse watched the proud muscular back of the youngster move toward the river. "Eagle Wing saved your life today, Grey Hair, and he counted coup on an enemy warrior."

"Two enemies today, his rifle killed one of the other Rics." Wolf's Head added.

"Come, we will check on Two-Eyed Dog." Walking Horse gathered the weapons and rifles of the dead Rics, then turned downstream. "The ones that escaped could try to reach their horses."

"These warriors were young and foolish. Now, they have paid for their foolishness." Grey Hair knelt at the river's edge to wash his wound.

"They were too young to die."

"They were Arickaree, never too young." Grey Hair frowned. "Now, they are good Arickaree."

"Perhaps you are right, Grey Hair."

"Did you see how easy the young one lifted the big Ric and slammed him to the ground?" Grey Hair shook his head in amazement. "As easy as I would lift a beaver hide."

Walking Horse looked across the river. "I saw it."

"He is very strong for one so young, my chief." Grey Hair nodded. "A very good thing for me."

"He is powerful like his father, Crow Killer." Walking Horse watched as the young men gathered their horses and rifles, then started back across the river. "I foresee many enemies falling to the young one."

"As do I."

As Walking Horse, Wolf's Head, and Grey Hair approached the camp, Two-Eyed Dog and the two squaws stood up from behind a dead drift log. The squaws had received bad treatment at the hands of the young Rics. Both were filthy, bloody, and bruised from the beatings they had received. Walking Horse nodded at the frightened women, then pointed at Grey Hair's wound. The oldest understood his meaning and moved to bind the wound that still bled freely. The other woman stood still, she was young, slender, and very beautiful. Although frightened, she stood her ground with her eyes showing fire as she gazed boldly at her captors.

"This one is a comely squaw for a Nez Perce." Two-Eyed Dog smiled as the girl hissed at him. "And she has spirit."

"She would gut Two-Eyed Dog like a fish." Grey Hair gritted his teeth, holding back the pain as the older woman cleaned and bandaged his wound.

"I believe you, my friend." The warrior laughed as the younger woman glared at him. "What will we do with them?"

Eagle Wing and Hide Belt rode the dripping wet horses from the river, dismounting beside Walking Horse. Only a trickle of blood ran from a small wound on the youngster's upper arm. Looking the two women over, Eagle Wing turned his attention to Grey Hair's shoulder.

"Will my friend be alright?"

The older squaw motioned with her hands fluidly, then spoke in broken English. "He will be fine, Arapaho."

Eagle Wing looked curiously at the woman. "You speak English?"

"I speak, and I know you. You are the son of the Crow Killer, the dog of an Arapaho." The woman shook her head. "The bear killer and killer of my people."

"He's my Father alright, but he is no dog." Eagle Wing was curious. "How do you know these things, squaw?"

The older woman squared her shoulders proudly. "I am Bird Woman the wife of Squirrel Tooth the Nez Perce. I saw you once when you came to the white village of Baxter Springs with the bear killer."

"Baxter Springs?" The words fell from Eagle Wing's mouth in surprise. "You are Squirrel Tooth's squaw. I never saw you at the white village."

"I was there and I was Squirrel Tooth's woman. These Arickaree cowards ambushed us and killed my husband as he tried to protect us."

"Squirrel Tooth is dead?" Eagle Wing was both surprised and glad. The Nez Perce had sent many a man, both white and red to kill his father.

The woman shrugged. "He is."

"The old devil caused my father much trouble over the years." Eagle Wing looked at Walking Horse. "What will you do with them?"

Studying the two squaws, Walking Horse looked over the horses that stood grazing along the river. He had heard the name Squirrel Tooth mentioned by Crow Killer several times, but he had never encountered the Nez Perce.

"What would my nephew have me do with them?"

"Tell me, old woman, the young squaw." Two-Eyed Dog spoke up. "Who is she?"

"She is my daughter." Bird Woman stepped in front of the younger woman to protect her. "Her name is Flower Leaf."

"Will your people be looking for you?" Walking Horse asked her.

The old woman shook her head. "We were on our way to Baxter Springs to trade our horses when the Arickaree attacked and killed Squirrel Tooth and my son Crippled Hand."

"So no one looks for you?" Walking Horse stared at the woman. "Speak, you will not be harmed."

"No one looks for us so soon."

"I claim the young one as my captive." Two-Eyed Dog grabbed the girl's arm. "I captured her. I claim her. It is my right."

"Two-Eyed Dog speaks the truth, my chief." Grey Hair spoke up. "His arrow killed the warrior who held her captive."

"Who wants the old woman?"

No words were spoken as Walking Horse looked around the gathered warriors. Kneeling down to examine the captured rifles and shot pouches, the chief nodded slowly. He knew it was the warrior's right to claim the girl as his captive. He had been the first one to attack the Rics and free her from them.

"I will give two horses, my captured rifles, and scalps for the one called Flower Leaf." All eyes turned to where Eagle Wing stood.

"No." Two-Eyed Dog shook his head, tightening his grip on the girl's arm. "I will not trade her."

"And I will add my horses and rifles for the girl." Grey Hair spoke up. "That is four good Appaloosa horses, four rifles, and scalps for one skinny squaw."

"A good price." Hide Belt nodded, looking hard at the warrior. "You do not need the headache of this squaw, my friend."

Looking over the beautiful spotted horses, the warrior turned the girl loose, pushing her toward Eagle Wing. "She is yours, young one."

Walking Horse breathed a sigh of relief at the words. He had stayed out of the talking. As chief, he could not take sides with either warrior on the war trail. Still, he could see Eagle Wing intended to take the girl from the older warrior even if he had to fight for her. The air had been tense, and he had no doubt there could have been a fight between the two warriors.

Walking to where the horses of the Arickaree grazed, Eagle Wing took the hair bridles of two of the lesser horses and led them to where the two women stood.

"You are free to return to your people, old woman." Eagle Wing handed the leads to the women. "Quickly, gather food and blankets, and leave this place."

"You gave four horses and rifles for them, then you give them their freedom?" Two-Eyed Dog was shocked.

"Their freedom was mine to give, my friend." Eagle Wing turned on the warrior. "Is that not so?"

Nodding, the warrior looked at the women and shook his head. "I return the horses and rifles to Eagle Wing and Grey Hair."

"The women are still free to leave?"

"They are free to go." Two-Eyed Dog nodded in agreement.

Walking Horse shook his head slowly. Truly this son of the Crow Killer was different. He could kill easily, but he showed mercy as well. To give away such valuable rifles and horses so easily showed there was no greed in the youngster. The old Cheyenne Medicine Man predicted great things for this one, surely this was one of the first. No warrior on the war trail had ever given up his captives or horses before.

"I will pray to the spirit people for you, son of Crow Killer." Bird Woman stopped in front of Eagle Wing. "But Crow Killer is still a dog."

"Ride safely, Mother."

"Tell me, Arapaho, how are you called?"

"I am called Eagle Wing." He looked down into her sad dark eyes.

"Ride safely, Eagle Wing." The old woman nodded. "May the spirits always protect you."

Lifting the startled girl effortlessly onto the horse, Eagle Wing nodded, then helped the old woman on her horse. "Your land lies to the west, four sleeps."

The warriors watched as the two women swam the river, then they started gathering the belongings of the dead Arickaree. Seven good rifles, eight Appaloosa horses, and eight Ric horses were loaded down with knives, bows, and pelts the enemy warriors no longer had need of. Pushing the dead bodies into the sluggish river, minus their hair, the Arapaho turned south toward their homelands.

"I thank Grey Hair for helping me free the women." Eagle Wing smiled at the wounded warrior, then looked over at Two-Eyed Dog.

"Today, Eagle Wing saved my life. Whatever I own is yours for the asking." Grey Hair continued. "But, your actions, I do not understand."

"I wanted the women to be free to return to their own people." Eagle Wing shrugged. "Tell me, how did Two-Eyed Dog get such a name?"

"Did you not see his eyes?"

"Yes, I have looked into his eyes."

"They are slit like the wolves." Grey Hair laughed. "One is blue and the other green. He is my friend and a great Lance Bearer, but his eyes make him look hideous to others. He has trouble finding a squaw."

"But, he is a great warrior?"

Grey Hair nodded. "Yes, the two-eyed one is a great Lance Bearer."

"Well, he did a good thing for the women today by killing the Rics."

"Don't be fooled, young one. Two-Eyed Dog can be a very dangerous warrior when he has to be."

"I believe your words, my friend."

"Eagle Wing has done great deeds this day." Grey Hair smiled. "The people will sing your praises."

"No more than Grey Hair did."

"You saved my life today. When you become a Lance Bearer of the people, I would like for our blood to mix. Then we will be true brothers."

"Not now?"

"No, my young friend, it is not permitted until you pass the rites of manhood and become an Arapaho warrior."

"It will be an honor to be Grey Hair's brother." Eagle Wing nodded. "It will be as you ask."

The miles passed quickly as Walking Horse led his warriors across the beautiful Yellowstone River and back into Arapaho lands. Several sets of dark eyes watched from the Crow side as they swam with the spotted horses across the clear river, but no challenge was shouted out.

Grey Hair smiled as they neared the dark topped lodges of the Arapaho. "Tonight, Eagle Wing, there will be a great feast and dancing in your honor."

"My honor, why?" The youngster was curious.

"Yes, for you, my young friend. You have saved the life of the great Grey Hair, and you are the son of Crow Killer." The warrior smiled.

Eagle Wing shook his head. The last thing he wanted was praise and bragging heaped upon him in front of the whole Arapaho village. Nevertheless, he knew it was the way of the people to bestow glory on their returning victorious warriors.

CHAPTER 5

Eight Crow warriors rode out from behind the brush and trees as Walking Horse and his party swam the Yellowstone River back into Arapaho lands. Sitting their horses as the Arapaho passed from their view, a heavily muscled warrior raised his clenched fist and shook it.

"Soon, Arapaho, you will not cross our lands so freely and live!" The Crow warrior, Long Leaper, growled in rage. "Soon!"

"They ride our hunting grounds like the land is theirs." Another warrior shook his head.

"Little Elk speaks the truth this day." The warrior agreed. "I, Long Leaper, will change this."

"Red Hawk our chief speaks different words." A slender warrior called Bull Calf spoke up.

"Red Hawk is a fool." Long Leaper turned his horse away from the Yellowstone. "Soon, I will be Chief of the Crow."

"Does Long Leaper plan to kill Red Hawk, our hereditary chief? Bull Calf frowned.

"Hear me, one day soon, I will be chief." Long Leaper slapped his chest.

"And you intend to fight the Arapaho Lance Bearers?" Little Elk questioned him.

"I have waited for revenge against the Arapaho for many moons." Long Leaper touched his throat, remembering the day Walking Horse had choked the air from his body.

"These are dangerous fighters you speak of."

"I am a dangerous fighter, Bull Calf." Long Leaper glared at the smaller warrior. "Look at my lodge, many scalps hang on my scalp pole."

"I know this, but the Lance Bearers are not Comanche or Pawnee."

"They bleed and die like any other warrior, my friend."

"Did you see the young warrior that rides with Walking Horse?" Crooked Arrow spoke up. "I believe he is the son of Crow Killer."

Long Leaper's head spun around. "How does Crooked Arrow know this thing?"

"My sister spoke with Red Hawk's squaw after he rode north with the Arapaho." The warrior shrugged. "Red Hawk went with the Arapaho to bring the young one back for his novice time with Chief Walking Horse."

"Red Hawk did not return?"

"No, our chief, Red Hawk, stayed with his great friend, Crow Killer, to hunt for a few days."

"Bah, an Arapaho for a friend. Red Hawk is a traitor to his people."

Bull Calf shook his head. "Our great Chief Plenty Coups looked upon Crow Killer as a son."

"Plenty Coups was old." Long Leaper frowned. "Plenty Coups had lost his mind."

"I would not say these words too loud." Crooked Arrow suggested. "Red Hawk might take your hair."

Long Leaper looked at the warrior. "I am no longer the young helpless one I was when Walking Horse and I last met."

"Be careful, Walking Horse and Red Hawk are both great warriors," Bull Calf warned. "Next time, he might choke the life out of you."

"Soon, my friends, I will be Chief of the Crow." Long Leaper gripped his rope rein hard. "When Red Hawk is dead, then I will go after your great Arapaho Walking Horse."

"Why not today?"

Long Leaper glared at Bull Calf. "If I had known the young one was the son of Crow Killer, I would have attacked Walking Horse and his Arapaho dogs today."

"You would have attacked them alone, Long Leaper." Crooked Arrow shrugged. "Red Hawk is still my chief."

"But, you ride with me today."

"Only because I was told to do this thing."

"Maybe, I should start with you, Crooked Arrow." Long Leaper turned his horse.

"Will Long Leaper fight us all?" The young Crow men all glared at the warrior.

Scowling at the young warriors, Long Leaper kicked his gelding and raced to the top of the knoll overlooking the Yellowstone.

"One day, he will get himself killed." Bull Calf shook his head.

"Hopefully, soon." Crooked Arrow nodded.

In the late evening, Oliver sat with Jed and Red Hawk around the oak table in front of the cabin drinking coffee, listening as the whippoorwills sang their songs down along the small creek. White fluffy clouds drifted across the blue skies, slowly disappearing into the darkening sky. The large herd of horses grazed peacefully on the valley floor as the western sun started to set over the mountains.

Oliver set up his surveying tripod. Red Hawk was fascinated as he looked at the telescope attached to the top of the tripod. He had never seen the magic of the far-looking glass before. The horses far away looked so close as if he could reach out and touch them with his hand. As Oliver tried to explain the use of the instrument and how it measured the distance of the land, the warrior shook his head.

"This is how you own land, Red Hawk." Oliver explained. "You first lay out the land and measure it, then you pay for it and it's yours."

"You cannot buy mother earth with buffalo hides or horses." Red Hawk refused to believe the words of the young white. "You can only take land because you are stronger than your enemies."

"Out here, maybe, but back east, you have to buy land to own it." Oliver smiled. "In the east, all land is owned."

Red Hawk picked up a bundle of papers and waved them at Oliver. "You say these marks make this land belong to my brother?"

"This valley and the next valley south belong to Jedidiah Bracket." Oliver nodded. "Surveyed, paid for, and recorded with deeds for all to see. These papers are the proof."

"And no one can take them from him?" Red Hawk questioned him. "Not even his enemies?"

"No one." Oliver continued. "Not ever, at least as long as he pays his taxes every year."

"What are taxes?" Red Hawk asked.

"A man must pay money each year to the leaders of our people to keep the land."

"And yet you say he owns the land?"

"Yes."

"What if they come here with many guns and warriors?" Red Hawk shook his head.

"No matter, this deed and land is recorded back east, it belongs to Jedidiah Bracket."

"I have never heard of such a thing as owning the ground the people walk on."

"Oliver is a lawyer and a surveyor, my friend." Jed laughed at Red Hawk's disbelief.

"What is this lawyer you speak of?"

"A lawyer is a man who knows the law of the whites and has knowledge in these things." Oliver replied. "And one that knows how to put them down on paper for all to see."

"Maybe this one can put the Crow lands on paper so the Comanche cannot raid our horse herds?" Red Hawk looked at Oliver. "That would be good."

"From what I have heard it is the Comanche who need protection from the Crow." Oliver shook his head. "Especially from one warrior called Red Hawk."

"Someone has been lying to you." In the four days, Red Hawk had been at the cabin, he had come to like the congenial young white.

"Oliver, don't you know the Comanche horses just follow Red Hawk home, like the children followed the Pied Piper." Jed laughed.

"This Pied Piper must have been a great warrior." Red Hawk agreed.

"Oh, he was, he was." Oliver gathered his instruments, removing them from the heavy night dew. "Make sure you put those deeds where they will be safe and dry, Jed."

"Where are you going?" Jed looked at Oliver curiously. "We were going hunting come morning, figured you and Red Horse might like to go."

Blushing slightly, Oliver turned to the doorway. "Ellie is showing me the south valley tomorrow, sorry."

Jed looked across the valley where Red Horse was driving in the horses, Jed wanted kept up for the night. "Don't venture too far."

"Yes, sir. I won't."

Red Hawk watched Oliver as he walked away, then turned his attention as the horses trotted through the tall green grass toward the cabin.

"Ellie Thunder has been spending much time with the young white." Red Hawk grew serious. "Is this a good thing, my brother?"

"They are only good friends." Jed watched Oliver as he followed the small trail to Wilson's cabin. "Their friendship is harmless."

"Perhaps." Red Hawk shook his head. "When does the young one return to the east?"

"He returns soon. We are trying to make a warrior out of him so the white hunters will not kill him."

"In his own lands to the east, he would not need protection. Send him away, my friend, before it is too late." The warrior warned.

"Ellie Thunder has a mind of her own."

"Tell me, do you think that paper makes you own these lands?"

"Yes, I do." Jed nodded, then smiled. "But, this paper may need a little help from my rifle."

Little Antelope greeted Walking Horse and Eagle Wing as they passed through the gathered villagers. Hugging her husband, she turned to her nephew. She hadn't seen the young one in almost two years and she was surprised at his height and the muscle he had put on.

"Nephew, welcome to our village."

"It is good to see my aunt." Eagle Wing smiled at the beautiful woman.

"Come, I have food for my warriors, and I wish to hear of your father and my sister." Little Antelope led the way to their lodge. Two young children in their seventh and tenth summers waited silently in front of the hide lodge.

Walking Horse grabbed the youngsters and pulled them to him. "This is my son and daughter."

"You have grown, my cousins." Eagle Wing smiled at the small children. "You are Grass Bee and your brother is Small Bow."

The shy youngsters looked down at the ground, smiling bashfully. Little Antelope pushed them forward. "Say something to your cousin, Eagle Wing, before he thinks you do not like him."

"Those are very pretty names for such pretty young ones."

"We know who he is, Mother." Little Grass Bee spoke up. "We were afraid to speak in his presence."

"Why would you be afraid of a cousin?" Little Antelope knelt before the children. "He will not hurt you."

"We have heard many scary tales of his father, Crow Killer." The little girl ducked behind her mother. "He might kill us as he did the great bear."

Smiling, Little Antelope turned to Eagle Wing. "It is true, he is the son of the great Crow Killer, but he will not harm you."

"We have heard about the great bear killer and his medicine, but I am not afraid." Small Bow stepped forward and looked up at Eagle Wing.

"You are brave."

Shaking his head, the youngster smiled. "Not brave, I just know you will not harm us with our father Walking Horse here."

"That is true, Small Bow, my uncle is a great warrior."

"Do you come here for your novice time?" The boy was inquisitive. "To become a Lance Bearer?"

"Enough questions." Little Antelope ushered the children and Eagle Wing into the lodge. "We will eat, then you can talk."

With their meal finished and after answering many questions from Little Antelope about his folks and more questions from the children, Walking Horse and Eagle Wing strolled through the large village. The Arapaho lodges were strung out in a large meadow. The lodges formed one large circle with the older warriors and their families placing their hide tepees in smaller circles inside the ring.

Horses, dogs, and children had trampled the once abundant grass flat as they grazed and played between the lodges. Over time, the grass had become short, causing the large horse herd to move further out onto the valley floor for forage.

Young boys, not yet old enough to be warriors, rode herd among the loose horses, preventing them from straying too far. Their sharp eyes were ever alert, ready to sound the alarm if danger or enemy raiders appeared. Horses were the most important part of the tribe's safety and well-being. Needed for transportation, warfare, hunting the shaggies, and defending the Arapaho, the horse was valuable. The younger boys watched over the vast herd of horses with great pride.

Walking Horse with Eagle Wing at his side strolled through the village conversing quietly. The older warrior grinned as he watched the young women stare openly at his nephew in admiration. Eagle Wing was still too young to take a wife, but the young girls wanted to be noticed anyway. He remembered well how the young women of the Arapaho and Cheyenne used to pass in front of Crow Killer, hoping to get his attention.

Walking Horse doubted there was a warrior in the tribes as handsome or as well muscled as Eagle Wing was. Already the youth was tall, muscular, and carried himself with the forbearance and aristocratic pride of one many years older. Grey Hair and Two-Eyed Dog had already told the story throughout the village of the fight at the big river. Now, the people were even more in awe of the youngster. Courage, bravery in battle, and honor were the most sought after traits a warrior could attain. Every village took pride in their warriors, young or old.

"There will be a large celebration tonight in Eagle Wing's honor." Walking Horse nodded at a passing warrior. "The people rejoice that the son of their beloved Crow Killer is here."

"My Father is liked here?" Eagle Wing looked around as he passed through the smiling villagers.

"He is more than liked, young one." The warrior nodded in pride. "Your father is loved here, and admired by all."

"It will be hard to live up to his reputation."

"Yes, very hard." Walking Horse nodded. "So don't try, instead live up to your own."

"When does my novice time start, Uncle?"

"It has already started." The warrior raised his great arm and pointed around the village. "How you conduct yourself is part of your training."

"I thought it was all about fighting and warfare."

"No, the people must learn and respect you first. Then, the trials against our enemies will begin." Walking Horse explained. "To become a great warrior, you must be accepted and trusted by all the people."

Nodding, Eagle Wing looked around the village. His sharp eyes took in the meat racks where strips of deer meat hung drying. Squaws, old and young, worked with their skinning awls scraping the dead scraps of meat from several dead deer hides, preparing them for tanning, needed for clothing. Others tended the large fires that boiled water under the large cooking pots that had been traded from the whites. A greasy water-like mixture bubbled as it boiled down into glue. His face tingled from the odor, as the smell it emitted was not pleasing to the nose.

"I will not disappoint, Walking Horse." Eagle Wing nodded. "I would die first."

Walking Horse knew the youngster wasn't bragging. He knew this young warrior meant what he said. He had seen many young men go through their novice time. Even the young white who would become the great Crow Killer had to go through the ritual to become a Lance Bearer. Somehow, this young man was different.

Walking Horse thought back, over twenty years ago, when Chief Slow Wolf had asked him to take the young white they had found by the raging Platte River and teach him the ways of the Lance Bearer. It had been asked only as a request from the old Arapaho Chief, but Walking Horse could not refuse his beloved uncle anything. He remembered at the raging river, the white lay at his feet in mud, soaking wet, and covered in blood. At first he had wanted to kill the wounded one. In his own youth, he had disliked anything white. But as the flashes of lightning lit up the night and showed the birth mark of a lance on the hurt one's shoulder, he had changed his mind. The flashing brilliance of light had shown the white carried the sacred mark of the lance upon his back, the same mark this young one carried.

Yes, he remembered, he had disliked the young white from the first time they met. But, with time, he had learned to respect Jedidiah Bracket and then it had turned into love, like he would have for his own brother. In time, Crow Killer had become his brother. So many times, they had held each other's lives in their hands. They even had the ceremonial exchanging of blood, making them true brothers. But, this young warrior was different, even from the great Crow Killer. Walking Horse could feel there was something special about the youngster walking beside him. He did not know what, but he could feel the inner strength, the power of self-confidence emitting from Eagle Wing.

Even more than Crow Killer, this youngster had an air of confidence that few warriors possessed. He did not swagger or outwardly display any kind of cockiness like a braggart. There was something about the young man. The calmness of his actions, the strength when he spoke, the traits others did not possess. Maybe not even Walking Horse himself or Crow Killer. If the old Cheyenne Medicine Man's prophecy came true, Eagle Wing was a born leader and a warrior that others would naturally follow.

The flames of the great bonfire leaped high into the dark night as warriors danced and promenaded themselves around the burning logs, pretending they were fighting their enemies. Women, young and old, called out their shrill shrieks as they yelled for their favorite warrior.

Eagle Wing sat beside Walking Horse, in the seat of an honored guest, watching the dancing and listening to the pounding of the hide drums beating a steady cadence for the dancers. Grey Hair slipped beside Eagle Wing and whispered over the noise of the drums.

"The young women look at you, my friend." The warrior smiled. "Maybe, one will ask you to dance the maiden's dance."

"I do not dance."

"It would be an insult to refuse should one ask you." Grey Hair replied. "The people will be watching."

Eagle Wing shrugged. "But, I do not know how to dance."

"Perhaps, none will ask, but I doubt it. If they do, just go out and do as the others are doing." Grey Hair suggested.

"Or they will be insulted?"

"Maybe not insulted, but very disappointed, I think."

The dance lasted for several hours and several of the young women pulled Eagle Wing into the circle of shuffling dancers, circling the watchers. Grey Hair and Two-Eyed Dog smiled and whooped as the embarrassed youngster passed in front of them.

Despite his initial reluctance to participate in the ceremonial dancing, Eagle Wing found himself enjoying the festivities. Throughout the night, the young warrior shuffled slowly in cadence with the drums, circling around the great fire.

Little Antelope knelt beside Eagle Wing. "Does my nephew enjoy the dancing?"

"Yes, but I think I would rather be hunting the shaggies."

"You are like your father." The small woman smiled. "He never really enjoyed the dancing or the attention the ceremonies brought."

"Knowing Crow Killer, I believe you."

"Hunting buffalo does not have the pretty maidens as the dancing does."

"No, it doesn't, but it isn't as tiring as jumping around in a circle."

"Dancing is part of being a warrior, my nephew." She smiled, thinking back on her younger days. "One day, you will wish to have a wife. This is how you meet them."

Walking Horse touched Eagle Wing and Little Antelope on the shoulder. "It is late, we go. We will ride south tomorrow."

"I will speak with Grey Hair, then I will return to the lodge."

"I heard." Grey Hair nodded as he walked up. "Tomorrow, your novice time begins."

"Walking Horse says we ride south."

"South, then he takes you to Pawnee country."

"Crow Killer has told me of the Pawnee." Eagle Wing nodded. "He said they are mighty warriors."

"I have fought the Pawnee many times." Grey Hair pointed to the grey strip in his scalp. "They did this to me in battle. They come here to steal ponies and women. There are many great warriors among them."

"Red Hawk says the Pawnee now have white friends."

"This is true." Grey Hair nodded. "The whites give them rifles and in return the Pawnee scout and fight for them."

"Then, they are our enemies."

"Ride with care, my friend, and keep your eyes on the skyline." The warrior started to turn. "Yes, they are our enemies."

Long before daylight, Walking Horse had them on the trail south. Both he and Eagle Wing were mounted on dark bay horses. The warrior had explained the spotted horse, Eagle Wing had ridden to Arapaho lands, would show up in the dark of night, whereas the bay horse would not. Traveling at a steady but cautious pace, Walking Horse surveyed every part of the trail they followed. Several times, he explained the importance of scouting out the meadows and woodlands they passed before riding out across the open places.

"The enemy can be anywhere in this country." Walking Horse nodded at the heavily wooded forest they rode through. Oak, willow, cedar, and every sort of tree dotted the flat landscape. Some of the trees were covered in dense brush underneath, making an enemy impossible to spot. "They can be on an unsuspecting warrior very quick."

Eagle Wing watched closely as they passed by the heavy foliage. His eyes and ears were alert, keen to any danger. The only sound heard from their horses was a swishing sound as they passed through the knee-high grass. Many times, Crow Killer had spoken the same words, warning his son of enemies lying in wait to attack any unsuspecting traveler.

The fifty-caliber Hawken rested easily across the horse's withers while the strong bow and quiver of arrows hung across his back. Jed had exchanged the thirty he had given his son with the fifty-caliber rifle, saying it was more fit for a warrior.

"Are we still on Arapaho hunting grounds, Uncle?"

"Yes, this is Arapaho lands, but the enemy could be here also."

"It is indeed a good place for an ambush." The brush was covered in heavy thickets of short cedar and briars making it extremely difficult to see any lurking enemy.

"We ride out today only to see if any enemy warriors ride our lands." Walking Horse kicked his bay into a trot. "We have not come looking for a fight."

For two hours, Walking Horse led them due south in an easy trot. Nothing showed on the flat grasslands except for a few deer and an occasional small bunch of wild horses. Dove, prairie hen, and coveys of quail flew up under their horse's feet as they passed.

"There have been no hunters here." Eagle Wing watched the small herds as they passed. "The animals do not flee from us in fear."

"You are right, my nephew." The warrior nodded approvingly. The young one was very knowledgeable of the wild ones. "These animals have not been hunted so they are not wary of us."

This was Eagle Wing's first venture alone with his uncle into the vast hunting grounds of the Arapaho. For the past year, Crow Killer had explained to him that he would be expected to perform and pass many obstacles on his vision quest to become a Lance Bearer. Today, he followed Walking Horse, keeping his thoughts to himself. It was a pleasant day and he was enjoying this time alone with the warrior. It made him feel proud to be treated like a man. The trials did not worry him. He had been training his mind and body many years for this day.

"Today, Nephew, we will hunt for meat to take back to the village." Walking Horse crisscrossed the grass filled meadows, looking for the herds of deer. "Near this place on our first hunt together many years ago, your father killed a huge bull elk. These grounds are rarely hunted so there should be meat animals out here today."

"In Crow Killer's valley there are many large elk."

"The largest elk I ever saw was the one Crow Killer killed across the Yellowstone in Crow Country." Walking Horse reminisced. "That was also the day he killed Long Leaper's father."

"Because of the elk?"

"Yes and no." Walking Horse continued. "That day the Crow, Wild Wind, was looking for a fight. He thought your father would be an easy kill so he used the dead elk to pick a fight."

"I thought the Crow and the Arapaho were at peace."

"Not back then." The big warrior nodded grimly. "Now, we are at peace, but that was before the Arapaho and Crow made a truce. Chief Plenty Coups took a liking to your father for his bravery. There were no shaggies on our side of the river. Crow Killer convinced Plenty Coups to let us hunt the north side. Now, since the old chief's death, there are ones in the Crow village that want to break the truce and make war on us again."

"But Red Hawk is my father's brother, as you are."

"Red Hawk does not want to break this peace." Walking Horse continued. "You will always have enemies in every tribe. Be careful and trust no one. Sometimes, not even the ones you think are friends."

"I hear your words, Uncle."

"Good, then let us look for a deer or elk."

CHAPTER 6

The hunt had been successful as two dressed deer lay across the withers of their horses as they entered the village. Hanging the deer from a pole scaffold, Walking Horse spoke to an old squaw, then led the horses to their lodge.

"Grass for the horses grows short in this place. Soon, we will have to move the village." Walking Horse could feel the short grass under his feet.

"Crow Killer puts up dry grass to feed our horses through the hard times."

"Yes, I know, but our people hold to the old ways. It would be impossible to put up grass for so many." Walking Horse explained.

"It is too bad, Uncle, the grass keeps our horses strong during the deep snows." Eagle Wing looked at the huge horse herd. "But, you are right, for this many it would require too much work."

"Take the horses to the herd and release them out of the village." Walking Horse did not want the horses to run over an elderly one if they were released among the lodges. "When you return, we will eat."

"You had a successful hunt." Little Antelope smiled as Walking Horse entered the lodge. "I watched as you gave deer to the old ones."

"Eagle Wing is a good shot with the bow." Walking Horse smiled as he reclined against his backrest. "Much better than Crow Killer was."

Little Antelope's eyes looked away as a smile came to her lips. Thinking of her warrior always brought good thoughts. "The young one is older than his years already."

"Yes, he is much older than his years." Walking Horse agreed. "He will be a great warrior."

"When will you send him to seek his vision?" The small woman set a bowl of steaming venison and greens beside the warrior.

"Tomorrow, I see no reason to wait." Walking Horse shrugged. "He is already wise in the ways of the forest. He is a good hunter and has already counted coup on many enemies."

"But, our nephew is so young." Little Antelope studied the warrior's face. "To ride alone in these lands is dangerous."

"You speak of the Pawnee?"

"They raid our pony herds and watch our lands." Little Antelope worried for the safety of Eagle Wing, alone on the high mountain.

"While Eagle Wing is at the sacred place of our ancestors, I will keep patrols watching for enemies." Walking Horse bit into the hot meat. "To seek a vision, he must be alone with his thoughts."

"I know this, Husband, but he is so young." Little Antelope argued.

"You would not have thought so if you had seen him at the river fighting the Rics. He is very strong and he fights like a demon." Walking Horse continued. "Besides, many of our warriors were even younger when they sought their vision."

"Like Crow Killer?"

Walking Horse nodded. "Somehow, I feel this young one will be even a more terrible fighter than my brother."

"Why does my husband say this?"

"I have seen his calmness in battle. I have heard the prophecy of Spotted Panther. Yes, Little Antelope, this young one is a fighter."

"My sister, Bright Moon, knows the prophecy and worries for him."

"As she should, a dangerous path lies before him." The warrior nodded. "But, only time will tell us his fate."

Grey Hair joined Eagle Wing as he led the horses past the lodges and out to the big herd that milled about on the huge meadow. No words were spoken as the two young men walked through the village. Dark eyes of every maiden followed the warriors. Nowhere in the tribes were there any physical specimens to match these two young men.

"Soon, Walking Horse will set you on your vision quest." Grey Hair let his eyes follow the horses as they trotted off. "Be brave, be patient, then the vision will come."

"How do you know? Have you had a vision?"

Grey Hair smiled. "It will mark you and sear into your mind forever."

"Sounds scary." Eagle Wing had been raised both red and white. He wondered if a vision from the spirit people would come to a half white.

"Be strong so when this time has passed, we will ride on the hunt and against our enemies." Grey Hair's dark eyes flashed excitedly. "In the days to come, we will have many great adventures."

Before the light came across the sky, Walking Horse brought Eagle Wing to the sacred mountain. Nodding with confidence, he turned and led his horse away. No words were spoken, none were needed. The young one knew why he was there. Armed only with his skinning knife, he climbed to the high sacred place.

From high above, on a rocky peak that almost reached the clouds, Eagle Wing could see the valley below for miles. Herds of buffalo, deer, elk, and wild horses looked like small ants as they grazed on the vast lands. The soft morning breeze blew through his hair and caressed his smooth face. Prostrating himself naked on the shelf of rock in the morning sun, he watched as an eagle floated on the winds. His mind drifted with the great bird and his body relaxed as he waited for his vision to come.

For centuries, every young man seeking his longed-for vision had suffered, prayed, and suffered even more, waiting for the spirit people to send a sign. No food or drink was allowed to pass his lips during this time as he prostrated himself on the high rocks.

For two days, Eagle Wing lay on the flat smooth stone, freezing at night and burning up in the daytime. He knew nothing of visions, for no warrior was allowed to tell their experience. To tell anyone or show fear would turn the spirit people away from the vision seeker.

From lack of water, Eagle Wing's mouth was parched and his stomach convulsed as he weakened. Would the vision come or should he walk away from this place and rid himself of this suffering? Rising to a sitting position, trying to find the soaring eagle, the youngster wiped his hand across his face. To fail and return to the village would dishonor both Walking Horse and Crow Killer. No, he would not be shamed. He would die on this ledge before dishonoring himself like a weakling. He would wait for the vision to show itself to him. Lying stiffly, he closed his eyes to the bright sun and let his mind drift and soar with the eagle. Crow Killer had always told his sons, something worth having was worth suffering for, perhaps even dying.

Another day and night passed as the strength and mind of the young vision seeker slowly weakened from hunger and thirst. Startled in his delirium, Eagle Wing moved sideways as he tried to get away from a herd of buffalo, charging forward to trample him. Waving his hands and screaming, he tried to divert the enraged animals away from him. Sharp horns pierced his side, pinning him to the cold rocks. Blinking his eyes open, the youngster watched as the dark shaggies stepped back from him with their black hooves pawing the ground in fury and their nostrils snorting fire and smoke. As the haze of fog lifted miraculously, their dark hides changed color. The vision seeker watched the shaggy heads and faces of the beasts as they turned snow white. Huge blooded tears fell from their eyes as they collapsed naked and died before him.

Suddenly, the herd vanished and a lone phantom rider appeared above him in the clouds. The warrior's whitish arm extended and pointed his finger in every direction. The phantom was ghostly white with fiery red eyes just as the buffalo had looked. No words came from the pale aberration's mouth, only his silent thoughts penetrated the foggy mind of the fevered Eagle Wing. For several minutes, the warrior's fiery red eyes had stared deep into the prone body, penetrating his very soul. With one last look and a knowing nod, the warrior vanished back into the clouds.

Eagle Wing awoke groggily from the dream, sitting up weakly and looking around. Unsteadily, he tried several times before he could stand. Finally, he staggered several steps as he tried to clear his head. Touching his side, he felt the sticky blood that seeped from several places where the horns had penetrated his side. Eagle Wing shook his head, and started back down the rocky path that led up to the high places of the spirit people. The same direction the ghostly warrior had pointed to before disappearing back into the clouds. Eagle Wing tried to clear his clouded mind. He knew he had seen his vision. He did not understand the dead buffalo, but somehow he knew the warrior in the clouds had become his protector. In their short encounter, the warrior had entered his mind as their thoughts had become one. The great strength of the ghost warrior had entered his very heart and soul. Eagle Wing had his vision and his prayers had been answered.

Below, where the flat valley stopped and the high cliff started, Walking Horse waited. Taking the staggering youngster by the arm, he led him to the small fire and placed him on a buffalo hide. Putting a water bag to Eagle Wing's mouth, he let the young one drink slowly.

"You have been seeking your vision for four days, Nephew." Walking Horse looked down at the sunbaked face and bloody side. "It was a long time, and I became worried. You have suffered much for your people."

Nodding, Eagle Wing tried to speak but the words were not forthcoming. Letting more water slip down his parched throat, he could only shake his head. For several hours, Walking Horse kept him drinking and finally, Eagle Wing ate some deer meat that Little Antelope had prepared.

As his voice and strength returned, Eagle Wing sat up slowly and looked around the valley floor. "It is good to see you, my uncle."

Walking Horse placed jerked meat in his hands, then pointed to the bloody marks on his side. "The rocks dug into you as you slept."

Eagle Wing looked down at his side and smiled. "Yes, Uncle, the rocks were very sharp."

"Your vision came on the winds?"

"Yes." Eagle Wing remembered his dream vividly; the buffalo with their sharp black horns and bloody eyes, the red-eyed horseman in the clouds, and his bloody side. Had the buffalo gored him or had it been the rocks? Eagle Wing knew the answer. There were no sharp edges on the smooth rock ledge.

"After you rest from your ordeal, we will ride to the village. We will let Soaring Bird interpret your vision."

"I thought no one was to know of my vision."

"Soaring Bird is the greatest of medicine men and he is the only one that can tell you the meaning of your vision and medicine." Walking Horse nodded. "No one else will know of your vision."

Eagle Wing shook his head. "Even I do not know exactly what I saw."

"The old one will know." Walking Horse assured him. "You should be proud, Eagle Wing. Very few warriors ever meet this old medicine man."

The small lodge of Soaring Bird stood near the village's edge. Several buffalo skulls perched atop poles lined the lodge entranceway. Others lay around the hide structure, warding off evil spirits.

Sliding from his horse before the lodge, Walking Horse held up his hand and looked over at his nephew. "The one inside can see into your mind, young one. Do not lie to him in any way."

"I do not lie, Uncle."

"I know this, Nephew." Walking Horse nodded. "But sometimes with pain, you might see things that are not real."

"I understand your words. What I will speak of will be only what I have seen in my vision."

Before they could announce their arrival, the raspy voice from inside the lodge bid them to enter. The lodge was dim, only the sun shining through the smoke hole above gave off any light. Eagle Wing waited a few moments, letting his eyes adjust to the dark interior. Focusing on the slender form sitting across from him, he tried to take in the old one's features. Never had he seen such a thin person. The face was lined with seams of age or old scars, and in the dark he couldn't be sure. The form before him seemed grotesque, and it was hard to look him in the face. The sharp piercing eyes were ablaze as they penetrated into not only his eyes, but even his mind. His thoughts could reach into his, draining his very soul. The medicine man was ancient with thin frail arms, bony knees, and the little hair left covering the bony head was completely snow white. Eagle Wing wondered what kind of aberration sat before him.

"Sit, my sons, both of you." The rattle in the old one's hands buzzed as Eagle Wing and Walking Horse took their places across from him. "The spirit people tell me Eagle Wing has had a vision."

"Shall I stay, Grandfather?" Walking Horse knew no one was to hear the vision except the seeker and the one interpreting the vision.

"Yes, Walking Horse will remain and hear these words." The old head nodded slowly. "This dream is different, very different."

"If it is your wish, I will remain." Walking Horse nodded.

Soaring Bird pointed to Eagle Wing's side. "The horn of the buffalo is sharp, but it gives you strength. Any warrior that can withstand its pain and live, will one day become invincible to mere mortal man. In your vision, Tatanka's horns have spoken."

Eagle Wing was covered by a leather shirt Walking Horse had brought for him. He was amazed how the old seer knew things. "Yes, Grandfather, they were very sharp."

The old one leaned slightly forward, gazing through the smoke into Eagle Wing's eyes. "Your eyes and the smoke tell me you have seen something phenomenal. A vision like no other has ever seen."

"Yes, I saw many things I cannot explain."

"Tell me more of your vision, young one."

Thinking back on his dream, Eagle Wing told of the buffalo herd appearing with their bloody black horns, turning white in color, the bleeding eyes, and their deaths. Then, the phantom horseman appeared in the clouds exactly as he could remember.

"That is all, Grandfather. It felt like the phantom one looked deep into my mind with his red eyes. Then, he pointed his bloody finger in all directions, nodded his head, and vanished back into the clouds."

"Did you not feel the horns cutting into your side?" Soaring Bird looked down where blood had appeared as it soaked through the leather shirt. "Was the phantom one ghostly white except for his eyes?"

"Yes, Grandfather, I felt the horns pierce my side." Eagle Wing nodded, but wasn't aware his side bled again. "There was pain, then the ghost warrior appeared out of the clouds."

"Your side bleeds, but it gives you strength." Soaring Bird stared into Eagle Wing's eyes. "Tell me of this pale warrior."

Remembering the ghost warrior astride a white horse with red blazing eyes and smoke coming from his horse's nostrils, Eagle Wing shook his head. Had the vision been real or had it been a dream? "He appeared in the sky, and held out his hand to me. His thoughts seemed to enter my mind. Then the warrior pointed in each direction before evaporating back into the clouds. That is all."

"The spirit warrior was completely covered in white except for his eyes?"

"Yes, Grandfather."

"Tell me again, what color were his eyes?"

"They were a yellowish red, like a fire." The youngster shrugged. He would never forget the image of the rider in the sky.

"What else does Eagle Wing remember?"

"This phantom or whatever it was did not feel threatening to me."

The youngster searched his mind for other clues. "He seemed to be a friend, a strong arm reaching out supporting me."

"Eagle Wing has seen what few others have seen." The old man explained. "The spirit world has sent the great one to your vision. The last one to see this warrior was our great Chief Slow Wolf."

"The great one?" Walking Horse spoke the words in awe.

"Yes, the great one. Flying Cloud was in your dream, young one."

"Is this a good omen or bad, Grandfather?"

The old medicine man thought several minutes before answering. "Most warriors only see this one when they are about to die. The spirit people call him the messenger of death. He leads our dead warriors to the hunting grounds in the next life."

Eagle Wing blinked. "Does this mean I am about to die?"

"No, I believe Flying Cloud wanted to gaze into your eyes to see your mortal spirit. To look into your heart before giving you his blessing."

"His blessing?"

"As the great Cheyenne, Spotted Panther, has revealed in his smoke, you will follow a dangerous path for your people." The thin one shook his rattle. "The dead buffalo at your feet shows them being killed. Their white faces show the ones that have killed them. The blood running from their eyes shows they plead with you to fight and take revenge against their killers. Walk proud, young one, protect the weak and never turn your back in battle. The Great One in the clouds will protect you from your enemies. Be mighty and fearless before all enemies."

"Do you mean never retreat?"

The old one reached behind him and pulled a gnarled-handled war club from behind him. Intricately decorated with strands of hair and sinew, the axe was lighter than the one Crow Killer had given him on his thirteenth summer. The stone head was made of a different kind of rock, but somehow Eagle Wing knew this axe was deadlier.

"This is the war axe of Flying Cloud himself. Once, the great warrior and Chief of the Arapaho, Slow Wolf, carried this war club also. Now, it belongs to Eagle Wing. The spirit people want you to carry this war club always." Soaring Bird prayed over the axe reverently, then handed the club to Eagle Wing. "It will always protect you from your enemies. It will honor you, providing you honor it."

Walking Horse sat in awe as he looked down at the war axe. Many times, he had seen Slow Wolf carry the weapon in battle. He had thought the war axe had been in the old chief's burial ceremony when he died, but here it was, the same axe Slow Wolf always carried.

"I do not understand your words, Grandfather."

"Carry the axe proudly, but only kill to protect your people or yourself. Never provoke a fight. The day it slips from your hands is the day of your death, Eagle Wing." The old man warned.

Eagle Wing studied the war club. It was beautiful, and the balance was perfect. He got the feeling the axe could strike an enemy by itself without help. The young one knew he held a special weapon in his hand. The old one said with the aid of such a weapon, he could not be defeated in battle. "Thank you, Grandfather."

"Go now, bring glory and victory to our people. Always walk proud, and never bend a knee to the killers of the buffalo or sign their papers."

Exiting the lodge, Walking Horse looked in awe at the young one beside him. He had heard stories of Flying Cloud, the great ghost warrior in the sky, but he knew Eagle Wing had actually seen him. Had the magnificent war axe been sent to Eagle Wing by the spirit warrior? He was not mistaken. He had seen the same war axe placed with Slow Wolf on his burial scaffold. If it was as Soaring Bird had foretold, it was a sign of great things to come for the young warrior.

"Is something wrong, Uncle?" Eagle Wing looked into Walking Horse's face. "You are troubled."

"No, Nephew, I am proud of you." The warrior shook his head. "Maybe a little awestruck is all."

"Uncle."

"Yes, Eagle Wing."

"What the old one speaks, is it the truth or was I dreaming?" Eagle Wing looked into the dark face of Walking Horse.

"The bleeding scars on your side were not made by a dream." Walking Horse nodded. "And you know as well as I there are no sharp places on the rocks where you lay."

Eagle Wing knew the marks were real and still seeped blood. The flat rock where he lay was smooth, and there was nothing on the ledge to injure himself on. The vision seemed so real. The pale warrior and buffalo showed themselves to him, their breath hot and rancid. Soaring Bird said it had been his vision, it must be so.

Greeting them outside the lodge, Little Antelope looked at the straight carriage of Eagle Wing. Her eyes glanced down at the leather hunting shirt where fresh blood showed. Coming home after four days of exposure to the elements uncovered, she had expected him to be weak and gaunt. She had seen other young men after coming back from their vision quests. They had been pale, thin, and unable to walk alone at times. The one standing before her was different, somehow transformed. He stood before her straight, strong, tall, and full of confidence. As Eagle Wing stepped through the entranceway with the children, Little Antelope took Walking Horse's arm, restraining him.

"What has happened to him, my husband? His carriage, his face, my nephew has changed. He seems older, matured."

The warrior smiled down into her upturned face. "He has received the strongest of visions from the spirit people. He is no longer a child. Now, he is an Arapaho warrior. After the ceremony, he will be a Lance Bearer for the people. Soaring Bird says he has seen what no other has seen. The old one said Eagle Wing will become one of the greatest of our warriors."

"Then, his novice time has ended?"

"This one is now a Lance Bearer of the Arapaho People." Walking Horse turned for the lodge. "I can say no more, but today humble yourself as you stand in the shadow of a great one."

Little Antelope felt weak as she wondered what this meant for her nephew, the son of her warrior. Crow Killer still held a place in her heart, but now, she worried for his son. "I will treat his wounds."

"No, just get him a clean shirt." Walking Horse nodded. "His wounds will heal themselves. Fold the bloody shirt and save it for Bright Moon."

Walking Horse wanted to waste no time. Tonight, he would announce to the village elders, the Lance Bearer ceremony would be conducted within ten sleeps. That would give plenty of time for the ones far away to arrive at the village. The Lance Bearer Ceremony was a great occasion, and this one would be even greater. One of the candidates to become an Arapaho Lance Bearer was the son of Crow Killer. Every warrior would welcome the young one into the Lance Bearer Society of the Arapaho with gifts and brotherhood. The people could see something special had happened as he had sought his vision far up on spirit mountain. Something supernatural changed the young one, and that is why Walking Horse cut short his novice time. None would ever know as they knew to speak of it was forbidden. Nevertheless, something definitely had changed the youngster's stature into a warrior seemingly overnight.

The celebration and dancing would last for days. Walking Horse sent runners to Crow Killer, Bright Moon, and the Cheyenne Village of He Dog and Dull Knife. He also sent runners to the Yellowstone to look for some of Red Hawk's warriors who patrolled the river. Seeing none and following their chief's orders, they returned to the village without crossing the river.

"There is plenty of time." Walking Horse listened as Two-Eyed Dog reported his failure to find any Crow warriors at the river.

"I could have crossed the river and ridden to Red Hawk's village, my chief."

"No, with Red Hawk away from his village, I do not know if our people would be safe." Walking Horse remembered how Red Hawk had warned of Long Leaper's threats against the Arapaho when they had talked at Crow Killer's lodge. "We do not want to provoke a fight now."

"Surely, Long Leaper would not disobey Red Hawk and attack us."

Walking Horse shook his head. "I am not sure. This Crow hates me, perhaps more than he hates Crow Killer."

"They say Long Leaper has become a mighty warrior over the past few years." Grey Hair shrugged. "They say he has taken many scalps from his enemies."

"Yes, I have heard this from Red Hawk." Walking Horse remembered the young warrior he had choked back on the river because he dared look at Little Antelope wrong. "I should have killed him many moons ago."

"What will we do?"

"I will ride to the river tomorrow and make smoke."

"At the river, I felt the Crow watching us. They were there alright, but they would not show themselves." Two-Eyed Dog cautioned.

"You are probably right." Walking Horse looked toward the river. "I fear this will only end with the death of Long Leaper."

Walking Horse and Little Antelope were not the only ones to notice the change in Eagle Wing. Grey Hair was deep in thought as he rode across the grasslands beside the young warrior. How a few days on the sacred mountain had made a change in the youngster's demeanor was astounding. His proud carriage was even more aristocratic, his head was held high, and he spoke even less than he had before his vision. The war axe he carried was different from any he had ever seen. Grey Hair asked to hold the beautiful weapon, but Eagle Wing refused.

"Eagle Wing has changed." Grey Hair looked at the calm face. "Tell me, what has happened, my friend?"

"Grey Hair knows it is not permitted to speak of such things." The younger one shook his head. "I have not changed; it's only in your mind."

"No, I sense something about you is different."

"Well, I washed my face this morning."

"I am serious, do not joke." Grey Hair looked at Eagle Wing's bare torso, nothing covered his chest. The scars from his time on the mountain showed plainly. "Your side has almost healed from its wounds."

"I am a fast healer."

"I am not blind." Grey Hair insisted. "You are somehow different from before."

"Come, let us ride to the river." Eagle Wing wanted to change the subject. Talking about his vision was not allowed and talking about himself was embarrassing.

Kicking their horses into a hard run, the two warriors made a mad headlong dash to the Yellowstone. Clods of fresh dirt flew up from their flying feet as they whooped and raced the straining horses along the path to the river. Reining in on the bank of the smooth running water, they peered out over the crossing.

Grey Hair laughed as he looked at the heaving Appaloosa. "He is too fast for my horse."

"His grandfather was the great spotted horse of Red Hawk the Crow."

Eagle Wing and Red Horse had raced many horses against the stallion, but only the paint horse of Crow Killer in his youth could match his speed. Once, their father had caught the boys racing the horses and forbid them from riding anything but the small black mule for a solid moon. That experience was enough to stop the horse racing, at least when

Crow Killer was anywhere near. Riding the small black mule was beneath their dignity, or so they thought. Anyway, there definitely had been no more horse races within sight of the cabin.

The horses were swigging deeply of the cool water when several Crow riders appeared, moving down from the high banks. Stopping at the riverbank, they sat their horses quietly.

"That is Long Leaper in front of the others." Grey Hair frowned. "Be careful, he is a treacherous one."

Kicking their horses, all but two of the Crow warriors waded into the water, raising their rifles and hurling insults across the water. Then, they laughed, and moved back onto solid ground. One of the younger warriors touched off his rifle, sending a loud clap reverberating up and down the river.

"Do we fight them or ride away?" Grey Hair glared at the Crow. "They have challenged us."

"They mouth insults from across the river, but their words do us no harm." Eagle Wing sat quietly on his Appaloosa watching the Crow. "Insults from ones like these are nothing."

"It does not make you mad, my friend?" Grey Hair was older, but somehow since Eagle Wing had returned from his vision quest he had matured beyond his years. Some warriors were natural born leaders, demanding respect, and this youngster was one of them.

"We will meet one day when the river does not separate us." Eagle Wing turned his horse. "For now, we will let them have this day."

Jeers came from across the river. "Arapaho dogs, why do you turn away? The cowardly son of the Crow Killer flees like a woman from a fight with real warriors."

"I cannot let Long Leaper insult us and ride away." Grey Hair reined in his horse. "There are only five of them, let us fight."

"No, across the river is my uncle's land and people." Eagle Wing shook his head. "I will not fight with them over mere words."

"They cross the river." Grey Hair looked toward the river where the Crow had entered the water again. "The Crow push this fight, my friend. They come onto Arapaho land."

Eagle Wing reined his horse around as the Crow warriors hit swimming water. Riding back to the edge of the river, he pointed his bow at

Long Leaper and pulled out his war club. Laughing, the Crow pulled up his breechcloth, exposing himself, then pulled his swimming horse around and started back for the bank.

"Another time, son of Crow Killer." The warrior taunted. "We will meet another day. I promise you."

Grey Hair smiled at Eagle Wing with pride. "I do not think this one really wanted to fight with you, my friend."

Slapping his horse with the bow, Eagle Wing started back toward the village. "Come, Grey Hair, we will look for a deer to bring the people."

"Walking Horse has sent many warriors to hunt for meat before the great celebration." Grey Hair took one final look at the retreating backs of the Crow. "There will be a great many mouths in the village to feed. Soon, Crow Killer and your mother will arrive."

"This is good. It will be good to see my father and mother."

"And your sister?" Grey Hair looked at Eagle Wing. "She will come?"

Eagle Wing smiled. "Yes, Ellie would not miss the celebration."

"Perhaps, I will play my flute for her."

"Your flute?" The young warrior shook his head. "Then, I wish Grey Hair luck."

"The flute is good. Girls like the music."

"Uh-huh."

Grey Hair stood talking to Walking Horse as Eagle Wing led the horse, carrying the deer, to several squaws standing near the drying racks.

"The Crow called names and insulted Eagle Wing."

"You did not fight with them?"

"No, my chief, we did not cross the river." Grey Hair replied. "Eagle Wing would not permit it."

"That is good."

"They acted like they were going to cross the river." Grey Hair laughed. "Then your nephew turned and challenged Long Leaper to a personal fight."

"Then what happened, Grey Hair?" Walking Horse questioned. "You said they did not fight."

"Nothing, Long Leaper laughed and returned to their side of the river." Grey Hair continued. "I think the Crow were testing Eagle Wing."

"That is good. Long Leaper is an older experienced warrior." Walking Horse looked to where Eagle Wing spoke with a warrior named Iron Bull.

"I do not think one lone warrior, no matter how old or experienced, could stand against this one." Grey Hair nodded. "He is young, but I believe the spirit people watch over him."

"I believe this also." Walking Horse agreed as they had seen the same thing in Eagle Wing. "Tell me, Grey Hair, why did you listen to Eagle Wing and not fight the Crow?"

"This I do not know, my chief." The warrior seemed puzzled. "There is something about this warrior. His spirit is so strong, that one has to respect his counsel and words."

Three warriors reined in, stopping at the creek before crossing. Jed stood watching from the doorway of the cabin. The black mule had already announced the new arrivals. Motioning for the warriors to cross, he held up his hand and welcomed them. Recognizing the warriors, he smiled. He had known these young Arapaho since they were children.

"Welcome, my friends." Jed was surprised. He didn't expect to see them return to the cabin so soon. "Has something happened?"

"It is good to see Crow Killer again." The young warrior, Broken Leg, smiled down from his horse. "No, there is no bad news, only good."

"Then, why have you returned to my lodge so soon?"

"Chief Walking Horse invites you to a celebration." The warrior smiled. "He wishes for you and Bright Moon to come to the village."

"Celebration?" Jed shook his head. "What celebration?"

"Your son, Eagle Wing, and two others will be the honored guests at the Lance Bearer ceremony, welcoming them into our society."

"So soon?" Jed was curious. It had been less than a month since Walking Horse had taken the youngster south to the Arapaho village.

"This son of yours is very special, Crow Killer." Broken Leg continued. "Walking Horse proclaims to all, the young one will someday be the greatest of Lance Bearers."

"Then he has seen his vision?"

"Yes, and he was summoned to the lodge of the ancient one, Soaring Bird." The warrior nodded. "Only the special ones ever speak with this old medicine man."

"Soaring Bird." Jed knew to have the old one interpret a vision was indeed an extraordinary thing. He himself had seen the old medicine man on several occasions, but had never spoken with him. "White Swan, another older medicine man of the Arapaho, had interpreted Jed's vision."

"Yes, Crow Killer, the medicine man who some say speaks with the spirit people."

"We will come." Jed knew something special had happened for the novice time to be cut so short. And to have his vision interpreted by Soaring Bird was indeed something very few could tell of. Looking to where Bright Moon had stood anxiously in the doorway, he nodded and turned his attention back to the mounted warriors. "Get down, my friends. The women will bring you food."

"Walking Horse says we are to wait and ride with you to our village." Broken Leg stood beside his horse.

"Has there been trouble?"

"No, but the Crow, Long Leaper seeks trouble."

"My brother, Red Hawk, is back with his people." The Crow chief had left days earlier to return to the south. "Surely, he will not allow this."

"It is not Red Hawk who causes trouble." The warriors sat down around the table as Bright Moon brought food. "Long Leaper has many warriors who follow him now."

"They don't listen to Red Hawk?"

"Most Crows do, but many still remember the Arapaho as being hereditary enemies of the Crow." Broken Leg shrugged. "Even the great, Red Hawk, cannot keep them from causing trouble. He is not Plenty Coups yet."

"Has Eagle Wing had trouble with the Crow?"

A warrior named Cut Arm nodded. "Grey Hair told us how Long Leaper challenged your son at the river."

"What happened?"

"Eagle Wing accepted the challenge and prepared to fight, but the Crow only laughed and rode away."

Jed remembered the young Crow warrior and his father Wild Wind. This one was a troublemaker and a warrior who hated the Arapaho. Like his father, Wild Wind, he bullied and threatened younger warriors into following him against weaker enemies.

Wilson and Oliver walked up and nodded at the newcomers. Oliver still remained at Wilson's cabin, content and in no hurry to return to the east. On several occasions, Jed had offered to return the young white to Bridger, but for three weeks Oliver had found excuses for not leaving the cabin. Jed knew only too well the reason for his delay. All he had to do was watch the way the boy looked with calf eyes at Ellie Thunder every time she appeared. When not helping Wilson or riding with Red Horse, he found excuses to hang around the cabin.

Jed wanted to help Oliver survive the wilderness. He had instructed his younger son, Red Horse, to teach the young white everything he could about being a woodsman. Still, there had been plenty of time for Oliver to sit around the cabin with Ellie, laughing and talking. The young white man was completely fascinated and captivated by the beautiful girl. Sometimes, Jed felt his daughter was enthralled with the attention of Oliver as well. Bright Moon was concerned about the relationship, but Jed only shrugged saying it was just two young people enjoying each other's company. He well remembered the innocent time he had spent with Ellie Medicine Thunder, now Red Hawk's wife.

"Where is my son?" Jed was curious why he hadn't come.

"He stays behind at the village, preparing himself for the great celebration." Looking as Ellie Thunder stepped from the cabin, Broken Leg smiled. Now, he knew why Grey Hair had been so disappointed when he hadn't been selected to journey north to Crow Killer's valley. "I think for some reason, Walking Horse keeps him close to the village."

"I figure Long Leaper is the reason." Jed nodded. "Walking Horse probably wants to keep Eagle Wing away from the river."

"Yes, to ride here, Eagle Wing would have to cross the Yellowstone where Long Leaper could be waiting."

"Yes, the Crow just waits to cause trouble." Cut Arm added. "But, Walking Horse does not want this until after the Lance Bearer Ceremony."

"Perhaps Long Leaper will be at the river when we return." Jed nodded slowly.

Broken Leg smiled. "This one is no fool. He will not confront the great Crow Killer."

"I guess there will be many at the celebration?"

"Many." Broken Leg and the others started to bite into the steaming meat as Ellie Thunder started toward the table. Jed smiled as the warriors seemed to freeze with their mouths agape. Jed knew his daughter was beautiful beyond compare. The warrior finally found his voice and continued. "He Dog and his Cheyenne, Dull Knife and his people, even Red Hawk and some of his people have been asked to come."

"We will prepare for the journey and leave with the new sun." Jed was surprised Red Hawk would be invited. Hereditary enemies of the Arapaho, a Crow had never been invited to the Lance Bearer Celebration.

"Where are you going, son?" Wilson had only heard the end of the conversation as he walked up. The old one smiled as Ellie Thunder pushed him down onto the table seat.

"There will be a large celebration for your grandson in the Arapaho village." Jed looked at the old farmer. "You must come too."

"Not me, no siree." Wilson shook his head. "My old bones are getting far too old to go traversing all over these mountains on the back of a horse."

"What about you, Oliver, will you join us?" Jed smiled. "You will get to see many Indians if you care to go."

"Many Indians." Oliver shook his head, then looked up at Ellie Thunder.

"Perhaps, it is something you should get used to, young man." Wilson looked at the girl and smiled.

Blushing, the young white nodded. "You are right, I will go."

"Good, it is settled." Jed nodded. "Load all your possibles. Perhaps, He Dog will see you safely to Bridger when he returns to his village."

"He Dog?"

"My uncle is Chief of the Cheyenne." Ellie Thunder smiled at Oliver.

"The blood-thirsty one that Red Horse has spoken of?" Oliver asked.

"Yes, but still he's my uncle." Ellie laughed knowing what the young white was thinking. "He will like you, Oliver. My uncle will not scalp you."

"I hope not." The young man tried to laugh. "I have grown fond of my hair."

Oliver had been around many Indians while at Bridger. He had lived with Jed and his family for over a month, but he still wasn't completely comfortable around them. Raised in the east, the young man was not overly confident. He was strong enough and wasn't a coward, but he knew he was completely out of his element in these mountains. He learned many things about survival from Red Horse, but he could not understand their language or even their ways at times.

Jed looked around for the ever-elusive Red Horse. His youngest was forever roaming the mountains alone, far away from the cabin. Bright Moon always fussed and scolded the youngster to remain closer to the cabin. Jed knew it was just in the boy's nature to ride the many mountain trails alone. There were different things in these forests and valleys that could do harm to an unwary hunter. Unlike Bright Moon, Jed didn't worry for his younger son. He knew Red Horse was already a good hunter and wise in the ways of the mountains.

"Eat now and rest, my friends. We will depart for the south with the new sun." Jed stood up and motioned Wilson to follow him. "Turn your horses loose with the others so they can rest and fill their stomachs."

Nodding, as Jed walked away, Broken Leg smiled at Ellie Thunder. "Grey Hair speaks of you."

"And what does Grey Hair say about me?" Ellie Thunder met his dark gaze.

"He said for me to send his greetings and wishes you a safe trip back to our lands."

"Why did he not come himself?"

"Our chief wanted him and your brother to stay close to the village." Broken Leg shrugged, smiling at the beautiful young woman. "He was very disappointed. When he heard he could not come, his heart fell to the ground."

"Yes, it did, and now, I know why." Cut Arm laughed lightly.

Ellie Thunder turned her dark eyes on the other warrior. "You should eat your food, warrior, before you choke on it."

Seeing the warrior drop his gaze, Oliver questioned her. They had been speaking in Arapaho. "What did he say, Ellie?"

"Nothing, only we are to leave with the new sun."

"Is it far?"

"Maybe three sleeps."

Oliver shrugged. "Three sleeps, I do not understand."

Ellie only smiled. "Three days, Oliver."

Jed walked with his stepfather along the trail, leading down to the creek. "You will be safe here in my absence, Father?"

"It will be as usual." Wilson nodded. "If strangers come, I will retreat to the rock cave."

"That is good." Jed nodded. "I do not know of any enemy that will come here, but one never can be sure of such things. Be alert and listen for the mule and wolf to warn you."

"Don't worry, boy." The old man remembered the trapper Squires and his Metis killers. "I will stay alert."

"Do so, for I do not trust the whites from Bridger." Jed looked across the broad valley. "I doubt they'll return, but they just might."

Smiling, Wilson skipped a flat stone across the water's surface. "It doesn't seem possible that our little warrior has grown to manhood so quickly."

Jed looked up at the tall quiet mountains. "I wish he could have stayed here in these mountains where he would be safe."

"Like you said, Jedidiah." Wilson nodded solemnly. "These valleys and forests as big as they are could not hold the spirit of one like Eagle Wing. He's been different from other boys since he was a babe. He's even different from you when you were his age."

"Yes, there is restlessness in him."

"Red Horse is wild and free." The old farmer smiled. "But he is not as restless as his older brother. There's just something about our oldest. His spirit will never be tamed."

"The old one, Spotted Panther, said it would be so." Jed shook his head sadly. "He foresaw Eagle Wing fighting many enemies. He predicted our son would be in dangerous battles with many enemies, red and white."

Wilson stopped and took Jed's arm. "You go see your son be honored in the Arapaho way. I will take care of things here."

"I know you will."

"Jedidiah, my son, I know your worries." The old shoulders seemed to sag. Jed knew Wilson thought of his sons, Billy and Seth, who now rested beneath the earth back at his farm on Pennington Creek.

"I will return as soon as I can." Jed placed his hand on the old farmer's shoulder. "You stay safe."

CHAPTER 7

*L*ook, Uncle, the seers of death float on the winds." Eagle Wing pointed at several vultures floating lazily in the sky. "Their sharp eyes have found something hurt or dead."

"We will go see. Be alert, Nephew." Walking Horse kicked his horse into the lead. Many times, he had seen the enemy use this trick. They would bait a dead animal to draw the carrion eaters. When a hunter comes to investigate what the large vultures had found, they would attack. This was Arapaho Hunting Grounds, but one could never be sure when interlopers could be lurking in the shadows of the woods.

Moving cautiously to where the huge black birds sat perched on limbs or floated in the air, Walking Horse studied the hidden places. Several big birds spread their wings, lifting their heavy bodies into the air as the riders approached. Pushing through a heavy thicket of brush, they spotted the body of a dead horse in a small clearing. Blood covered the ground underneath the animal's neck. By all the blood, Walking Horse could tell the horse's throat had been cut.

Seeing movement to his right, Eagle Wing pushed Walking Horse sideways, just in time to save him from a flying arrow, missing only by inches. Raising his rifle, he looked into the dark eyes of a young warrior. Blood covered the body and one leg protruded awkwardly at an angle from the injured warrior. Aiming his rifle as the hurt man pulled his skinning knife, Eagle Wing slowly lowered his weapon.

"You have saved my life this day, Nephew." Walking Horse stepped closer to the hurt one. "This one is Pawnee."

"His leg is broken." Eagle Wing reached out his hand, motioning to the warrior. "He is young."

"Yes, he is young, but as dangerous as a young rattlesnake, Nephew."

"What will we do?"

"He is the enemy of the Arapaho. Do you wish to kill him or leave him?"

Eagle Wing looked over at the dead horse. "He is a merciful man. The horse had a broken leg. This one put him out of his misery."

"He is still Pawnee." Walking Horse was curious how the youngster would answer. "They have no heart."

"He is Pawnee, but a warrior with a good heart, Uncle." Eagle Wing quickly motioned with hand signs to the injured warrior. "A cruel one would have let the horse suffer."

"He will not put the knife down." Walking Horse watched as Eagle Wing moved closer to the defiant warrior. "Use caution, Nephew."

"Do you speak our language, Pawnee?"

"I understand your words." The dark head nodded slowly.

"Put your knife away so I can look at your leg."

"So you can kill me, Arapaho?"

Walking Horse stepped closer to the hurt one. "If we wanted you dead, Pawnee, we could just shoot you."

Nodding, the warrior laid his knife aside as Eagle Wing knelt beside him. "Your leg is badly broken."

"Put me out of my misery as I done the horse."

"No, you will live. It can be mended."

"What happened?" Walking Horse looked into the pained eyes.

"I was foolish. I was chasing a lone shaggy when my horse stepped into that hole and broke his leg and mine." The brown finger pointed to the hidden gopher hole.

"Where are your people?"

"We were separated on the hunt. They must have thought I had already returned to our village."

"This is Arapaho lands." Walking Horse shook his head. "Why do you hunt here?"

"The Arapaho are weak. We, Pawnee, hunt where we please."

"What is your name, Pawnee?"

"I am called Weasel."

"Then, Weasel, put this in your mouth and prepare yourself." Eagle Wing handed the hurt one the shaft of an arrow. "If you try to stab me with it, I will do to you as you did to your horse."

"I believe you, Arapaho." Weasel placed the broken shaft in his mouth.

With Walking Horse's help, Eagle Wing slowly straightened the leg. He could feel the young warrior's body tense and tighten when the broken bone grated together. He knew the pain had to be excruciating, yet no word or cry came from the warrior's mouth. Pulling the leg steadily, Eagle Wing felt the broken bones go back in place. Using arrows from Weasel's quiver, he quickly splinted the leg. The Pawnee was an enemy, but he had to admire the young one's courage.

"You are a strong man, Pawnee."

"You have done this before?" Weasel dropped the arrow from his sweating face. "Yet, you are so young."

"I have a young brother who is always breaking something." Eagle Wing looked up as Walking Horse released the Pawnee's shoulders and stood up. "What will we do with him, Uncle?"

"What would Eagle Wing do with him?"

"How close is your village, Weasel?"

"There." The brown hand pointed. "A short journey."

"Your village is on our land?" Walking Horse's face hardened. "Why?"

"Only temporary, we were on our way to Bridger's Post to trade horses for powder and lead for our rifles." Weasel shrugged. "We needed food and thought we would be away from these lands before you found us here."

"Moving east you will enter Cheyenne lands." Walking Horse shook his head. "He Dog of the Cheyenne does not put up with trespassers on his lands."

"Our people have to eat."

"A whole village goes to Bridger?" Eagle Wing handed the injured one a water skin.

"No, there are only a few lodges with us."

"You do not have white traders in your own lands?"

"We have white traders." The dark head nodded. "But, they cheat us on our trades. Bridger treats us fair."

"Leave him, Nephew, his people will find him."

Eagle Wing looked down at the injured warrior. "I would take him to his lodge with your permission."

"They would attack you before you could explain."

"We cannot leave him here to die."

Walking Horse looked down at the hurt warrior, then back up at Eagle Wing. "We will take him closer and leave him for them to find."

"Can you sit a horse, Pawnee?"

"Leave me here, Arapaho. It is too dangerous for you to take me closer." The warrior shook his leg. "You have done enough. My people will find me."

"Perhaps they will, but another enemy not so understanding as us may find you first." Eagle Wing warned.

"Who is your chief?"

"Limping Fox."

Walking Horse nodded. "He is a bad enemy, Eagle Wing. Your father killed his brother, Wet Otter, many summers ago."

The Pawnee's head snapped up, looking at the young warrior before him. "You are the son of Crow Killer?"

"Yes, I am Eagle Wing, son of Crow Killer."

"You have done good by me." The dark eyes stared at Eagle Wing. "My grandfather hates Crow Killer for killing Wet Otter. You must leave this place quickly. You and Walking Horse are in much danger."

"You know who I am, warrior?" Walking Horse looked curiously at the dark face.

"I know the great Chief of the Arapaho." Weasel nodded. "I saw you at Bridger's Post once when we went there to trade."

"Why should there be trouble, warrior?" Eagle Wing questioned. "We have helped you."

"I fear for you and Walking Horse." Weasel sat up straighter. "My grandfather, Limping Fox, will kill you."

"We cannot let the Pawnee run us from our own lands." Walking Horse knew he should forbid his nephew from riding closer to the Pawnee with the hurt one.

"Then, we will take this one to his people." Eagle Wing looked at Walking Horse.

"I think it is a foolish thing to do, Nephew. We may have to fight." The warrior looked at the helpless one. Then, he remembered Spotted Panther's words. Maybe, this would show if the old medicine man's stones spoke the truth.

"My father says an enemy recognizes compassion even in their enemies." Eagle Wing looked down at the Pawnee. "We shall see."

Walking Horse also wanted to see how the Pawnee would react. It would be very dangerous, but perhaps this young one did have the spirit people helping him. Today would be a good day to learn of this prophecy, Spotted Panther and Soaring Bird, both had foretold.

"We will go."

Helping Weasel up before him on the bay horse, Eagle Wing followed Walking Horse to the east in a slow walk. Weasel pointed out the direction of the village with his finger. The broken leg had been bound tightly to keep the bones inline. Still, Eagle Wing knew the Pawnee was in severe pain from the jolting of the horse.

Hardly an hour passed before the shrill cry of alarm sounded and six warriors raced out toward them. Their leader was a bulky warrior with scars covering his chest and arms, showing he had been in battle many times. Checking the priming of his rifle, Eagle Wing reined in his horse beside Walking Horse and waited as the Pawnee advanced toward them.

"More come from our side." Walking Horse nodded as three more warriors rode in from the north side. "Are you ready, Nephew?"

"I am ready." Eagle Wing nodded.

"If they attack, I will kill their leader, then we will flee this place." Walking Horse showed no emotion as he sat his horse calmly in the face of his hereditary enemy. "Pull the hurt one from your horse, Nephew."

Sliding Weasel from the bay horse, Eagle Wing helped the warrior limp several feet toward the oncoming Pawnee warriors. Leaning on his bow for balance, Weasel held his arm high, halting the warriors. A single rider rode to within thirty feet of the injured man and stopped his horse.

"Do these Arapaho no harm, Grandfather." Weasel grimaced. "They have brought me back to my people. They have saved my life."

The dark face of the big warrior studied the splinted leg and then the two Arapaho waiting before him. "What is this? Why would you not kill this one?"

"We are warriors not killers of helpless ones." Walking Horse spoke up.

"You are Arapaho, the hated enemy of the Pawnee."

"Today, we will have a truce so this one can live, Limping Fox, great Chief of the Pawnee." Eagle Wing spoke.

"Perhaps, Walking Horse Chief of the Arapaho knows he is badly outnumbered."

Walking Horse nodded slowly. "Yes, but my first bullet has your name on it, Pawnee, and the Weasel will be second to die today."

Several minutes passed before the big warrior finally nodded. "We will have a truce for today. Ride to our village and eat with us."

Walking Horse hesitated, as he well knew the Pawnee for deceivers and liars. Looking at the mounted warriors, he knew if Limping Fox wanted to fight he could easily kill him and Eagle Wing. He thought of Crow Killer, he should never have brought the injured warrior home.

"My grandfather speaks the truth, Walking Horse." Weasel looked up at the warrior. "If he lies then he will have to kill me, his favorite grandson, for I have pledged my word for your safety."

Looking at Eagle Wing's calm face, the warrior nodded. "We will share your food, Limping Fox."

"This is good." The Pawnee motioned his warriors forward to help Weasel. "Today, we will lay aside our old hatreds and eat in peace, but only today, Arapaho."

The big Pawnee was a formidable looking warrior with scars covering almost every inch of his torso. This one had seen many battles. He wondered if his words of truce would hold once they were in the Pawnee village surrounded by his people.

Six hide lodges dotted the small meadow where the Pawnee had camped. Walking Horse knew this was no raiding party as women stood around the fires cooking. Children stopped their hoop games and stood watching the newcomers as they rode in. Walking Horse counted only ten full-grown warriors, but still a formidable fighting force against only two.

Sliding from their horses, Walking Horse and Eagle Wing were ushered to a circle of robes and given the place of honor. Eagle Wing glimpsed at the women before the cooking fires. Not as pretty as the Arapaho maidens, these squaws were stoutly built, suited for a harsh and hard life of work. None looked at the newcomers as all kept their eyes cast downward on the meat they were preparing.

"My grandson says I am right, you are Walking Horse, Chief of the Arapaho."

"Yes, I am Walking Horse and this young one is Eagle Wing."

"You have found a helpless enemy and helped him." Limping Fox nodded as he took his seat. "Why would you do this thing?"

"My nephew, Eagle Wing, wished it so." Walking Horse shrugged. "As I said, we do not make war on the injured or helpless ones."

"Your people and the Cheyenne have always made war on the Pawnee as we have made war on your people." Limping Fox shook his head.

"Today, we will share your food and be friends."

The big Pawnee nodded. "For today only. Tell me, Arapaho, where is Crow Killer, the enemy of the Pawnee?"

Weasel looked at Eagle Wing and shook his head. The truce was a fragile one day affair. If Limping Fox knew the son of his hated enemy was eating his food, things could turn deadly. It was best for all not to reveal his identity.

"My brother, Crow Killer, is far away to the north."

"One day we will meet at Bridger's Post." Limping Fox scowled. "He has killed many Pawnee and I have sworn I will kill him."

"He kills only when he is attacked." Walking Horse, even though outnumbered, would not back down or condemn Crow Killer.

"You say he is your brother?"

"Yes, he is my brother."

Limping Fox shook his head. "It is good we have a truce this day or I would kill you as he killed, Wet Otter, my brother."

The food was good. The Pawnee women made up in their cooking what they lacked in looks. Eagle Wing could taste the delicious spices as he consumed his second bowl.

Setting aside his empty bowl, Walking Horse stood to his feet. "We will leave now. Thank you for the meal."

"It is good to see an enemy eat as you did." Limping Fox smiled cruelly. "One day, I will meet you in battle and I want you strong."

"The Arapaho are a strong people." Swinging on his horse, Walking Horse nodded. "Do not let me catch Limping Fox or his people on Arapaho lands again."

"The truce will hold until the dark times come again, then it is finished."

"Agreed."

"Wait, Eagle Wing." A squaw had brought a beaded arrow quiver and handed it to Weasel. "This is my most cherished possession. I want you to have it for what you have done this day."

Taking the quiver, Eagle Wing marveled at the beautiful beadwork that decorated the deer hide arrow holder. "It is indeed beautiful."

"Wear it and always remember I, Weasel, thank you for saving my life."

"One day, we will meet again."

"I hope your words come true."

Chapter 8

Wooden platters of food were placed on the oak table as Wilson and Oliver walked down the path to the larger cabin. Jed and the warriors greeted the two men as they found seats at the table. Jed didn't miss Oliver's searching eyes as they looked to the cabin for Ellie.

Broken Leg caught the young white's seeking eyes also. Speaking in Arapaho, he laughed. "I think Grey Hair has competition for her hand."

"I think you are right, my friend." Cut Arm nodded.

"It's not polite to talk about your friends in Arapaho." Jed scolded the two young warriors.

"We are sorry, Crow Killer." Broken Leg smiled. "But, Arapaho is the only language we speak. Our white words are very few."

"I assume they speak of me?" Oliver glanced across the table.

"It is nothing, young one." Jed shook his head. "Eat hearty, we leave at first light."

"I will be ready."

The south pass had been crossed and the small column made its way slowly down the mountain, heading for the big river. Jed had sent Broken Leg and Cut Arm ahead to scout out the trail. Many times in the past, Jed had learned that an enemy could be hiding anywhere. These vast mountains were empty of enemy tribes, but a traveler could never let down their guard.

Oliver looked at Ellie and smiled. "I believe these warriors think I have romantic intentions toward you, Ellie."

The girl's dark eyes questioned him as her voice spoke softly. "Why would you think that, Oliver?"

"I cannot understand their words, but I feel that is what they speak of." The young white blushed. "Would you mind?"

"No, but for now let's just be good friends."

"We are already friends, Ellie. But, yes, I can wait."

"Wait for what, Oliver?" Red Horse got in on the last of the conversation.

"None of your business, little brother."

Broken Leg sat his horse in the middle of the trail, waiting as Jed and the others rode toward him. Normally, always happy, but today the young warrior was serious as he held up his hand. "We found an injured woman ahead at the river. She is hurt bad."

"Let's go." Jed kicked his bay horse forward.

Sliding from his horse as Cut Arm motioned to them, Jed hurried to where a young woman lay covered in a trade blanket. Blood covered her shoulder and soaked her filthy doeskin dress.

"She is Nez Perce." Cut Arm looked down at the girl. "She has lost much blood."

Kneeling beside the wounded girl, Jed examined the ugly wound. He could see the shaft of a broken arrow showing through her clothes. By the lump and swelling, he knew an arrowhead was imbedded deeply in the girl's shoulder. The wound was bluish and infected.

Speaking softly to the pain-racked girl, he nodded. "What has happened to you?"

Pain gripped the tight face as she spoke feebly. "The young warrior, Eagle Wing, freed us from the Arickaree and sent us back to our lands."

"Eagle Wing?"

"Yes, but two Rics still lived and ambushed us several sleeps downriver." The sweaty head nodded. "They killed my mother."

"How did you escape?"

"One arrow knocked me, from my horse, into the river." The eyes closed. "They thought I was dead. I hid in the water and watched as they took our horses and blankets, then rode away."

"Where is your mother?"

"Wolves carried her away during the night." Tears came to the dark eyes as she looked away.

"How did you get away from the wolves?"

"I remained in the water. Wolves do not like water unless they are very hungry."

"How many sleeps ago was this?" Jed cut the dress away from the nasty wound. "Ellie, build a fire and heat some water quick."

"Many sleeps. The Rics followed us, then waited for the Arapaho to get far away before they attacked us. Maybe ten sleeps, I do not know. After a few days, my mind did not think so well."

"How did you get back here?"

"I have no idea. I got turned around and lost my way." The small shoulders shivered. "When I awoke this one was beside me."

"It is good Cut Arm and Broken Leg found you." Jed washed the wound softly. "I will have to dig the arrow from your shoulder."

"What is your name, warrior?"

"I am Crow Killer of the Arapaho." Jed watched the eyes narrow. "And yours?"

"I am Flower Leaf, daughter of Squirrel Tooth, the Nez Perce."

"Squirrel Tooth?" Jed was shocked at the name. "You are far from your own country."

"The Rics captured us and brought us here." Flower Leaf turned her face away. "Let me die, Arapaho. Do not dishonor me."

"If I can, I aim to save your life, young one." Jed spoke softly. "There is no dishonor in living."

"But, my father was your enemy."

"Yes, but his daughter is not."

Bright Moon knelt beside the girl with water. "Another sleep and she would have perished."

"The arrow has been in her shoulder many days." Nodding, Jed looked at the girl. "She still may."

Holding the knife over the flames, Jed sterilized the blade, then motioned to Bright Moon. He knew the pain would be terrible as he cut into her soft skin. Flower Leaf moaned softly as the sharp knife made its first cut, causing blood and pus to gush from the wound. Slowly, her eyes rolled in her head as she passed out from the pain.

While the girl was unconscious, Jed quickly opened the wound, cutting muscle away from the imbedded arrowhead. After pulling the flint out, Jed probed for any foreign object in the shoulder. Heating the blade to a red heat, he seared the wound to stop the bleeding. Even unconscious, the girl moaned and tried to shrink away from the intense pain.

Covering the cauterized wound with a salve, Ellie had given him, Jed wrapped the wound, then stood up. "She is a brave one."

"And a beautiful one." Cut Arm nodded.

"Will she live?" Ellie Thunder saw a heavy rush of blood from the wound. "She has lost much blood."

"I don't know. Now, it's up to her. We have done all we can." Jed shook his head. "I wish Ellie was here to help."

"I think this one will live." Bright Moon wiped the Nez Perce girl's forehead. "She has much courage."

"If infection and fever does not set in."

"Can she be moved?" Broken Leg looked down at the girl.

"Not for many days." Jed looked across the broad river. "She is too weak. Moving her could kill her."

"I will stay behind with her." Cut Arm spoke up. "Crow Killer and Bright Moon must not miss their son's Lance Bearer Ceremony."

"I cannot leave you here alone, my friend." Jed shook his head.

"I will hide her in the downed trees over there." Cut Arm pointed to the small barricade where Big Elk and the Comanches had been killed. "None will dare look for us there. It is sacred grounds now."

"Cut Arm is not afraid of the spirits that walk the ground?"

"Big Elk was my uncle. He will protect us."

"I will stay with Cut Arm." Broken Leg volunteered.

"And I will stay also." Oliver held up his rifle.

"You, Oliver?" Ellie looked surprised at the young white.

"When the woman is strong enough to travel on a travois, we will ride for the village." Cut Arm motioned to Flower Leaf.

Jed nodded at Broken Leg. "So it will be. We will make camp here tonight, and then ride on in the morning."

"Should we leave them, my husband?" Bright Moon looked down at the girl as she moaned.

"We must."

Broken Leg shrugged. "You cannot miss the most important time in your son's life."

Jed studied the river, then looked at Bright Moon and Ellie. He had to look out for their safety. "We ride in the morning. I will send warriors back here in three sleeps."

With the coming of the new sun and after wiping the ground clear of fresh horse sign, Jed walked back to the river where Bright Moon and the others waited with the horses. Before departing the barricade, he looked down into the fevered eyes of Flower Leaf.

"How do you feel, girl?"

"My shoulder burns like fire." The dark eyes looked up. "Thank you, Crow Killer."

"The pain will end soon." Jed handed Cut Arm the jar of salve. "You are young and you will grow strong again."

"You are a good man, like your son Eagle Wing." Flower Leaf tried to smile. "My father was wrong about you."

"I will send warriors here for you." Jed nodded at Oliver and the others. "Stay quiet and out of sight."

With Fox Ear and Red Horse in the lead, Jed led the women to the Yellowstone. Not a Crow or any other warrior was spotted as they forded the beautiful river. Jed studied the high banks closely as their horses hit swimming water. He knew somewhere up there, hidden by the huge willows and cottonwoods, Crow warriors were watching closely as they crossed. Jed couldn't figure out Long Leaper's hatred for him. Yes, he had killed Wild Wind, but the Crow had pushed the fight on him.

Riding into the Arapaho village, the small party was quickly surrounded by villagers, yelling and jumping in joy at their appearance. Little Antelope raced up and hugged Bright Moon and Ellie.

Staring at Jed, she smiled. "You have had a safe trail?"

"We have." Jed smiled at the pretty woman. As always her appearance brought a warm smile to his face. "Where is my brother, Walking Horse?"

"My husband and Eagle Wing hunt the shaggies for the celebration."

"And Grey Hair?"

"He is with the horse herd, catching horses."

"Catching horses? Is there trouble?" Jed was curious. The horses were normally caught by the younger boys.

"Walking Horse has ordered that each warrior keep a spare horse by his lodge during the night hours." Little Antelope nodded. "Grey Hair is selecting the best horses."

"So, there is trouble?" Jed asked.

"There is always trouble." Little Antelope shrugged.

"I will ride to the herd."

Turning, Little Antelope pushed Bright Moon and Ellie toward her lodge. It had been many moons since the sisters had seen each other. Jed knew the women would have plenty to talk about and Bright Moon was excited to see her nephew and niece.

Finding Grey Hair with the young horse herders, Jed pulled the warrior off by himself. "Walking Horse is not here. We must send warriors to the big river and bring back the ones we left behind."

"What has happened, Crow Killer?"

Jed quickly told the warrior about finding the wounded Nez Perce girl, and leaving Broken Leg and the others behind to care for her. Grey Hair nodded, remembering the pretty young woman with the fire in her eye. He also remembered they had completely forgotten about the Ric warriors that had escaped into the densely thicketed river bottom. He figured the two Rics had watched from hiding as the women crossed the river, then had followed and attacked them when they thought it would be safe. They had been foolish not to hunt down the enemy warriors and kill them.

"How many do you wish me to send?"

"Six warriors will be enough."

"You are here now so I will lead them myself with Two-Eyed Dog, Hide Belt, and some others." Grey Hair turned his horse.

"I will tell Walking Horse when he returns."

Grey Hair smiled. "Two-Eyed Dog rescued the woman. He will want to go. He has looked at the young Nez Perce squaw."

"Yes, she is something alright." Jed smiled.

"I go."

Walking Horse and Eagle Wing circled the valley where they had last seen the Pawnee. The meadow was vacant. Only trampled grass left any sign that anyone had been camped there. Nodding, Walking Horse turned back west toward the village. Passing where the dead horse had broken his leg, they found his carcass picked clean by the buzzards. Only bare bones remained of the once-beautiful animal. Eagle Wing nodded, the big birds were the cleaners of the earth, keeping mother earth pure.

"Come, young one, we return to the village." Walking Horse kicked his chestnut gelding. "Your parents arrive here soon."

"We return without any meat, my uncle?"

"Tomorrow, we will hunt with Crow Killer." The big warrior smiled, remembering the many times he and Jed had been out on the hunt. "He is a great hunter."

"Was he as great a warrior as everyone says, my uncle?"

Walking Horse looked at the young one and nodded. "Crow Killer was the greatest of warriors. None could stand against him."

"And many have tried?"

"Many." The warrior remembered Bear Claw, Wild Wind, the Frenchman, the white trappers, and all the rest dead by Crow Killer's hand. "Yes, Nephew, there have been many."

"He never speaks of his battles."

"No, counting coup and killing is not something he would brag about. It is not his way." Walking Horse nodded. "That is why I am proud to call him my brother."

"I hope I can walk in his steps with honor as he has."

Walking Horse thought of the old medicine man, Spotted Panther, as he looked at the valley they were crossing. "His are big steps to fill, but I believe Eagle Wing will do it."

"Sometimes, I think my father is saddened by killing so many enemies."

Nodding, the warrior looked away. "Crow Killer has lost many friends and killed many enemies in battle, enough to sadden any man."

Reining in hard, Walking Horse looked to where five warriors had emerged from the tree line, bordering the meadow. These people were complete strangers and a tribe unknown to Walking Horse. The riders were almost naked and painted for war, moving straight at them in a slow walk. The valley grass brushed their horse's bellies as they rode to where the two Arapaho were sitting their horses.

"We were very foolish, young one." Walking Horse studied the approaching horsemen. "We talked too much. We were not alert, watching as we should have been."

Eagle Wing surveyed the different directions, then turned his attention on the five warriors. "Who are they, Uncle?"

"I do not know these people." Walking Horse studied the short cropped, black hair, banded with hide across their foreheads. "I have never seen these strange ones before."

"They are painted for battle." Eagle Wing looked at the painted faces. "They have no rifles, only bows."

"I do not know what tribe they are from."

"Do we fight, Uncle?"

"We will wait until they come closer to see what they want." Walking Horse checked the powder in his rifle. "Five to two are not bad odds for Arapaho Lance Bearers, and our rifles will reach far if they choose to fight."

"Their horses are small and they wear only breechcloths to cover their bodies."

"I have heard of a tribe of small people that live south beyond the Comanche lands." Walking Horse watched the riders with curiosity. "Watch closely, Nephew. Even our enemies say they are ferocious fighters."

"You think they come to fight with us."

Walking Horse stiffened. "This is the second time we have ridden to this place, and both times we have found enemy warriors. This cannot be. Prepare, Eagle Wing. Today, we will fight."

Raising his rifle in warning, Walking Horse turned his horse sideways and waited for the newcomers to turn away. Finally, as they approached within bow shot, he kicked his horse forward. The Arapaho's pride would not let him turn from these strangers. Finally, the five warriors reined in their horses and waited, strung out in a single row, facing the two Arapaho. All the small warriors had an arrow notched in their short powerful bow.

Walking Horse was shocked, in less than the blink of an eye, two arrows buried into the chest of his bay horse, bringing him to the ground. With a defensive reflex as the horse reared, Walking Horse fired his rifle toward the warriors. The lucky shot brought down one of the screaming riders. The horse fell sideways atop Walking Horse, pinning the warrior's leg, then kicked his final death throws and lay still. Raising his rifle as the remaining warriors charged forward, Eagle Wing knocked another backward from his racing horse. Pulling his war axe and screaming his war cry, he raced forward directly into the remaining three warriors. Walking Horse, pinned under his horse, watched helplessly as the bay horse charged into the three fighters, knocking one from his horse.

Walking Horse shook his head as he watched the fight unfold before him. The young one looked like his father, Crow Killer, as he fought with a fury, slashing and hacking his way through the warriors, making them turn their horses away. Whirling his horse, Eagle Wing plunged again between the two remaining fighters, slashing at them with the war axe Soaring Bird had given him. The smaller warriors were brave, but they were no match for the screaming demon that fought them. Finally, with a cry of defeat both warriors turned their horses and tried to run. The speed of the smaller horses was no match for the swifter bay horse Eagle Wing rode.

Twice the war axe slashed downward as the bay horse ran alongside the fleeing warriors. With two terrible blows, Eagle Wing split the heads of both of the strange warriors. Walking Horse stared in disbelief as the young one turned the bay and rode back toward him. A young warrior, maybe even more ferocious fighter than Crow Killer, rode across the bloody field toward him. The youngster was covered in blood, but only a small scratch showed on his right arm.

Dismounting, Eagle Wing raised the dead horse enough for Walking Horse to free his pinned leg. The warrior stood slowly to his feet and shook his head. He had never seen a warrior fight with so much ferociousness.

"Are you hurt, Uncle?"

"Hurt, no." Walking Horse limped around, loosening up his cramped leg. "Just embarrassed that I let them kill my horse."

"It was not your fault." Eagle Wing caught one of the dead warrior's smaller horses. "They may have been small in stature, but their bows were mighty."

"That they were." Walking Horse agreed as he retrieved one of the short bows. "I would like to take these weapons back to our village. They are powerful."

"Anything else?"

"Leave them their hair, Eagle Wing." The warrior knew what the young one asked. "They were foolish to attack us, but they died bravely."

"Take my horse, I will ride one of theirs." Eagle Wing handed Walking Horse his rein, remembering his disgust at having to ride the black mule. "The Chief of the Arapaho should not ride such a puny animal."

"The Chief of the Arapaho should not have let his horse be killed so foolishly." Walking Horse looked around at the dead bodies. "We do not even know who they were or why they attacked us."

Leading the other four horses before them, Eagle Wing and Walking Horse crossed the small stream and entered the village. Seeing the bloodied horses and warriors, the villagers became excited and called out their shrill cries. They knew their chief had been in a fight and had been victorious. Eagle Wing slipped from his horse at the creek, washing most of the dried blood from his torso. Still, the villagers could see the slash on his arm and the blood covering the captured horses. Jed stood up quickly as he heard the uproar from where he sat with Bright Moon and Little Antelope. Turning his attention to the north end of the village, he watched as Walking Horse and Eagle Wing rode through the throng of people.

"My brother and our son come. Something has happened." Jed stood concerned.

"There has been a fight." Little Antelope noticed the dried blood on Eagle Wing's arm.

Smiling, Walking Horse slid from the bloody bay horse and shook hands with Jed. "It is good to see you here, my brother."

"It is good to be back with my people once again."

Bright Moon stepped tentatively forward, not knowing exactly how to greet her son. She could plainly see the change only a few sleeps had made in the youngster. Before her stood a confident Arapaho warrior, a man that demanded respect even from his mother.

Stepping forward, Eagle Wing embraced Bright Moon and Little Antelope. "It is good to see my mother and my aunt."

"It is good to see my son."

"Father."

"Who have you fought with?" Little Antelope asked, looking at the bloody horse, then at Eagle Wing's arm.

Walking Horse nodded as he looked at Eagle Wing proudly. "Today, my young nephew saved my life and counted coup on four enemies."

"Tell us, Husband."

"Today is the second time Eagle Wing has saved me from death. This one is a mighty warrior!" Walking Horse exclaimed proudly.

"What has happened, Husband?" Little Antelope insisted on hearing the story.

"Bring food, woman, then I will tell you of the bravery and courage of Eagle Wing."

"Come, Eagle Wing, I will bandage your arm."

Eagle Wing looked around the village. "I have not seen Grey Hair."

"He has gone to bring Oliver, Broken Leg, Cut Arm, and the Nez Perce girl back to the village." Ellie Thunder seemed to pout. "She was attacked and left for dead at the big river."

"The Nez Perce girl?" Eagle Wing looked at Ellie. "You mean the one called Flower Leaf?"

"Yes, Brother, Flower Leaf." Eli frowned. "Cut Arm thinks she is very beautiful."

"Yes, I remember her. She is very beautiful." Eagle Wing smiled. "For a Nez Perce."

"Yes, she is very pretty." Red Horse chimed in innocently. "Perhaps, Grey Hair, will think this too."

Ellie Thunder glared at her little brother. Jed was curious at her actions. He thought his daughter was interested in the young white, Oliver, but what did he know. He was just a father and a young daughter was hard to figure. Any woman was hard to figure. Even Bright Moon had surprised him many times.

As Walking Horse finished his meal, he related the tale how he had been saved from the hands of the unknown enemies by his nephew. Eagle Wing shook his head as the tale was embellished more with each retelling. Jed listened closely as Walking Horse described the small warriors.

"Red Hawk has spoken of a vicious tribe from the south called the Apache." Jed continued. "He says their horses are not worth stealing."

"Apache, that's a funny name." Red Horse laughed.

"Maybe a funny name, my nephew, but these warriors were fierce fighters." Walking Horse pointed at Eagle Wing. "I was pinned under my horse and helpless, and your brother had to fight four of them."

"Pinned under your horse?" Red Horse was curious.

Walking Horse looked over at his embarrassed nephew. To kill four warriors in hand-to-hand combat was something to brag about. Few warriors, not even the great Crow Killer, Red Hawk the Crow, or Walking Horse could brag of such a feat. He looked at the strange war axe, hanging from Eagle Wing's belt. Perhaps, it did hold some magical power as the old medicine man had said.

"Yes, young one, I lay helpless under my dead horse and could not help your brother. No matter, this one did not need my help. He fought like a wildcat, killing the enemy with just his axe."

Once the tale of the battle with the Apache was finished, Jed and Walking Horse spoke of the fight at the great river with the Rics. Eagle Wing excused himself and walked toward the horse herd.

"Wait, Brother, I will go with you."

"You can come, but no more talk of the fight, Red Horse."

"Why? You are a hero to our uncle and the people." The youngster shrugged. "You should be proud."

"One does not speak about himself." Eagle Wing explained. "People will think I am a braggart."

"Then everyone will know I am a braggart." Red Horse laughed.

"Silence, young one, or I will throw you in the creek."

"The Lance Bearer Ceremony is only three days away." Red Horse nodded. "There, you will be talked about for sure."

"Perhaps, but I will not be doing the talking."

CHAPTER 9

Grey Hair sat his horse at the bank of the great river and studied the jumbled dead logs that made a solid barrier he could not see through. Finally, he nodded as Broken Leg rose above the downed trees and waved. Kicking his horse into the sluggish water, the warrior swam with his men across the wide river. Splashing out onto the sandy bank, he trotted the tired animal to the barricade.

"It is good to see Grey Hair and Two-Eyed Dog." Broken Leg smiled at the others as they rode up. "You have made good time."

"It is good to see my brother has not been scalped." Grey Hair looked at the downed trees. "Is everyone safe? Does the woman still live?"

"She lives." Cut Arm spoke from the barricade. "She is still weak, but she will recover."

"Can she travel?"

"Maybe, with a travois drag." Broken Leg shrugged. "But, it would be better to let her rest here a couple more sleeps."

Grey Hair nodded. "I would like to return to the village quickly."

"To be at the ceremony for Eagle Wing?"

"Yes." Grey Hair replied. "I will look at the woman."

Broken Leg and Two-Eyed Dog stood over Flower Leaf and looked down into her drawn face. Both warriors could tell she was still weak from her terrible wound, and moving her to the village on a drag would be slow and dangerous for the wounded girl. Once they cross the big river, there would still be several smaller creeks to cross and two more rivers. Dragging the slow bumpy travois would take at least four days and possibly even more to reach the village.

"She is very weak, Grey Hair."

"Yes, she is. We will have to wait longer before we leave this place."

"If we move her, she could die." Two-Eyed Dog spoke up. "I will not do this."

Oliver listened as the warriors talked, but he had no way of knowing what they were discussing. He picked up a few words of Arapaho from Red Horse and Ellie, mostly about food or hunting. This subject was different and he knew these warriors were talking about the girl.

"I wanted to see the young one receive his lance." Grey Hair nodded. "Something mighty had been seen in his vision that Walking Horse will not speak of."

"I know, my friend, but I must remain here with this one. I want her to live." Two-Eyed Dog looked at the girl.

"No matter, whatever it was, it is forbidden to speak of." Grey Hair shook his head. "Perhaps, one day we will know."

"We must hunt. We are out of meat and our stomachs growl from hunger." Cut Arm spoke up. "We had to remain unseen, but now with more warriors to defend the woman, we can hunt."

Grey Hair looked at Oliver. "The white will watch over the Nez Perce. The rest of us will hunt."

"We will not use rifles. An enemy could be near." Broken Leg warned.

"The enemy is always near, my friend." Two-Eyed Dog laughed.

Quickly pairing off, the warriors disappeared in the high reeds, bordering the riverbank. The woods and meadows along the banks of the big river were far from any tribe's hunting grounds. The meat-bearing animals were in abundance, bounding from the high grass along the river. Less than two hours passed before the warriors returned to the barricade with two deer, several rabbits, and prairie hens. Quickly, a fire was built and meat was sizzling over the open flames.

Cut Arm and Two-Eyed Dog caught their horses and rode out to scout the surrounding land, leading down to the river crossing. No enemy had been spotted, but with the much-needed fire throwing off smoke, every warrior knew they had to stay alert and watchful in this wild untamed land. Returning to the barricade, after a quick scout, both warriors were handed huge pieces of roasted deer and rabbit.

"The woman ate several pieces of meat." Broken Leg nodded. "She will grow strong soon."

Grey Hair looked toward the river. "We will set watchers near the river tonight."

"I will take the white man." Cut Arm spoke up.

"He knows nothing of watching for an enemy." Two-Eyed Dog shook his head.

"It is time he learns. Besides, my friend, you should stay and protect the woman." Cut Arm grinned.

Walking Horse and Jed walked through the village as the people moved about the morning cook fires. Both looked to the south, hoping to see Grey Hair and his warriors riding into the village. The much-celebrated Lance Bearer Ceremony was only two sleeps away. Both men wanted Grey Hair to be at the ceremony since they knew he and Eagle Wing had become great friends.

"They have been gone too long." Walking Horse looked around the village. "Perhaps, I should send warriors to the south."

"The Nez Perce woman was very weak." Jed nodded. "Grey Hair may have had to wait for her to regain her strength before moving her."

"This could be true. I will wait another sleep."

"Let us ride to the river and send word to Red Hawk."

"We go." Walking Horse knew time was running short and Red Hawk must know of the ceremony.

The great Yellowstone River flowed smoothly as its clear water calmly moved downstream. Jed, Eagle Wing, and Walking Horse sat their horses, looking out across the great river. Nothing moved or stirred on the far bank. For several minutes, Jed waited, looking to see if any Crow warriors would ride down to the crossing.

"They are there. They're just not showing themselves." Jed frowned.

"I can smell Long Leaper even from here." Walking Horse nodded.

Kicking his horse into the water, Jed smiled at Walking Horse. "Well, we'll just go find Long Leaper."

"Then prepare yourself for a fight, my brother."

Ten Crow warriors rode their horses from the high cliff as the three Arapaho rode out of the river. Holding up his arm, Jed circled his gelding three times. He waited as they plunged their horses in breakneck speed, down off the high bank. Jed had to admit, the Crow were some of the best horsemen among the tribes. The bank was steep and sandy with poor footing, yet the fast moving Crow warriors held onto their horse with only their legs. They were born horsemen, the best.

Walking Horse recognized Long Leaper as soon as he cleared the tree line. In the years since the Blackfoot Chief, Bear Claw, had stolen Little Antelope, the warrior had matured and was more muscular. There was no mistaking the hate-filled face of this warrior. It was the same face that had turned red when Walking Horse choked the young warrior into submission so many years earlier.

"The Crow has become a full-grown warrior." Walking Horse nodded. "Be careful with this one, my brother."

"I see now why some of the Crow follow this one."

"Perhaps to their deaths."

Long Leaper reined in his high-spirited buckskin horse and glared at the three warriors. The hate emitting from his eyes as he studied Jed and Walking Horse could not be missed.

"Why do you cross onto my land, Arapaho dogs?" The voice was deep guttural, filled with hate. "These are Crow lands."

Nodding, Jed looked calmly at the warrior. "We have come seeking Red Hawk."

"Red Hawk, bah." Long Leaper slapped his chest. "What do you want with him?"

"This does not concern Long Leaper." Jed nodded slowly. "Just tell him his brother, Crow Killer, wishes for him to come to the river."

"His brother, an Arapaho. Why should I do this thing for you?"

"Because I ask it and because Red Hawk is your chief."

Crooked Arrow kicked his horse forward and nodded at Jed. "I will take Crow Killer's word to Red Hawk."

"Thank you, warrior."

"I am Crooked Arrow, nephew of Red Hawk, and my uncle is still our chief." The young Crow scowled at Long Leaper.

The ferocious looking face of Long Leaper glared at Walking Horse. "For now, he is. Go, Crooked Arrow, do these dog's bidding."

Jed shook his head as Walking Horse moved his horse forward. "Tell Red Hawk, we will meet him here at the river with the new dawn."

Crooked Arrow nodded. "I will tell him this."

"Tell him to bring Ellie Medicine Thunder and his children." Walking Horse added.

As Crooked Arrow rode away, Jed looked at Long Leaper. "One day, warrior, your mouth will get you into trouble."

"Why not today, Crow Killer, or are you scared like your son?" Long Leaper raised his war axe.

"Not today, Crow. I have better things on my mind." Jed shook his head as Eagle Wing glared at the Crow.

"Kill this loudmouth, now!" Walking Horse was shaking with rage.

"No, my brother." Jed calmly refused. "This is a time of celebration, not killing."

"But, he insults you."

"Yes, but I will not kill any people of Red Hawk this day."

"He knows this and that is why he is so brave." Walking Horse glared at the smirking Crow.

"No, I do not believe this." Jed looked at the warrior. "I think Long Leaper would fight. He is no coward."

"No, this one is not a coward." Eagle Wing rode his horse alongside Long Leaper's buckskin horse. "One day soon, warrior, we will fight."

"You are just a papoose yet." Long Leaper looked into Eagle Wing's dark eyes. "You are not worthy of one, such as I, to kill."

"One day, Crow, soon."

Jed looked at the village as they rode in. In their absence since early morning, the village had grown immensely. He could see the lodges of the Northern Cheyenne of He Dog, the lodges of Dull Knife, the great Cheyenne Chief, and even a few lodges of Sioux. The valley was alive with riders showing off their skills in horsemanship. Children were running everywhere, covering the open grounds as they played.

Walking Horse reined in his big bay horse. "I think we will need more meat, my brother, much more."

"Peers that way to me." Jed agreed. "We will cross the river and bring in some shaggies."

"What about Long Leaper and the Crow?" Eagle Wing questioned.

"I will speak with Red Hawk with the new day."

"You know, my brother." Walking Horse shrugged. "One day, one of us will have to kill Long Leaper."

"No, my uncle, he has insulted me and I will kill this one." Eagle Wing declared.

"He is an experienced and older fighter than you, my son." Jed shook his head. "Perhaps, you should leave this one to us."

"Sometimes older is better, but sometimes it is not, my father." Eagle Wing replied.

Red Hawk with Ellie Medicine Thunder and their children waited on the bank of the Yellowstone as Jed, Walking Horse, and Eagle Wing waved at them from across the river. Crooked Arrow and several Crow warriors sat their horses, surrounding their chief and his family. Long Leaper was not seen anywhere.

Jed watched as the Crow kicked their horses into the current of the river. Smiling, he watched the little children slip from their horses, laughing as they hung onto the manes of the swimming horses. They were born horsemen, even the girls. Jed admired their complete lack of fear. Dripping water as they exited the river, Jed stepped forward to take the hand of Red Hawk. Ellie smiled as Eagle Wing slid from his horse.

"You have grown, Nephew."

Eagle Wing nodded. "It is good to see my aunt and her children."

For several minutes, the two parties, Crow and Arapaho, mingled and greeted one another as old friends. Pulling Red Hawk away from the others, Jed and Walking Horse spoke with him about their need for meat.

"Deer and elk are not enough, my brother." Jed explained their problem. "We need meat from the shaggies, much meat."

"Your village must be large."

"Very large." Walking Horse nodded.

"Long Leaper is across the river." Red Hawk looked to the far bank. "He is full of hate."

"Yes, we spoke with him yesterday."

"I will send Crooked Arrow and others, and they will bring meat."

"How do we thank you, my brother?" Jed asked.

"This one is as my own son." Red Hawk grasped Eagle Wing's arm. "We will make his celebration one to remember."

"I will ride with Crooked Arrow to bring in the shaggies." Eagle Wing spoke up.

Red Hawk held up his arm. "No, my nephew, this could cause a fight and these days are only for celebrating."

"As my uncle wishes."

Everyone in the village was in a festive mood. Little Antelope, Ellie Thunder, and Bright Moon fussed over the children of Ellie and Red Hawk, hugging and bragging on what pretty children they were. Cook fires roasted chunks of meat for the celebration, and drums beat out a rhythm, keeping time with the dancers already celebrating. The tribes celebrated many things, such as warriors returning from a successful raid, newborn children, a successful hunt, but none compared with the yearly Lance Bearer Ceremony. Never had the tribes come together in such numbers except for the peace-signing treaties the whites had the tribes attend.

A great circle, comprised of the head chiefs of the tribes, was spread with buffalo robes laid on the ground in front of Walking Horse's lodge. He Dog and Dull Knife represented the different camps of the Cheyenne people. They had all come to pay their respect to Eagle Wing, the son of Crow Killer. Many were surprised when Red Hawk, a Crow and hereditary enemy, took an honorable place among them. Few outside of He Dog and Walking Horse knew of the friendship that existed between the two men. No hard looks or insults were spoken as Red Hawk was treated with respect.

The long pipes of the nations were brought out and lit, paying homage to the spirit people and wishing for good fortune for the people. Jed listened intently as the chiefs spoke of the encroachment of the whites into their hunting grounds. Dull Knife, a great warrior, talked calmly saying a war with the whites would be dangerous for all. Other lesser chiefs talked in anger, calling for war. They wanted the yellow iron hunters and the pony soldiers protecting them to be run out of their country or killed.

From the north edge of the village a sudden hush quieted the normal activities of the boisterous children as they played. Jed stood and turned his attention with the others as several mounted warriors entered the village. Decked out in their eagle war bonnets, the newcomers sat their high-stepping horses proudly, arrogantly.

He Dog stepped beside Jed and uttered one word. "Gall."

Jed had heard of this great Sioux warrior, the right fighting arm of Sitting Bull, the medicine man, and leader of the Hunkpapa Sioux. He wondered what a Sioux and great war chief as Gall was doing there. Gall was indeed a great chief and a magnificent built warrior. A heavily-muscled, middle-aged man slid gracefully from his horse and stood proudly before the gathered chiefs. The dark flashing eyes and broad face took in the gathered leaders of the Arapaho and Cheyenne people.

"The Arapaho welcomes Gall and his warriors." Walking Horse greeted the Sioux. "We are honored with your presence, brothers."

"It is our honor to be here." The voice was deep, commanding attention. "We have heard of this celebration and wanted to come."

"You are welcome, join us." Walking Horse offered the chief an honored place beside him. "With the new sun, our Lance Bearer Ceremony will begin."

Gall looked around at the gathered chiefs and nodded. "It is good to see He Dog and Dull Knife again. Some of you, I do not know."

Introductions were quickly made to the gathered ones who did not know Gall. All knew the name, but many had never met the Sioux Chief. To be in the company of a leader as Gall, made each warrior proud.

"Gall has traveled many days to come here." He Dog looked across the circle to where the Sioux had seated himself between Jed and Walking Horse. "He and his men are just in time."

"We heard of this huge gathering of the Cheyenne and Arapaho." The chief nodded. "Sitting Bull asked me to come here and speak with you, and I also wish to see this young warrior who is to be made an Arapaho Lance Bearer. We have heard of him on the winds."

"You make us proud." Jed spoke softly. He wondered how Gall could have heard of Eagle Wing so far from Sioux lands.

"And we have heard of Crow Killer." Gall smiled. "In our country, the great bear killer is a legend."

"Speak, Gall, great Chief of the Sioux." Walking Horse motioned at the chief. "Our ears will hear your words."

Gall looked to where Red Hawk sat beside Jed. "Are we among friends here? Will my words be heard?"

"This is Chief Red Hawk. He is Crow, but he is my brother." Jed looked straight into Gall's eyes. "He is to be trusted."

Gall smiled. "We have heard of Red Hawk. We have to protect our horse herds from him."

Red Hawk nodded at the Sioux warrior. "And I have heard of the great Gall, War Chief of the Hunkpapa."

Gall stood up and looked around the circle of warriors. "I thank you for this honor, my brothers. Our great leader, Sitting Bull, sends these words for your ears." The strong voice of a born leader was heard as Gall spoke of the decimation of the buffalo herds. "If the depredations and killings are not stopped, the great herds will be gone and the horseback people will starve. Already, the southern herds are almost nonexistent. Killing only for hides and tongues of the animals is senseless waste. We must band together to remove the whites from our hunting grounds."

"Does Sitting Bull wish our warriors to ride with his people against the whites?" Dull Knife spoke up.

Jed listened as Gall spoke the inflammatory words of war against the intruding whites, and the war chief spoke the truth about the buffalo. Also, Sitting Bull and Crazy Horse, another great leader of the Sioux, wished to protect their lands and people from the incursions of the whites. They would fight, but Jed knew it would be futile. The whites were too powerful. In the east, they had just fought a war with armies that outnumbered the warriors of the tribes by thousands. Jed knew in the end to fight, the white soldiers would bring death and destruction to his red brethren. He also knew this was what Spotted Panther had spoken about when he foretold of Eagle Wing becoming a great warrior.

Many times during the long nights in his cabin, he had thought of a way to stop the fighting and bloodshed he knew was coming, but there was no way. Crazy Horse was proud, Gall was proud, Sitting Bull was proud, and they would fight. They would have to be defeated, beaten into submission before they would succumb to the white's demands to move their people onto a reservation. All were revered leaders with followers that would follow them to their death. As he listened to the chief speak, he knew the people were heading to their destruction. In his youth, back east many years ago, he had seen the power and fighting strength of the whites. Now, with so many years passing, he knew they would have become even stronger. Still, he understood, this was their land and they were proud and free. To let the whites come in unopposed would shame the great leaders. It would also be the end of a way of life for the horse culture of the people.

After Gall finished speaking and took his seat, Walking Horse stood to his feet. "In two sleeps, we will have the Lance Bearer Ceremony, then we will speak more of this."

Grey Hair looked down at the travois as Flower Leaf was laid upon it. Covered in blankets, the drag was the only way the injured woman could safely return to the village. It was still too soon to move the girl, but they had no choice. They had already stayed too long, hidden behind the barricade. Any day an enemy raiding party could discover them and they were too few to defend themselves. Crossing the great river, Two-Eyed Dog had held the weak girl safely in his strong arms, keeping her high out of the water.

"She is a strong woman. She is in pain, but says nothing." Grey Hair nodded at the warrior as the travois dragged across the rough ground.

"Yes, she will be my woman when she is well." Two-Eyed Dog looked back at the girl.

"She is Nez Perce, my friend."

"No matter, Grey Hair, she will be mine." The warrior shook his head. "I know I am not pretty to look at, but she will be mine."

"Have you spoken to her about this?" Grey Hair asked.

"When she is well, I will speak with her."

Grey Hair knew Two-Eyed Dog spoke the truth; he was not pretty. His two different colored eyes set him apart from other warriors, but the warrior had other qualities far better than looks. He was a great hunter and fighter with an erect, heavily-muscled body. He had a caring heart for his family and he was loyal to a fault. As an enemy captive, the girl had no choice if Two-Eyed Dog wanted her for a wife. However, this one was different and would not force himself on the Nez Perce girl.

For two days, the small party steadily made their way south to the Yellowstone and Arapaho Country. At first, Two-Eyed Dog was worried, but Flower Leaf became stronger as the days passed. Making camp as the sun went down on the second day, she sat up by herself and spoke a few words to Two-Eyed Dog. With the coming of the new sun, Grey Hair decided there was no longer any need to drag the cumbersome travois. The young woman was now strong enough to ride with one of the warriors.

Grey Hair helped the small woman onto a horse in front of Two-Eyed Dog. Ahead, lay the Yellowstone and home. The warriors were excited and hoped the lance ceremony had not been held yet. They all wanted the attentions of their favorite young women they knew would be forthcoming at the dancing.

The Yellowstone was only a short distance ahead as Grey Hair raised his hand and halted his small cavalcade of riders. Nodding and pointing his jaw at Hide Belt, he held the party back as the young warrior loped ahead to check the crossing for any danger. For several minutes, the horses fidgeted under the warm sky, swishing their tails, freeing themselves from the pesky red head flies that bit them relentlessly.

Returning, Hide Belt frowned at Grey Hair. "The Crow, Long Leaper, waits at the crossing. He says we are to find another place to ford the river."

"There is no other place closer than five miles downriver." Two-Eyed Dog growled. He knew Flower Leaf was very tired and weak.

"The Crow knows this." Hide Belt shrugged. "He wants to fight."

"How many warriors does he have with him?"

"I counted ten Crow."

Grey Hair looked at Two-Eyed Dog. "We go to the crossing. The white will wait here with the woman."

Oliver knew something was amiss as the warriors seemed agitated. Moving closer to Grey Hair, he shrugged. Using hand signals, the Arapaho leader finally made Oliver understand he was to wait with the woman while they rode ahead.

"Enemy." Grey Hair pulled his index finger across his throat, then pointed to Oliver, the girl, and then the ground.

Nodding, he understood and took the rifle Two-Eyed Dog handed him. The signs, to shoot any enemy, were plain as the warrior pointed at the girl. Oliver knew Two-Eyed Dog was placing the girl's safety in his hands. The warrior placed Flower Leaf under a large oak tree in the shade and rode away. Oliver checked the priming on both rifles he held.

Oliver watched as Grey Hair, Two-Eyed Dog, Broken Leg, Hide Belt, Wolf's Head, Small Bow, and Cut Arm disappeared as they headed toward the crossing on the Yellowstone. Looking down at the girl, he noticed she was watching Two-Eyed Dog with concern.

Grey Hair reined in as Long Leaper, followed by his warriors, rode out and blocked their way to the river crossing. Most of the Crow riders were young, but with the rifles they carried, they were still deadly. Behind him sat five Lance Bearers and one young warrior of the Arapaho.

Grey Hair smiled. "Ten Crow against seven Arapaho. Those are good odds, my friends."

"Too good, Grey Hair, but I could fight these dogs with Broken Leg alone." Two-Eyed Dog kicked his horse forward.

"Two-Eyed Dog would not deprive the rest of us a chance to count coup and keep all the glory to himself, would he?" Hide Belt raised his war axe and laughed.

"We all go." Grey Hair nodded. "Do not pick a fight with these warriors unless they start it."

"The warrior, Long Leaper, is crazy with hate." Broken Leg warned. "He will try to stop us from using the crossing."

"Then he will die." Two-Eyed Dog growled. "Flower Leaf is weak and needs to go straight to the village, not downriver five miles."

"If they refuse to let us pass, only then, will we fight." Grey Hair watched the riders, blocking their path.

Long Leaper sat his horse, watching as the Arapaho warriors approached across the small clearing. Crooked Arrow frowned as he looked at the dark face of the leader of these warriors. Kicking his horse, he reined in front of Long Leaper.

"If you fight these warriors, Red Hawk will be dishonored."

"I lead this war trail, not Red Hawk."

"War trail, bah!" Crooked Arrow shook his head. "We are only here to protect the crossing from enemy raiders that come to steal our horses and women."

"Is Crooked Arrow afraid of a few Arapaho?" Long Leaper looked at his warriors. "Is he a coward?"

"No man can call Crooked Arrow a coward." The warrior flung his arm at the muscular Long Leaper.

"Then fight them, Crooked Arrow, prove your courage."

"I will fight Long Leaper and prove my courage, but I will not betray Red Hawk, my chief." The young warrior slid from his horse.

Long Leaper looked to where Grey Hair's warriors had reined their horses in and were watching. "So be it. First, I will kill Crooked Arrow, then the Arapaho."

Grey Hair watched in curiosity as the two Crow warriors faced off in front of them. He did not understand what they were doing until both men pulled their war axes and skinning knives.

"Long Leaper fights with the nephew of Red Hawk." Hide Belt shook his head. "I have seen him before."

"Is Broken Leg sure?"

"I am sure." Broken Leg confirmed. "This one is still very young and no match for Long Leaper."

"If he kills Red Hawk's nephew, he is a dead man." Two-Eyed Dog grinned. "That would be a good thing."

"I think the young warrior tries to stop the rest from attacking us." Grey Hair kicked his horse forward. "We must not let him die for us."

Both Crooked Arrow and Long Leaper stepped back from each other as the Arapaho warriors rode within thirty feet of where they stood. Not one of the warriors moved as they faced one another over a short distance.

"If Long Leaper wants to fight so badly, let him fight me." Grey Hair slid from his horse. "Or let us pass in peace."

"I have been insulted, Arapaho, this is my fight." Crooked Arrow argued.

"Not today, young one. We were insulted first." Grey Hair declared.

Long Leaper kicked at the ground, then mounted his horse and looked down at Crooked Arrow. "Another day, coward."

Watching Long Leaper and his followers ride away, Crooked Arrow looked at Grey Hair. "You have probably saved my life this day, but I am shamed before you and my people."

"You carry no shame, young one." Grey Hair smiled. "You were willing to face Long Leaper even if you lost your life. Your uncle will hear of your bravery."

"Perhaps you are right, but eventually, I will have to fight him."

"There is always time for fighting." Grey Hair sent Two-Eyed Dog back for Oliver and the girl. "Today, you will ride with us to our village."

"You think to protect me, warrior?" Crooked Arrow frowned. "I need no protection from an Arapaho."

Grey Hair shook his head. "Red Hawk will be at our village, and you can tell him what has happened."

"I will not ask my uncle for help."

Two-Eyed Dog rode up with Flower Leaf and Oliver as Grey Hair swung on his horse. "Come with us, Crooked Arrow, we may need your help to get safely across the river crossing."

Nodding, the young Crow agreed. "Then, I will ride with you."

Long Leaper and his warriors watched, from the heights, as Grey Hair and his warriors swam across the Yellowstone. Pure hatred showed in the eyes of the Crow.

Little Elk smiled as he watched the swimming horses. "We are lucky Crooked Arrow stopped the fight with them."

"Do you think I was afraid?"

"You should be afraid, my friend." Bull Calf chimed in. "To fight against the Lance Bearers is a dangerous thing. Many of us could have died this day."

Long Leaper glared at the disappearing backs. "They would have died too."

Little Elk laughed. "Call me a coward too, my friend, but it is good to be alive on such a fine day."

Glaring and trembling in rage, Long Leaper kicked his horse into a hard run to the south.

"One day, he will get us all killed."

"Little Elk is right. He did not miss it by far today." Bull Calf chimed in.

CHAPTER 10

Grey Hair was relieved as he rode into the huge village. Preparations for the Lance Bearer Ceremony were still going on. Squaws hustled about everywhere in the village, putting the final touches on the meat and vegetables they had gathered.

Reining in where Red Hawk, Walking Horse, and Crow Killer sat under a large shade tree, Grey Hair slid from his horse. "We have brought the hurt one."

"It is good you have returned." Walking Horse nodded. "We have waited for you to start the ceremony."

Little Antelope listened from where she had been working over a cook fire. "Bring her into the lodge."

Walking Horse watched as Two-Eyed Dog carried Flower Leaf into his lodge. Turning to where the warriors sat their horses, he nodded. "Grey Hair and his warriors have done well."

Red Hawk looked curiously to where Crooked Arrow sat his horse. Walking over to the young warrior, he looked up into the downcast eyes.

"Tell your uncle." Hide Belt spoke.

"Speak, Nephew." Red Hawk's voice became firm. "What has happened? Why are you here with these warriors?"

Sliding from his horse, the young warrior finally spoke about the trouble across the river. Finishing, he looked into Red Hawk's eyes. "You must permit me to fight Long Leaper." The eyes pleaded. "Until then, I will be shamed by the people."

"If what you speak is true, there is no shame in your actions."

"There is shame for me here." Crooked Arrow clenched his fist and pounded his chest. "After the ceremony for your friends, I must challenge Long Leaper if I am to live with the Crow people."

Listening, Jed knew the young warrior spoke the truth. Even knowing a fight with the older and stronger warrior would result in his death, Crooked Arrow would have to fight. There was no other way if he was to retain his honor and respect of his people. He had been called a coward and no warrior could allow the word to stand. The challenge had been presented, and now, there was no way out but death if he failed. For a brave man, death was better than living in shame.

Jed watched as the dejected Crooked Arrow walked away with Hide Belt and Broken Leg. Sitting back down against his backrest, he looked at Grey Hair. "Long Leaper was waiting for you at the crossing?"

"Yes, Crow Killer." Grey Hair nodded. "Crooked Arrow is brave. He stopped many deaths this day."

"It is time for me to kill Long Leaper." Red Hawk nodded.

"My brother cannot do this thing." Walking Horse warned. "That would disgrace the young one even more. You cannot fight his fights."

"Crooked Arrow is still too young to fight such an experienced warrior as Long Leaper."

Walking Horse agreed. "Yes, he is young, but still, he is a man and he must fight his own battles."

"I will decide this after the ceremony." Red Hawk looked at Jed. "We must watch over Crooked Arrow tonight so he will not try to slip across the river."

"I will have Hide Belt and Broken Leg watch over him." Grey Hair nodded and stood up.

"The squaw of the Nez Perce looks stronger." Jed looked at the lodge.

"She is much stronger." Grey Hair assured. "Two-Eyed Dog watches over her like a mother."

"What does she think of Two-Eyed Dog?" Walking Horse questioned the warrior.

"She has said nothing, but I do not think his face matters to her." Grey Hair smiled. "I would not like to come between her and my friend."

"Nor would I." Cut Arm laughed. "I think there would be a fight."

Grey Hair looked around the village. "Where is Eagle Wing?"

"Soaring Bird has summoned him to his lodge before the ceremony." Jed replied.

"I will go meet him and let him know we have returned."

Grey Hair walked past several lodges when he spotted Eagle Wing walking along the creek that bordered the village. The ever-present war axe was stuck through his leather belt. Hitting a fast trot, he caught up to the preoccupied warrior.

"You are in deep thought, my friend."

Eagle Wing nodded in surprise. "Grey Hair, you have returned."

"We have brought the Nez Perce woman back."

"Then she lives?"

"Yes, she is stronger." Grey Hair answered.

"I have just spoken with Soaring Bird."

"I know, Crow Killer said you were with the old one, and I know, I am not to ask what he wanted." Grey Hair smiled.

"I'm glad you have returned before the ceremony."

"Tonight, Walking Horse and Crow Killer said we will become true brothers." The warrior nodded. "Is that your wish too, my friend?"

"It is my wish, Grey Hair." Eagle Wing strolled slowly along the creek bank. "Have you seen Ellie Thunder yet?"

"No, I have been in talks with your father and uncles."

"There must have been trouble?" Eagle Wing asked. "Something keeps you from seeing my sister."

"Yes." Grey Hair quickly told of the trouble with Long Leaper and Crooked Arrow. "I fear Red Hawk will kill Long Leaper and shame the young one forever."

"Long Leaper is still at the crossing?"

"He and his warriors wait at the crossing to cause trouble with anyone that tries to cross."

"There is a way out of this for Crooked Arrow."

"Tell me what way, Eagle Wing? One day, he will make a good man. He does not deserve to die or have to live in shame."

"The ceremonies will be finished tonight." Eagle Wing continued. "After that, I will be a Lance Bearer of the Arapaho. Then, only I am responsible for my actions."

Grey Hair smiled. "And if you kill Long Leaper before Crooked Arrow returns, he cannot be blamed."

"I have not met this Crooked Arrow. He will know nothing of this."

"That is good. He is still young, but he is a proud man for a Crow." Grey Hair nodded.

"Then, after the ceremony, we will ride to the crossing."

"And be there with the coming of the new sun." Grey Hair grinned. "That is a good plan."

"Stay silent, my friend."

"Eagle Wing does not want to take any warriors with us?"

"No, no one must know of this. We accidentally rode into Long Leaper and had to kill him."

Grey Hair looked across the village. He knew what Eagle Wing proposed was dangerous. Long Leaper was no mere warrior. He was big, strong, and full of hate. If the followers of the Crow warrior joined in the fight, they both could be killed.

"This is good. Now, I go to play my flute for your sister, if I can get her away from Oliver."

"Good luck with both." Eagle Wing smiled. This day, Grey Hair will become his blood brother as well as his great friend. He would be a welcomed husband for Ellie Thunder.

"What does my brother and Grey Hair speak so quietly about?" Red Horse stepped from behind a tree. "You're up to something."

"We speak about the ceremony tonight." Eagle Wing frowned. "Why are you sneaking around this place like a coyote after a rabbit?"

"Eagle Wing lies. I'm not stupid." Red Horse pretended to pout. "Tell me, I will say nothing."

"No, you won't, because I'm not telling you anything."

"That's why I sneak around. It's the only way I can find out anything." Red Horse pouted before breaking out his smile. "I'm no longer a child, my brother."

Early dark had come and the village was in a festive mood. People pushed in and surrounded the huge bonfire that roared in the middle of the village. The people were dressed in their finery, from the beautiful hand-worked dresses of the women to the long eagle-feathered head-dresses of the chiefs. Aromatic smoke from the clay bowled pipes drifted into the night air as the warriors smoked and waited patiently for Walking Horse, Chief of the Arapaho and Lance Bearers. It was his duty as village chief to start the ceremony by summoning to the fire, the young warriors who would become Lance Bearers.

Tonight, before all the people, the new Lance Bearers would be presented their traditional lances. Each lance was carved with the ceremonial figure of his vision. For the remainder of their lives, each Lance Bearer would carry their lance as a badge of honor.

The younger maidens were dressed in all their finery in preparation for the dancing to come. Each would set her eyes on the young man they wished to dance with, hoping one day the young man would bring horses to her father for her bride price.

Finally, as darkness fell over the village, the time had come and Walking Horse stood before the great fire in all his finery. An imposing figure, the Arapaho Chief stood well over six feet in height with a sculpted body and a handsome face. Raising his hands for silence, the tall warrior summoned the three young men forward who were to be inducted into the Lance Bearer Society.

Eagle Wing was dressed in beautiful handmade soft doeskin decorated with porcupine and pine needles, and beads. The tallest and most muscular of the three participants of the ceremony, every eye was glued on him. The young son of Crow Killer was indeed an imposing and handsome figure as he stood proudly before Walking Horse.

Wolf's Head was presented his short lance first. The figure of a bear decorated the end of his lance. Black Crow was next, and his lance was decorated with the head of a wolverine, the most ferocious of the wild ones. The village became even quieter as Eagle Wing stepped before Walking Horse.

The lance presented to him was decorated with the head of a bull buffalo, the strongest and bravest of animals. The lance was beautiful, and tears seemed to run from the eyes on the carving. All eyes focused on the lance and all were curious about the carving. They wondered what the tears represented as they guessed and had their own thoughts, but none would ever know.

As the three new Lance Bearers raised their lances in triumph, the tribal drums began to beat out their rhythmic throbbing. The ceremony was finished. Now, the dancing, eating, and celebrating would continue throughout the night until utter exhaustion sent the villagers to their lodges. Suddenly, the watchers separated as the old medicine man, Soaring Bird, limped slowly toward the fire. The noise was subdued. Few had ever seen the feeble one this far from his lodge. For him to be present meant something out of the ordinary would take place.

Summoning Eagle Wing and Grey Hair before him, the old one unwrapped an ancient hunting knife. Looking into the two warriors' eyes, he had them hold out their arms. A quiet prayer was spoken to the spirit people above, then the knife made two quick cuts and the arms were placed together.

"From this day forth, my sons, you share the same blood. Only death can ever separate you." With these few words, Soaring Bird released their arms and walked slowly away.

"You did not tell me Soaring Bird himself would perform this ceremony." Grey Hair looked down at the cuts on their arms.

Eagle Wing smiled. "You did not ask, my brother."

Dull Knife, He Dog, Gall, and Red Hawk complimented the new Lance Bearers and blood brothers honoring them. He Dog and Dull Knife were Cheyenne Dog Soldiers equivalent to the Lance Bearers of the Arapaho. Eagle Wing looked to where Jed and Bright Moon waited for their son to finish being honored by the chiefs. No honor could be more rewarding than to be welcomed by his father and mother. Crow Killer was the most celebrated of all Lance Bearers and Bright Moon had stood by his side in many battles.

Jed looked proudly at his son and clasped his shoulders. "I am proud of my son."

"Thank you, Father."

"What will you do now?"

"My uncle, He Dog, has asked that I accompany him when he takes the white man back to Bridger."

"Will you do this thing?"

"It is He Dog's wish." Eagle Wing nodded. "If Oliver wishes to return east, I will ride with my uncle."

Jed nodded slowly. "Then we will take the east trail back to our valley. We will accompany you and Oliver to Bridger."

Bright Moon smiled happily. "I need flour and sugar, and I will see my old friend Alex again."

"This will be a happy trail." Eagle Wing knew his parents wanted to be close to him for a few more days.

Red Horse touched the buffalo head lance in his brother's hand. "Why does the buffalo cry, my brother?"

Eagle Wing held up the lance and smiled. "Because, young one, he is sad."

"Are you sad, Eagle Wing?" Ellie Thunder asked as her and Little Antelope moved closer.

"No, my sister, how could anyone be sad at a time like this?" Eagle Wing smiled. "I am now a Lance Bearer of the people and I have a new brother."

"And maybe a new brother-in-law." Red Horse kidded.

Glaring at her younger brother, Ellie blushed and looked over at Grey Hair. "Your mouth runs too much, little brother."

"I don't think so." Grey Hair smiled. "I like his words."

"Both of you talk too much." Ellie looked to where Oliver stood listening, but did not understand their words.

A beautiful dressed young woman touched Eagle Wing's arm and he moved away with her toward the dancers.

"Your son has become a man, Sister, quite a man." Little Antelope smiled.

"Yes, he has, so soon though." Bright Moon nodded sadly, but proudly.

Red Horse watched as Grey Hair and his brother slipped silently through the village toward the horse herd. Following at a distance, he stayed out of sight as they caught their horses. Quickly racing to catch his own horse, Red Horse followed them west, away from the village. He had no idea where they were heading, but he knew it was why they had been so secretive earlier in the day.

The celebration and dancing lasted most of the night. The hour was late, but the trail was lit up by the brightness of the full moon. Red

Horse followed the two riders easily as they rode slowly to the Yellowstone, unaware of his presence.

"We will reach the crossing with the first light." Grey Hair spoke as the whippoorwills told of their nearness to the great river. "It is not much further now."

"This is good."

"Did you see Oliver dancing with your sister?" Jealousy could be heard in Grey Hair's voice.

"I think they danced well together." Eagle Wing smiled.

"It is a good thing you take him to Bridger's Post soon."

"You will not come with us, my friend?"

"Perhaps, if Walking Horse permits it."

"To leave Ellie Thunder alone so long with Oliver could be dangerous."

"Surely, she would not take a white as a husband, would she?" Grey Hair asked worriedly.

"I guess not. Oliver doesn't have a flute."

"This is not a funny thing to speak of."

Reining in as the shimmer of the river showed, both warriors sat quietly, listening to the night sounds and the movement of the river. The crossing was peaceful as the current moved slowly downstream, making small ripples across the water. The river crossing where they sat was deserted, showing no new tracks or evidence that anyone had crossed in the night.

"Perhaps, Long Leaper is not here." Grey Hair shrugged.

"Then, I will ride on to the Crow village." Eagle Wing's face hardened. "This must be finished before Crooked Arrow comes. Today, one of us will no longer walk this land."

"Because of the insult he spoke to you, or because of his threat to Crooked Arrow?"

"Crooked Arrow is the nephew of Red Hawk, and he has helped you. The young one will not be killed by Long Leaper." Eagle Wing declared.

Whirling their horses as a horse nickered lightly behind them, both warriors raced back up the trail to find Red Horse. Only a guilty smile came from the young one's face as they approached him.

"What are you doing here?" Eagle Wing frowned. "You are far from the village."

"My horse needed exercise."

"Go back, Red Horse, this is a dangerous place for you."

"I am not afraid of danger, Grey Hair. Maybe, I can help." Red Horse suggested.

"Crow Killer will help your backsides when he finds out."

"Where are we going?"

"He cannot be trusted to go back." Eagle Wing shook his head in disgust.

"What will we do?"

"We cannot return him to the village, Crooked Arrow will come soon." Eagle Wing frowned at his brother. "He'll have to ride with us."

Returning to the river crossing, Eagle Wing circled his Appaloosa several times and studied the far bank. Several minutes elapsed before five riders appeared on the high bank, then rode their horses to the river's edge. Long Leaper was not among the young warriors.

Raising his bow, Eagle Wing pointed at the riders. "I have come to take up Long Leaper's challenge."

Bull Calf raised his own bow. "Long Leaper is not here. He has returned to the village."

"Remain here, Red Horse." Kicking his horse, Eagle Wing started across the Yellowstone with Grey Hair beside him.

Keeping his eyes focused on the Crow warriors as he rode up out of the water, he did not notice his younger brother following close behind him. Bull Calf and the others waited quietly as the Arapaho reined in their horses.

"Why does the son of Crow Killer seek Long Leaper?"

"Ride to your village and tell the dog of a Crow that Eagle Wing, the Arapaho Lance Bearer, challenges him to fight." Grey Hair spoke to the Crow.

"Go, Little Elk, tell Long Leaper he has his wish." Bull Calf waved his arm. "Hurry."

"I will wait above on the flats." Eagle Wing nodded as the warrior turned his horse. "Tell him if he is not a coward to come to this place."

A half grin came to Bull Calf's face as Little Elk thundered away. "Eagle Wing will share our fire and meat while we wait for our glorious leader."

"You do not like Long Leaper?" Grey Hair looked at the warrior.

"No, he is trouble. He causes much dishonor for Red Hawk."

"Why do the mighty Lance Bearers of the Arapaho bring a child along today?" Another warrior looked over at Red Horse. "Do you need his help?"

"After Eagle Wing is finished with Long Leaper, then you and I will fight, Crow." Red Horse glared at the warrior. "I am no child."

"I told you to wait across the river."

"My horse was lonely over there." The contagious smile crossed the young one's face.

The Crow warriors all laughed. "This one has courage for one so young."

"Yes, he has courage, but no brains." Eagle Wing shook his head.

"We will not fight this day, young one." The Crow warrior laughed. "I like you."

Sitting around the fire, Eagle Wing refused the meat he was offered. Crow Killer had always told him never to eat before a fight. A full stomach dulled your reflexes and slowed your movements. Also a deep wound on a full stomach was bad.

Two hours had passed when Bull Calf spotted a rider crossing the flat plains in a hard run. "It is Little Elk returning."

Reining in his blowing horse, the Crow swung from the animal. "Long Leaper comes."

"Good."

"He says he will meet you there, over the low hill." Little Elk pointed behind him.

Eagle Wing looked out across the waving prairie grass at a small rise that obscured the land beyond it. From where they stood, he could see only a few sparse trees dotting the prairie. Nodding, he removed his war shirt and tossed it to Red Horse. "Stay here, Brother."

"No."

The warrior, One Bull, nodded at Red Horse. "Let your brother watch Eagle Wing. I, One Bull, give you my word the young one will be returned safely to your village after the fight."

"No matter who wins?" Grey Hair spoke up.

"No matter." One Bull nodded. "We do not fight children."

"I told you, warrior, I am not a child." Red Horse's face turned red.

"Crow Killer will have your pants for this, little brother."

Red Horse shrugged. "I will not let you go alone."

"No, young one, you are not a child." One Bull smiled and nodded at Red Horse.

Jed walked from his lodge and looked around for Eagle Wing and Red Horse. Finding neither one near the lodge, he walked toward the horse herd. Red Hawk fell in beside him as he made his way through the village.

"Where does my brother go in such a hurry?"

Jed greeted Red Hawk, then motioned at one of the young horse guards. "I look for my sons."

"They took their horses and left the village many hours ago, Crow Killer."

"Left, who left the village?"

"Eagle Wing and Grey Hair first, then the young one, Red Horse, followed them."

"Which way did they ride?"

The young horse guard pointed his thin arm. "That way, toward the river."

Jed looked at Red Hawk. "Why would they ride to the river?"

"This is bad." Red Hawk frowned. "I fear Eagle Wing goes to challenge Long Leaper."

"Why would he do that?"

"My people tell me Long Leaper insulted, then challenged your son to fight a few days ago before he was a Lance Bearer." Red Hawk continued. "Now, I fear he goes to take up that challenge, and maybe, because of Crooked Arrow."

"Crooked Arrow?"

"He helped Grey Hair get the woman across the Yellowstone and Long Leaper has insulted and threatened to kill my nephew."

Jed spoke to the startled horse guard. "Bring our horses to the lodge of your chief, quick."

Eagle Wing was shocked when he looked out across the flat grassland as his horse cleared the high knoll. Over one hundred Crow warriors sat their horses in a semicircle about the flats. Crow warriors of all ages, some wearing their eagle feather war bonnets sat quietly, watching as Little Elk followed by the Arapaho rode toward them.

"We are a little outnumbered, my brother." Grey Hair checked his rifle priming.

"Do not worry, Arapaho. They are not here to fight for Long Leaper." Little Elk turned to the warriors. "They have come to see the great Crow Killer's son fight."

"I give you my promise." Bull Calf nodded. "No one will interfere."

"Thank you, Bull Calf." Eagle Wing nodded.

Bull Calf took in the powerful Appaloosa and the muscular frame of Eagle Wing. "Kill him quick, Arapaho. Make him look like the fool that he is."

CHAPTER 11

As Eagle Wing and the others rode forward, the Crow warriors closed the circle, completely encircling the two combatants and one older warrior. No words were spoken as Eagle Wing and Long Leaper sat their horses, fifty feet apart, staring at each other. Eagle Wing, seeing Long Leaper armed only with his war axe and skinning knife, handed Red Horse his rifle and bow. Sliding from his horse, he pushed the buffalo headed lance deep into the soft fertile ground.

"When this is over, papoose, I, Long Leaper will have your lance and be a Lance Bearer myself." The Crow laughed as he sat his buckskin horse.

"Perhaps, but I am no longer a child, Long Leaper." Eagle Wing nodded down at the lance.

"The lance will soon be mine along with your hair."

"Come and take it, Crow, if you can." Eagle Wing swung back on the Appaloosa and pulled his axe.

The older warrior sitting between the two combatants held up a hand and looked at each warrior. Nodding sternly, he dropped his arm and retreated, rejoining the other watchers. Both horses surged forward at the drop of the hand. Before the watchers could blink, the two fighters clashed together, with their horses pushing hard against each other.

The ringing war axes were heard across the grasslands as the dangerous warheads collided together. Both warriors were strong and fast as they parried and thrust at each other. The Appaloosa horse Eagle Wing rode was a powerful, well-trained animal, but so was the buckskin Long Leaper was mounted on. Neither warrior had the advantage in horseflesh. Locked together in mortal combat, the two men fought with all their strength, and both knew the slightest mistake would be their last.

Bull Calf had been wrong as Long Leaper fought bravely, not giving an inch as the Appaloosa pushed against him. Blood streamed down the arms of both fighters as the horses reared and plunged mightily. Grey Hair had to restrain Red Horse from going to the aid of his brother as the fight swayed back and forth. Eagle Wing was knocked sideways on the great Appaloosa several times when struck by the powerful blows of Long Leaper's heavy war axe.

Each warrior tried to unseat the other, pushing and shoving as the horses repeatedly charged into each other. Only the great heart and strength of the Appaloosa kept Eagle Wing safe as he reared and pushed against the buckskin horse of Long Leaper. To hit a horse intentionally was considered cowardly so both warriors hacked only at their opponent.

Feeling the accidental bite of Long Leaper's axe, the great spotted horse reared as the blade bit into his shoulder. Lashing out with both front feet, he reared from the pain. As the Appaloosa came down across the back of the buckskin, he pawed Long Leaper from his horse's back. Lunging from his horse, Eagle Wing chased after the unseated warrior. Swinging his axe powerfully, as Long Leaper tried to rise and shield himself from the vicious attack, Eagle Wing's axe clashed hard against the other axe. Swinging the war axe with all his power, Eagle Wing snapped Long Leaper's axe off at its head. Lunging forward as Long Leaper switched his skinning knife to his right hand, Eagle Wing cut Long Leaper deep across his stomach. Retreating from the vicious attack, the Crow tried to defend himself, but to no avail. The Crow's face was a blank mask as he looked into the face of death.

Jed, Walking Horse, and Red Hawk pushed into the circle of warriors just in time to see Eagle Wing bury his war axe into the head of Long Leaper. Twice more the war axe of Flying Cloud descended, almost decapitating Long Leaper. Filled with adrenaline and rage, exhausted from the terrible fight, Eagle Wing stood wobbly as he looked at the warriors.

Red Hawk rode forward and stopped his horse for all to see him. Raising his hand, he looked slowly around the circle of Crow warriors. Many were shocked to see a vicious fighter as Long Leaper, one of their best fighters, killed by such a young warrior.

"It was a great battle, mighty Chief of the Crow." The older warrior who had started the fight rode in front of Red Hawk and looked at Eagle Wing. "This one is a mighty and valiant warrior, and truly a great Lance Bearer of the Arapaho."

"Yes, Running Elk, this one is a great Lance Bearer and he is also my nephew." Red Hawk spoke proudly.

A mighty cheer went up from the gathered Crow as the warrior Running Elk raised his hand, then turned and rode his horse to the circle of warriors. Jed kicked his horse forward and dismounted beside Eagle Wing.

"Come, we will ride to the river and clean your wounds, my son." Jed knew exactly what he was going through. Many times, he had been in the same situation.

Eagle Wing took one last look at Long Leaper, then swung on the bloody Appaloosa. Passing Red Horse, Grey Hair, and Bull Calf as he rode away from the bloody ground, he noticed a look of awe on his younger brother's face.

Crooked Arrow, who just arrived, reined in his horse as Eagle Wing passed him. "What has happened, young one?"

"My brother, Eagle Wing, has killed Long Leaper."

"Long Leaper is dead?" Crooked Arrow asked from shock.

"He won't get much deader." Red Horse grinned.

Red Hawk stopped Jed as he started for the river. "I cannot leave my people right now. I must return to the village and calm my people. I must take my place as chief where I belong, like my father before me."

"I will bring Ellie Medicine Thunder to the river in two sleeps, my brother."

"It is time for me to realize my responsibilities. I am no longer free to roam as I wish." Red Hawk looked at the retreating back of Eagle Wing. "That one may be a greater warrior than any of us, my brothers."

"I believe you are right, Red Hawk." Walking Horse remembered Soaring Bird's words and vision. "Long Leaper was already dead when he challenged that one, but did not know it."

"My son fights with more rage than we did." Jed nodded worriedly.

Bright Moon and Little Antelope watched as the riders approached the lodge. Jed had washed Eagle Wing's wounds at the Yellowstone, but still the many cuts and abrasions from the fight oozed blood. Sliding stiffly from the Appaloosa, he looked over the horse.

"Smear bear grease on his wounds, then turn him loose."

Nodding, Red Horse led the big horse to the herd.

Bright Moon looked at Jed, but said nothing as she ushered Eagle Wing into the lodge. Ellie stood looking toward the river.

"My husband?"

"Red Hawk has returned to the village." Jed could see the worry in her face. "Bright Moon and I will take you and the children to the river to meet him in two sleeps."

"Eagle Wing has been in a fight."

"He has defeated Long Leaper in battle today." Walking Horse nodded proudly.

"Does it always have to be this way with all the killing?" Ellie looked at Little Antelope.

"A warrior fights for his people." Jed explained. "Long Leaper would have killed Crooked Arrow if your nephew hadn't killed him."

Ellie and Oliver passed Red Horse as he led the bloody Appaloosa to the creek. Hurrying to the lodge, she looked worriedly at Jed.

"What has happened, Father?"

"Your brother has killed the Crow, Long Leaper, in battle." Jed nodded at the lodge. "He is inside with your mother."

"Is Eagle Wing okay?" Oliver questioned.

"My son is okay."

Two days later, Bright Moon and Jed escorted Ellie Medicine Thunder and her children to the Yellowstone. They waited as Red Hawk and some of his warriors swam their horses across the magnificent river.

"How is Eagle Wing?" Red Hawk asked as he splashed from the water.

"Your nephew is sore, but fine." Jed smiled at the warrior. "When the sun comes again, I will take Oliver to Bridger's Post, then we will return home along the immigrant road."

"And Eagle Wing?"

"He will not go on to Bridger. He has been asked to stay at He Dog's village. He will not return to our valley." Jed replied sadly.

"Is Gall still at the Arapaho village?" Red Hawk frowned.

"Yes, he waits to ride with us as far as He Dog's village."

"The Sioux are trouble, my brother." Red Hawk shook his head. "Tell my nephew not to follow him into battle with the whites."

"We have spoken of it."

"Some of my people will scout for the white soldiers." The warrior looked down. "They do not wish to fight Eagle Wing."

"Nor does he wish to fight his uncle's people." Jed assured him.

"Tell him to return to your valley and live in peace." Red Hawk suggested. "The whites are too mighty in war."

"I have spoken to him of this already."

"He will not listen?"

"No."

After shaking hands, Red Hawk nodded at Bright Moon and Red Horse, then motioned for Ellie and the children to follow him back across the river.

Eagle Wing rode with Jed and Bright Moon several miles past He Dog's village. After shaking hands with Oliver and hugging Ellie, he turned his horse toward the village. Red Horse nodded as he passed his brother.

Reining in her horse, Bright Moon called out to the proud warrior. "Come home safe, my son."

No word came from the warrior.

"My brother is deep in thought, Mother." Red Horse assured her. "Sometimes, when he is this way, he hears nothing."

For three days, Gall spoke in council with the tribal elders of He Dog's village. Dull Knife said nothing as he listened to the fiery oratory of the fierce Sioux. His words were bitter, full of hate and vengeance, against the oncoming tide of whites.

"They must be stopped or we will have no hunting grounds left."

"Tell us, Gall, can the pony soldiers be stopped?" Dull Knife stared into the fire. "Their weapons are many."

"Red Cloud stopped them many sleeps ago." Gall replied. "They left our lands and we burned their forts."

"That was many summers ago. Now, they are stronger." Dull Knife shook his head. "Now, Red Cloud and his people are on a reservation."

"Red Cloud lost heart." Gall strode in front of the elders. "Sitting Bull and Crazy Horse will live free like our ancestors, or die fighting."

"What has Sitting Bull seen?" All present knew Sitting Bull was a great medicine man of the Hunkpapa Sioux.

"He has not spoken yet." Gall shrugged.

"And Crazy Horse?" He Dog asked.

"Crazy Horse says we will defeat this enemy. His medicine is strong. He cannot be defeated in battle." Gall explained.

"We will speak of this more." He Dog would not be pushed into war by Gall or Sitting Bull's words.

"No more talks. With the new sun, I will take my warriors and go." Gall looked around. "We have been gone too long. Those who wish to follow me, be ready with the new day. We ride north to join Sitting Bull."

Eagle Wing and Grey Hair were standing off to the side of the council, listening intently. Both Dull Knife and He Dog had spoken with words of caution while Gall's words were heated and passionate. They knew he would fight as long as he drew breath.

"Do you ride with Gall?" Grey Hair looked at Eagle Wing.

"I ride with Gall." Eagle Wing nodded. "It was in my vision."

"Then, I too will ride with Gall." Grey Hair smiled.

"And my sister?" Eagle Wing asked. "There will be much danger."

"I will win much glory fighting the white soldiers." Grey Hair laughed. "Then, I will not need my flute."

Eagle Wing looked back to where the council was breaking up. Seeing He Dog walking toward them, he greeted his uncle.

"Gall leaves with the new sun." The Cheyenne leader nodded. "Will my nephew and his Arapaho warriors ride with him?"

"Yes, my uncle." Eagle Wing replied. "You heard Chief Gall speak about a great council with the white peacemakers."

"You will go to this council?"

Eagle Wing nodded. "Gall has asked me to speak for him so his words will be spoken with a straight tongue."

"Is this wise, my nephew?" He Dog asked. "The whites will learn your face and hate you."

"This is a small thing if I can prevent a war with the whites." Eagle Wing shrugged. "You do not like my going to this council?"

"I fear for you, Eagle Wing." He Dog touched his shoulder. "If you go, be crafty like the fox, wily like the coyote, and smart like the owl."

"I must help my people protect their lands."

"Gall is a strong war leader. Go with him to translate their words. Then, come back to your people safely."

"My uncle does not go north to fight?"

"No, we have many enemies here." He Dog frowned. "The Arickaree, Pawnee, and Shoshone wait for us to become weak so they can attack us."

"And your warriors?" Eagle Wing knew many of the younger Cheyenne warriors wanted to fight with Gall.

"Many will follow Gall, but there will still be enough to keep the people safe from attack."

"And Dull Knife?" Eagle Wing looked to where Gall talked with several older men.

"Dull Knife is a wise chief." He Dog shook his head sadly. "He does not wish to fight, but his people push him into this battle."

"Good-bye, Uncle."

"Good-bye, Nephew." He Dog took the extended hand.

For four days, Eagle Wing and his warriors followed Gall and his Sioux north, crossing the great rivers and broad grasslands. Eagle Wing never realized the prairies were so vast and beautiful. Herds of buffalo raced away as they passed through the flower-covered meadows. There appeared to be no end to the sea of grass and lonesome prairie before them. Topping a small hill that wound down to a small river, he was astounded to see thousands of lodges on the valley floor.

"I didn't know there were this many lodges in the tribes." Grey Hair dropped his jaw in shock. "Look, there must be thousands of horses roaming across the pastures."

"And there are so many people." Eagle Wing nodded.

Gall rode up beside the bewildered warriors. "The great Sitting Bull has summoned people from all the agencies and the roaming tribes for the council."

"He thinks the whites will see all these people and leave our lands?" Eagle Wing looked into Gall's broad face.

"It is a good thought, young one."

"And they all came." Grey Hair couldn't believe his eyes. "How can the whites defeat so many?"

"They won't. We will drive them from our lands." Gall kicked his horse and rode toward the village. "Follow me, Lance Bearers."

"Crow Killer said back east the whites have numbers like this, maybe even more." Eagle Wing added. "And they have many weapons of war."

"Maybe, but they are not here, we are." Grey Hair laughed. "And we are great fighters."

"Two-Eyed Dog should be here." Cut Arm continued. "There will be many maidens for him to look at. Not all would find his face ugly."

Grey Hair shook his head. "He has already found his woman, and he would not leave her even for a good fight."

"Women, they have ruined many Lance Bearers." Cut Arm growled.

Grey Hair thought of Ellie and when the fighting was over, he would ride to the valley and bring her to his lodge. Cut Arm was right, then again, he was wrong. A good woman made a warrior great, but she could also get a warrior killed thinking of her. Until the fighting was finished, he would think only of war. He grinned, well, most of the time.

The closer they rode to the huge village, the larger it loomed. From where they sat their horses, the lodges stretched for many miles down the small river. None of the horses or warriors were painted for war since this was a time for the peace council. If the council with the whites failed and the soldiers refused to remove the gold seekers and buffalo hunters from the Black Hills and Sioux Hunting Grounds, then there would be war.

Gall had ordered the women of his people, the Hunkpapa Sioux, to furnish Eagle Wing and the Arapaho warriors with lodges. Tethering their horses to pegs, to keep them close, Eagle Wing and Grey Hair accompanied by several others strolled through the lodges curiously.

Children played their hoop games or swam in the small river. The women worked deer hides or were busy cooking over their fires. Warriors sat around in small groups, making arrows or smoking their pipes. Eagle Wing noticed the newer rifles the Sioux warriors carried.

"Those rifles will shoot many times." Grey Hair pointed to a Henry repeater a warrior cleaned. "It will kill many enemies before it is empty."

"Will it shoot as far or straight as this one?" Eagle Wing looked at his Hawken single shot rifle.

"It does not have to, my brother." Grey Hair shook his head. "This weapon is used to kill men up close, not to hunt game with."

"Who told Grey Hair of this weapon?" Wolf's Head spoke up.

"One of Gall's warriors carried such a weapon in our village."

"Where do they get such a rifle?" Broken Leg asked.

"White men trade guns for gold and buffalo hides like the white fur traders at Bridger."

Eagle Wing looked at Wolf's Head curiously. "You mean whites trade these weapons to us so we can kill other whites?"

"Gall's warriors say white soldiers try to stop this, but there are too many traders here."

Passing a large white lodge, Grey Hair elbowed Eagle Wing. A lovely young woman stepped from the lodge and focused her dark eyes on Eagle Wing.

"She is beautiful."

Eagle Wing nodded. "What of Ellie?"

"She looks at you, my brother, not me. Perhaps, you should practice with my flute." Grey Hair laughed.

A shocked look came across the face of the tall warrior. Glancing quickly at the slender woman, his heart seemed to miss a beat. She was indeed beautiful, very beautiful. Turning once more as they walked away, he noticed her dark eyes still followed him. Embarrassed, he dropped his eyes as his face turned red, then followed Grey Hair.

"Who is she?" Eagle Wing wanted to turn once more but didn't dare.

Grey Hair laughed. "I do not know, my friend, but you have finally found something that interests you."

Stopping at the river, Eagle Wing looked to where several white tents flapped in the soft breeze. Soldiers spaced at intervals, stood guard around the white man's lodges. Whites in black coats and army uniforms sat about the tents at tables, laughing and talking.

"Crow Killer says to be very careful around these white soldiers." Eagle Wing shifted his dark eyes, taking in everything in the white camp. "He says they are dangerous. They distrust us."

"They distrust us." Cut Arm spat. "They are the ones that come unasked and unwanted into our lands."

"They fear us is why they distrust us." Grey Hair nodded. "Look, they are all so young."

Wolf's Head laughed. "We are not so very old, my friend."

"No, but we are Lance Bearers and have counted coup." Grey Hair studied the sentries. "Let us approach them to see their faces."

A sentry spotted the group of warriors as they approached his place on the perimeter of the camp. Never had he seen such a handsome group of young warriors, but these warriors were also fierce looking men. He couldn't help notice the lances with the carved emblems on them, sticking out from the arrow quiver of each warrior. One warrior in particular grew his attention. The one that carried the beautiful bead-covered arrow quiver across his broad shoulders. Taller than the others, the soldier knew this one, with his proud carriage, was the leader of these warriors. Raising his weapon, the soldier nervously blocked the ten warriors from coming closer.

"Halt." The soldier barked the order. "Sergeant of the guard, post number two."

Eagle Wing stood less than five steps from the nervous white and looked him straight in the eyes. The soldier was even younger than he was. Turning as an older white with yellow markings on his coat walked toward them, Eagle Wing nodded, then led his warriors away.

"You people want something?" The yellow-striped soldier spoke gruffly. "You there."

Eagle Wing pretended not to understand and continued away.

"What did he say?"

"He invited us to eat." Eagle Wing smiled.

"Then why do we leave?" Cut Arm asked.

Grey Hair shook his head. "I think my brother means they were going to have us for their meal."

A young boy ran up to the Arapaho as they walked away from the river. "Gall wishes you to come to the lodge of Sitting Bull."

"We will follow you, young one." Eagle Wing nodded.

"Man, weren't they something, Sarge? Magnificent looking creatures." The sentry nervously watched the warriors stroll away.

Staring closely at Eagle Wing, the three stripe soldier nodded. "They're fighters, I'll bet."

"They're Arapaho Lance Bearers, Sergeant." A buckskin clad white walked up. "Those boys are the most ornery fighters on the plains."

"You know the tall one, Howard?"

"No, Sergeant, not right off." The scout shook his head. "But, I'll make some inquiries and find out who he is."

"He looks like a fighter to me."

"Bank on it." Howard agreed. "You see that lance with the buffalo head sticking out from his arrow pouch?"

"I seen it."

"He'll stick it in the earth and die fighting, right there, unless another warrior frees it from the ground."

"You don't say." Sergeant Hufnagle spat. "Death before dishonor?"

"You could say that, and deadlier than a rattlesnake before his death." Howard grinned.

Eagle Wing and Grey Hair followed the young boy into the center of the village while the rest returned to their lodges. Every eye turned as the proud, tall figures walked past the painted lodges. Very few in the Sioux Nation could match the physical stature of these two warriors. The young women of the Sioux couldn't tear their eyes from them. Gall stood up as they approached the huge white lodge of the older man sitting before it with several others.

"Today is good, for my Arapaho sons have come." Gall greeted the newcomers. "This is our great Sioux leader, Sitting Bull."

"I have heard much of the great Sitting Bull." Eagle Wing acknowledged the stocky older man as he stood up. "We are happy to be here and meet you, my uncle."

"Gall has told me of Eagle Wing and Grey Hair of the Arapaho. It is good for you to come, my sons." The voice was deep, but not gruff.

"Thank you, Uncle. We are honored."

"Sit, my friends, we will smoke and talk."

Eagle Wing puffed lightly on the long pipe as it was passed to him. Passing it to Grey Hair, he looked about the circle of older warriors. He was curious which one was Crazy Horse, the War Chief of the Oglalas. Most of these men were older like Sitting Bull. He had heard the Oglala chief was young, only a few years older than he was.

For several minutes, the pipe was passed, offering its blessings to the spirit people before important talks were started. Finally, Sitting Bull laid the pipe aside and cleared his throat.

"I thank all my brothers for coming to these talks with the whites. I thank American Horse, Spotted tail, Iron Breast, Man Afraid of his Horses, Tall Bull, and Touch the Clouds who represent Crazy Horse and the Oglalas." Sitting Bull looked around at all the chiefs.

Gall nodded at Eagle Wing and Grey Hair. "These two young warriors are Eagle Wing and Grey Hair of the Arapaho Lance Bearers. Eagle Wing knows the white tongue. He has agreed to be our tongue at the council with the whites to translate their words for us."

"We are honored the great warriors of the Arapaho are here." Sitting Bull nodded. "This is good, not always are the words we speak and hear are translated correctly in our tongue."

"It is a good thing Eagle Wing speaks for us. Their talker has spoken our words wrong many times in the past." American Horse spoke up. "In the past, their ears have been closed to our words."

"Tomorrow, we meet with the whites in their camp. We will listen to their words and maybe they will listen to ours." Sitting Bull shrugged.

Iron Breast looked at Touch the Clouds. "Why does Crazy Horse not come to this council? Is he too proud?"

"Crazy Horse will never come to a council with whites. He says their words are empty and our words fall on deaf ears." The warrior shook his head.

"He is missed, He is a power to be listened to." American Horse spoke again.

Touch The Clouds shrugged. "My chiefs, he will not be missed when he is needed, when the fighting starts."

"With the new sun, after they fill their stomachs, we will go to their camp." Sitting Bull looked at the stern faces. "We will carry no weapons."

Every head nodded as the medicine man stood up. Sitting Bull was a fiery speaker who could foretell the future and see what the coming days would bring. A born leader that all men would follow.

Gall looked at his mentor and nodded. "Does Sitting Bull think these talks will get the whites to leave our lands?"

"No, I think they wish us to move onto their reservations and leave our old ways behind." The chief spoke sadly. "I think there will be war."

"Then why do we waste our time with these talks?" Iron Breast growled. "Let us kill these whites."

"No, I have given my word we will hear their talk." Sitting Bull raised his voice. "We will not dishonor our people by attacking the peacemakers."

Eagle Wing looked at Iron Breast as the warrior spoke only one word. "Peacemakers, hah!"

Walking away from the council, Eagle Wing let his eyes find the warrior, Iron Breast. "That one seems to hate everything."

"He does." Grey Hair nodded.

The new sun brought a beautiful sunny day for the council. Birds sang along the clear stream with meadowlarks and doves calling out their songs across the grasslands. Horses by the thousands could be seen and heard, nickering for their colts or stallions challenging their rivals for mares. The lodges they passed by on the way to the council were breathtaking. Most were covered with fresh new hides and painted with different symbols, showing the great valor of the warriors who lived in them. As Eagle Wing moved with the others, toward the white camp, the commotion of the huge village was new to him. The Arapaho people were happy, but not nearly as boisterous and loud as the Sioux.

Today was a big day for the tribes. He hoped, for the people, the peace council would go well. The little he knew of war was only what Crow Killer had spoken of. The different tribes were always fighting with one another, mainly to count coup on their enemy, or to steal horses or women. Killing to subjugate an enemy was very rare.

A big semi-circle of the lead chiefs with Sitting Bull at the center was laid out before the wooden tables and chairs the white's sat at. Eagle Wing shook his head as the white men would not lower themselves to sit on the ground as the chiefs did. They were all great chiefs and none of the frail whites were their equal in battle. No warrior, unless he was brave and fearless in battle, could speak for his people. All the Chiefs of the Sioux and Cheyenne were present, only Red Cloud was missing. He already had moved his people to the reservation near Fort Robinson.

A white soldier with eagles on his shoulders stepped before the chiefs and presented them each with a bundle of smoking tobacco. With the help of a translator, he invited them to smoke. Eagle Wing sat beside

Gall and studied the one that translated the words of the whites. The man wore the typical buckskins of a hunter. Tall and thin, the speaker's face was lightly covered in hair. Carrying a dark complexion as he did, Eagle Wing knew this one was what the whites called a half-breed, half white and half Indian. Later, he was to find out the man was Goruard, the half-breed son of a white trader.

With the smoke finished, all eyes turned to where a short, balding white stood nervously before the chiefs.

Gall shook his head and mumbled to Eagle Wing. "How can the people trust one such as this?"

Many councils had been held before, but each chief knew this council could be one of the most important. Goruard translated slowly as the chiefs listened carefully. Several times, Sitting Bull looked at Eagle Wing to see if his words were true. The chiefs' jaws hardened as the white spoke of the tribes moving onto designated reservations or their removal would be with force. Goruard's words hardened as the white made demands, then threats toward the chiefs.

Sergeant Hufnagle and the scout Howard listened to the words and watched the chiefs' expressions. Eagle Wing stood up and raised his hand as Goruard interpreted the last few words.

"This one has not spoken the words straight, my chiefs." The young Arapaho looked at the interpreter. "His words say if you return to the reservation, you will be free to roam and hunt at will. This is not what the no-haired white one speaks."

Sitting Bull ignored Goruard and spoke to the white leader of the peacemakers. "Ask his half-breed to speak his words once more."

Goruard looked at Eagle Wing, wondering how he knew English. "I am sorry, my chiefs. I should not have spoken for the white chief."

"Tell him." Sitting Bull's words came out hard and sharp.

Again, the white spoke, repeating his speech. This time Goruard translated his words exactly as he had spoken them. Nodding, Eagle Wing sat down.

"That one seems educated and a force to be reckoned with." Hufnagle spat a stream of tobacco.

"I do believe you're right, Sergeant." Howard nodded. "At least he speaks English, how I don't know."

For several minutes, Sitting Bull sat without moving, then finally, he stood up and stared at the assembled whites. Not a man of great height like Touch the Clouds, still he was a man of great strength and pride. The pin-like eyes seemed to burn a hole through anyone he disliked. Now, they were centered on the little white.

"You say we are to go to a reservation and be counted like cattle." The chief's words were calm. "You say if we do not do this thing, you will come with your white-eye soldiers and drive us before you. Look around, white man; we hold your lives in our hands right now. This was our land long before you came here. We are not people to be spoken to as you have or be treated like children. You say we are to go now. Hear this, you will leave our lands and take your soldiers with you. Do not cross the wide Missouri or we will fight."

Eagle Wing listened to Goruard translate the chief's words, then watched as all the chiefs, except Spotted Tail, followed Sitting Bull back to the village. The scout, Howard, walked to where Eagle Wing and Grey Hair stood listening as Spotted Tail spoke with the white peace council.

"What is your name, warrior?"

"Why do you want to know my name?" Eagle Wing looked at the scout's twinkling blue eyes and remembered He Dog's words of warning.

"Curiosity only." Howard smiled. "I have been told you are Eagle Wing, the son of Jed Bracket or Crow Killer."

"How do you know of Crow Killer?"

"Me and your pa came west together on Chalk Brigg's wagon train many years ago." The eyes twinkled. "You're almost the spitting image of him."

"You were friends?"

"I didn't say we were friends, but we weren't enemies. You are Eagle Wing?" Howard asked.

"I am Eagle Wing."

"And this one?"

"He is Grey Hair, Lance Bearer of the Northern Arapaho Tribe."

"A great society of fighters." Howard smiled. "Old Lige Hatcher used to speak of them with great respect."

"You knew Lige Hatcher?"

"I knew him. He taught me the ways of the plains. He was a great scout." Howard nodded.

"Yes."

"Do you ride with Sitting Bull and Crazy Horse?"

"I am here to translate the white man's words."

"You know as well as I that they'll fight before going on a reservation." Howard's words were not threatening. "Can't say I blame them."

"They have not told me their thoughts."

"They might win a battle or two, but in the end, they'll lose." Howard shrugged. "Go home, Eagle Wing, and take your warriors with you. This is not your fight."

"They are my people."

"Yes, I suppose they are. Is your mother Arapaho?" The scout asked.

"Cheyenne."

"A great people." Howard nodded. "Tell your pa I said hello."

Watching the white scout walk away, Eagle Wing replied. "I will tell him your words."

Turning, Howard stopped. "Go home, this is bound to get nasty."

Eagle Wing, Grey Hair, and the rest of the Arapaho waited beside Gall as the huge village tore down their lodges and separated in different directions.

"Where do they go?" Grey Hair watched the people disband.

"We are too many to feed." Gall replied. "We must scatter the villages and hunt the shaggies. The cold times will bring hunger if we do not store meat and hides."

"What will you have us do?"

"Come with my people. We will watch over our eastern hunting grounds and keep the whites from our lands." Gall flattened his huge hands. "Sitting Bull does not believe the pony soldiers will come against us until the new grass grows in the spring."

Eagle Wing looked at Grey Hair. "I will follow Gall east."

"We came here together, my brother. I will stay." Grey Hair turned to Cut Arm and Wolf's Head.

"We cannot let you have all the fun." Both warriors laughed. They would follow Gall too.

CHAPTER 12

Three days after saying farewell to Eagle Wing; Jed, Bright Moon, Ellie, Red Horse, and Oliver rode into Bridger's Trading Post. Maud and Percy stood under the blacksmith awning, watching as Jed led the small party of riders up to the porch of the trading post. Ellie and Bright Moon had replaced Oliver's store-bought suit with buckskins. Ellie said the suit changed his looks from pilgrim to hunter.

Maud looked closely at the tall man. At first, he didn't recognize him as the same pilgrim he had taken back into the mountains. The tripod from his surveyor's equipment tied to the packhorse jarred his memory. The young white had changed considerably, becoming more muscular since their last parting, but he was definitely the pilgrim.

Maud elbowed Percy in the side. "Lookee, Percy, it's our pilgrim in the flesh."

"He sure looks different in them buckskins, don't he?"

"Yep, he do." Maud's eyes found Ellie Thunder, riding one of the loudly-colored Appaloosa horses. "But, she sure ain't."

"Don't do anything foolish, Maud." Percy warned. "We barely escaped with our hides intact last time we tangled with that Injun."

Maud counted the riders, and only the one that had shot Joe and sliced his ear was missing. "You know what this means, Percy?"

"What?"

"This means nobody is guarding his cabin or valley except the young buck that cut me and killed Joe." The big hunter laughed. "She's wide open for sure."

"No, Maud, I ain't going back there on a bet." Percy shook his head. "No, siree."

"Think of all that gold stashed there." Maud grinned slyly. "Old McGraw shared a jug with me once. He got himself a little drunk and told me about all the fine pelts old Crow Killer has traded to Caldwell over the years. There must be hundreds of dollars in gold coins, not counting the gold in them mountains. What would an Indian spend money on?"

Percy shook his head. "You think we're gonna have enough time to prospect for gold? No, sir, not me."

"Would you ride back for the money he's got socked away?" Maud tempted Percy. "We'll be in drinking money for a mighty long spell. I'm telling you."

"I don't know." Percy looked at the store where Caldwell was talking with Jed and Bright Moon. "That one scares me."

"Round up Case and find Frank Elder." Maud's eyes stared hard at Ellie. "We'll ride out while he's here trading."

Percy noticed the trapper looking at the girl. "And the squaw?"

"She'll wait. Right now, we're going after the gold he's got cached."

"Alright, but I don't like it one bit."

"You like drinking and carousing without working, don't you?"

"That I do."

"Then get. Have Elder get our supplies so that Injun won't recognize us."

"We pulling out tonight?"

"We are." Maud looked again at Ellie. "I'll wait for you west of here on the immigrant trail."

Otis McGraw worked over a hot forge, scalding an iron rim onto a wagon wheel. From his anvil, he watched as Maud and Percy talked quietly with their heads close together as they nodded to where Jed Bracket just rode up. Unable to stop his work to go greet Jed, he continued with the fire, not wanting the iron to cool without being seated snugly around the wooden wheel. Curiously, he watched as the two hunters were cooking something up. The old blacksmith figured it had something to do with Jed.

He remembered last spring when Maud had made improper advances toward Jed's young daughter. Maud was no good so he decided to keep an eye on the two men. When he had finished repairing the wheel, he would find Jed. Dropping his eyes, McGraw acted uninterested as the one called Maud walked to the corral and haltered his horse.

Paying the blacksmith money, owed for stable rent, Maud placed a saddle on his sorrel horse. McGraw couldn't help but notice the torn ear that had never grown back together. When asked about the ear, Maud had said it was torn by a Hackberry thorn, but to McGraw it looked like a knife cut. He remembered when the three hunters had returned to Bridger on their last hunting foray. The ear had been crudely wrapped and never meshed back together properly.

Two hours later, McGraw was still working over the wheel when Percy and two other men came from the trader's post. Heavy packs loaded with enough food for several days were loaded onto a pack animal. Saddling their horses, they paid McGraw and waved good-bye.

"You boys leaving out I see."

"Going after buffalo hides." Percy smiled.

"Maud going with you?"

"Nah, ain't seen him today."

McGraw nodded as he caught the hunter in a lie. Two hours earlier, he had watched Percy and Maud talking just outside his stable. Yep, he knew they were definitely up to something. It couldn't be the girl, she was still at the post.

As the sun set in the west, McGraw finished replacing the wheel on the supply wagon and removed his leather apron. He would grab himself something to eat, then go seek out Jed. His old body was exhausted, and the wheel had been hot and heavy work. Lying down tiredly on his cot, the blacksmith fell asleep almost immediately.

The rooster's crowing brought McGraw slowly awake. Shaking the cobwebs from his head, he sat up from bed. Cussing to himself for falling asleep before speaking with Jed, he looked about the smithy. It was daylight and he had slept all night. Wiping the sleep from his eyes, he headed for the Post Store.

"Good morning, Otis." Alex Caldwell studied the blacksmith. "Man, you look like you had a rough night."

"I reckon I did at that." McGraw looked about the store. "I'm looking for Jed."

"You been hitting the bottle?" The store man shook his head. "You want some coffee?"

"No, I ain't been drinking. I just need to find Jed."

"Bright Moon and Ellie Thunder are out back." Caldwell shrugged. "Jed, his son Red Horse, and that pilgrim Oliver rode out, right before daylight."

"Pilgrim, you mean the young white surveyor that disappeared last spring?"

"The same." Caldwell nodded. "Why do you need Jed?"

McGraw shrugged. "Reckon it'll keep. Just tell him to come see me, soon as he gets back."

"I'll do it."

McGraw turned for the door, then stopped. "Keep a sharp eye on the girl until Jed returns, will you?"

"Why, is something wrong?"

"Just watch her, Alex." McGraw swore. "Watch her close."

It was almost dark when Jed, Oliver, and Red Horse rode through the lodges, lining the grounds outside the post gates. Reining in where he had last seen Silent One's mother, he sat his horse and waited. A younger squaw exited the opening and looked to where Jed sat his horse.

"I look for Elk Woman." Jed looked down at the woman. "I have meat for her lodge."

The woman shook her head glumly. "Elk Woman has gone to meet her ancestors."

"This is a sad thing to hear. Then, this meat is for you, woman."

"I thank, Crow Killer." The little squaw smiled slightly. "The meat is welcome."

Reining in at McGraw's stable, Jed slid from his horse and looked for the blacksmith. Handing Red Horse the reins to his gelding, he walked into the shop.

"Otis where are you?"

McGraw entered the shop from a back door. "Alex finally sent you."

"No, I haven't seen Alex today. We just came to buy some feed for our horses." Jed shook hands with the old blacksmith. "And, I didn't bring the mule."

"Never you mind about the mule for now, old friend." Otis wiped a dirty hand across his face. "You may have greater problems."

"What do you mean, Otis? What problems?"

"You remember that hunter, Maud and his cronies, hanging around here last time you were at the post?" Otis continued. "Did your son tell you the trouble we had with that bunch over Ellie Thunder last time you were here?"

"I remember him. And yes, Eagle Wing told me about you helping him against the hunter last spring. Thank you, old friend."

McGraw quickly told Jed what he had seen and heard, then told how the hunters had ridden from the post the evening before loaded with supplies.

"They were sure eyeing you when you rode into the post." The blacksmith shook his shaggy head. "I think them skunks are up to no good, Jed."

Jed thought about Wilson being alone, back at the valley. He worried Maud and his men might be heading for the cabin. McGraw had said they had seen him and his people enter the post earlier. They would guess the valley was unprotected. Wilson had only come with Jed to Bridger one time and doubted they would know about him. He wondered if the old farmer would be able to fight off the hunters if he knew they were coming. There was a good chance the hunters weren't riding for his valley, but he couldn't take the gamble. One thing he knew for sure, they weren't going after buffalo this time of year. Thanking McGraw, Jed bought a sack of grain, then turned from the shop. Leading his horse, Jed walked quickly to the post store.

"What's wrong?" Red Horse could see the apprehension on his father's face.

"Feed and water the horses, Red Horse, and do not ask questions. Hurry!" The youngster never had his father speak so short to him before.

Finding Bright Moon and Ellie Thunder cooking food in Caldwell's backroom, Jed and Oliver set their rifles against a door jam.

Seeing his worried face, Bright Moon turned from the stove. "What has happened, my husband?"

"The white hunter, Maud, the one Eagle Wing cut, I think he's riding for our valley and has a whole day's lead." Jed looked at Oliver.

"What will you do?"

"I must ride quickly to our lodge."

"We will ride with you." Bright Moon nodded.

"No, not this time." Jed shook his head. "I must ride fast and hard to reach our valley in time to help my father."

"I understand. Take Red Horse, he is almost a warrior." Bright Moon placed plates of food on the table.

"Yes, Red Horse will ride with me." Jed nodded. "Otis and Alex will look after you and Ellie."

"I will take care of Ellie, my husband." Bright Moon frowned.

"I know you will."

Oliver cleared his throat. "I will ride with you, Jed."

"I thought you wanted to go back east?"

"Not now." The young white shrugged. "I will go with you."

"Eat first, I will fix food for the trail." Bright Moon offered. "Ellie, go bring your brother."

Alex stood in the doorway, listening to the conversation. "Don't worry, Jed. We'll take care of the women."

"Thank you, my friend."

"This white hunter you speak of is an evil man." Ellie turned for the door. "You should have killed him."

Jed, followed by Red Horse and Oliver, rode as fast a pace as the darkness would permit. There was little moon to light their way which slowed the riders. With the coming of daylight, Jed could plainly see the trail leading down to Blackhorse Crossing and the hoof prints of five horses on the sandy trail beneath them.

"They are riding for the valley." Jed's words were harsh. "I should've killed them before."

"They'll reach Grandfather before we can warn him."

"Yes, but hopefully he'll find out when they enter the valley."

"The wolf and mule will warn him." Red Horse nodded.

"Providing he listens to them." Jed was worried. He wanted to hurry, but he couldn't push the horses too fast. The valley was a long way off and the horses had already traveled from He Dog's village to Bridger with little rest.

Maud grinned as he looked down from the high ridge at the cabin far below. Several horses and a lone cow grazed peacefully out on the broad valley floor. Maud was curious, even from this height, he could see smoke coming from the chimney.

"Someone's home, boys."

"It can't be Crow Killer." Percy replied. "We left him back at Bridger. He don't know we're out here."

"Like I said, it's probably the Injun that cut me and killed old Joe." Maud spat a stream of tobacco. "That'll be good. I've got a score to settle with that one. We'll be on him before he knows we're here."

"I hope so. He's pretty good with that rifle." Percy remembered the hard-faced youngster.

Wilson heard the mournful cry of the old wolf and then a little later the small black mule started braying. The wolf could be calling his mate, but not the mule. He knew she sensed something. Someone must be coming toward the cabin. Grabbing his rifle and shot pouch with some hardtack, Wilson raced from the cabin, hurrying up the trail.

A shot rang out as a bullet buzzed through the branches over his head. Kneeling briefly, Wilson looked back as four riders crossed the small creek below the cabin. Cussing himself for letting the unknown riders get so close before discovering them, Wilson fired a hurried shot, then ran for the rock cave.

"It's just an old man." Maud reined in at the cabin. "Percy, you and Elder go after him while I search the cabin."

"He may be an old man, but he dang near nailed me with that shot." Elder cussed.

"We'll get him, Maud." Percy dismounted. "You and Case find the gold quick and let's get our tails out of here."

Hurrying into the cave, Wilson reloaded his rifle, then fixed the priming in the other rifles stacked against the stone wall. Every week, Jed made a point to fire the stacked rifles, then clean and reload them. All they needed to fire was to prime their firing mechanism. The small cave was a natural fortress, easy to defend with a good field of fire up and down the narrow trail.

Racing up the rocky trail, Percy and Elder knew they could easily overtake the old man. Too late, they heard the close blast from a rifle, then Elder was flung backward, stone-cold dead on the trail. Percy ducked back behind a curve in the narrow passageway. Never a brave man, he always followed Maud and did as he was told. Now, alone on the trail with Elder dead, the hunter was scared. Retreating down the trail, Percy hurried back to the cabin.

"I heard the shot. Did you get him?" Maud stood in the doorway.

Shaking his head, Percy dropped onto one of the chairs. "No, he's done killed Elder."

"That old man killed Elder?" Case cussed in shock.

"Yes, that old man." Percy cussed. "That old man as you call him has a natural fort up that canyon, and he can shoot."

"Well, we've got to get him." Maud spat. "There's no gold here so it must be up there somewhere and he'll know where it is."

"Well, Maud, good luck digging him out of there."

"Let's go."

For a few hours, after several shots had been fired at him, Wilson waited quietly watching the trail. There was no other way for the men below to reach him unless they scaled down the steep cliff walls above him. Even if they did that, they would be in his sights for several minutes. For now, it was a standoff, providing he didn't fall asleep. Several times, he had fired as the attackers had shown themselves, trying to locate exactly where he was hiding. Finally, he held his fire and waited for a clean shot at one of the men.

"Come out, old man, and we'll let you live." Maud hollered at Wilson. "We just want the gold we know you've got up there."

Not a sound came from the rocky trail which enraged Maud. He had to know where the old man was hiding before he could attack. Raising his filthy hat on an oak branch, Maud cussed as the hat went spinning through the air.

"He done ventilated your hat, old hoss." Case giggled.

"Shut up, Case." Maud looked at the hole in his hat.

Percy wanted to run. The old man meant business. From where he was holed up, he could kill everyone of them. They didn't dare stick their heads out to try to locate the shooter or they might end up with a hole in them just like the hat.

"That old geezer can sure shoot."

Maud nodded, then studied the surrounding mountain. "We might flank this place and get above him."

"Yeah, and we might just wind up like Elder."

"Percy, we sure can't sit around here waiting for him to show himself."

Percy snorted. "No, sir, but we sure enough can ride out, right now."

"I ain't leaving without that gold." Maud leveled his rifle. "And I'll gut shoot the first one that tries to run out."

Percy shook his head in disgust. He knew this was pure folly from the very first. "Well, tell me Maud, just what are we gonna do?"

"You stay put right here and cover us." Maud studied the trail. "Me and Case are gonna keep low, belly up this trail and get us an old man."

Percy shook his head as the two men started up the rock path on their bellies. Five minutes passed before the first shot sounded. Quickly peeking around a rock wall, Percy saw Case laying belly down on the rough trail, less than fifty feet away. Half of his head was blown off. Maud was nowhere in sight. Pulling back as another bullet ricocheted off a boulder, Percy raced down the hill. He hadn't wanted any of this and he was getting out while he still had his head in one piece.

Jed could hear far-off rifle fire from the high ridge overlooking the valley. The sound of a lone horse coming their way sounded on the north trail. Quickly retreating, where they could hide their horses, the three riders waited for the oncoming rider.

Intent on escaping the valley and death, Percy hurried up the mountain never expecting anyone on the trail above. He was afraid of Maud, but the old man shooting at him was even deadlier. Pushing his horse hard, he rode right into Jed before he knew he was even on the trail.

Dropping his rifle, he raised his trembling hands. "I ain't in this, mister."

"Have you killed the old one?" Jed's voice was cold and hard as nails.

"Not as far as I know, but he's killed two of us." Percy swallowed hard. "Who's left down there?"

"Just Maud. That old man done for Elder and Case."

Jed's eyes blazed as he looked at the terrified man. "Where is the old one?"

"Up a rocky trail somewhere behind the cabin."

"Red Horse, bring this one down to the cabin." Jed leaned over and picked up Percy's rifle and checked the priming. "Oliver, come with me."

Kicking his big bay into a hurried trot down the steep trail, Jed never looked behind him. Two more gunshots went off as he questioned Percy. Red Horse held his rifle on Percy as he listened to the horses move down the trail. Again, the roar of a rifle blast came from far away.

Percy couldn't meet the cold, dark eyes of the youngster. Watching as he notched an arrow to his powerful bow, Percy swallowed hard.

"What are you gonna do, Injun?" The face was terrified as the bow was lifted.

"Well, white man, I'm sure not gonna sit here and wait for my grandfather to be killed." The force of the bow drove the arrow halfway through Percy's thin body.

"I'm dead, killed by a kid." Percy clutched at the arrow in his chest and held onto his saddle horn. "By a kid."

The sharp blade of the skinning knife sliced across Percy's throat as he fell sideways from his horse. Sliding from his horse, Red Horse rolled the dead hunter's body off into the deep canyon that fell away from the trail. Taking the reins of Percy's horse, he swung back on his Appaloosa.

"You shouldn't have come back, white man. But, I don't think you'll make that mistake again."

The rifle fire from below quieted as Red Horse hurried down the mountain pass. Reining in, as he crossed the creek, he slid from his horse and started up the narrow trail leading to the cave. Halfway to the cave, he found Oliver lying beside a log with a bullet through his leg.

Kneeling beside the injured man, Red Horse examined the wound. "It bleeds, but it's not serious."

"Jed told me to stay here."

"How many whites are left?" Red Horse checked the priming in Oliver's rifle pan and handed the rifle to him.

"Your father says only one, but I don't know. The one that shot me was up there somewhere." Oliver took the weapon.

"Stay alert and watch the trail."

Oliver nodded. "Where is the one you were watching?"

"He fell into the canyon." Red Horse shrugged, then started up the trail. "Stay alert, Oliver. We will return."

Jed eased slowly along the rocky trail, watching for any motion above him. Since the bullet that hit Oliver had been fired, there had been total silence. He feared Wilson was dead, if not there would be more firing from above. Cautiously, he slipped along the path using the rocks as protection from the white. The narrow path leading to the cave went past where Wilson should be for several hundred feet before coming to a sheer wall. Step by dangerous step, Crow Killer once again turned into the bear killer, stalking his prey without a sound.

"I know you're down there, Injun. I seen you and the pilgrim." Maud's voice sang out from above. "Come on, I'm waiting for you."

Red Horse heard the voice as it reverberated up and down the trail. Stopping where the trail took a steep climb upward, the youngster turned off the trail and started working his way up the rougher mountainside. Many times, he had climbed this passageway while out hunting, discovering new places on the rough mountain. His stout young legs climbed over the rocks and brush silently as he made his way to the top which should bring him out above the voice. He knew the trail, the white was on, and there was no way he could pass the rock wall without a rope. Crow Killer had his escape blocked from below, and now, Red Horse would block his escape from above.

Climbing steadily over the treacherous rocks, he finally reached the top where boulders lay strewn along the mountainside. Moving back where he would be above the white, Red Horse stopped and pulled an arrow from his quiver. The red mark of a horse head was painted on the shaft of the arrow. A horse's head, his mark, same as the great Lance Bearers bore on their lances. Nodding, he started forward, trying to be silent as he intersected the trail where he figured the white should be waiting.

Moving into the cave as he kept his eyes on the trail, Jed found the old farmer face down on the sandy floor, his body soaked in blood. Turning the old one over easy, he watched as the blue eyes blinked open.

"You're here, boy." The voice was raspy, weak.

"I'm here, Pa." Jed nodded as he examined the wound.

"They finally got me, Jed, but I didn't let any of the skunks get into the cave."

"Rest easy, don't talk." Jed looked at Wilson's bloody shirt. "You'll be fine."

"No, son, I won't." Wilson replied weakly. "Leave me, go get him."

Jed knew Wilson was right as he was bleeding out. "There's time for that after I get you down to the cabin."

"I'll never make the cabin, Jed." Blood came in bubbles from the old one's mouth. "Take good care of my cow."

The voice trailed off as his head fell to the side. "I'll take care of her, Pa. I'm sorry for leaving you alone."

From above, on the trail, an anguished scream sounded making Jed rush from the cave and up the narrow passageway. Maud lay against the rock wall with an arrow protruding from his throat. Blood ran down his face and body as Red Horse stood over him, holding his scalp. The brown eyes of the big hunter widened as Red Horse pried his mouth open and pushed the skinning knife slowly down his throat. Again, the gagging muffled scream came from the man's mouth.

"You will come to our valley no more, white man." Red Horse plunged the knife all the way into Maud's throat. "Or look at my sister."

Jed blinked as he walked to where Red Horse stood over the hunter. Taking the scalp from his younger son, he flung it behind the rocks. "Where is the other white, my son?"

"Dead, as this one is." Red Horse turned his back and stood quietly. "Grandfather is dead?"

"Yes, he has gone to be with his sons."

"He was a good grandfather." Red Horse's shoulders shook silently. "This one's dying was too easy. He should have suffered more."

Jed looked down at the dead hunter. "Yes, but he's dead now."

"Not dead enough!" Red Horse pulled his knife from Maud's throat. "I'll check on Oliver."

Jed looked at the dead white, then at the retreating back of his youngest son. In one day, Red Horse had become a warrior. Jed hoped he would not lose his charm and happiness as He Dog had after the death of his brother, Yellow Dog. He shook his head as he walked back to the cave. One never knows the path their life would follow. After today, he wondered what Red Horse's path would be.

Oliver sat at the wooden table outside the cabin as Jed and Red Horse dug a place for Ed Wilson below the cabin. Few words had been spoken by either of them as they helped him to the cabin, then carried the body of the farmer down the trail for burial.

"Take him into your arms almighty one. He was a good father and grandfather. We will see him again one day." Jed cleared his throat and started covering the grave. Oliver limped slowly down to the grave and stood respectively beside Red Horse.

"Grandfather has a beautiful place to rest." Oliver looked out across the creek and meadows.

Nothing had been said about the whites that lay along the path to the cave, but Oliver knew they were dead. He had seen the hard look on Red Horse's face covered in blood. For once, the youngster was quiet. With the killing of Ed Wilson, he had changed. Where once a young boy stood, now there was a warrior.

Jed sat drinking coffee outside the cabin after washing up in the creek. Looking at the bloodstained Red Horse, he started to speak, but then held his words.

"With the new sun, I will ride for your mother and sister." Jed looked at the quiet youngster. "You stay here and take care of Oliver."

Only a nod came from Red Horse.

Oliver lifted his cup of coffee and tried to ease his leg. "We'll be here, Jed. For sure, I ain't going far with this leg."

"Stay off the leg, Oliver, and keep it elevated." Jed remembered Ellie giving Walking Horse the same advice many years ago.

"Yes, sir."

Red Horse didn't question his father as he disappeared back up the path to the cave. An hour passed before Jed reappeared and washed his hands in the clear water of the creek. At one place, high up the pathway, the canyon wall fell into a narrow crevice far below.

CHAPTER 13

Sitting Bull's camp lay in a vast valley, west of the broad Missouri. Buffalo roamed the grasslands in great numbers, but the white hunters had almost eradicated the great animals east of the river. Sitting Bull and Gall knew it was only a matter of time before the white's greed would have them crossing the Missouri for more hides. Even though the tribes had dispersed to hunt the shaggies for winter meat, Sitting Bull's village was still huge.

Crazy Horse and his Oglala camped to the north, near the Black Hills. Eagle Wing, Grey Hair, and their warriors camped on the Rosebud, along a small tributary bordering the great village. As dusk arrived, Gall had ridden into their camp and dismounted. Greeted by the Arapaho, he took a seat in front of their lodges.

"Sitting Bull has called for the sun dance and wished for his nephews to come to the celebration." Gall explained. "The sun dance is spiritual like the Arapaho Lance Bearer Ceremony. Perhaps, Sitting Bull will have a vision to foretell our future."

"We know of this sun dance. When will it be held?" Grey Hair asked.

"He will give the other villages time to gather." Gall looked out across the prairie. "Perhaps, three sleeps."

"Should we hunt for meat for the celebration?"

"No, with the new sun, I will lead warriors to the east along the Missouri to scout the river." Gall looked hard at Eagle Wing. "It is my wish the Arapaho would ride with me."

"We will be ready with the new sun." Eagle Wing nodded. For a week since arriving, his warriors had sat idly around their camp, caring for their horses and weapons.

"Gall's face was hard." Grey Hair watched as Gall and his warriors rode away. "He is going to the river for some reason."

"Yes."

Through the early morning, a fine mist covered the wide prairie as Eagle Wing rode alongside the silent Gall. Thirty warriors, Sioux, Cheyenne, and Arapaho rode in a lope to the east. For several miles, riding up and down the slopes and gullies covering the land, Gall alternated the horses from a trot, then into a slow lope. Buffalo and deer raced from the passing riders in fear.

In a low hollow, running parallel to the Missouri, the chief stopped the warriors and dismounted. Motioning for Eagle Wing and Grey Hair to follow, he crept forward and peered over the grassy ridge. Below, two wagons sat alongside the river. Buffalo hides were stacked in piles on the wagons.

"This is what Sitting Bull speaks of." Gall growled. "These whites are on our side of the river, killing our game."

"They have killed many shaggies… many!" Grey Hair took in the piles of hides.

"They kill and waste meat that would fill the stomachs of our people."

"What will Gall have us do?" Eagle Wing could see the anger in the chief's face.

"Follow me. These will kill no more." Motioning for the warriors to spread out along the bank, Gall led the charge from the hollow and onto the unsuspecting skinners.

Gunfire disrupted the silent tranquility of the river as the warriors raced through the white camp. Whooping and screaming their war cries, they shot down and bludgeoned the hide hunters without mercy. Quickly searching the camp and surrounding brush for more whites, Eagle Wing found an old man cringing under a buffalo robe. Dragging the whimpering man to the others, Eagle Wing let him fall at Gall's feet.

"I let you live old one." Gall looked down at the shaking man. "Tell your people to stay on their side of the river or they will die as these whites did."

Eagle Wing translated the words and watched as the white was placed on a work horse and sent back across the great river. Gall handed Eagle Wing and Grey Hair each a captured Henry repeater with shells.

"They are fine gifts." Eagle Wing looked down at the rifle. "We thank you, my uncle."

"Your warriors fought well today." Gall looked around at the dead whites. "Your arrows found many. You deserve the rifles."

Eagle Wing knew Gall had asked that he and his warriors accompany him so he could see for himself the fighting abilities of the Lance Bearers. He nodded slowly as he watched the warriors go through the dead men's belongings. Everything of value was removed before the camp was set on fire. Gall rode his horse to where they waited and held out three Sioux breast plates.

"We came here today because yesterday our hunters found three of our young warrior's dead downriver." Gall showed the chest plates. "These belonged to the dead ones."

Now, Eagle Wing knew why these whites had been killed. Not so much for trespassing and killing buffalo on Sioux lands as it was for killing three young warriors. Gall had the killers tracked to this white camp, and now, these breast plates had been found in one of the tents.

"The whites deserved to die." Grey Hair frowned.

"All whites deserve to die." Cut Arm nodded slowly.

"Not all, my friends, but these did." Eagle Wing thought of his grandfather.

"Will the white soldiers come across the river?" Grey Hair looked across the broad river as the lone white waded ashore and mounted a horse. "Will their soldiers make war on our people?"

"Who knows what the whites will do." Gall shrugged. "The Treaty of Laramie gave this land to us on paper. No white is to hunt our side of the river, and now, they have killed our young men for beads."

"These whites will kill no more." Now, Eagle Wing understood why Gall and Sitting Bull hated the white interlopers so.

"Tomorrow, we will ride to the village of Crazy Horse." Gall looked around at the burning tents and wagons.

"The hides of the shaggies?" Grey Hair looked at the piles of buffalo hides.

"I will send women back to bring them to our village."

Eagle Wing had heard of the great Crazy Horse ever since Gall had come to Walking Horse's village. The warrior was already a legend among the tribes. His medicine was strong, and legend had it that he could never be killed or defeated in battle. Eagle Wing would be honored to meet one such as this Oglala.

Three days later, after a hard, fast ride from the valley, Jed rode through the overhead gates as he passed into Bridger's Post. Sliding from his horse, he turned the tired animal into McGraw's stable with Bright Moon and Ellie's horses. After latching the wooden gate, he walked to where McGraw worked over an anvil.

"You're back pretty quick, Jed." McGraw laid aside his hammer and looked up at the tall warrior with curiosity.

"I have traveled fast, my friend. My business is finished, and now, I come for Bright Moon."

"Where is your young son and Oliver?" McGraw looked around the compound, seeing Jed was alone.

"They both remained at the valley." Jed started to walk to the post. "And Maud?"

"I don't think he will come back here." Jed shrugged.

"Ever?" McGraw rubbed his chin.

Ignoring the last question, Jed crossed the post grounds and entered the store to find Ellie and Bright Moon working behind the counter. As always, they were a beautiful and welcomed sight.

Seeing him darken the doorway, Bright Moon smiled and hurried to greet him. "My husband, you are back."

"I am back, and starving." Jed picked her up and held her to him. "What are you and Ellie doing?"

"They're both helping me clean this place up." Caldwell greeted Jed. "You can leave both of them with me forever."

Jed looked about the large store and it was cleaner and more organized. "Can't do that, Alex. I'm afraid I need them at home."

"I know." Caldwell grinned. "But, if you should change your mind."

"I'll never do that, old friend." Jed smiled as he looked into his beautiful wife's face.

Ellie looked questioningly at her father. "Where is Red Horse and Oliver?"

"They stayed behind at the valley to hunt. With the new sun, after my horse rests, we will ride for home." Jed turned his eyes from Bright Moon. She could read his thoughts and moods. Today, he didn't want to talk about his father's death or Oliver's wounds.

Looking at him curiously, Bright Moon nodded. "Come, my husband, I will fix you something to eat."

Entering the warm kitchen behind the store, Bright Moon poured Jed a cup of coffee and started side meat to frying. "Is my son, Red Horse, okay?"

"He is fine, but Oliver has been wounded. I must get back to see about him." Jed swallowed the hot coffee.

Breaking eggs into the iron skillet, Bright Moon shrugged slightly. "Tell me, Husband, what is wrong?"

"Our father is dead." Jed spoke the words softly. "The whites killed him before I could get there to help."

"And the whites?"

"Dead." Jed nodded. "Red Horse killed two and my father killed two."

"Red Horse!"

"He has become a man. A warrior to be proud of."

The small shoulders seemed to sag. "He hasn't even had time to enjoy his youth. First, Eagle Wing, and now, Red Horse."

"Be proud of your sons." Jed swallowed the hot liquid. "They have made me proud."

Bright Moon shook her head sadly. What was pride? For eighteen years, she had lived with Crow Killer and her beloved children secluded in their beautiful mountains. There had been peace, pride was not needed.

The village of Crazy Horse sat in a small valley, only a few miles from the sacred Black Hills. In the distance, a sharp eye could see the silhouette of the dark mountains. All Sioux people believed these mountains were the home of the spirit ones, the givers of life. Every Sioux warrior would defend these sacred lands with their lives. As they approached the village, several mounted warriors rode out to greet Gall and his followers.

Eagle Wing could tell by the greeting, they had been expected. He knew Gall must have sent a rider ahead to tell the Oglala they were coming.

Dismounting before a small, humble lodge, Eagle Wing looked at the warrior, he knew, was the great Crazy Horse of the Oglala Sioux. The warrior stood erect with the air of a powerful leader. A scar ran down the face, as the scar on his own face did. His complexion was lighter than most, and the warrior before him seemed humble, a man of few words. This one, despite the scar, was handsome and dignified. Yes, this had to be Crazy Horse.

The voice was soft and friendly as the great one greeted his guests and asked them to sit at his fire. Food was brought, then the long stemmed smoking pipe. Eagle Wing noticed the chief, neither smoked nor ate. Somehow, just sitting quietly, he emanated a magnetic charm, all around him with such a powerful persona. As he ate, Eagle Wing, watched and listened to the chief's words. He knew why his people loved their strange one so.

"It is good of Gall to come to our village."

Nodding, Gall returned the compliment. "It is good to be in the village of Crazy Horse."

"You have fought?" Crazy Horse looked down at the bloody breast-plates held in Gall's hand.

"White buffalo hunters came into our country, killed our buffalo, and killed three of our young ones, just boys." Gall laid the bone chest coverings before him. "We killed all but one. He will warn the others to stay away from our lands."

Crazy Horse let his eyes study the breastplates for several minutes before speaking. "This will not stop the whites from coming. They have greed in their hearts. They want our lands, the yellow iron in our mountains, and the hides from our buffalo."

The voice was neither bitter nor hateful, but spoke with a sad foreboding of things to come. Eagle Wing thought about the greed of the white hunters at Bridger. He knew Crazy Horse's predictions would come true.

"Sitting Bull wanted me to counsel with you, and I wanted to introduce you to these Arapaho allies." Gall nodded and looked to where Eagle Wing, Grey Hair, and Cut Arm sat.

"Our Arapaho friends are welcome." Crazy Horse studied the three young warriors. "Soon, we will need all the brave hearted ones who will fight."

"It is good to meet Crazy Horse, and greet the great Touch the Clouds once again." Eagle Wing nodded then looked at Touch the Clouds, whom he had already met at Walking Horse's village.

"My friend has told me about the Arapaho Lance Bearer who speaks the tongue of both red man and white. I am curious, how did you learn the white tongue?" Crazy Horse questioned him.

"My father is Crow Killer." Eagle Wing nodded proudly. "He taught me the words and how to make marks on paper."

"We have heard of the great Lance Bearer, Bear Killer, and killer of his enemies, even here." Crazy Horse nodded. "He is said to be a mighty warrior."

"He is the greatest of warriors."

"Yet, he will not make war on the whites?" Mighty Bow sitting beside Crazy Horse asked.

"No, he stays at his lodge unless he is attacked." Eagle Wing looked at the warrior. "But, I and my friends have come to fight with Gall and Crazy Horse."

"Touch the Clouds has told me about the courage of Eagle Wing and the Lance Bearers. We thank you for coming. This will be a hard fight. This is an enemy that is strong and wishes to end our way of life." Crazy Horse explained.

"You have fought the white soldiers before?"

Crazy Horse continued. "I rode with Red Cloud. We killed many whites that followed the one called Fetterman. Now, the great Red Cloud lives on a reservation, eating the white man's meat and flour."

"Why does Gall honor us with his presence?" Touch the Clouds' voice was as deep as he was tall.

"Soon, Sitting Bull will hold a Sun Dance, and a huge celebration for all. He wishes for Crazy Horse and his people to come and honor the brave ones that dance."

"Our people will come."

"That is good. I fear we will need great strength and all the help the spirit ones can give us." Gall handed Crazy Horse a Henry repeater.

"This is for Crazy Horse. The white hunters we killed had many of these rifles that shoot many times without reloading."

The chief's strong hands turned the rifle many times examining it.

Gall explained how it worked and presented it as a gift. "Come, we will shoot this weapon."

The Sun Dance always brought a great multitude of tribal members to watch the warriors, old and young, suffer and show their spiritual strength. Hoping for a strong vision to be shown to them, each participant danced, blew his whistle, and chanted his song under the glaring sun and sometimes through the cold of night. As a spiritual ceremony, one's heart had to be pure to take part. Not all were allowed to partake in the painful ritual. A warrior had to be both strong of body and spirit to survive the ceremony, and tear loose from the leather thongs and wooden pins that kept him tethered to a stout pole.

Others drug buffalo skulls behind them. Their backs were pierced by sharp wooden awls a medicine man attached through holes in their skin. The ceremony was not for the weak of heart, and only the strongest would break loose and survive the ordeal. A religious ceremony, the Sun Dance, was the most reverent ceremony of the Sioux Nation.

Sitting Bull had danced the Sun Dance Ceremony many times, seeking visions to protect his people and to tell them what to do. This time was no different as Eagle Wing watched as the wooden pegs were attached to the medicine man. The sharp knife cut four times into his chest, yet Sitting Bull never made sound nor did he flinch in pain. This was not a religious ceremony of the Arapaho, though some participated.

Each participant danced for the people, hoping for a vision that would drive out the hated whites. Some, who could not break the rawhide thongs holding them, were cut loose and slunk away in shame. Others collapsed onto the ground as their skin parted, freeing them from the ordeal. Eagle Wing marveled at the dancers as they circled the pole with blood running down their chests and backs.

"Look, my brother." Grey Hair nudged Eagle Wing. "Cut Arm is painted in white, and he will join the dancers."

"I wish him much strength and endurance." Eagle Wing watched as the medicine man attached the rawhide thongs into Cut Arm's chest.

"He's gonna need it."

"One has to have great faith in the spirits to pass such a test." Gall stood next to the warriors, observing Cut Arm and the others. "We will watch as Sitting Bull takes his place beside your friend."

All day, Cut Arm danced and shuffled around the pole occasionally leaning back hard, attempting to break the bonds that held him. Eagle Wing and Grey Hair stood watching, trying to give their friend strength. Both could feel the pain and torture Cut Arm was feeling. Several times, one of the elders would ask him if he wanted to be released from his bonds. Shaking his head, the Arapaho danced into the night, making Eagle Wing and Grey Hair proud of him.

"Will he break loose?" Broken Leg shook his head as Cut Arm threw himself against the leather thongs again and again.

"He is stronger than I thought." Grey Hair shook his arm.

"I do not have enough faith to suffer as he does." Wolf's Head shrugged.

"Nor I." Broken Leg agreed as he watched Cut Arm continue.

Finally, with a last powerful lunge, the skin holding the wooden pegs parted, letting Cut Arm sink to the ground. Two women helped the weakened warrior to a buffalo robe and ministered to his wounds. The slits where the pegs were attached would heal, but cords of knotted skin would leave their mark. The warrior would proudly carry these scars for life. Sitting Bull's body was covered in scars he had inflicted on himself as he danced, seeking a vision. The dance was spiritual, and afterwards, many foretold several things revealed to them that the future would bring.

Eagle Wing and Grey Hair sat their horses beside Gall on a high knoll, watching the string of wagons and hundreds of horse soldiers, making their way across the flats in a long column. Each warrior was amazed as the massive caravan moved like a snake toward them.

"Soon, they will enter the beginning of the Black Hills, the Paha Sapa." Gall growled. "They are not turning this time."

"Why would they come here and break the treaty Red Cloud signed?" Eagle Wing asked.

"The treaty was put on paper many years ago." Gall shrugged. "Now, Red Cloud moved his people to the reservation, and the whites think he has given up our mountains."

"But, the treaty gave you the Black Hills for as long as the grass grows and the water flows."

"To the whites, words on paper are just that, Nephew." Gall sadly shook his head. "Just words on paper."

Several of Gall's warriors, along with the five Arapaho that rode with Eagle Wing, sat in plain sight, atop the high ridge above the white column. Cable Howard and an Indian scout leading the column rode toward them, then pulled out his farseeing telescopic lens and studied the watching warriors.

"Gall the Hunkpapa and Eagle Wing of the Arapaho." The scout looked at the Arikara warrior, Bloody Knife, sitting beside him. "I can almost read their thoughts from here. They are not happy with our presence."

"We trespass on their lands. Why should they be happy?" The warrior looked up the hill and shrugged. "I would not be happy if you invaded my lands."

"You better ride back and tell Yellow Hair we've got company."

"He will know. The Crow are with him, and they have sharp eyes." Bloody Knife took the offered glass and studied the warriors. "Eagle Wing is the one on the spotted horse?"

"Yes."

"For one so young, he is a magnificent looking warrior." The Arikara handed the glass back to Howard. "He sits his great spotted horse proudly."

"Bloody Knife, can tell that from here?" Howard grinned.

"He will be a dangerous fighter. A bad one to do battle with." The warrior reined his horse around and rode away.

"I feel you may be right about that." The scout mumbled.

Gall frowned. "Come, we will tell Sitting Bull and send riders to Crazy Horse."

Eagle Wing, seeing the lone white scout and Arikara studying him with the long glass, remembered meeting the white scout at the peace treaty. Both men studied each other, then Eagle Wing raised his rifle as Howard waved at him. Looking at the caravan of wagons and soldiers, he knew in the end Crazy Horse and Sitting Bull would lose their land.

The whites were just too numerous and powerful. They would win battles, but in the end, he knew they would be forced onto reservations. Red Cloud had already seen this, so he had saved his people the death and destruction a war with the whites would bring. The old chief was wise and once a great war chief like Crazy Horse and Sitting Bull. Red Cloud was not afraid to fight and he was not a coward. However, he had ridden the iron horse to the east, and he could see how hopeless it would be to fight against the might of the coming whites.

Eagle Wing knew what was coming, but he had given his word so he was committed to helping the Sioux. Crow Killer had tried to warn him against fighting the whites. Death, he did not fear, but the destruction of his people, the Arapaho and Cheyenne, would come sooner if he did not help Crazy Horse. The whites were hungry for land, and after the Sioux and Cheyenne were defeated, they would come for Arapaho lands.

Returning to his lodge, Eagle Wing looked around at the gathered warriors. "My friends, we have seen the might of the whites. They are strong, and I fear we are looking at death. Crow Killer said we could not defeat this enemy."

"What would Eagle Wing have us do?"

"Return to your lands." Eagle Wing looked at Grey Hair and shrugged. "Then, my brother, take your flute and go win my sister for your wife."

"And what will Eagle Wing do?"

"I have given my word to help Gall in this fight." Eagle Wing looked down at his rifle. "I will stay and fight, but I did not speak for you."

"No, we will not run like the coyote. We will all stay and fight beside Eagle Wing." Wolf's Head declared.

Shaking his head, Eagle Wing looked at the young Lance Bearers. They were the bravest of the brave. "Then, my brothers, we may die, but we will die with honor."

The small skirmishes between the encroaching pony soldiers and the warriors of Crazy Horse and Gall happened daily. The warriors attacked the woodcutters and the patrols of soldiers guarding the whites who walked the land and dug in the ground. Eagle Wing knew they were surveying the lands of the Black Hills. They used the same tripod and long seeing glass that Oliver carried with him. These whites were here to make maps. He knew they would leave when they finished, but one day, they would return. He also knew they were seeking the yellow iron as they dug holes in the ground.

Two Arapaho, Wolf's Head and Little Fox, had been wounded in the skirmishes. Both warriors lay in lodges back at the village. Neither carried serious wounds, but they would be out of the fighting for several suns. Over the past three weeks, the fighting had been only minor, with few deaths on either side. Mostly, it was sniping and harassing the whites, just letting the whites know, the Sioux were watching. A few horses had been stampeded, stolen from under the very eyes of the pony soldiers. The younger warriors were eager to show their bravery against the Crow, Arikara, and Pawnee that scouted for Yellow Hair Custer.

Each day, Eagle Wing, using his Lance, had counted coup on many whites as his powerful Appaloosa had charged through their wagons, unhorsing the white soldiers and Indian scouts. From the knoll, Crazy Horse nodded as he watched the young Arapaho fighting his way clear through a squad of whites. In battle, the whites were still green soldiers. They had been taken by surprise at the sheer bravado of the daring warrior on the spotted horse. Now, after being embarrassed by the daring warrior for days, many waited with their rifles ready to get a clear shot at this warrior on the beautiful Appaloosa.

"He fights like Crazy Horse, not for glory, only to help the people." Touch the Clouds grinned.

Nodding, the warrior carrying the blue hailstones painted across his arms and chest, kicked his horse forward. "While they watch Eagle Wing and his warriors, we will hit them from the rear."

"Why do we not quit playing war and kill these whites, my chief?"

"Sitting Bull is the head chief of all the Sioux." Crazy Horse spoke. "He says we will not attack these pony soldiers in force. But, we can harass and count coup on them. Hoka Heye."

Eagle Wing whirled as he saw Broken Leg fall from his horse. Racing the Appaloosa into the melee, he pulled the hurt warrior in front of him and raced away. Howard raised his rifle and took aim at the powerful back as the horse thundered away.

"Whose side you on, Howard?" A young Lieutenant yelled as he fired several times with his pistol. "Ours or theirs?"

"So far, Lieutenant, that warrior hasn't killed, nor will I." Howard smiled as he watched Eagle Wing carry the wounded warrior to safety.

"No, but he's making fools of all of us."

"You still got your hair." Howard turned. "And we're fools for even being here."

"The army is paying you to protect their property scout." Lieutenant Fields shook his head. "You had that heathen dead to right, but you let him get away."

"Yes, sir, but if we kill too many of them, they just might get serious and quit playing with us." Howard warned.

"We've wounded a few of them and killed a couple." The officer nodded.

"Yes, sir, but that's not yet a full-fledged battle." Howard argued. "And they've left plenty of knots on our men's heads, haven't they."

"I've seen that same warrior on that Appaloosa several times in the last days. He's caused more headaches and destruction among us than all the others combined." Fields shook his head.

"Yes, sir, he's something, ain't he, Lieutenant?"

"That he is. I wish I had a whole company of fighters like him." Fields agreed. "But, we've got to kill him."

"Not we, Lieutenant. You can kill him, but I ain't." Howard replied.

"Are you squeamish, mister?"

The scout shook his head and turned away. "Try me sometime."

Eagle Wing laid Broken Leg on the ground as Grey Hair and Cut Arm rode up.

"Is he dead?"

"No, but our friend is wounded badly."

Eagle Wing looked up as Crazy Horse and Touch the Clouds slid from their horses. Kneeling over the wounded Broken Leg, Crazy Horse examined the wound.

"Take this one to the village. The medicine men will tend to his wound." Crazy Horse nodded at Touch the Clouds. "Hurry, he is hurt badly."

Lifting Broken Leg gently, Touch the Clouds placed the wounded man in front of another Sioux warrior. "Take him, go."

"What brave hearts ride with me against the white soldiers?" Screaming his war cry, Crazy Horse charged across the small knoll that blocked the woodcutters' view, and charged straight into them. Eagle Wing followed the mighty warrior as he ran his racing horse through the circle of woodcutters and pony soldiers. Rifles fired and bullets screamed by him as he followed the warrior. Twice, they circled the whites, then Crazy Horse broke off the attack.

Later, as he sat with Grey Hair beside their cook fire, Eagle Wing spoke of the bravery of Crazy Horse. "It's like this one cannot be killed. Today, I have seen bullets pass harmlessly by him."

"Several times, I have seen him ride right through the whites without a scratch." Grey Hair nodded.

"We must send Broken Leg back to our village." Eagle Wing looked to where a medicine man of the Sioux worked over the wounded warrior.

"Who will take him?"

"Wolf's Head and Little Fox are both hurt and cannot fight, but they are strong enough to return him to his people." Eagle Wing poked at the small fire.

"They will not like this." Grey Hair shook his head. "They will know you are just trying to get them away from this battle."

"They can return when their wounds heal, but for now, it is important to get Broken Leg back to the village safely."

"I will tell them. I do not understand why we do not kill these whites." Grey Hair stood and walked off.

Several warriors rode through the village and raced to Sitting Bull's lodge, then slid from their horses. The medicine man walked from his lodge and waited for the warrior to speak.

"The whites leave our lands, my chief." Howling Coyote spoke excitedly. "Crazy Horse watches them as we speak. He sends these words."

"Bring my horse." Sitting Bull nodded. "I will see this for myself."

Following Sitting Bull, Eagle Wing and Grey Hair rode to the base of the Black Hills where the whites had been camped many miles east of the Sioux village.

Only the trailing dust, and tracks of the wagons and horses showed the whites had ever been in the valley. Crazy Horse and some of his warriors rode from the east and reined in their horses.

"The soldiers have left this place." Crazy Horse looked at Sitting Bull and shook his head. "We followed them. They leave our lands."

Sitting Bull nodded slowly. "We will let them leave without further fighting."

"There has already been fighting. Some are dead and many are wounded." Gall shook his fist. "Let us follow them and attack their wagons."

"No, we will let them go." Sitting Bull spoke. "There has been no real fighting. But, if we attack them as they leave, they will return and fight us."

Eagle Wing looked at Gall and then down the trail to the east. "I will ride down to see their diggings."

"There is nothing there, Eagle Wing." Gall was curious. "Only a muddy creek with holes in the mother earth where the whites have dug."

"I will see these holes." Nodding at Grey Hair, he started down the ridge.

"What do you look for, my brother?" Grey Hair followed.

"What the whites call yellow iron."

"And if we find it?" Grey Hair shrugged.

"If the golden metal is there and the whites have found it, they will return to this place in great numbers." The Arapaho frowned.

"Rocks will make them return in great numbers?" Grey Hair asked.

"They will cover the ground like locusts."

Eagle Wing walked along the bank of the small stream, searching out the diggings the whites had left behind. Five Arapaho Lance Bearers stood on the bank and watched him curiously. For two hours, he plunged his hands into the cold water, moving up and down the stream. He had to know if the whites found the yellow iron they coveted so much. Standing erect, he opened his hand and showed Grey Hair several small, dull yellowish pieces of rock.

"This stone is what the whites seek?" The warrior took one of the small pieces from Eagle Wing's hand.

"Crow Killer has some of these rocks." Eagle Wing explained. "He says to the white, this yellow iron is more valuable than horses, hides, or women."

"Why? You cannot eat it, nor will it keep you warm."

"What good is it?" The others stood about looking at the gold.

"They have found what they look for." Eagle Wing dropped the gold into his bullet pouch. "They will return."

"Whites are crazy."

"No, my friends, they are greedy." Eagle Wing continued. "This is gold, and it makes the white man go crazy."

Sitting Bull, Gall, and Crazy Horse looked at the gold pieces Eagle Wing held out to them. Nodding their heads slowly, they listened as he explained the value of these yellow looking rocks.

"These small stones, my chiefs, are much more valuable to the whites than the hides of the shaggies." Eagle Wing shrugged. "Crow Killer says the whites will kill for this yellow iron."

"My warriors report Yellow Hair has taken his men east toward the big river."

"Then we will split up and hunt for our winter meat." Sitting Bull nodded.

"What will the Arapaho do?" Crazy Horse looked to Eagle Wing.

"I will take my wounded home. For now, the fighting is finished."

"Will you return if the fighting starts again?" Crazy Horse looked deep into Eagle Wing's eyes. "We need brave hearts like the Lance Bearers."

"I have many hurt warriors, none dead. I do not know if they will follow me back to this place." Eagle Wing shook his head.

"And Eagle Wing?"

"I will fight with my Sioux brothers." Eagle Wing replied. "Send word when you need my help."

"That is good to know. None fight with Eagle Wing's bravery. When will you depart?" Crazy Horse asked.

"With the new sun."

"You are welcome in my lodge anytime, my friend."

CHAPTER 14

None of the Lance Bearers that rode east, following Eagle Wing and Grey Hair, had been killed, but many carried wounds on their bodies. Broken Legs' wound was great. Every Lance Bearer had counted coup on the whites, Pawnee, Arikara, and Crow scouts of Yellow Hair. All carried the new Henry repeaters, Gall had given them as gifts, as they departed their camp for the west. Shells filled the saddlebags taken from the white soldiers. Many horses stolen from the soldiers and branded with the U S mark were led by the Arapaho. No scalps had been taken. However, there was much glory, honor, and many trophies to show for their fighting.

The Arapaho warriors knew Eagle Wing felt guilty about them being wounded. Grey Hair and the others spoke with Eagle Wing over their campfires at night when they stopped, letting Broken Leg rest.

"We carry no shame, Eagle Wing. You carry no shame. We have won much honor fighting with Gall and Crazy Horse."

"In battle, men are killed and wounded." Wolf's Head smiled. "We will follow you on the war trail again."

Eagle Wing nodded. "In a few sleeps, we will be back in our lands. I am thankful none have been killed."

"I do not understand why we did not kill the whites. We fought, but were not allowed to kill." Cut Arm shook his head.

"Sitting Bull is much wiser in these ways than we are, my friend." Eagle Wing chewed on a piece of dried meat. "I think there will be plenty of chances to kill the white soldiers in the days ahead."

"Will you return to fight with Crazy Horse?"

"You have seen the might of the whites." Eagle Wing shrugged. "I have given my word to fight with the Sioux, but you, my friends, should think on this."

Cut Arm agreed, shaking his head. "They do not come to our lands yet."

"After they take land from the Sioux, they will come for our lands next." Wolf's Head spoke up.

"This is so." Grey Hair nodded. "Then, we will have to fight to save our own lands."

"I speak only for myself, but I will fight." Cut Arm added. "It is better to fight them before they make beggars of us."

The morning was peaceful and beautiful as the small party of warriors passed through the aromatic meadows. The land was painted with every colored flower; it was indeed picturesque. Grass, belly deep on the horses, gave off its sweet smell as the horse trampled it down in their passing. Birds of every kind flew up underneath the hard hooves as they passed. Several times throughout the day, resting deer, hidden in the tall grass, bounded away after they had been aroused from their resting places.

Grey Hair and Cut Arm rode in front of the small caravan that crossed the grass-covered lands, leading the party west. Eagle Wing was deep in thought. He had fought with the Sioux and counted coup many times, but had they accomplished anything? There had been no decisive battle, and the whites had only departed Sioux lands after finding what they came for. The whites were not defeated. They came and went like they already owned the Sioux lands. He rode beside the travois that carried Broken Leg across the prairie.

"I know your thoughts, Eagle Wing." The wounded one looked up. "You have led us well and you fought as no other. Do not feel ashamed."

"Thank you, Broken Leg."

"I will show my scars to my new woman with great pride." The warrior smiled.

"I did not know you had a woman."

"Not yet, but after I tell the glory of this fight, I will have one soon."

Gray Hair raised his arm in warning as several Pawnee warriors rode from their place of concealment and fired into the Arapaho party. Charging forward, Eagle Wing watched Cut Arm fall from his horse as the Pawnee rifles fired again. The new repeating rifle he carried spoke many times as he raced the Appaloosa straight into the enemy warriors. With a scream, Grey Hair and Wolf's Head hurried after Eagle Wing as he closed with the enemy warriors, fighting hand-to-hand combat with his war axe.

Seeing Cut Arm fall, Eagle Wing fought with a vengeance as he pushed into the enemy warriors, knocking them from their horses. Their bullets miraculously missed him and hit their own warriors many times. Screaming, Grey Hair charged fearing for his friend as he watched Eagle Wing being surrounded by the Pawnee. Reaching the melee, Grey Hair, Wolf's Head, and the rest of the Arapaho used their war axes as they pushed forward, knocking the Pawnee from their horses.

Every warrior was amazed. Never, had they seen a warrior fight with such fury and rage, killing enemy warriors without compassion. Eagle Wing fought like a demon, fearing nothing, only wanting to close with the enemy and kill them. In terror of the madman that seemed invincible, the Pawnee finally retreated, leaving many of their number lying dead or dying, strewn about the ground.

Grey Hair looked at the blood-covered body of Eagle Wing and the blood-splattered Appaloosa, almost turning him red. Eagle Wing ran one final Pawnee to the ground, cleaving his head as the powerful spotted horse caught up with his laboring horse. Pulling alongside the crazed warrior, Grey Hair held out his lance and stopped the Appaloosa.

"You have killed enough this day, my friend." Grey Hair looked into Eagle Wing's enraged eyes. "They are running."

"Did Grey Hair not recognize this enemy?"

"No, my friend, I was too busy fighting." Grey Hair shook his head.

"I recognized their leader. These Pawnee scouted for the pony soldiers of Yellow Hair." Eagle Wing wiped the blood from his face. "They knew we would ride this way with our injured ones. They waited here to ambush us."

"Attack Lance Bearers, why would they be so foolish?" Hide Belt questioned.

"They wanted our weapons and horses." Grey Hair shook his head. "They lost face, fighting for the whites and when we counted coup on them, so they followed us to this place to take scalps and horses."

"And they died for their foolishness." The warrior grinned.

"They left many behind on the ground." Grey Hair looked around.

Wolf's Head rode to where Grey Hair spoke with Eagle Wing. "Our brother, Cut Arm, is dead."

"Who else?"

"Iron Bull also."

"There are over twenty Pawnee dead or wounded. What will we do with the wounded ones?" Another warrior asked.

"Leave them." Eagle Wing turned back to where Cut Arm lay. "Come, we must build a travois to carry our dead."

"We could carry them on their horses."

"No, Wolf's Head, they will be carried with honor, not thrown over the back of a horse."

Suddenly, the blast of a rifle came from across the flat meadow. Grey Hair slumped slowly from his horse. Several Cheyenne warriors raced toward a wooded area as Eagle Wing leaped from his horse and knelt beside the wounded warrior. Turning Grey Hair over, Eagle Wing could see the bloody hole in the warrior's side.

"We missed one of the enemy, my brother, but he did not miss me." Grey Hair tried to smile.

The bullet had passed clean through Grey Hair's side, exiting his back. Quickly ripping a trade blanket into strips, Eagle Wing stemmed the flow of blood. "No, my brother, you did not duck."

"No, I did not see this one coming." The warrior gritted his teeth as pressure was put on the wound.

"The wound is clean. You will watch better next time."

"Yes."

As the Cheyenne warriors returned, Eagle Wing saw they led a Pawnee horse and waved another rifle and scalp in triumph.

"That one will kill no more of our friends." Two Bears, the Cheyenne, swung down from his horse beside Grey Hair, handing the wounded one the bloody scalp.

"Thank you, my brother." Grey Hair accepted the grisly trophy.

As the combined party of Cheyenne and Arapaho warriors neared the Cheyenne hunting grounds, some of the warriors split off with a wave at the Arapaho. Eagle Wing would not ride into He Dog's village. He wanted to hurry to take his dead and wounded home. Grey Hair was badly hurt and needed the help of a medicine man. Eagle Wing looked down at his friend and nodded. He would ride for Ellie Medicine Thunder as soon as they returned to the village.

Walking Horse stepped from his lodge as he heard the wailing and loud crying of the village. Looking toward the creek to the east, the tall warrior watched as four travois were pulled across the shallow creek. Hurrying quickly to the center of the village, he looked up into the bloodstained face of his nephew.

Moving to the travois, he looked down into the pale face of Broken Leg and Grey Hair, then at the dead forms covered in trade blankets. Shaking his head sadly, he knelt beside the wounded and placed his hand on their shoulders.

"How do you feel, Broken Leg?"

"I am okay, my chief." The warrior tried to smile. "It is good to be back among my people."

"And, Grey Hair, my nephew?"

"It is good to see you again, Uncle."

"We are glad you are home." Walking Horse looked over at a few gathered warriors. "Take these warriors to the lodge of Ghost Man."

Eagle Wing slid from his horse and motioned for a young horse guard to take the Appaloosa. "Bring me a fresh horse quickly."

"Yes, Eagle Wing."

"Where does my nephew ride to?"

"Grey Hair has a bad wound and fever. I go after Ellie Medicine Thunder."

"Ghost Man cannot heal his wound?"

"I fear for my brother." Eagle Wing waited as the boy brought a fresh horse from the herd. "His wound is bad."

"You have ridden far. I will go myself."

"No, Uncle, you are needed here to take care of the dead." Swinging on the horse, he nodded at Grey Hair. "Be strong, I will return quickly."

"Do not worry. I will play my flute again for Ellie Thunder."

Eagle Wing crossed the Yellowstone and passed the startled Crow warriors who now followed him south to the Crow village. No one tried to stop him. They only followed the hard-running bay horse. Riding into the Crow village, Eagle Wing slipped from the lathered horse. With the commotion outside, Red Hawk almost ran into Eagle Wing as he exited his lodge. Quickly explaining why he was there, Eagle Wing waited as Red Hawk summoned Ellie and sent for the horses. Hurrying from the lodge with her medical bag, the tall woman spoke with Red Hawk.

"We must hurry, Ellie." Eagle Wing swung up on a fresh horse. "I fear for Grey Hair."

"I will ride with you to the river." Red Hawk helped Ellie on her horse, then swung on his Appaloosa. Seeing the splattered blood all over Eagle Wing, the Crow Chief asked. "You have been in battle?"

"Yes." Kicking his horse, Eagle Wing raced for the Yellowstone. "We go."

Ellie knelt beside Grey Hair and examined the inflamed wound in his side. Shaking her head, she daubed at the bluish torn flesh with a clean cloth. Grey Hair flinched slightly as she probed into the festered bullet hole.

"I am sorry, Grey Hair, if I hurt you."

"Thank you for coming here, Medicine Thunder." Grey Hair nodded his sweaty head. "Will I live?"

Ellie looked into the feverish eyes and smiled. "You will live to ride with Eagle Wing again."

Eagle Wing, who had been ushered from the lodge, sat outside talking with Walking Horse. "The Pawnees came on us as we neared our lands."

"They grow brave with their new rifles and white friends."

"They have fewer rifles now." Eagle Wing handed Walking Horse one of the new Henry repeaters.

"These are the ones that shoot many times?" Looking at the rifle, the warrior nodded slightly.

"Yes, and they kill many times."

"Our warriors, who have gone to be with their ancestors, were killed with these weapons?"

"Yes." Eagle Wing thought of Cut Arm, the laughing one, and Iron Bull. "Both were brave Lance Bearers."

"Now, both are dead." Walking Horse's voice grew cold. "Two times they have invaded our lands and have killed. This cannot stand."

"We killed many Pawnee warriors."

"They were on our lands?"

"They were on Cheyenne hunting grounds."

"First, we will see if Grey Hair lives, then we will ride against the Pawnee. They must be punished hard before they grow braver and come to our hunting grounds."

"Does my uncle think they would be so foolish?"

"They are more numerous than the Arapaho, and now, they have these rifles that shoot many times." Walking Horse nodded solemnly. "Yes, they will come here. They think the new rifles give them strong medicine."

Rising, as Elli walked from the lodge, Eagle Wing stared at her worried face. "Tell me, Aunt, will my brother live?"

"I do not know. He has a high fever and the wound is infected." Ellie shook her head. "I have given him medicine and cleaned the wound. Now, we have to wait."

"Thank you for coming."

"I wish I could do more for him." Ellie frowned. "If he had gotten back sooner…"

"He is strong, and he has a reason to live."

"A reason to live?" Ellie looked curiously at her nephew.

"Your niece, Ellie Thunder is his reason." Eagle Wing replied.

Smiling slightly, the tall woman returned to the lodge. Yes, love was a powerful medicine, but this time would it be enough?

Eagle Wing returned to his place outside the lodge.

"Tell me of the fighting to the east, Nephew."

Eagle Wing started telling about Sitting Bull, Crazy Horse, and the skirmishing with the white soldiers, and of the gold. "I fear the real fighting has not started yet. This time they only came to look for yellow iron and make their maps through Sioux lands."

"You say the Crow and Pawnee fought alongside the whites?"

"Yes, they scouted for the white soldiers."

"Then, they are allies now?"

"I fear this is so."

"And Red Hawk?" Walking Horse looked across the village.

"Red Hawk will not attack the Arapaho, Uncle."

"Can we be sure of this? You say some of his people fought with the whites against Sitting Bull and his people."

"This is true, but I don't think he will attack you." Eagle Wing shrugged. "He is married to your sister."

"No, he wouldn't, but his young warriors might."

"They are no danger to the Arapaho."

Walking Horse nodded. "I wish Crow Killer was here."

"I would like to leave my father in peace at his valley." Eagle Wing suggested. "Crow Killer has seen enough battles and blood. Now, he should live out his days in peace."

"The Arapaho are his people." Walking Horse shook his head. "If they are in danger, he would want to know."

"Would you have me ride after him?"

"No, we will punish the Pawnee first." Walking Horse replied. "But, first we will wait and watch over Grey Hair."

Three days later, Red Hawk with three warriors rode into the Arapaho village. Many Lance Bearers had escorted them as they crossed the Yellowstone River. Ellie and Eagle Wing greeted them as they dismounted.

Hugging her husband, Ellie asked. "What does my husband do here?"

"I have come to see if Grey Hair lives and to see my wife."

"Red Hawk is welcome." Walking Horse spoke as he and Little Antelope walked up.

"He is very ill, my husband." Ellie replied.

"Will Grey Hair live?" Red Hawk knew the wounded one and Eagle Wing were more than brothers, as each had shared hardships as he and Crow Killer had.

"I don't know. The fever is still in his body." Ellie shrugged. "Only time will tell."

"This one will live." Eagle Wing nodded. "He is strong."

"My children, are they well?"

"They miss their mother."

Excusing herself, Ellie went back into the lodge. Walking Horse ordered food brought to the Crow warriors, then sat down with Red Hawk and Eagle Wing.

"The Pawnee say they were attacked by Arapaho warriors east of here as they rode to their village." Red Horse looked at Eagle Wing. "They say an Arapaho Lance Bearer, riding a spotted horse, killed many of their warriors for no reason. They say this Arapaho killed like a crazed demon."

"They speak with split tongues, my uncle." Eagle Wing flattened his hand in denial. "They lie!"

"Tell me about this fight, my nephew."

Eagle Wing quickly related the short fight to Red Hawk as he had to Walking Horse. "The Pawnee shot Grey Hair and killed two others. After that, they ran like cowards. We did take the horses and weapons of the dead and wounded ones."

"It was their blood that covered your body when you came after Medicine Thunder?"

"It was, but the Pawnee attacked my warriors from ambush first."

Red Hawk nodded. "I believe you, Nephew. The son of Crow Killer would not lie."

"It happened just as I have said."

"Eagle Wing has told you that he fought against some of my young warriors that scouted for Yellow Hair?" Red Hawk asked Walking Horse.

"He did."

"They say the Lance Bearer on the spotted horse counted many coups and much honor." Red Hawk nodded. "They say he was a demon fighter, unable to be shot, protected by the spirit people."

"It is as Soaring Bird said." Walking Horse looked at Eagle Wing.

"Tell me, Walking Horse, are we still brothers?" Red Hawk looked into the warrior's eyes. "My warriors scouted and fought with the white soldiers without my blessing."

"Red Hawk is still my brother."

"This is good." The Crow nodded. "My warriors say Yellow Hair retreats across the Missouri. Perhaps, the fighting has ended."

"No, my uncle." Eagle Wing produced the yellow nuggets. "The white, gold hunters will return soon."

"Eagle Wing is probably right. The whites lust after the yellow iron." Red Hawk examined the small rocks.

"Just like a Crow, I know, lusts after horses." Walking Horse smiled.

"Have you met Sitting Bull and Crazy Horse of the Sioux?"

"Yes, Sitting Bull is a great medicine man."

Red Hawk nodded. "And Crazy Horse?"

"He is the greatest of fighters." Eagle Wing nodded, remembering the quiet one who rode straight through the whites and Indian scouts. "No warrior is greater."

Walking Horse spoke quietly as he looked at Red Hawk. "The Pawnee attacked and killed my people. I say this, Red Hawk, as a friend, they must be punished. Soon, I will raid their villages."

"I understand the words of Walking Horse." The dark head nodded slowly.

"This will not cause trouble between our people?"

"The Pawnee fight for the soldiers, not the Crow." Red Hawk shook his head. "The Crow also scout for the whites, but we do not honor each other."

"That is good."

"I will say nothing of your plans."

Walking Horse nodded, then stood up. "You and Eagle Wing will eat with me tonight."

Little Antelope walked from the lodge and motioned at Eagle Wing. "Grey Hair wishes to speak with you, my nephew."

"Will he live?" Red Hawk asked the small woman as Eagle Wing passed into the lodge.

"His fever has broken. My sister believes his chances are good." Little Antelope smiled.

Eagle Wing sat next to the buffalo robe bed Grey Hair rested on. "You look much better, my brother."

"I feel better." The face was still pale, but there was no fever. The warrior was stronger. "Thanks to Medicine Thunder and Little Antelope."

"My aunt is a good medicine woman."

"Yes, I owe her my life." Grey Hair nodded. "Now, I can play my flute for Ellie again."

"When you feel better, my brother, we will ride to the valley of Crow Killer."

"Then, I must hurry and get well."

Two days later, Red Hawk with Ellie and his warriors had returned to their village. Grey Hair was stronger, and his wound was less inflamed and starting to heal. Walking Horse led Eagle Wing and thirty Lance Bearers south and east toward Pawnee lands. The Arapaho Chief was determined to punish the Pawnee for invading Cheyenne hunting grounds and killing Cut Arm and Iron Bull. As Chief of the Arapaho, Walking Horse had to move against the Pawnee. He knew they would come into Arapaho lands if they were allowed to kill without being punished.

The midsummer days were hot as the Arapaho entered Pawnee hunting grounds. Stripped down to their breechcloths and weapons, the Lance Bearers sat their horses as they looked out from the woods at the huge Pawnee village. For four days, their best tracker had followed the dim tracks of the Pawnee warriors that had attacked Eagle Wing and his returning warriors. Black Bird, the Lance Bearer with the eyes of a hawk, led the warriors, following the trail of the Pawnee to this village. There was no mistake this was the village of the evildoers, the killer of the Arapaho warriors.

Walking Horse held up his rifle as his black eyes riveted on the village. "Today, we avenge Cut Arm and Iron Bull. Eagle Wing, take five warriors and run off their pony herd."

"What will Walking Horse do?" Eagle Wing asked.

"Kill." The voice was hard and cold. "We ride through their village and kill any warriors we see. After today, these Pawnee dogs will not dare come into our lands and kill our people. Be brave, Lance Bearers. Make the people proud."

The line of warriors nodded as they held up their rifles. The ornamented Lance heads showed from each arrow quiver. These assembled Arapaho were the greatest fighters on the plains and they were eager to attack the Pawnee.

"I will ride with Eagle Wing so he does not get lost." Wolf's Head laughed quietly.

"Eagle Wing will go first, to run off their horses so they cannot follow us." Walking Horse motioned with his rifle. "If there are any left alive."

Black Bird pointed. "See, the lazy ones do not even keep horses tied by their lodges."

The great horse herd grazed the lush prairie grass on the south side of the village. A muddy stream with high, steep banks separated the herd from the Pawnee lodges. Slipping along the wooded side of the village, the five raiders with Eagle Wing watched as young horse herders sat around the herd.

"Do not kill the young ones guarding the horses if you do not have to."

"Eagle Wing shows mercy to these dogs?" Little Fox spoke up. "I say we kill whoever comes before us."

"They are just children. Kill all the warriors you see." The hard eyes stared down the warrior. "No children will die."

"Children grow up to be warriors."

"We will slip across the gorge and run the horses to the west." Eagle Wing motioned the warriors forward. "They will run straight and not try to leap down the high banks."

"It is a good plan." Wolf's Head agreed.

Crossing the deep gorge at the end of the herd, the raiders were discovered as soon as they rode up out of the creek bed. The frantic warning cries of the young horse herders brought a few mounted Pawnee warriors racing toward the herd.

"Start the herd running, Wolf's Head." Eagle Wing turned his Appaloosa. "If Little Fox wants to kill, he will ride with me to cut the Pawnee off."

"Eeeoh!" The scream came as Little Fox whipped his horse, racing to confront the oncoming warriors. Eagle Wing had to admire the young warrior as he showed no fear as they cut in front of the Pawnee. Hearing the sudden outburst of rifle fire coming from the village, the Pawnee facing them turned their attention momentarily toward the village. Surging forward, Little Fox brought a Pawnee down with his rifle, then struck another with his war axe. Eagle Wing killed a third and watched as the other warriors raced back to the village.

"Hurry, Little Fox, we follow Wolf's Head and the horses."

"The cowards run like rabbits." Little Fox taunted the fleeing Pawnee.

"They are not cowards. They go to protect their women and children."

Wolf's Head had the horses running swiftly down the edges of the deep gorge, pushing the herd hard to the west. Racing the flying Appaloosa, Eagle Wing caught up with the two blanket-waving warriors that rode with Wolf's Head. Behind them, they could hear the loud gunfire coming from the village. Little Fox fired his rifle into the air and yelled his war cry.

"Save your shells, the horses are running." Wolf's Head admonished the excited warrior.

An hour later, the huge herd had tired, slowing to a trot as Walking Horse and his warriors caught up to them. Far behind, Eagle Wing could see a few Pawnee following at a distance, waiting for more of their warriors to catch up. Two hundred or more horses ran before the raiders as the warriors whooped and hollered. Many older horses, colts, and slower broodmares had become stragglers, falling away from the herd.

Walking Horse rode up beside Eagle Wing. "We have done well this day, Nephew."

"Yes, we have many horses."

"There will be more Pawnee villages near." Walking Horse looked over his shoulder at the distant Pawnee and shook his head. "If a Lance Bearer held back because of so few warriors like they do, they would be dishonored."

"They wait for others to come." Eagle Wing motioned to Wolf's Head, Little Fox, and a warrior named Rides His Horse. "We will send them back."

"Be careful, Nephew."

"I remember my friends, Cut Arm and Iron Bull, this day."

Rifles roared from behind the herd as Eagle Wing ran his Appaloosa straight at the following Pawnee. Seeing the warrior on the spotted horse approaching at a run, they knew him to be the crazed one. Hesitating, the Pawnee turned and raced back to their village.

"Look, my brother." Wolf's Head jeered as he reined his horse in beside Eagle Wing. "Twenty run from four."

"Cowards." Little Fox spat, and started forward.

"Be careful, Little Fox, they may be trying to lure us into another ambush." Eagle Wing held up his hand. "We return to the herd."

"Does the great Eagle Wing fear these puny Pawnee?"

As Eagle Wing turned and rode back to the west, Wolf's Head warned. "You are lucky, warrior, he does not kill you."

Little Fox shook his head. "He rides away from danger. Perhaps this one is a coward."

"I would not speak these words again, warrior, if I were you." Wolf's Head pulled his war axe.

CHAPTER 15

*B*lack Bird rode far behind the weary horse herd as they were pushed to the safety of the Arapaho hunting grounds. The Pawnee could come in great numbers as soon as reinforcements arrived from other villages. With winter coming, losing so many valuable horses would endanger the whole village. Starvation in the cold times was harder on a tribe than losing warriors, trying to bring back the horses needed to hunt the shaggies. Knowing the Pawnee were in a frenzy, Walking Horse sent the warrior to watch their back trail for any enemy warriors.

"What will we do when they come, my chief?" Wolf's Head asked as he watched the warrior ride away.

"Tell the warriors to catch two of the best buffalo runners and lead them." Walking Horse nodded. "When Black Bird warns us, we will stampede the loose horses and turn away as they pass."

Eagle Wing nodded. "That is a good plan, Uncle."

"Catch two extra horses for Black Bird. We are not enough to fight so many."

"I will catch you two horses also, my chief." Wolf's Head laughed and rode away.

"He is a brave warrior." Eagle Wing nodded. "He has fought well in every battle."

"Yes, but sometimes the brave are foolish and die an early death. We need all our warriors." Walking Horse explained.

Two days from the Pawnee village, the herd had to be abandoned. After receiving reinforcements, many Pawnee warriors had closed in on the raiders. Walking Horse led his warriors away after stampeding the tired horses into a slow run to the south. Hiding with their captured horses, the Arapaho watched as the Pawnee passed. Nodding, the Lance Bearers turned and rode for home.

"They have lost many of their best buffalo runners, many warriors, and a few rifles." Walking Horse looked proudly at his warriors. "That is enough."

"It is never enough." Little Fox shook his head. "Never."

"One day, your mouth will get you in trouble." Wolf's Head warned.

Eagle Wing and Grey Hair sat in front of the lodge, enjoying the warm sunshine. Several young maidens passed by, smiling coyly. Two-Eyed Dog sat beside them, whistling softly as he braided a rawhide rope. The warrior with the two different colored eyes was in high spirits. His wedding was only two sleeps away.

"Why does Two-Eyed Dog braid a new rope?" Grey Hair eased against the backrest. "I thought you had already caught Flower Leaf."

Shaking his head, the warrior smiled and continued working on the rope. It was customary for warriors to harass and banter the one about to be married. However, no words would bother him today.

Eagle Wing looked at Grey Hair. "When will my friend be strong enough to travel to Crow Killer's valley?"

"Soon." Grey Hair replied. "Very soon."

"Do you need me to play the flute for Ellie Thunder?" Two-Eyed Dog asked harmlessly.

"You, my friend, are far too ugly to play a beautiful flute."

"Perhaps your words are true, but I would not sit here and let a weak white steal my woman." Two-Eyed Dog smiled. "Maybe, he already has."

Frowning at the warrior, Grey Hair turned his attention on Eagle Wing. "Two-Eyed Dog is right. While I sit here, the white has more time with Ellie."

"And?"

"I will speak with Walking Horse. With the new sun, we will ride to the valley of Crow Killer."

"You cannot leave so soon, my friends." Two-Eyed Dog seemed hurt. "Do you forget my wedding?"

"Then, we will leave as soon as you are married." Grey Hair replied.

"That is good." Two-Eyed Dog smiled. "My friends make me a happy man."

As the friends talked, Black Bird rode in and slid from his horse. Taking a seat beside Eagle Wing, he held out a beautiful skinning knife. "I found this where we fought with the Pawnee."

"You have ridden far into their lands alone and that is very dangerous, my friend." Grey Hair frowned.

"Walking Horse sent me to see if they come to attack our people."

"Do they ride here?"

"They do not leave their village." The warrior passed the knife to Eagle Wing. "Their women still wail and mourn the death of their warriors and loss of their horses."

"It is a beautiful knife." Eagle Wing tested the sharpness. "The steel blade came from the whites."

"I make a wedding present for Two-Eyed Dog. He may need to cut his bonds and run from Flower Leaf."

"Not you too, Black Bird." Two-Eyed Dog acted hurt.

"It is only a joke, my friend, but the knife is yours."

"I thank you, Black Bird."

The wedding ceremony took little time, but the dancing and celebration lasted throughout the night. Flower Leaf had recovered and was beautiful in her new wedding clothes. With all the celebration and noise, Walking Horse had sent several of the younger warriors, not yet Lance Bearers, to guard the horse herd and watch for any raiders. The Pawnee had lost many horses, warriors, and much pride. He knew one day, they would ride against the Arapaho in revenge. A night like tonight would be the perfect time to attack an unsuspecting village.

"My uncle, with the new sun, Grey Hair and I will travel to the lodge of Crow Killer."

"Is Grey Hair strong enough to make such a journey?" Walking Horse looked at Grey Hair.

"Love makes one strong." Eagle Wing looked to where Two-Eyed Dog and Flower Leaf were dancing. "See how happy they are."

"I thought after you saved the Nez Perce woman from the Rics, she would want you as a husband." Walking Horse remembered the way Flower Leaf looked at Eagle Wing back at the big river.

Eagle Wing shook his head and smiled. "They looked at each other the first time they met. No, their hearts touch only each other."

"We will ride out with the new sun." Grey Hair suggested. "If you think the people will be safe while we are gone."

"The village will be safe." Walking Horse assured him. "Perhaps, one day, the Pawnee will come, but not until after the meat taking times."

Eagle Wing sat his horse beside Grey Hair as they looked north, across the huge valley of Crow Killer. Elk, deer, and a few wild horses dotted the vast meadows. Eagle Wing missed these lands and it was good to be home.

Kicking their horses, they made their way down the steep grade that leveled out onto belly deep grass. They had been four days on the trail. The ride back had taken longer than usual. Eagle Wing had held the horses to a slow walk most of the way so Grey Hair would be in less pain.

"How are you, my friend?"

"I feel fine, and soon I will see Ellie." Grey Hair smiled.

Eagle Wing heard the mule's long bray as they neared the cabin. Red Horse came across the meadow, racing toward them. Whooping and hollering, he reined in hard as he passed them and whirled his horse.

"You're alive, my brother. You have come home."

"I'm alive alright and I'm home." Eagle Wing smiled.

"And you brought Grey Hair." Red Horse laughed. "I don't think Oliver will be happy."

"How are the folks?"

The smile left the face. "They're fine."

"What's wrong, Red Horse?"

"Come, I'll race you to the cabin."

Eagle Wing held up his hand. "Grey Hair has been wounded and must go slowly."

"You have been in battle!" Red Horse exclaimed. "How were you wounded?"

"I did not duck, young one."

"Was it a great battle? Did you kill many? Tell me, Grey Hair!"

"It will wait until we speak with Crow Killer." Grey Hair replied. "I will only tell the story once."

"Did you kill many?" Red Horse was persistent.

The horses splashed across the creek and on toward the cabin where Jed, Bright Moon, Oliver, and Ellie waited excitedly. Sliding from their horses, Eagle Wing shook hands with Jed, then hugged his mother and sister. Nodding at Oliver, he turned and helped Grey Hair to a seat at the wooden table.

"Grey Hair has been wounded in battle." Red Horse blurted out.

"I am fine. Ellie Medicine Thunder took care of my wounds."

"My Aunt is a good medicine woman." Ellie brought Grey Hair a cup of water.

"She is that." Grey Hair looked at the beautiful girl. "Thank you, Ellie."

"We will fix you something to eat, my son." Bright Moon turned to the cabin.

"Thank you, Mother."

Taking a seat, Jed looked across the table. "Tell me, how you were wounded?"

"I will let Eagle Wing tell the story." Grey Hair looked toward the cabin. "I was knocked out through most of the fight."

Eagle Wing quickly told of the attack by the Pawnee, how Grey Hair was wounded, and Walking Horse's raid on the Pawnee village. Finally, he told about their fights with the whites to the east and the gold he had found. Pulling the small nuggets from his bullet pouch, he laid them out on the table.

"This is high-grade ore." Oliver picked one up and examined it.

"Then the whites will know this also?"

"They will know, my friend. Believe me, they will know." Oliver picked up another small nugget.

Eagle Wing looked at the tall one. "Then, the whites will return to the land of the Sioux?"

"They will if I know my greedy, white brethren. I've seen men go mad looking for gold. Yes, Eagle Wing, they'll return and soon, that's if they ever left." Oliver explained.

"What do you say?" Eagle Wing looked at the young white man.

Looking at the nuggets, Oliver shook his head. "When white men see nuggets like these, they go crazy. I figure some of the white soldiers and maybe the surveyors stayed behind, hidden in the hills."

"This is what I told Crazy Horse and Sitting Bull."

"You fought with these chiefs against the whites?" Jed picked up his cup.

"It was not fighting, my uncle." Grey Hair spoke up. "Play fighting mostly. Your son counted many coups and took much honor on this battlefield."

"But, there was no killing?"

"A few on both sides were killed, but the Arapaho did not kill." Eagle Wing shook his head.

"Not until the Pawnee attacked us on our way back to the village, then we killed." Grey Hair spoke.

Eagle Wing stood up and walked over to where he had laid his blankets and rifles against the cabin. Returning, he placed a Henry repeater in Jed's hands.

"This new rifle is for you, my father."

Taking the Henry, Jed ran his hands over the walnut stock softly. "I have seen one at Bridger. It is a thing of beauty."

"That beauty kills many times." Grey Hair watched as Eagle Wing turned and entered the cabin. "Your son is a great warrior among the Sioux, Cheyenne, and Arapaho. He counted many coups, took horses and rifles, and fought with much bravery against the whites, Pawnee, and Crow."

"Crow?" Jed looked hard at Grey Hair.

"Yes, the Crow scouted with the Pawnee against the Sioux."

"Were any Crow killed?"

"No, Crow Killer, but we had great fun counting coup on them." Grey Hair nodded proudly. "Later, we did kill many Pawnee or Eagle Wing did."

Red Horse smiled as he listened to the warrior brag on his brother. Because of his youth, Crow Killer forbade him from riding with his brother to fight with Gall and Crazy Horse. Nothing excited him more than the thought of riding into battle against his enemies. Soon, when he became of age, he would become a Lance Bearer and fight.

Jed looked at the cabin, then back at Grey Hair. "Will my son return to the east and join Crazy Horse?"

"If the whites return, he has given his word to help."

"The whites are powerful."

"The ones we counted coup against were young and weak."

"Do not be fooled, Grey Hair." Jed frowned. "They are mighty in war and they outnumber our people."

"We cannot just give our lands to them."

"No, Crazy Horse would not do that without a fight." Jed smiled as Eagle Wing rejoined them.

"Where is Grandfather?"

Red Horse looked at his father, then looked away. Jed sat quietly for several minutes, then looked at his son. "Your grandfather is dead."

"Dead?"

Sadly, Jed told about the fight with the whites from Bridger and how Wilson had died. "Your grandfather killed two whites before he died and Red Horse killed the other two."

"It's always the whites who kill and destroy. I should've killed the trapper instead of just cutting his ear." Eagle Wing clenched his fists.

"Your grandfather rests in peace now with his sons." Jed shook his head. "His killers are dead."

Dawn broke brightly over the valley as Eagle Wing walked from Wilson's cabin and joined Jed and Bright Moon at the table. Looking out across the pastures, in these high mountains, everything was peaceful and serene as it should be. Elk could be heard bugling, sounding their call across the valley. Occasionally, during the night, the high-pitched call of a wolf was heard. Trees lining the small creek were filled with birds, calling out their songs. A woodpecker, busily at work on a defenseless mountain pine, sounded his pecking across the treetops.

Looking out over the grazing herd and pastures, life here was peaceful. Yet, the outside world and its battles called to him. He often recalled Soaring Bird's prophecy as he thought of the old medicine man's words. He knew these mountains and valleys could not hold him. His spirit was too wild. Something, he couldn't understand, summoned him from across the high places.

"It is good to have you home, Brother." Ellie brought coffee and sweet cakes, then poured everyone a cup.

"It's good to be home." Eagle Wing bit into a cake. "Thank you, Ellie."

"How long do you stay?"

"Only a few days until Grey Hair regains his strength."

"Do you return to Walking Horse's village?" Jed asked.

"Yes." Eagle Wing smiled and told about Two-Eyed Dog and Flower Leaf's wedding, and how the Lance Bearers had sewn their lodge flap so they couldn't get out.

"She was not like Squirrel Tooth at all." Jed smiled, remembering the young Nez Perce.

"No husband, she was a woman." Bright Moon shook her head.

Eagle Wing looked at Ellie and smiled. "Today, I will take Oliver and Red Horse hunting."

A frown came from the beautiful face as she understood his reasons. She knew he wanted to give Grey Hair time alone with her, away from the others. The frown worried him. Maybe, Grey Hair was too late.

"If you hunt, watch for the black mountain cat. He still stalks the land." Jed noticed the look that passed between the siblings.

"I will watch for his tracks."

"Red Horse knows where the cat sleeps during the day. His lodge is on a lower trail, leading from the north ridge."

"I know the place." Eagle Wing nodded. "Red Horse almost killed himself trying to jump his horse over the ridge once while you were away."

"You did not tell me of this." Jed frowned.

"Father, if I told you everything that one did, you'd lock him up for good."

"I imagine some things are better off not knowing." Jed laughed.

"If Crazy Horse and Sitting Bull go to war against the whites, Chalk Briggs will have trouble bringing his wagon trains west."

"Has Eagle Wing heard this?"

"Only that the Bozeman Trail would be closed to all whites, and that's the immigrant road that goes past Bridger." Eagle Wing replied.

"Did Crazy Horse speak these words?"

"Gall."

Oliver walked up and to Grey Hair's disgust, smiled brightly at Ellie. He could see from her looks, she welcomed the white's advances. Perhaps, he had waited too long in playing his flute.

"Where is Red Horse?"

"He's milking the cow." Oliver smiled as Ellie handed him a cup of coffee.

"I thought perhaps, the young one still sleeps."

"No, sir, he'll be here directly."

"Today, Oliver, we will hunt the black cat."

"Hunt?" Oliver looked at Ellie. "But, I was going to ride."

Eagle Wing frowned at the young white, then looked at Ellie. "Today, you, me, and Red Horse will hunt."

"Yes, sir." Oliver nodded. "I reckon my riding can wait."

Jed looked curiously at his son, then at Ellie. Picking up his coffee cup, he walked to the cabin where Bright Moon was preparing breakfast. The cabin smelled of side meat and potatoes cooking and fresh coffee.

"Our son tries to play Cupid." Jed smiled.

"What is Cupid?" Bright Moon pulled brown biscuits from the fire.

"Cupid is someone who tries to get two people together, I reckon."

"You mean Ellie and Grey Hair?"

"Yes."

"His Cupid will fail." Bright Moon flipped the side meat. "I think Ellie has looked at Oliver."

"He would take her back east." Jed frowned. "He won't stay here."

"She has talked to me about the east. I think she wants to go."

"And leave our valley?"

"Our valley, my husband, not hers." Bright Moon turned to face Jed. "She is young, just as Eagle Wing. This valley cannot hold their spirits."

"Will we lose all our children?" Jed questioned. "All of them?"

"Yes, in time, I fear even Red Horse will leave." Bright Moon smiled sadly. "He already has dreams of battle and glory."

"Battle and glory." Jed repeated. "What has battle and glory done for me?"

"You have this valley, my husband, and me." Bright Moon looked into his dark eyes. "Do you regret that?"

"Of course not."

"Our children will choose their own path. There is nothing we can say or do to stop it."

"How did you become so wise?"

"By living with the greatest and wisest warrior of all." She hugged him, then ushered him from the cabin. "You will make me burn breakfast."

Eagle Wing, with Oliver and Red Horse in tow, rode their horses to the north pass, then turned them loose to return to the herd. His young brother knew the haunts of the big cat and exactly where to find him.

Earlier, Eagle Wing had nodded toward Grey Hair as they ate. He wanted to get Oliver away from Ellie so the warrior could have time alone with his sister. After the looks she had given Oliver over coffee, he feared Grey Hair had come too late.

How could his sister look at Oliver when a great warrior and Lance Bearer like Grey Hair wanted her for his wife? Women! He shook his head, knowing he would never understand them.

"This cat is smart, Brother." Red Horse pulled Eagle Wing back from his thoughts. "Even the great Crow Killer and Red Hawk have not been able to kill this one."

"Even the smart ones will sometimes make a mistake."

"Well, we'll see. His lodge is down there." Red Horse pointed down the small steep path.

"Oliver, wait up here while we go down." Eagle Wing nodded at the tall white. "Watch closely."

Red Horse laughed. "Yes, Oliver, this one is big enough to have you for his dinner."

Treading their way slowly and quietly down the gravel path, both hunters studied the tangle of bushes and trees that lined the high side of the gorge. Somewhere ahead, they knew the cat waited and had probably already sensed their being down in his lair. Eagle Wing had seen the huge cat before, when he was out hunting, but this was the first time he hunted the animal. It's hard to slip up on a cat this old without him knowing of their presence. Crow Killer had told him how the whites hunted the big cats with dogs that treed them. He was a hunter and didn't need dogs.

Today, the black hide of the cat would hang in the barn, next to the bear hides. Moving cautiously, Red Horse pointed to the wall with the flat overhang fifteen feet above where they stood. Eagle Wing could see the claw marks and slight path the cat used to climb the vertical wall.

"He's up there." Red Horse whispered. "Father and Red Hawk tracked him here to his lodge once before."

"Ready your arrow, little brother. I will flush him out for you."

Before Eagle Wing could take his first step upward, a black form passed over their heads in a mighty leap, then in a mere flash, bounded up the trail out of sight. Red Horse's arrow missed its target by inches as the cat disappeared into the undergrowth. Shaking their heads, the two brothers laughed and started back up the trail when they heard the sound of a rifle go off. Racing up the steep trail, they found Oliver trying to extricate himself from under the body of the dead cat. Blood covered the hunting shirt and britches of the tall white.

Red Horse whooped. "You got him, Oliver! Are you hurt?"

"No, I don't think so." Oliver looked down at his bloody clothing.

"You counted coup on him for sure." Red Horse helped Oliver to his feet.

"I was lucky. I thought he had me for sure." Oliver shook his head.

"Oliver has done well this day." Eagle Wing praised the shaking hunter. "We will skin the cat and return to the cabin."

Ellie and Grey Hair sat at the table talking when they spotted the three hunters crossing the creek. Seeing Oliver kneel at the water with bloody clothes, Ellie jumped from her seat and raced to the creek. Grey Hair watched as she grabbed him and looked at his clothes.

Walking to where Grey Hair sat, Eagle Wing looked at his friend's sad face, then down at the broken flute, burning on the outside fire.

"I did come too late, my friend."

"I am sorry, Grey Hair."

"I too am sorry."

Jed walked from the cabin and looked to where Ellie was walking with Oliver from the creek. "Has Oliver been injured?"

"No, Father. He killed the black cat, and it's the cat's blood that covers him." Red Horse placed the hide on the table.

Relieved, Jed straightened out the huge black hide across the table. "We will cure the hide for Oliver."

"Yes, it will make a good wedding present and covering for his bed." Red Horse teased.

"Be quiet, young one." Eagle Wing frowned.

Ellie looked curiously at Eagle Wing as Grey Hair walked toward Wilson's cabin. "Where does Grey Hair go?"

"He leaves, to be alone." Eagle Wing pointed down at the beautiful flute consumed in fire.

"Come, Oliver, we will peg the hide and scrape it." Red Horse sensed the tightness in the air. "It will keep you warm in the cold times."

Ellie looked at the broken flute, then at Eagle Wing. "Why has Grey Hair burned his flute?"

"You should know, Sister."

"But, what have I done?"

"You have taken his heart." With one look at the burning flute, Eagle Wing followed Grey Hair to Wilson's cabin.

Two days later, the little mule's braying brought Jed from the cabin as the sun was beginning to set in the west. Five Arapaho warriors and three Sioux rode across the creek and reined in before the cabin. Jed greeted the warriors as they slid from their tired horses and bade them welcome. He could tell by the condition of the horses, the warriors had ridden hard to the valley.

"Turn your horses loose and sit at my table." Jed asked Ellie to bring hot coffee for the riders. "You have come far and in a hurry."

Wolf's Head nodded. "Walking Horse has sent us to bring these warriors to your lodge to find Eagle Wing and Grey Hair."

"Drink, my friends, then we will smoke and talk." Jed watched as Ellie poured coffee for the warriors. "Red Horse, get your brother and Grey Hair."

Walking up to the seated warriors, Eagle Wing recognized Stone Fist, the nephew of Gall. Greeting the Sioux and Arapaho warriors, he fixed a place for Grey Hair to sit.

"My friends, it is good to see you again."

"It is good to see you and Grey Hair again." Two-Eyed Dog smiled.

Eagle Wing knew whatever brought the warrior, so far away from Flower Leaf, had to be important. Plus, Gall's nephew this far west, he knew they came for him. They must need him in the east. Introducing Jed to Stone Fist, he waited as the men smoked and drank their coffee.

"It is good to see Broken Leg has healed from his wound." Grey Hair spoke to his friend.

"And Grey Hair, how is the wound?" Broken Leg looked at Ellie and smiled. "And how is Ellie Thunder?"

After several minutes of small talk and smoking, Wolf's Head looked across the table at Jed. "As I said, Walking Horse has sent us to bring Stone Fist to your valley."

"Your words must be important for you to ride your horses so hard."

"They are important." Stone Fist spoke up. "Gall wishes for the mighty Eagle Wing and his warriors to return to his village."

"There is more trouble?"

The dark head nodded. "The whites move into the Black Hills. Crazy Horse says they must be stopped before more overrun our sacred mountains."

Jed looked at the warrior. "Why is my son needed?"

"Eagle Wing is great in battle. He gives our warriors strength with his presence. He is a great leader, and they will follow him." The Sioux explained. "He also speaks the white tongue."

"Crazy Horse needs him to help lead our people against the pony soldiers." Another warrior spoke up.

Stone Fist nodded. "This is true. Eagle Wing is a great war leader."

"Has the fighting begun or do they still just pretend at war?" Grey Hair questioned.

"Crazy Horse has already killed several of the ones that dig in the ground." Stone Fist frowned. "This is no longer play, my friend. These whites desecrate our sacred lands."

"You will eat and rest here today." Eagle Wing glanced at Bright Moon. "We will leave with the coming of the new sun."

"This is good, Eagle Wing." Stone Fist smiled.

As Bright Moon and Ellie brought food for the new arrivals, Jed motioned for Eagle Wing to walk with him down to the creek. Jed and his son had always been close until they had been separated on his eighteenth birthday. Always an obedient son, Eagle Wing wanted his father, Crow Killer, to be proud of him. Even at a young age, Jed could see the inner strength and steadiness of the youngster.

"A fight with the whites will be dangerous, my son."

"I have seen the great strength of the whites." Eagle Wing nodded. "I know this, my father, but Soaring Bird has seen me riding this trail in his smoke, and I have given my word to fight with Sitting Bull and Crazy Horse."

"A warrior is only as good as his word."

"Would Crow Killer have me break my word to the Sioux and stay here, safe in your valley, while others fight and die?" Eagle Wing asked.

"Your mother and I worry about you." Jed shook his head. "Yes, my son, I wish you would reconsider riding to the east. Stay here in our valley and live in peace."

"Would you really have me do this?" Eagle Wing looked questioningly at Jed. "I have given my word to help the people in this fight."

"Even if it means your death?"

"Soaring Bird did not speak of my death or my life, only that the Spirit ones wanted me to help the people."

"I can say no more. Tell me, does Grey Hair look at your sister?" Jed asked.

"He came here to ask her to be his wife, but that time has passed." Eagle Wing replied.

"Something has happened?"

"I think Ellie prefers Oliver for a husband."

"Oliver is white. He would take her from our mountains." Jed shook his head. "What has she told Grey Hair?"

"Grey Hair has broken his flute and threw it into the fire." Eagle Wing shrugged. "You know what this means."

"I know, my son. The flute is a warrior's most valued possession when seeking a squaw." Jed frowned.

"Did you play the flute for my mother?"

"No, I never could master the flute, but your mother took me anyway." Jed smiled. "Perhaps, one day you will find a woman to play the flute for."

"My father knows I do not play the flute."

CHAPTER 16

*E*agle Wing studied each warrior as they sat around the small fire outside the cabin. All were young and most had ridden with him when he rode to Gall's village. With the coming of the new sun, he would lead these fine young men again to the east and maybe to their death. Eagle Wing was still young himself, and yet, these Lance Bearers looked to him for leadership. He wondered if they followed him because of the words of the old medicine men, Spotted Panther and Soaring Bird.

The light of the fire reflected off each face as the warriors sat listening intently as Jed told how he had become the owner of the paint horse grazing with the herd. Now, the paint was too old to carry Crow Killer on a hard campaign. However, Jed still rode the old horse when he was riding the valley. He had been a great one in his day, the strongest war horse Jed had ever ridden. Only the spotted Appaloosa of Red Hawk could match the speed and strength of the paint horse.

Stone Fist looked at Jed. "It would be good if Crow Killer would join Crazy Horse in this battle."

"No, my friend, my place is here, unless the Arapaho people need me to fight their enemies." Jed shook his head. "I have fought my battles and I will remain in this valley."

"You do not believe Crazy Horse is right to fight the whites?"

Jed looked at the Sioux. "Crazy Horse is right to protect his people and hunting grounds."

"Then, why do you not fight?"

"Hear me, Stone Fist, the whites are mighty in war. I fear the Sioux people will suffer greatly, and in the end, they'll have to move onto a reservation anyway."

"At least we will fight, and maybe, die like men." Stone Fist glared.

"At one time, I too thought as you do, but not anymore." Jed did not let the hot words make him angry.

"I apologize for my bad manners." Stone Fist dropped his head. "None can deny the loyalty and bravery of Crow Killer. Your words are probably true, but we have to try."

"I know you do. Good luck, my friends."

The early sun found Eagle Wing, Wolf's Head, Stone Fist, and several others on the north trail leading out of the valley. Surprisingly, halfway up the grade, Eagle Wing spotted Oliver following them with his surveyor equipment loaded on a pack animal. Something must have happened. Earlier, Broken Leg, Two-Eyed Dog, and others had ridden south to take Grey Hair back to the Arapaho village. After a great deal of arguing, Grey Hair finally agreed, knowing he was not strong enough. Eagle Wing would take the shortest route to Bridger's Post, Then, he would pick up Cheyenne warriors at He Dog's village and wait for Broken Leg and the Arapaho warriors to ride east with him.

Reining in at the ridge, where he could see the large valley below him, Eagle Wing studied the distant cabin for several minutes. As Oliver rode up and joined them, Eagle Wing looked at him curiously.

"We did not know you were riding with us, Oliver."

Shrugging, the tall young man would not look at Eagle Wing. "I will go with you as far as Bridger. It's time for me to return to the east."

"You are welcome, my friend." Eagle Wing could see Oliver was dejected, but said no more.

"Thank you." Oliver was surprised Eagle Wing acted friendly to him.

"Take care of the folks, little brother."

"You take care of yourself and you too, Oliver." Red Horse sat his horse watching as Eagle Wing led the warriors and disappeared around the first curve in the north trail. For once, he didn't have a smile on his face as he worried for his brother.

The eight riders had ridden their horses hard to reach Blackhorse Crossing on their second day. Swimming the Snake River at the narrow ford, they dismounted and made camp for the night. They were in no hurry since Broken Leg and his party would take longer to drop off Grey Hair at the Arapaho village, then ride on to He Dog's village.

Broken Leg reined in his bay horse at the big river and called a halt for the day. They made camp near the crossing, staying away from the jumble of logs, where the fight with the Comanche had taken place. All the warriors knew this place was where so many warriors had died. They were all brave warriors, but still superstitious of the dead. They feared the dead ones who guarded this hallowed place. The river was peaceful, so they camped along its bank, away from the barricade, trying not to disturb the dead ones. They built up a warming fire as the river's cool water flowed slowly along.

Washing his body, Grey Hair returned to his blanket roll and untied the rawhide binding. Unrolling the trade blanket, he blinked in surprise as he found the burned ends of his old flute and a wooden reed to make a new flute. Looking at Broken Leg, he shook his head in confusion.

"Ellie Thunder sent this for you." The warrior handed Grey Hair a beautiful pouch made to hold a flute. "She said she will be waiting when you return to play your new flute for her."

"But, the white one, Oliver." Grey Hair shook his head. "I do not understand."

"No one understands women, my friend." Broken Leg grinned. "Oliver is her friend. She saw the blood on his shirt and feared for him is all."

"I was foolish to be jealous and misjudged her feelings."

"Yes, you were, but her beauty would make any man jealous." The warrior nodded. "But, I do not think there will ever be any reason for you to be jealous again. The white one, Oliver, rides east with Eagle Wing to Bridger."

"I did not know this."

"You can turn around and go back to her." Broken Leg suggested.

"Not yet, I would be too ashamed. I must prove my bravery to her."

"You are a Lance Bearer. No one doubts your bravery in battle."

"I acted stupid and childish." Grey Hair studied the burned flute. "I must prove I am a man to her."

Holding the pouch in his hand, the warrior stood awestruck for several minutes. Shaking his head, he moved slowly to the river's edge. Broken Leg smiled as his friend was happy once again.

Bridger's Post hadn't changed as Eagle Wing, Wolf's Head, Oliver, and the Sioux passed through the gates. Reining in at the post store, Eagle Wing slid from his Appaloosa horse and studied the post. Several Arikaree men stood along the porch walls, staring at them with hatred in their eyes.

"I do not think we are welcome here." Wolf's Head shook his head.

Eagle Wing didn't want to ride to Bridger, but in his haste to leave, he'd forgotten several items. He needed supplies, plus flint and steel for his fires, but mainly, he wanted to make sure Oliver would be safe at the post.

"Bridger allows no fighting around this post." Eagle Wing looked at Stone Fist. "Have your warriors wait outside, and make no trouble here."

"I do not like the Ric dogs."

Wolf's Head shrugged. "Is there anybody you do like, Stone Fist?"

Only a frown came from the warrior as he followed Eagle Wing into the store. Alex Caldwell was standing behind the counter. Setting down a large vase, he hurried over to the warriors.

"Heavens to Betsy, it's you, Eagle Wing." The store man grabbed him by the shoulders. "You have grown like a weed. Is your pa with you?"

"No, Mister Caldwell, he's back in his valley." Eagle Wing nodded at Wolf's Head and Stone Fist. "They are my friends."

"Then, they are welcome." Caldwell smiled.

"And you know Oliver."

Caldwell looked at the tall buckskin-clad Oliver in surprise. "We worried you might be dead when you didn't return with Jed, young fella."

"Not yet, Mister Caldwell." Oliver tapped his leg. "Maud got a slug in my leg is all."

"Maud shot you?" Caldwell shook his head. "Why?"

"Maud and his men came into Crow Killer's valley." Oliver explained. "They were up to no good."

"Maud and his men have disappeared too."

"I wouldn't know anything about him or his men. Last time I seen that killer, he was headed for here."

"They didn't return and ain't been seen since."

"Beats me… probably out hunting." Oliver lied.

"Tell me, what brings Eagle Wing to Bridger?"

"We're headed east and need a few supplies." Eagle Wing looked at Oliver. "And we're gonna leave Oliver with you until he goes back east."

"Oliver won't be heading east for some time." Caldwell nodded slowly. "Old Gabe said Crazy Horse is kicking up a fuss back to the east, and now, I fear you're riding to join up with him."

Only a nod came from the tall warrior as he looked at the rack of rifles and pouches standing along the wall. "We need flint and hardtack."

"Alright." Caldwell nodded solemnly. "How are your folks?"

"Fine." Eagle Wing didn't speak of Wilson's death, not wanting to answer the many questions he knew would be forthcoming.

Otis McGraw, the post blacksmith, bumped into Oliver as they exited the store. Not recognizing the tall man dressed in buckskins, McGraw excused himself as he started forward.

"Have you forgotten me, Mister McGraw?" Oliver asked.

After looking closely at the tall man, a smile spread across McGraw's face. "Oliver Bass, well, I'll be jiggered. Is that you?"

"It's me alright, Otis."

Pumping Oliver's hand, McGraw looked at the warriors behind him. "My how you've changed from pilgrim to mountain man."

"I reckon I have at that."

Not recognizing Eagle Wing, the blacksmith looked questioningly at Oliver. "These your friends?"

"It's me, Mister McGraw, Eagle Wing."

"The son of Jed Bracket and Oliver show up here, all in one day." McGraw was shocked. "Man, y'all sure have filled out."

"So have you, Mister McGraw." Oliver patted the blacksmith's belly.

McGraw looked at Stone Fist and the Sioux sitting at the tie rack, then at Oliver. "You boys bring your horses to my shop and I'll feed them."

Following the old blacksmith, Eagle Wing noticed a Ric warrior hurrying toward the post gates. Turning their horses into the corral, they laid their blanket rolls under the roof. Pushing some sticks together, Wolf's Head borrowed a pot from McGraw and started coffee to boiling.

Oliver unpacked his horses and walked over to Eagle Wing. "Looks like I won't need your pa's packhorse anymore."

"Crow Killer gave the horse to you." The hardness returned to his voice. "He's yours."

"Thank him for me."

"When I return home." Eagle Wing watched the same warrior come back through the post gates with two white hunters following him.

The filthy dressed hunters stopped short of where Oliver stood. Looking the tall man up and down, one of the men spat a stream of tobacco onto the ground. Turning as he seen the brown juice splatter on the ground, Oliver nodded at the men.

"Can I help you?" Oliver politely asked.

"You're Oliver Bass, ain't you, boy?"

"I'm Bass."

"Changed a mite." The skinny hunter grinned a toothless grin. "Where's Maud and his men?"

"How should I know?" Oliver shrugged.

"You left here with them, that's how you would know." The man stepped forward threateningly.

Eagle Wing started forward when Oliver stopped him.

"I've got to live here a spell, my friend. This is my problem."

"It sure is." The hunter spat another stream of tobacco. "Yep, you've changed some. Almost didn't recognize you."

"What do you want, mister?"

"Done told you what I want."

"And I told you I didn't know." Oliver took a step back from the man. "Why do you want to know?"

"He's my boss and friend, that's why." The hunter pulled his skinning knife. "You better start talking right now."

Eagle Wing stepped forward as the other white cocked his rifle.

"No, Eagle Wing, this is my fight."

"This is a dangerous one, Oliver."

"After you ride out, no one will be able to protect me."

"You become an Injun lover, boy?"

"You might say that, mister."

Nodding, Eagle Wing stepped back, then looked at the other white.

Wolf's Head had slipped around the corral and placed his knife against the man's throat. "He is all yours, Oliver."

Oliver's razor-sharp knife slipped silently from its sheath. Moving forward, he flicked the blade out at the hunter. Seeing the warriors behind the tall white, the hunter swallowed hard and put his knife away.

"We'll talk about this later, boy."

"We'll settle this now." Oliver slapped the hunter. "Right now."

Wiping the blood from his face, the man backed away. "Next time, Bass."

Eagle Wing nodded as the two hunters retreated across the grounds. "You'll have to watch these men, Oliver."

McGraw stepped forward. "We'll be here with him, Eagle Wing."

"I'm proud of you, my friend."

"Your father and Red Horse helped make a man out of me while you were away."

"And my sister?" Eagle Wing wanted to know what happened. He worried for his friend Grey Hair. "It's none of my business, but what happened? I thought…"

"We talked." Oliver dropped his eyes. "She said she loved me, as she would a brother. She will marry Grey Hair."

Nodding, Eagle Wing walked to where McGraw was placing a plate of buffalo tongue and potatoes on a bench. He wondered if Grey Hair knew since he had left before they had headed out. He thought the same as Grey Hair, thinking his sister was in love with Oliver.

"What will Oliver do now?"

The tall man smiled and took the plate of food handed to him. "I believe I'll join Chalk Briggs and head further west."

"You will not return to the east?" Eagle Wing asked.

"No. One day, I think they'll need lawyers and surveyors in the west." Oliver replied sadly.

"We'll ride out with the new sun." Eagle Wing looked at the tall man. "Be careful and take care of yourself."

"And you take care of yourself." Oliver nodded. "And tell Ellie and Red Horse, I'll never forget them."

"I will tell her. You will come and visit someday?"

"Perhaps I will, someday."

No warriors of any tribe were seen on the trail south and east from Bridger to He Dog's village. The days of late summer were on the land. The once green grass had turned brown and wilted with the hotter days. It was eerie as complete silence covered the land. Eagle Wing had sent Wolf's Head and Stone Fist to ride ahead to make sure there were no surprises hidden in the heavy growth of trees lining the trail.

Their first night on the trail, they camped at the canyon Crow Killer always stayed his first night out from Bridger. Standing over the burned campfire, Eagle Wing's memories went back to his days with his father and mother. The next morning, he watered his horses at the crossing where the Pawnee had attacked just as he was being born. The trail held many memories, Crow Killer had told him of the battles along this path.

The white lodges of He Dog's village came into sight on their third day. Young horse herders rode out with their shrill warnings as Eagle Wing and the warriors rode into view. Reining in, he waited until the young boys recognized him.

"Is it you, Eagle Wing?" The oldest boy looked around at the Sioux.

"It is me, young one."

Several older warriors rode up and after greeting the newcomers, escorted them back to the village. He Dog walked from his lodge and took the arm of Eagle Wing.

"It is good to see my nephew and his friends."

"It is good to see my uncle."

Having the horse herders take their horses, He Dog motioned the warriors to sit. Sitting in a semicircle before the chief's lodge, Eagle Wing watched as villagers passed curiously by the lodge. All wanted to see the son of Crow Killer, the warrior they had heard so much about.

"Broken Leg and the others haven't come here yet?"

"No, only you and these warriors."

"These men are from Gall's village." Eagle Wing introduced each of the warriors to He Dog and Crazy Cat. "We ride to the east."

"You will make war on the whites again?"

"Yes, Uncle, again."

"Some of my people will ride with you, but I fear this time some will not return." He Dog nodded sadly. "I hear the whites cross the Missouri in great numbers."

"In battle, there are always losses." Stone Fist shrugged. "It is the way of a warrior."

He Dog nodded at the Sioux. "It is easy to die, my friend, but sometimes harder to live."

Two days later, Broken Leg with Grey Hair at his side, rode into He Dog's village and slid from their horses. Eagle Wing could not believe the wounded one rode with the warriors. Looking hard at Broken Leg, he shook his head as he embraced his friend.

Broken Leg pointed at Grey Hair. "We could not stop the hard head from riding this trail."

"I am a Lance Bearer, not a child." Grey Hair smiled.

"But, your wounds?"

The grey headed one shrugged. "Before this trail is finished, my friend, I will probably have many more."

With the coming of the new sun, Stone Fist was in a hurry to leave. With a night's rest, the warriors of the Cheyenne, Arapaho, and Sioux waved at the villagers who came to see them off on their trail to the east.

He Dog held onto Eagle Wing for several minutes before releasing him. "Have courage, Nephew, but return to your people safely."

The horses weren't spared as Stone Fist drove them relentlessly to the east to Gall's village. Even the great Appaloosa of Eagle Wing was tired from the long trail. Several times, Eagle Wing cast worried looks as he rode alongside Grey Hair. He didn't know how the wounded warrior could be holding up under the strain of such a long, hard journey. Eagle Wing knew Grey hair was hurting and exhausted, but his great heart kept him riding without complaint.

Reining in his horse, Stone Fist looked at Grey Hair. "With the new sun, we will be at Gall's village… there, you can rest."

Eagle Wing knew the warrior only worried about his chief and his people, but Stone Fist had a way of saying his words in a harsh way.

Grey Hair gritted his teeth. "Do not worry about me, Sioux, I will be there."

Nodding, the warrior looked at Eagle Wing and kicked his horse back into the lead. "This is good."

"If he were not an ally, I would kill him."

"He only worries about his people." Eagle Wing made excuses for Stone Fist. "I think he is a good man."

"Perhaps, but he has a way of making me angry."

"I know." Eagle Wing smiled. "Why are you here, my friend?"

"I would not be a brother if I let you ride into battle alone."

"You know about Oliver and Ellie?"

"Yes, Wolf's Head told me after we arrived at the big river."

"Then, why did you not return to her?"

Grey Hair nodded tiredly. "I will have to carve another flute before I can return to her."

"Flutes… don't wait too long again, my friend."

"When the whites are defeated, then I will ride with you to Crow Killer's valley."

Sitting Bull had moved his village closer to the Rosebud Range. The dark mountains loomed over the landscape as the riders pushed their horses across the dry grass. Shaggy buffalo stampeded before the tired horses as they passed. Now, Eagle Wing was eager to reach the village. Grey Hair was weaker and needed to rest after the long trail.

The village looked larger since the last time they were there. Eagle Wing wondered if all the villages had been reunited. He doubted it, from what Stone Fist had said. Crazy Horse only fought with a few gold diggers, not the soldiers of Yellow Hair. To feed so many gathered in one place would take huge supplies of meat and grass for their horses.

Greeting the new arrivals, Gall nodded at Stone Fist and smiled at Eagle Wing. Helping Grey Hair to a backrest beside the lodge, Eagle Wing took the extended hand of the Hunkpapa Chief.

"Grey Hair is still not healed of his wound?" Gall looked down at the warrior.

"It has been a long trail, my chief."

"You made good time coming here."

"Yes, Stone Fist pushed us hard to get here."

Gall could hear the coldness in Eagle Wing's voice. "My nephew is a good man, a great fighter, but his manners need improving."

The sun was setting in the west over the far mountains as Gall and several warriors sat smoking and talking. With their stomachs full and bodies rested, Eagle Wing and Grey Hair relaxed against the backrests.

"Does Crazy Horse still fight with the whites?" Stone Fist spoke up.

"A soldier chief with a few pony soldiers has come to protect the ground diggers." Gall nodded slowly.

"Yellow Hair?"

"No, it is another. This one has only a few soldiers riding with him."

"How many whites dig for gold?" Eagle Wing asked. He knew the whites were crazy, putting the yellow iron before their own safety.

"Many more come to our country every day." Gall shook his head. "And this white soldier chief will fight to protect them."

"Then, we will kill them." Stone Fist growled.

"The white scout that led Yellow Hair leads them. He has many Arickaree warriors." Gall nodded. "More Arickaree than soldiers."

"Why has Gall sent for me?" Eagle Wing questioned the chief.

"The white scout named, Howard. He has asked that we bring you to have council with him."

Eagle Wing remembered the white scout from the treaty talk at Gall's village, months before. The white man seemed friendly, but anyone riding with Arickaree were not friends. Ever since he had been old enough to listen to the war stories of Walking Horse and Crow Killer, he had heard they were the enemy. Even Red Hawk hated the Rics.

"Why does he wish to talk with me?"

Gall shook his head. "He would not say."

"Talk, talk." Stone Fist shook his head. "There has been enough talk."

"If talking can prevent another war, I say we talk." Gall glared at the warrior. "It will hurt nothing."

"Nothing, unless it is a trap." Grey Hair spoke up. "I do not trust this two-tongued white scout."

Gall raised his hand as several tried to speak at the same time. "Why would this scout want to trap Eagle Wing with lies?"

"I do not know, but this white knows who my brother is." Grey Hair looked at Eagle Wing. "If he were a prisoner, perhaps they think he would tell the plans of Crazy Horse and Sitting Bull."

"The only plan needed now is killing, not talk." Stone Fist glared.

Eagle Wing stood up and looked at the warriors. "I will meet with this scout. Send him these words. We will meet alone with no warriors."

Gall nodded as the tall warrior turned and walked away.

The village was shrouded in darkness, except for the many cook fires glowing about the grounds. Deep in thought, he accidentally bumped into a young woman carrying firewood. Apologizing, Eagle Wing helped the pretty girl pick up the scattered pieces of wood, but kept several of the larger pieces. Looking closer, Eagle Wing was surprised. Before him stood the beautiful young woman he had seen the last time he was there.

"These are heavy. Let me help you with them."

"You are Eagle Wing, the Arapaho?" The flames of a fire lit up their faces as she looked up at him.

"Yes, how are you called?"

"I am Morning Dove." The girl looked around bashfully as she reached for the wood. "You cannot carry the wood to my father's lodge."

"Why, it is heavy?"

"I am not married. It is forbidden for maidens to talk with young men." The young woman looked around again. "Especially at night and in the dark."

"It is the same in my village." Eagle Wing smiled. "But, the wood is still heavy."

"If my father sees us together talking, after the sun has gone down, he would punish me."

"Well, we wouldn't want that, Morning Dove." Eagle Wing placed the wood back in her arms.

"But tomorrow, after I do my work, I will be down by the creek checking on my father's horses."

"Perhaps, I will have to check on my horse too." Eagle Wing smiled. "Tomorrow, then."

Grey Hair still sat against the backrest alone as Eagle Wing came walking up. Neither spoke as he took a seat beside his friend.

"Gall has sent a runner to the white scout."

"Good."

"I hope it is safe, my friend." Grey Hair frowned. "I do not trust these whites."

CHAPTER 17

The morning sun broke bright and warm as Eagle Wing walked along the creek bank where the great horse herd grazed. Already, the land heated up, it would be another hot day. Soon, the autumn rains should come and cool down the blistering prairies. And soon, the tribes would begin hunting the shaggies for their winter supply of meat. Hopefully, the talks with the scout, Howard, would produce a peace settlement. Maybe the scout could get the gold seekers to leave the Black Hills.

"Eagle Wing is in deep thought." A soft voice spoke from behind him.

Turning, he looked at the tall young woman standing at the creek's edge. Tall, lithe, and straight, she was even prettier than she had been last night in the dark. Long black hair cascaded down her back, reaching below her slim waist. Eagle Wing swallowed as he had never seen such beauty.

"You are here, Morning Dove."

"Yes, but I cannot remain here long." The girl's eyes seemed to twinkle as she spoke. "My brothers or father might see me."

"Morning Dove, a beautiful name for a beautiful woman." Eagle Wing could feel his heart pounding inside his leather hunting shirt. "Who is your father?"

"Iron Shirt, brother of Gall."

"I know Gall."

Morning Dove nodded. "Yes, I have heard him and my father speaking about Eagle Wing the great Arapaho Lance Bearer."

Embarrassed, Eagle Wing cleared his throat, but still could not take his eyes from the girl. "Can we walk? You need to find your father's horses?"

"No, not here, but tonight at the celebration, we can talk during the dancing." The snow-white teeth showed again as she smiled. "If I am seen with you, I might be punished and not permitted to come to the dance."

"Dance?" Eagle Wing had heard nothing about a dance.

"This night, Gall will hold a ceremony for the warriors who go to fight with Crazy Horse."

"Tell me, Morning Dove, I know you cannot talk with me now." Eagle Wing fumbled to get the words out. "But, have you been spoken for?"

Nodding, she looked deep into his eyes. "Many older men have asked for me."

"You did not accept any of them?"

"I have waited for the great warrior, I watched this spring, riding with my uncle." She smiled bashfully. "After that, I have only seen Eagle Wing in my dreams."

Stepping closer, Eagle Wing looked down into her oval eyes and took her hand. "I never knew such beauty existed."

"Stone Fist says your sister is very beautiful."

"Perhaps, Stone Fist is right, but she is my sister." Eagle Wing smiled. "Why hasn't Stone Fist or younger warriors asked for you?"

"Stone Fist is my brother and the others do not have the wealth my father would ask for me."

Starting to say more, Eagle Wing was bewildered as the woman darted swiftly down the creek bank. Turning, he watched as Stone Fist approached.

"You speak with, Morning Dove, my sister." The warrior looked to where the girl had disappeared.

"A few words was all."

"Be careful, Eagle Wing. My father, Iron Shirt, has a terrible temper and is very protective of his only daughter."

"She told me this."

"And yet you still spoke with her?"

"And I will speak with her again."

Stone Fist smiled as he turned away. "It is good. I know my sister wishes this."

Gall approached and looked down at the warriors as Eagle Wing and Grey Hair sat talking. "The white scout, Howard, will meet with you to the north in what the whites call Skull Canyon."

The sun was high overhead as Eagle Wing stood up to face the chief. "When do we ride?"

"With the coming of the new sun." Gall looked at the tall one. "You can take warriors with you only as far as the canyon mouth."

"And the white scout?" Grey Hair asked.

"He too will bring warriors, but not into the canyon."

Grey Hair looked up at Gall. "I fear a trap."

"It will be as the white scout says." Eagle Wing agreed.

"If this meeting does not turn out well, Stone Fist will take his warriors north to join Crazy Horse." Gall looked down at Grey Hair. "Will you and your warriors ride with him?"

"We will ride to speak with Crazy Horse." Eagle Wing nodded. "After this talk, then I will decide."

"Tonight, there will be a celebration and dancing." Gall smiled at Eagle Wing. "But, I believe you have already heard this."

"I've heard." Eagle Wing watched as Gall strolled away, wondering how the chief had known he knew of the celebration. "Skull Canyon?"

"That is what the whites call the place you are to meet." Stone Fist walked up. "I fear this is a bad omen, Eagle Wing. It is a boxed canyon with only one way out."

"It is a trap."

"Grey Hair worries too much."

"One of us has to worry." Grey Hair looked at Eagle Wing. "You are in a good mood this morning. Why?"

"I feel like this is going to be a good day."

"You are up to something."

"Not me, Grey Hair."

Stone Fist grinned. "Yes, he is up to something, Grey Hair."

"What is he up to? Tell me."

The village was in a festive mood as the people danced and cele-brated with the warriors. Most of the time, celebrations were held after a victorious raiding party returned. Tonight, they celebrated their warriors going off to join the Great War Chief, Crazy Horse. Grey Hair sat and watched as several young women asked Eagle Wing to dance, only to be turned down politely.

"What is wrong with you tonight, my friend?" The warrior ques-tioned. "You do not dance."

"Nothing, I am just tired is all."

As the tall, beautiful young woman stepped before Eagle Wing, Gray Hair nodded. "Now, I know what has been wrong with you all day. She is the same maiden we saw in the spring."

Morning Dove and Eagle Wing danced almost every dance as the night wore on. Several times, passing where Gall and Iron Shirt sat, Eagle Wing could see the dark scowl on her father's face.

"My father does not approve of me dancing with Eagle Wing."

"As I would not approve of you dancing with any other warrior, old or young."

Only a smile came from the beautiful face as they danced around the fire. Finally, as the drums silenced, Morning Dove leaned close to Eagle Wing. "I will be at the water's edge in a few minutes."

Nodding, Eagle Wing turned and walked to where Grey Hair sat. "She is a very pretty maiden."

"Yes, she is."

"Be careful, my friend." Grey Hair smiled. "Or you too may wind up with a broken heart as I did."

"Your broken heart will be mended as soon as we return to Crow Killer's valley."

"Where does Eagle Wing go?" Grey Hair asked as his friend walked away.

The calm waters of the small creek shimmered in the glow of the moonlight as Eagle Wing approached. Morning Dove appeared out of the shadows and moved toward him. Holding her tightly, Eagle Wing looked down into her face. The moonlight glow made her even more beautiful.

"I should not be here."

"But you are, and it makes me happy you have come."

"I have never been so brave." The voice was soft inviting. "Eagle Wing does not fear my father?"

"No, when I return, I will speak for you." Eagle Wing smiled. "If you wish to be my wife?"

"Warrior, I would not be so bold if I did not wish that."

"Come, I will walk you back before you are missed."

"You will ride to the north with the new sun?"

"Yes."

"Be careful and come back to me safely."

Holding her hand, Eagle Wing smiled. "Wild horses could not keep me away from you now."

Grey Hair sat outside the lodge as Eagle Wing walked up. Looking up at his friend, the white-haired one shook his head. "Now, what have you been up to, my brother?"

"Why?"

"The father of the girl you danced with and showed so much attention to came here looking for her. He did not look very happy. Be careful with this one, Eagle Wing." Grey Hair warned.

"I will make the girl my wife."

"But, you just met her today." Grey Hair was shocked. "How can this be?"

"Was it not the same with you when you first met Ellie?"

Grey Hair had to admit, it was love at first sight when he had met Ellie Thunder for the first time. Still, he worried since they were not Arapaho people or Arapaho customs. He knew the Cheyenne and Sioux people guarded their young maidens zealously. When it came to their young women, strict protocol had to be followed to prevent trouble.

"Just be careful with this one, my brother." Grey Hair shook his head. "She could be dangerous for you."

Eagle Wing laughed. "That is why I brought you along, to protect me."

"This, my friend, is serious, not funny."

Many Arapaho, Cheyenne, and Sioux warriors sat their horses as Gall and Iron Shirt stood in front of them. Gall spoke a few words of encouragement, then stepped back. Iron Shirt walked up to the Appaloosa and looked up at the proud Lance Bearer astride him.

"You are leaving on a dangerous journey to speak with the white man for my people." Iron Shirt looked up into Eagle Wing's face. "Now, is not the time for words, but when you return, we will speak."

"I would like that." Eagle Wing watched the squat, heavily-muscled, older man walk away.

"Maybe you would and then again, maybe not." Stone Fist laughed, then turned his horse. "I warned you, my friend."

Skull Canyon, the whites had named the place for the piles of buffalo bones that lay bleaching in the sun at the base of the high cliff. Before the horse was introduced to the plains tribes, the great herds of bison were driven off the cliff by fire or driving them with blankets. Fear crazed, the wild shaggies would plunge to their deaths in panic. The huge plunder of meat would be used to feed and clothe the people.

Stone Fist held up his hand and stopped the warriors that rode behind him.

Many Arickaree warriors sat their horses on the east side of the canyon mouth. Lined up in a long line, the warriors looked fierce. War paint covered the warriors and their horses, and feathers fluttered in the wind as the opposition glared at the warriors sitting behind Stone Fist and Eagle Wing.

"The white man waits there, my brother." Stone Fist pointed. "I think it is a trick. The Arickaree are painted for battle and they outnumber us."

"Brother?"

"Morning Dove told me this last night after our father finished yelling at her." The warrior laughed. "She will marry Eagle Wing so yes, you will become my brother."

"This is a good thing." Eagle Wing looked toward the canyon. "And your father?"

"He will fight it at first, but my sister is hardheaded." Stone Fist nodded. "She has looked at you since the last time you were here."

"I did not know."

"No other has ever turned her head as you have."

"We will talk about this later."

"My words carry no weight in this. It is my father that you must deal with." Stone Fist shrugged. "Be careful today. I do not trust this white. Something is wrong, I feel it."

"I will." Eagle Wing nodded. "Brother."

Cable Howard had scouted for the army for several years and was getting along in age. Soon, the army would retire him for a younger man. The pay was lean and the danger was extreme in many cases. Still, he loved the freedom of riding the plains and fighting if he had to. Not prejudiced against the tribes, as many of the whites were, he still enjoyed his job.

Today, Captain Karr had sent him out to talk to the one warrior that was fluent in English and many Indian dialects. Finding out Howard's mission, to have him talk with the warrior, he had been approached by Lieutenant Daniels. There was money to be made. If a war with the Sioux was started, then the Indians would be driven from the Black Hills, allowing the gold hunters to search the mountains in safety. The gold seekers had offered much if Howard would kill the young warrior and then attack the warriors with him, knowing it would start a war. He didn't like what he was about to do, but he needed the money to buy a small place to retire, once his services for the army was no longer needed.

Howard watched as the proud warrior rode forward to meet him. Few in the tribes could match this one. His body was massed in muscle, tall, and erect. The young warrior's father was the Arapaho Lance Bearer, Crow Killer, also known as Jedidiah Bracket. He remembered Jed years ago when they rode the wagon train of Chalk Briggs to the west. He remembered the beating he had once received from Bracket for making fun of a settler girl on the train. He also remembered Jed being lost and supposedly drowned in the North Platte River during a vicious storm.

Captain Karr had been given a suicidal mission to stop Crazy Horse from killing the greedy prospectors, digging in the ground along Grass Creek. He did not have the pony soldiers to remove the crazed gold miners, nor did he have the soldiers to stop the killing. Howard, as well as Captain Karr, knew to confront Crazy Horse with so few soldiers would not end well. He couldn't understand the Generals back east sending a handful of soldiers on such a foolhardy assignment. Still, Karr was a soldier and no fool, but he had his reputation and career to remember. He was hoping this talk with Eagle Wing could get Crazy Horse to come in for a council.

The scout liked the young Arapaho Lance Bearer, but he needed the money. Howard touched the bag of gold coins resting in his bullet pouch as his sharp blue eyes watched keenly as Eagle Wing rode at a walk toward him. The dark eyes of the warrior were steady, unblinking in the hot sun, and his back ramrod straight. The scout could plainly see the rippling muscles in the warrior's arms and chest. The short lance with the buffalo head carving stuck out plainly from the arrow quiver. The Henry repeater rested across the horse's withers. No other weapons, just the rifle, lance, war axe, and his skinning knife showed.

Raising his hand, he motioned the peace sign to the warrior. "It is good to see Eagle Wing again."

Eagle Wing nodded. "It is good to see Scout Howard again."

"Did you express my greetings to your father from me?"

"I told Crow Killer that I had met with you at the peace council."

Howard looked at the warriors who had ridden with Eagle Wing. "Arapaho, Cheyenne, and Sioux… quite a mixture."

"My brothers ride here to see why you have asked me to come so far to talk with you." Eagle Wing nodded. "Speak, Scout Howard."

"My commanding officer wants Eagle Wing to speak with Crazy Horse and stop the killing of the white gold hunters."

"And what will Crazy Horse benefit from this?"

"Captain Karr will immediately remove all prospectors from the Black Hills."

"My chiefs say he has few soldiers and he cannot do this with so few." Eagle Wing responded.

"Your chiefs speak the truth, but if we didn't have to protect them from Crazy Horse there would be enough to run them from this place."

"Tell me, Scout Howard, do you speak the truth? Are your words honorable?"

"I speak these words for my captain." The scout's face turned red.

"Only for your captain?" Eagle Wing shook his head. "So you don't really know if he intends to keep his word or not?"

"What will a few days matter?"

"A few days will give your captain time to get more pony soldiers here and for more whites to come into our lands."

"Then you will not help?"

"This is not for me to speak on." Eagle Wing noticed the Appaloosa pricked his ears to the north. "I will take you to the camp of Crazy Horse, and there you can talk with him."

"No, I will not meet with Crazy Horse." Howard touched the heavy bag again. "And neither will you, my friend."

Howard pulled a white bandanna from his pocket and pretended to wipe his face. Both rifles, Howard and Eagle Wing's, discharged at the same time. Leaning sideways on the Appaloosa, Eagle Wing felt the bullet graze his side as the white scout was thrown back from his horse.

"Why have you done this thing, white man?"

The light from the blue eyes slowly faded. "Money... I was given much money to kill you."

"Why would they pay for my death?" The words were lost as the scout's head fell sideways in death. "You were foolish, Scout Howard."

Whirling the big horse, he watched as several warriors rode out of the canyon and the banner of the white soldiers came from the north. This is what the spotted horse had sensed. Racing the horse back to where Stone Fist and Grey Hair sat their horses, Eagle Wing reined in hard.

"It was a trap." Stone Fist growled. "The words of the white eyes cannot be trusted."

"They have us surrounded, Eagle Wing." Broken Leg looked to where the Arickaree and white soldiers had separated, making a line north and south."

Grey Hair looked at the bloody side. "You have been wounded."

"Follow me, brave hearts." Whipping the Appaloosa hard, Eagle Wing screamed and charged straight at the Arickaree that blocked their escape to the open prairie. Rifles roared as the spotted horse closed with the Rics in what quickly became hand-to-hand fighting. Both sides were so intermingled, rifles could not be used in fear of hitting one of their own. The war axes plunged deep. Now, was not coup taking time, but a life-and-death struggle as death lay on the land.

Fighting their way through the Arickaree, the warriors turned and fired into the confused ranks of the Rics. Eagle Wing watched as the soldiers raced their horses toward the fight. Two Sioux warriors had been knocked from their horses as they fought their way clear of the ambush. Eagle Wing watched as one tried to rise. Kicking the Appaloosa, he raced to the warrior's side. Sliding from the excited Appaloosa, Eagle Wing plunged his lance deep into the prairie sod.

"Hoka Hey!" Grey Hair screamed and charged into the tangle of fighting warriors. "We fight!"

Stone Fist led his Sioux to cut off the soldiers as they neared the battle. The Rics were everywhere. There was not enough room to fire his rifle without hitting one of his own warriors so Eagle Wing pulled out the war axe. Standing over the downed Sioux, he watched as complete pandemonium broke out as Grey Hair, Wolf's Head, Two-Eyed Dog, along with their Cheyenne and Arapaho allies, screaming their war cries, joined the fight.

Fighting with the courage and strength of many, the Lance Bearers and Dog Soldiers broke the ranks of the Rics, reeling them backward. Finally, seeing the white soldiers had been stopped, the Arickaree retreated from the battleground, then sat their horses watching. Too many of their warriors had been killed. Of the many bodies lying across the bloody ground, most were Rics. The Arickaree, thinking the whites would help win the fight, shook their heads as the white leader ordered his men from their horses instead of charging into battle. Stone Fist and the pony soldiers exchanged fire, but the range was too far to be effective.

Bloody from many wounds, Eagle Wing looked at the carnage as the gunfire ceased. Men were strewn about on the ground, some dead and some wounded. Horses lay on the field, kicking in agony from wounds. Shaking his head, he helped the wounded Sioux warrior, he had saved, to his feet.

Stone Fist held his warriors in a line between the wounded and the white soldiers. Broken Leg held the Arickaree at bay on the east side of the field. Looking at the carnage, Eagle Wing recognized the body of Grey Hair and raced to where the warrior lay crumpled across his lance.

Rolling the warrior over, Eagle Wing screamed and shook his head in grief as he looked at the lifeless eyes of his brother. Laying Grey Hair's body back softly on the grass, Eagle Wing turned in rage at the whites.

Grabbing the trembling warrior, it took three others, besides Broken Leg and Two-Eyed Dog, to hold back the crazed Eagle Wing from charging straight into the rifles of the soldiers. Stone Fist rode up and slid from his horse.

"We will help you kill the whites, my friend." The Sioux spoke to the struggling warrior. "You alone saved the life of Bear Walker."

"Their treachery has killed my brother, Grey Hair." Hate spilled from the bloody lips.

"Yes, but we will fight them another day." Stone Fist, the normally bloodthirsty one spoke caution. "They have us badly outnumbered today, my friend."

Slowly the rage and urge to kill left Eagle Wing's shaking body as he walked back to where Grey Hair lay. Yes, there would be another day. Broken Leg and Two-Eyed Dog stood beside the body and shook their heads sadly.

"He was a great Lance Bearer."

"Place our dead on horses and we will leave this place."

"Where do you go, Eagle Wing?" Broken Leg watched as he mounted the spotted horse.

Everyone across the battlefield watched as Eagle Wing rode to where Howard's body lay. Sliding from his horse, he scalped the white scout. Raising the bloody hair over his head, he rode the Appaloosa up and down in front of the white soldiers, then in front of the Arickaree, challenging any one of them to come out and fight. For several minutes, he sat his horse only yards in front of the enemy, but none rode forward to take up his challenge. None even discharged their rifles at the enraged warrior. Broken Leg worried that Eagle Wing, in his rage, might charge alone into the whites.

Finally, the Rics raised their arms in salute to the courage of the bloody warrior on the spotted horse, then turned their horses and rode away. Seeing the Rics leaving, the leader of the whites mounted his men and followed them. Eagle Wing screamed his war cry and flung the bloody scalp to the ground.

"The whites do not even take their dead scout." Broken Leg watched as the soldiers moved away. "At least the Rics will return after we are gone to pick up their dead and wounded."

"He lured us into this trap to kill Eagle Wing. Let the coyotes and birds have him." Two-Eyed Dog spat. "Why would he do this thing?"

"I do not know, my friend." Wolf's Head shrugged. "But, he did."

"I think they wanted something from this one and when he refused, they tried to kill him." Stone Fist watched as Eagle Wing rode away, leading the horse carrying Grey Hair. "He is the greatest of warriors."

"We will sing his praises over our fires." Black Bird nodded.

Two-Eyed Dog shook his head. "No, my friends, he would not want that. Today, he has lost one who was as a brother."

"Did you not see his face?" Broken Leg looked sadly after the warrior.

"I saw it." Stone Fist nodded. "He had the look of death and the Arickaree saw it as well, and that is why they left the field."

Gall watched as the bloody warriors, leading the horses of their dead, rode into the village. Mourning cries rang out across the lodges as women recognized and mourned their sons and husbands. Eagle Wing stopped the Appaloosa and the horse carrying Grey Hair before the lodge of Iron Shirt and waited until the warrior emerged from his lodge.

Stone Fist, sitting beside Eagle Wing, spoke first. "The whites lured us into a trap."

After looking up at the bloody warrior and blood-splattered Appaloosa, Iron Shirt looked over at the dead body of Grey Hair. "I am sorry for your loss, warrior."

"I have come for Morning Dove." Eagle Wing looked down at the warrior. "I take my brother home to his burial ceremony. I will not leave here without her."

"My daughter?"

"I do not want trouble." Eagle Wing trembled. "Do not force a fight."

Iron Shirt could see he looked into the eyes of death. "Does Morning Dove wish you for a husband?"

"I do, father."

"Let her go." Stone Fist helped the injured Bear Walker from his horse. "This day Eagle Wing saved the life of your other son."

Nodding solemnly, Iron Shirt looked to where Gall had walked up. "If this is so, I thank you, warrior."

Bear Walker spoke up from where Stone Fist helped him against a backrest. "It is true, father. This one killed many Rics and the white scout. He fought with the strength and courage of many."

"If it is your wish, Daughter, then go."

Swinging the tall girl up behind him, Eagle Wing nudged the Appaloosa and started out of the village.

"Will Eagle Wing come back to fight with his brothers the Sioux?"

Looking at Grey Hair's blanket wrapped body, the dark face nodded. "Tell Crazy Horse to send for me. I will come."

Stone Fist shook his head sadly as he watched the Arapaho and Cheyenne depart. "There goes a great war leader, but a man that is now full of hate for any enemy."

Knowing it would take several days of riding to reach the Arapaho village, Eagle Wing had the squaws in Gall's village sew the bodies up tightly in buffalo hides before they rode from the village. Two heavy poled travois were needed to carry the bodies of the warriors so many miles. Few words were spoken by the returning party as they made their way west to Arapaho lands. Days later, as the travois carrying Grey Hair and Wolf's Head was pulled through the Arapaho village, women hacked at their hair and screamed in sorrow as the medicine men sang their death songs and rattled their gourds.

Eagle Wing and Morning Dove looked up at the scaffolds the bodies had been placed on. Grief showed on Eagle Wing's face. He had lost one he loved as he did Red Horse. What would he tell Ellie? Grey Hair was still too weak from his wounds and should have remained in the village. Eagle Wing should have insisted, and he blamed himself for his loss.

"He died a Lance Bearer's death, Nephew." Walking Horse placed his hand on the broad shoulder. "He made us proud. His praises will be sung and he will always be remembered."

Nodding, Eagle Wing took a last look up at his friend and brother before turning away. Guilt weighed heavily upon his shoulders. He had lost one dear to him.

"Take Morning Dove to your lodge, Uncle." Eagle Wing walked away. "I will return soon."

Walking Horse watched him walk away. "My nephew has changed."

"He has lost one that was as his brother." Morning Dove nodded sadly. "Your words were well meant, but they cannot stop his grief."

Soaring Bird sat before his small fire as Eagle Wing entered the large lodge. Taking a seat across from the old one, he waited to be greeted.

"You have lost friends?"

"I have."

"You have suffered many wounds for your people." The old medicine man looked at the warrior. "You have killed many enemies."

"I have." Eagle Wing nodded. "But not nearly enough."

"Why has Eagle Wing come here?" Soaring Bird asked. "You already have my blessing. Your friends died for their people, and they died with honor. They will go to hunt the great places in the sky. Do not grieve for them, Eagle Wing, they are happy."

"Are they, Grandfather?"

"An honorable death is wished for by all warriors, my son."

Nodding slowly, Eagle Wing looked at the bony old man. "I have brought a maiden back with me. We wish to be married before I ride to my father's valley."

"You wish me to perform this marriage?"

"It is my wish."

"Is this woman a captive?"

"No, she is the daughter of Iron Shirt the Hunkpapa Sioux."

"My words have caused you much grief." The old one nodded sadly. "When do you wish this ceremony?"

"I will leave with the new sun."

"My medicine smoke sees you fighting with the Sioux again. She might become a widow if you fight the whites." Soaring Bird warned.

"We will marry."

"Bring her here as the sun goes down." Soaring Bird looked across the fire. "Perhaps this marriage will bring you some happiness."

After Eagle Wing had walked away, Little Antelope, who had stood back from the scaffold, took the tall woman by the hand and made her welcome as they walked to the lodge of Walking Horse. "My nephew, Eagle Wing, brought you back here with him?"

"Yes."

"You will be his wife?"

"Yes."

Little Antelope nodded. "You know of the prophecy? His life will be filled with fighting and danger."

"No, I have heard nothing, there has been no time." Morning Dove shook her head. "It does not matter, nothing matters. I love him and that is all I know."

"That is good." Little Antelope smiled, thinking of Crow Killer. "He is a great warrior as his father is."

Jed and Red Horse spotted the two riders as they descended the south pass leading down into the valley. Easing behind a stand of oak, they waited until they could make out the riders plainly.

"It is your brother." Jed kicked his bay horse forward in a lope.

Yelling and waving his arm, Red Horse kicked his Appaloosa into a hard run toward the trail. Eagle Wing could hear the yelling and knew it was Red Horse, but the trail's view was blocked from where they rode. Clearing the short brush, he could see the two riders coming at him in a hard run. Nodding at Morning Dove, he hurried the horses down the rough trail.

CHAPTER 18

Jed sat his horse smiling as Red Horse leaned over and hugged Eagle Wing. The youngster had matured, but seeing the safe return of his brother, he couldn't retain himself from his boyish outbreak. Moving alongside Eagle Wing's horse, Jed held out his arm.

"Welcome home, my son."

"It's good to be home." The voice was quiet and sad.

"And who is this?" Red Horse smiled at Morning Dove. "A captive?"

Eagle Wing smiled. "Yes, a captive. This is my wife. She is the daughter of Iron Shirt, the Sioux."

"Your wife?" Red Horse almost fell off his horse. "Does my new sister have a name?"

"My name is Morning Dove." A pretty smile broke out as she looked at the youngster. "Do not fall off your horse, warrior."

"I'm Red Horse and this is our father, Crow Killer."

Nodding slightly, Jed looked at the girl, then back at Eagle Wing curiously. He was surprised his son had taken a wife. He never seemed interested in girls when they had visited the Arapaho village, and he had been gone only a short time. The romance must have blossomed quickly. He could see his son had deep feelings for the beautiful woman.

"Morning Dove is welcome in my valley and my family." Jed nodded. "Come, Eagle Wing, we'll introduce my new daughter to your mother and sister."

Red Horse laughed. "They're going to be shocked. My brother only thought of war, not women."

"Ride ahead with Morning Dove. I will speak with Father." Eagle Wing nodded at Red Horse.

As Red Horse and Morning Dove rode out of hearing, Jed looked at his oldest. "You have a new wife, my son, but your face is sad."

Eagle Wing's shirt covered the scars from battle, but could not cover the sadness on his face. "In battle, I lost my brother and best friend, Grey Hair. How can I tell my sister?"

"Grey Hair was a great Lance Bearer." Jed understood as he had lost many friends over the years.

"I shouldn't have let him ride east with us. He was too weak from his wounds."

"It was his decision, as a man, not yours."

"What will I tell Ellie?"

"That he died a warrior's death, unless she asks more." Jed changed the subject to get Eagle Wing's mind from the sadness. "Now, tell me what possessed you to marry so quickly?"

"We bumped into each other in the dark and here we are."

"Where did you get the horses to give her father?"

"She was a gift from Iron Shirt."

"A gift?" Jed knew the Indian culture well. Morning Dove was a very beautiful maiden and her father would ask many horses for her.

Eagle Wing rode up beside Morning Dove. "Has my brother talked your ears off yet?"

"He reminds me of my brother, Bear Walker, the one you saved from the Arickaree." She smiled.

After hearing her words, Jed nodded knowingly. Now, he knew why she had been given to Eagle Wing, without a bride price.

Bright Moon and Ellie Thunder stood before the cabin, watching as the horses splashed across the small creek. Motioning for Red Horse to be silent for once, Jed slid from his horse as the women raced to greet Eagle Wing. For several minutes, the air buzzed with greetings and laughter.

Pulling Morning Dove in front of him, Eagle Wing presented his new bride. Bright Moon welcomed Morning Dove into her family as Ellie embraced her.

"Now, I have a sister to help against Red Horse." Ellie laughed as she walked with Morning Dove to the cabin.

"Around here, she'll have to learn English, my brother." Red Horse laughed. "Ellie forgets, some don't understand English."

Supper was finished as Eagle Wing took Ellie's hand and led her from the cabin. Seeing the serious look on his face, she paled slightly as they walked to the creek.

"Has something happened to Oliver?"

Eagle Wing turned to face her. "Oliver?"

"Your face is so serious, I thought."

"You ask about Oliver, not Grey Hair?"

"Yes, I was worried for him."

"You still care for Oliver?"

Dropping her eyes, she nodded. "Yes."

"But, Broken Leg said it was Grey Hair you wanted for a husband." Eagle Wing shook his head. "I do not understand."

"Grey Hair was the one you and father wanted me to marry." Ellie explained. "I wanted to please you."

"Please us?"

"Tell me, Brother, has something happened to Oliver?"

"Oliver was fine, last we seen him. It's Grey Hair." Eagle Wing thought of Grey Hair. Perhaps, his death was meant to be after all.

"Oh, no!" Her small hand went to her face in shock. "Grey Hair is dead?"

"Yes, he died a warrior's death fighting against many enemies." Eagle Wing replied sadly.

"I'm sorry for you and Grey Hair."

"And I'm sorry, Sister, that I took Oliver from this place and you."

"I will say a prayer for Grey Hair." Ellie turned and hurried back to the cabin. "I'm so ashamed, my brother."

Red Horse carried his sleeping robes from Wilson's cabin and dropped them near the horse barn. "The cabin is all yours, Brother."

"Only for a few nights." Eagle Wing sat at the table talking with Jed.

"Where do you go now?"

"We will ride to the western valley and stay there for a while."

"Why? There's plenty of room here, and if you go there, we'll have to build another cabin." Red Horse shook his head.

"We have skins for a lodge."

"Winter is coming and you're gonna live in a lodge and freeze your bottoms off?"

"I was born in a hide lodge." Eagle Wing frowned at his brother. "And, I'm Indian."

"I guess." The youngster laughed. "But, the cold times are coming and hides are not as warm or dry as logs."

Listening to the conversation, Jed knew Eagle Wing had to get away. "When will you take Morning Dove across the mountain?"

"First, I will take Red Horse and ride to Bridger." Eagle Wing looked toward the cabin. "If my father will take care of my wife in my absence?"

"You do not ride back to the east?"

"If I am needed, Crazy Horse and Gall will send warriors for me when the warm times come again."

"In the spring?"

"Yes, if the pony soldiers come back to his lands." The warrior nodded. "Then, I will gather warriors and go."

"Tell me, why do you ride to Bridger?"

"To right a wrong, I have committed." Eagle Wing looked down.

"Oliver?"

"Yes, if I can find him."

"Red Horse will remain here, and I will ride with you to Bridger."

"The women will need protection."

"Your brother is a man now. He can protect them as well as I can." Jed reminded him how Red Horse had killed Maud and one of his men. "I trust my son with their lives."

"As I do." Eagle Wing agreed. "We will not tell Ellie why we go."

"We must go quickly. The meat taking time is close and we have to ride to Turner's Hole before the snow comes."

"I will kill many shaggies this year." Red Horse was excited at the prospect of the hunt. "Maybe, we will be attacked by the Arickaree."

"Red Horse is young and does not know war." Eagle Wing shook his head.

"You are still young too, my brother."

"I feel old, little brother, very old." The warrior nodded slowly.

Jed knew exactly how his older son felt. He carried the same feelings in his own heart. Over the years, the terrible battles and conflicts had taken their toll on him. He hoped Red Horse would be able to avoid such a future.

Bridger's Post came into view several days later as Jed and Eagle Wing passed down the dusty immigrant trail. The cold fingers of winter were close. The mornings were chilly and the leaves started turning color and falling from the trees along the road. The horses already had begun to hair out, putting on their heavy winter coats. The small campfires, they sat around at night, were welcomed as Jed listened to his son tell about the fighting he had been in.

Reining in at the hitching post, in front of Bridger, both men slipped easily to the ground. Jed looked around the post, studying the compound. The buildings and stockade walls had aged with time, but warriors, squaws, dogs, and chickens still wandered about the grounds. Caldwell limped out onto the porch and greeted them.

"Jed, you're beginning to be a steady customer this year." Caldwell pumped Crow Killer's hand. "And so is Eagle Wing."

Jed nodded as he greeted the store trader. "Is that a bad thing, Alex?"

"No, no." Caldwell looked around. "You didn't bring the ladies this time?"

"We're not here for supplies, Alex. This is a more personal trip." Jed replied.

"Then, what has brought you so far, old friend?"

"We've come looking for Oliver Bass."

"Oh yes, Oliver." The store man nodded.

"Is he here?" Eagle Wing was eager to find Oliver and return to Morning Dove.

"He was, but Otis McGraw would have to tell you where he went." Caldwell motioned toward the livery. "I'll walk over with you."

"There's no need, Alex. We'll find him alright."

Holding up a broken butcher knife blade, Caldwell smiled. "I was fixing to get a new tip on this knife anyway."

The forge was red hot as the big blacksmith pumped the ballast, blowing air into the hot coals. Jed noticed McGraw hadn't changed, maybe older, but just as strong looking as he ever was.

Greeting the man, as he laid aside his rounding hammer, Jed told him why they had come. "You know where he went, Otis?"

"Not exactly, Jed. How about you boys have a cup of coffee?" McGraw offered.

"We're kinda in a hurry to find Oliver, old friend."

"All I can tell you for sure is one morning he saddled up and loaded all his possibles, then headed out."

"He didn't say anything at all?" Caldwell looked exasperated at the blacksmith.

"Nope, just that he'd been loafing too long and needed to get to work." McGraw nodded. "And, he thanked me for helping him out."

"Helping him?"

Caldwell cleared his throat. "I forgot to mention he had a little trouble with a couple trappers after Eagle Wing left last time."

"The same two trappers he was arguing with last time I was here?" Eagle Wing looked at McGraw.

"The same pair alright."

"What happened?"

"Wouldn't have believed it if'n I hadn't seen it with my own eyes. Oliver got mad and whooped both those loudmouths right there in the corral. After that, they lit out and haven't been back here since." McGraw grinned.

"You have any idea which way he went, Otis?" Jed spoke up.

"Nope, couldn't say. But, I don't figure he's planning on returning."

"How do you know?" Caldwell asked.

"Because, he took with him all that heavy junk. If'n he was planning on returning, he'd of left it here with me, and that's how I know."

Turning their horses loose in the corral, Jed tossed them some hay, then followed Caldwell back to the store.

"I'll fix you some food, Jed."

"Thanks, Alex, we'll be back shortly."

"He could have left out in any direction." Eagle Wing shook his head as they walked. "Where do we start looking?"

"Beats me, Otis didn't know." Jed shrugged. "We'll ask around and see what we can find out."

Moving about the compound, Jed studied the faces of the men sitting against the log walls. It was the wrong time of year for the roaming tribes to bring in their pelts. These were mostly loafers, hoping to receive some supplies the post trader would hand out. Most were Assinboine, and a few others lived close to the post.

Walking outside the gates, Jed stopped where he had talked with the small Assinboine squaw on his last trip and had given her a deer. If she would talk, perhaps she could tell them which direction Oliver had taken when he left the post. The villagers were naturally curious and very little passed their lodges without them knowing.

"You have returned, Crow Killer."

"Yes, Mother, but I didn't bring you any fresh meat today."

"Perhaps, another time."

Jed let a gold coin show briefly, catching her attention. "I'm looking for the young white man that left here a couple days ago."

"The tall one who fought with the ugly ones?"

"Yes."

Looking at Jed's hand, she nodded. "He rode west."

Jed looked in the direction she pointed. Nodding, he handed her the coin. "Thank you, Mother."

"Will you kill the young one, Crow Killer?"

"No, he is our friend."

"That is good, he is a good man. He gave us fresh meat. He will be missed." She smiled a snaggled-tooth grin. "And he defeated the trouble-makers that were mean to us. Too bad he did not kill them."

"Thank you, little mother." Turning back for the post, Jed heard her words of warning.

"Be careful Crow Killer. You and your son have many enemies here."

"Thank you again, Mother."

With the coming of the new sun and a hearty breakfast, Jed and Eagle Wing swung on their horses and looked down at McGraw and Caldwell.

"We'll see you in the spring, Alex."

"Is there any word from the east?" Eagle Wing knew that travelers passed through Bridger frequently from the east.

"Nothing much. After you killed Cable Howard and after the licking you and the Lance Bearers gave the Rics and the soldiers, everything has been quiet." Caldwell shook his head.

"You know about the fight?" Eagle Wing was shocked the trader knew.

"Shucks, everybody in these parts has heard about you." McGraw laughed. "Out here, word spreads like wildfire."

"You be careful, Eagle Wing. Now, the army hates you as it does Crazy Horse and Sitting Bull." Alex frowned.

"Then, let the army stay east of the Missouri."

"You know as well as I, they won't do that." Caldwell shook his head. "No, sir, come spring, those gold diggers will swarm those hills like ants."

"Then, they'll die."

"I expect there will be a lot of dying next summer."

"Be seeing you, come spring." Jed turned his horse.

"Hope you find Oliver." Caldwell waved as they passed through the gates.

"Where will we look now?" Eagle Wing studied the dusty immigrant trail as they rode west.

"Baxter Springs is the closest settlement." Jed nodded thoughtfully. "We may find out something there."

"And if we don't?"

"That's up to you." Jed shrugged. "We can keep looking or go home."

"He couldn't have gotten too far."

They had ridden past Carter's homestead in the darkness and reined in behind Doctor Zeke's office as the sun showed its brilliant light in the early morning. Knocking on the door, they heard shuffling behind the door and waited. The old grey-headed doctor, holding his spectacles in his hand, opened the door slowly.

"Jedidiah Bracket, you're here in the flesh." Doc Zeke was beside himself, pumping Jed's hand. "And, little Eagle Wing, who's not so little anymore. Come in, come in."

The room hadn't changed any since he had last brought Bright Moon into Baxter Springs for some fine cloth that couldn't be bought at Bridger.

"You're looking well, Doctor Zeke."

"You've really grown, boy." Zeke looked up at Eagle Wing. "Sit down and I'll fry y'all up a bite."

"Thank you, it's been a long trail." Jed smiled.

Pouring coffee from his old blackened coffeepot, Zeke looked over his glasses at the two men. "Have you seen Ellie? Tell me, how is she?"

"She's fine and the children are growing like weeds."

"I can imagine." The old doctor nodded. "And your family?"

"Fine, just fine." Jed didn't tell of Wilson's death.

"I would like to see them." The voice seemed sad.

"I'm sure she'll come to see you. Maybe, next spring after the thaw."

"What brings you so far west, Jedidiah?"

"I'm looking for Oliver Bass, a tall thin white man dressed as we are."

Flipping the side-meat, Zeke looked over at them. "You aiming on killing him?"

"No, he's a friend of ours." Jed laughed. "Why does everybody think we're killers?"

"Well, boy, you've been known to put a few under."

"I reckon, but like I said, Oliver is a friend of ours." Jed nodded. "We've come to take him home."

"I see."

"Have you seen him, Grandfather?" Eagle Wing asked as the old man set plates of food in front of them.

"You boys eat up, then we'll go take a walk."

Early morning risers in town watched curiously as Jed and Eagle Wing followed the old doctor along the dusty street. Most knew Jed, but it had been a long while since they had seen him in Baxter Springs. A few didn't know him at all and were nervous. Since Bate Baker had been killed and the fur trade had gone under, very few Indians rode into town. All had heard about the Indian problems in the east and these two following Doc Zeke made them skittish. Moving down the dusty street, Doc Zeke turned into what used to be Bate Baker's old fur trading store.

Turning, as the door opened, Oliver smiled in surprise, then hurried to where Jed and Eagle Wing stood. Pumping their hands, he shook his head. "What are you two doing here so far from the valley?"

"We've come to see you, Oliver." Jed smiled and looked around the empty room where hides used to line the walls and counters. The pelts were gone but the faint smell of raw hides remained.

"So far from your valley, you have me worried." Oliver looked at them curiously. "But now, tell me the real reason."

"What are you doing here?" Eagle Wing asked.

"Well, after the previous owner didn't have any use for the place anymore, I bought it from Doc Zeke."

"What will you sell?" Jed knew he spoke of Bate Baker.

"I'm going to open my law practice, a surveyor's office, and I'm going to start a land business with Doc Zeke's help."

"I see." Jed looked at Zeke. "So you two know each other?"

"We do now, Jed." Zeke laughed. "He told me all about the valley, Red Horse, Bright Moon, Ellie, and he told me about Ed Wilson's death."

"And you didn't say a word back at your house."

"Didn't see no need." Zeke shrugged. "Besides, I wasn't sure you weren't here to kill the boy, whom I have taken a liking to."

"So you're setting up a business for yourself?" Jed looked around the room.

"Yes, sir." Oliver looked at the two men. "How is everybody at home? How is Ellie?"

Jed nodded at Eagle Wing, then led the doctor through the doorway. "We'll be at the good doctor's office."

Oliver looked at Eagle Wing curiously as the door closed. "You're acting odd, Eagle Wing. Is it about Ellie?"

"Yes, my friend, it is."

Reining in, the three riders looked down from the high ridge, overlooking the vast valley as the herd of horses, one mule, and a cow grazed out on the browning grass. Smoke curled from the cabin's chimney as they kicked their horses down the rocky northern trail. Nearing the bottom, Jed heard the little mule bray as the wind brought their smell to her.

Nearing the cabin, Jed sensed something in the trees, then watched as Red Horse stepped into view. Figures with rifles stood in the cabin door, looking up the trail. Crossing the shallow creek as the women raced toward them, Jed smiled. Once again, he was home with his family.

Ellie Thunder stood in front of Oliver as the others walked back to the cabin, leaving them alone. Bashful for the first time, the two looked into each other's eyes. Turning, they walked slowly along the creek.

Red Horse shook his head as he watched them move away. "There goes, my sister."

"You do not like the white man?" Morning Dove asked.

"I like Oliver, but I don't think he'll stay here in our mountains."

Bright Moon looked at Jed. "Will they leave our valley, my husband?"

"Yes, they will live in Baxter Springs when they marry." Jed nodded. "Oliver has a business in the settlement now."

Bright Moon looked at Eagle Wing. "Walking Horse has sent runners here to speak with you."

"Runners, is there trouble?"

"They did not say, only that they wished you to come to the village in the spring after the snows melt and free the passes."

"They have left?"

"Yes, they are needed for the meat taking times."

Morning Dove looked at Eagle Wing with worry. "They want you to fight with them again."

Eagle Wing nodded at the beautiful woman. "I have given my word to Crazy Horse. If it is his wish, I will go."

Jed looked about the cabin. "Now, we have meat to hunt and then Ellie's wedding."

"If she will marry Oliver this time." Red Horse laughed. "She may change her mind again if she finds out he'll take her away."

Bright Moon shook her head sadly. "No, my son, she will go to the white village to live."

"Where will they be married?" Red Horse was curious. "Will we ride to Walking Horse's village?"

Jed shook his head. "No, they'll marry in the white church at Baxter Springs, as me and your mother was."

"Then, you will have to ride there soon, before the cold times come." Eagle Wing spoke up.

"If they are to marry, we'll leave in two suns." Jed looked at the valley.

"We'll stay here and look after the horses and milk the cow."

"That's good." Jed looked at Red Horse. "Will my youngest go?"

"If they marry in a white lodge, I'll go." The youngster grinned. "I want to see this."

"We will find a place for our lodge in the west valley while you are gone."

"I fear this will be a bad winter, my son." Jed shook his head. "Perhaps, you should stay here."

Looking at Morning Dove, he smiled. "We thank you, Father, but we would like time alone."

Jed, Bright Moon, and Red Horse watched while Oliver and Ellie Thunder were married by the white preacher. After their wedding feast, with Doc Zeke and a few of the older settlers, Red Horse wandered about the town, looking curiously at the new things the whites sold in their stores. The white village was definitely something to behold, but he wouldn't want to live as the whites.

Two weeks later, Ellie, Oliver, and Zeke waved as the group rode from Baxter Springs and headed home. A packhorse carried the supplies Eagle Wing and Morning Dove would need for the coming cold time. Bright Moon stated her worry for them to Jed.

"They are young and they wish to be alone." Jed smiled. "You know how it was when we first came here."

"But, across the mountain it will be so cold." She shrugged. "We had a warm cabin."

"It'll be just as cold on this side."

"Yes, but a hide lodge is not a warm cabin."

"They'll have each other to keep warm."

The cold times were approaching as the temperature dipped suddenly, causing frost to form on the creek banks. Crossing the mountains, Jed reined in at his usual campsite in Turner's Hole. Looking around the valley, he noticed nothing changed as the buffalo still roamed the valley floor in small herds. As they slipped from their horses, Eagle Wing started unloading their sleeping robes before hobbling the horses out on the brown grass. Jed had brought six pack animals and the black mule.

The small fire spat sparks into the air as the embers flew from the hot coals. As drippings from the deer steaks fell into the fire, the flames rose, making the meat sizzle.

Red Horse brought in more wood and piled it beside the fire for heat during the night. "Mother said you fought with a Frenchman and the Rics here long ago."

"Right over there by the rocks." Jed pointed with his chin.

"She also told how one time you almost froze going home."

"I fear if it hadn't been for the little mule, we would have." Jed nodded thoughtfully.

Eagle Wing looked at Jed. "You had a rough life, Father."

"Yes."

"Was it worth it?"

"Yes." Jed smiled. "I have a beautiful family and home, much happiness, and maybe some grandchildren soon."

"Mother and Morning Dove will miss us." Red Horse laughed. "They'll have to milk the cow."

"In two sleeps, my son, we'll head home, providing you can kill a shaggy." Jed shook his head.

"He may talk one to death." Eagle Wing threw a stick at Red Horse.

The shaggies had been found, and now, Eagle Wing and Morning Dove traversed the rough trail leading through the cold high pass. From the high elevation, they could see for miles, the west valley Jed had purchased and now, with Oliver's help, held title to. Not as large a valley as the one where Jed's cabin was located, but it was still vast. Two small creeks split the valley with their cold water coursing their way through the tall grass that grew abundantly across the meadows.

"It is beautiful, my husband." Sitting her horse, Morning Dove drew the fresh cold air deep into her lungs. "So beautiful."

"Will you be happy here?"

"If you are here, yes, I will be happy." She smiled.

"Maybe, we should stay at the cabin until we get a cabin of our own built." Eagle Wing looked across the wide valley. "We will be snowed in when the passes close."

The woman smiled again as she looked into the strong face of her warrior. "The snow will be welcome, then no one can come for you to fight their battles."

"It is your people's battles too."

"Yes, but I fear for you, my husband." She nodded. "You are always in front, leading the others. Your life is always in danger."

"Then, we will live here." Eagle Wing kicked the big Appaloosa forward. "Come, I will show you the place where we will set our lodge."

Riding into a heavily wooded cove, blocked on three sides from the harsh winter winds, Eagle Wing pulled Morning Dove from her horse. A smaller creek, a tributary of the other two ran past the shelf. Low enough so its spring runoff wouldn't flood the flat place, the lodge would be high and dry. The site of the camp, with its view of the mountains and valley, was picturesque.

Tying the pack animals, carrying supplies, meat, and hides for their lodge, he walked with Morning Dove to the edge of the clear, cold, rippling creek and looked up at the mountains. The valley spread out before them for miles in all its majestic splendor.

"It is so beautiful and peaceful here, my husband."

"Yes, I have camped here many times." Eagle Wing held her close.

"So quiet." Nodding thoughtfully, she smiled and laid her head against him. "I hope it remains so always."

The long wailing cry of a great grey wolf sounded along the mountainside, welcoming them to his domain. They were home.

The End